Colonel Erdington's Daughter

By

M P Middleton

Published by New Generation Publishing in 2016

www.newgeneration-publishing.com

 New Generation Publishing

My thanks to:

David H Keith (deceased)
Elizabeth Rowan Keith
John Middleton
and
Anna Robinson
Who all supported me in writing
The St Vere Quintet.

This book has been produced with assistance from
The London Borough of Barking and Dagenham
Library Service Pen to Print Creative Writing Project
2014/15 with funding from The Arts Council England
Grants for the Arts.

Supported using public funding by
**ARTS COUNCIL
ENGLAND**
LOTTERY FUNDED

London Borough of
Barking&Dagenham
lbbd.gov.uk

PROLOGUE

The weather was cold with a light drizzle in the air.

Colonel Aubrey Courtney decided it was not a morning for riding. He would pay a visit to his club instead.

The Horatio, in St James's Street, was the exclusive domain of infantry officers.

Aubrey ordered brandy and went to sit by the fire in a comfortable leather-upholstered chair. As he lit up a cheroot, he noticed a small pamphlet on the table before him. He picked it up. It was a compilation of articles featuring the Army's recent employment of "descents".

He began to read.

The London Chronicle July 1757

Mr Pitt has long been an advocate of the use of amphibious strikes, or "descents" against the French coastline in which a small British force may be landed. Settlements are then captured, fortifications, munitions, and supplies destroyed.

The London Chronicle August 1757

We are reliably informed that the British government has received an urgent request from Brunswick to endeavour to relieve the pressure put on them by the French. Mr Pitt has suggested that diversionary operations should be employed; namely, Mr Pitt's favoured "descents". Thus, the French would be forced to withdraw troops from the northern front to defend their coastline.

The London Chronicle September 1757

A British raid has been launched against Rochfort in Western France. For reasons not disclosed, it was not a success. Nevertheless, Mr Pitt is determined to press ahead with similar raids.

The London Chronicle April 1758

Another British raid in Western France. The current raid was organised under Lord Sackville. A landing at St Malo was partially successful. It was cut short by the appearance of French troops. The British force withdrew to Britain.

The London Chronicle August 1758

Mr Pitt's tenacity regarding his making use of descents has to be admired. As a diversionary tactic against the French, the same method has once more been employed. On this occasion, it was under the command of Thomas Bligh. This month, a raid on Cherbourg was successfully prosecuted. Ships and munitions were burned, and the town's fortifications were destroyed.

The London Chronicle September 1758

Despite previous "descents" at St Malo being unsuccessful, and only one descent anywhere else being successful, Mr Pitt could not be dissuaded from employing this method at St Malo again. After disembarking the troops, it was realised that St Malo was too heavily fortified. The operation was therefore abandoned. However, bad weather prevented the ships from re-embarking the troops. They marched overland to the safer harbour of St Cast. During the embarkation, the force was attacked by over ten thousand French troops resulting in an enormous loss of life and eight hundred British soldiers taken prisoner. A small auxiliary battalion camped above St Cast under the command of Colonel Erdington also took part in the battle, where Colonel Erdington lost his life.

Aubrey finished reading, picked up his brandy, and took a mouthful. He frowned at the Pamphlet and placed it back on the table.

A desire to strangle Pitt filled his mind.

They should all be hanged, or put up against a wall and shot. Damn them to hell, he thought. *Damn all politicians and damn all incompetent Army hierarchy.*

Aubrey stood, knocked back the rest of his brandy and left the Horatio.

He walked back to Army Headquarters, to his boring administrative duties.

His mind was so preoccupied with the senseless loss of life, that pride, self-aggrandizement and incompetence constantly caused, he hardly noticed the rain.

CHAPTER ONE

Major Edmond St Vere reined in his horse on the clifftop. Below, thousands of British soldiers waited on the beach for the small flat-bottomed boats, which would ferry them, seventy at a time, to ships anchored off the coast.

A movement on the cliff in the distance caught Edmond's eye. Raising his chin, peering, he looked, and his breath caught. Eyes wide, hands tightened on the reins, 'God Almighty,' he whispered.

A vanguard of French troops, in full battle array, was approaching across the cliff from the North.

Edmond wheeled his horse and galloped at breakneck speed back to his camp.

He rode to the Colonel's tent and gave the alarm.

'French troops. On the cliff. About to attack,' he panted.

The small battalion swiftly mustered for battle. They arrived at the beach, in time to see the French slaughter the unprepared men.

Riderless horses, with wild eyes and flying manes, galloped through the horrifying confusion, whinnying in fear. The wounded screamed in pain, calling for their mothers, imploring aid from Man and God. Men lay dead; others lay dying, with none to comfort them; their blood seeping into the sand in darkening patches. The smell of death pervaded the beach. At the shoreline, the waves flushed crimson.

Dark storm clouds, out to sea, moved towards the land, shedding sheets of rain. The deluge spattered the beach, washing away stains left by fighting.

Medical orderlies moved among the fallen soldiers. They carried off the dead to a communal grave, situated away from the field hospital and the main camp. For the rest, an endless stream of stretcher-bearers carried blood-soaked wounded from the site of the battle to the temporary field hospital, set up on the springy turf above the beach.

Here, in one small tent, Colonel John Erdington lay dying.

For several weeks before the battle, a small battalion of four hundred men lay camped outside the little French village of St Cast. The battalion's orders were to reconnoitre the area, and assist troops from St Malo, if necessary. Colonel John Erdington was in command; Major Edmond St Vere his second.

Colonel Erdington had hoped their presence at St Cast would go unnoticed by the French, who were preoccupied elsewhere.

English frigates and bomb ketches, out to sea, fired on the French, driving some back. But the weight of French troops was too great to overcome.

Edmond, Colonel Erdington, and four captains did their best to bring some order to the chaos. Yet, against over ten thousand French, victory was impossible. The soldiers fought bravely, but a terrible foreboding hung over the men on the beach, and on Colonel Erdington's small battalion.

Death. Her remorseless scythe thrust the soldiers into oblivion. They saw her, and they accepted her as in their hundreds they fell. Many died. Still more survived as maimed half-men.

Edmond fought bravely, hacking and slashing at the enemy.

His horse, Jet, was shot in the neck. Blood gushed from the wound as Jet reared. The horse fell. Edmond was thrown and knocked unconscious.

When Edmond came to, the battle was over.

An orderly helped him to his feet.

'Major St Vere, Sir, are you wounded?'

'No, I do not think so.'

Edmond looked about him.

'God, there are so many wounded. Have the French retreated?'

'Yes Sir, and taken hundreds of prisoners with them.'

Edmond, frowned, bemused.

'Have you seen Colonel Erdington?' he asked.

'Yes, Sir. He was badly wounded, Sir,' the orderly said, and moved off to help more injured men.

Edmond walked towards the field hospital, asking everyone he met whether they knew the whereabouts of Colonel Erdington. One orderly knew and led Edmond to a small tent.

'He's not expected to live out the night, Major,' the orderly said and hurried away.

Colonel Erdington had lost a lot of blood. In the half-light, the dark red bloodiness swamping his shirt heightened the stark, ivory pallor of his face. His breath rasped in his throat with a quick, panting rhythm that told Edmond death would not be long.

Edmond knelt beside the bed.

The dying man raised a hand, gripping Edmond's lapel.

'Edmond …' he whispered.

'Do not try to talk, John,' Edmond said.

Tears stung Edmond's eyes as he took a cloth, and staunched the blood oozing from the wound in the Colonel's chest.

Erdington coughed, tensing with pain, blood welling on his chest. He uttered one word.

'Sophia …'

'I shall take care of her, John. I promise. I shall treat her as my own daughter.'

Tears ran down Edmond's face as he spoke, leaving tracks in the dirt on his cheeks. He tried to control his ragged breathing.

He had seen enough men dying to be used to it by now, but never one he was so close to. He loved this man, both as leader and friend.

Another cough convulsed the Colonel's chest, as blood trickled from his mouth.

7

Edmond wiped away the blood and laid a hand on his colonel's arm.

'She will want for nothing, John,' Edmond said.

The words of a prayer echoed in Edmonds mind. *Eternal rest grant unto him, O Lord ...*

John grimaced, his body wracked with pain.

Rough gasps sounded in John's throat as he struggled to breath.

Edmond's eyes never left his friend's face.

Ah, God! Has he not suffered enough?

The Colonel's chest rose on one final harsh breath.

John Erdington's life left him in an echoing sigh.

Edmond placed a trembling hand on John's pale face, closing the sightless eyes. Stretching forward, he kissed the clammy forehead.

Edmond, still kneeling, bent his head, hands clasped together. He tried to pray, but couldn't.

'Goodbye, John,' he whispered, as he raised his head.

Standing, he looked at the empty body that had been his friend. So many good times they had shared, in combat and in peace.

Sadness engulfed Edmond. He sighed deeply. Reaching for a blanket, he bent forward to cover the lifeless form.

He sniffed hard, swallowed, and dashed a hand across his eyes.

I cannot be seen by the men like this.

He sat on a chair at the end of the bed. In the dim light, he looked about the tent. Apart from the Colonel's rent, bloody jacket, there was nothing in the tent belonging to John to take as a keepsake.

Edmond rose from the chair, going once more to look at his colonel's face. He lifted the blanket. Peaceful now, his struggle over, John's stillness calmed Edmond's agitation. He replaced the blanket, went to the tent flap, turned to take one last look at his colonel, and left the tent.

Outside, Edmond put a hand to his throbbing temple. The rain had stopped. Stifling air told of another storm brewing.

Edmond, some thirty years of age, stood tall, well-built, dressed in the uniform of a British officer. His scarlet coat, symbolic of the British Army, had cuffs and facings of sea green; his regiment's identifying colour. His waistcoat, shirt, and breeches were white, the stock at his neck, black. The symbol of a senior officer, a silver gorget, hung at his throat.

His black Hessian boots, normally kept shining by his batman, were covered in grime. Mud and blood spattered his breeches. Beneath his torn coat, unidentifiable stains covered his waistcoat and shirt. His dark hair was dishevelled, his green eyes bloodshot.

Havoc lay before him. The groans of the injured and dying filled Edmond with unease.

The confident voices of the surgeon, his assistants and their orderlies rang out. They called for support as they cut, sawed, stitched together and bandaged the remnants of men after battle.

Adding to the cacophony, incessant urgent shouts of orderlies calling for stretcher bearers to retrieve more casualties from the beach, where men lay in agony; some bleeding to death; others with hacked limbs; still more with gaping wounds. Their cries and moans mingled with distant thunder.

On the paths running between the tents, the muddy track shone, where spilt blood formed dark slicks.

Edmond shook his head as he assessed the carnage. His nostrils filled with the sweet, sickly smell of blood. A breeze wafted the pungent odour of men's sweat to mingle with the sharp stench of stale urine. On a following gust, the smell of approaching rain combined with the heavy reek of defecation. And over all, the terror of dying men rode on the wind.

Edmond had seen it all before. Yet, today, the shock of his colonel's death brought home to him the stark reality of senseless death. The cruelty of vigorous young lives lost, and for what?

God, how I hate the aftermath of battle.

Edmond slowly walked from the field hospital to make his way to his own tent.

He glanced up at the menacing clouds and walked on.

Wading through a stretch of bracken, Edmond came across the burial detail. They carried bodies to a pit, eight feet deep and twenty feet long. With care, they delivered the scores of incomplete gore-covered dead, to those arranging them in the bottom of the pit.

Edmond covered the lower half of his face with his sleeve, as he passed corpses cushioned in the bracken, awaiting the tender attention of their comrades.

Removing his sleeve from his face, Edmond began to climb the steep path up the cliff. He glanced down towards the beach. The sight was appalling. Many had been taken away, some to have their wounds tended, some to be buried. Yet, an enormous number of men still covered the beach.

Edmond continued on his way, eager to reach his own tent.

He arrived on level ground at the edge of the encampment. In still air, a pall of smoke hung over the area, fed by many campfires. The acrid odour filled his nostrils.

Edmond moved with easy grace. Not for a moment did he let his despondent mood show in the way he carried himself.

As he continued in the direction of his own tent, at the middle of the camp, he saw his batman, Sergeant Wilson, coming towards him.

The Sergeant's uniform was in disarray after the battle. His forehead bore a frown; his mouth pulled down.

At sight of his Major, Wilson's face broke into smiles.

Daniel Wilson, a crack shot, had been one of a platoon stationed on a ridge above the beach, picking off French troops. He had escaped the carnage of the main fight.

Wilson was almost as tall as Edmond, with a shock of brown hair, turning white at the temples. A thick-set man, with broad, strong shoulders, his honest face was kindly and expressive. He was a soldier through and through, having joined the Army as a boy of sixteen. He was now almost forty, and although he knew no other life, he longed to taste civilian freedom before he was too old to enjoy it. He saw no way of it being possible, so resigned himself to his fate.

Wilson hurried forward towards Edmond.

'Major, I've been searching for you. You're unharmed?' he said, relief on his lined, round face.

'I am, Wilson. Colonel Erdington is not. He is dead.'

'Damn them bleedin' Frenchies' eyes. How did it happen, Sir?'

'I do not know, Wilson, a bayonet I think,' Edmond replied.

'Ah, Major! The Colonel will be sorely missed. A fine officer. At least you're all right, though, Sir,' Wilson said, running his gaze over Edmond.

Wilson's keen eye detected a slackness about his Major's shoulders. Edmond's voice sounded weary, hoarse from fatigue. His face, under a layer of grime, was pale.

Edmond disregarded his fatigue and dishevelment. The thought uppermost in his mind was his need to inform Sophia of her loss.

'Will you fetch me another horse, Wilson? Jet was shot from under me,' Edmond said.

'I will, sir,' Wilson said. 'But we need to mend you. You present a sorry sight.'

As he spoke, Wilson brushed at his Major's shoulders, pulled bracken from a sleeve, and fiddled with a loose button on Edmond's waistcoat, his relief at finding his Major alive driving him to attend to Edmond's disarray.

'Stop fussing, Wilson,' Edmond said, as, with a flick of a hand, he stepped back to release himself from Wilson's ministrations.

'And fetch me my horse.'

11

CHAPTER TWO

Wilson picked up a large, well-worn metal ewer from the Major's tent. He went to a nearby campfire over which hung a hefty cauldron of bubbling water. He filled the ewer and returned.

He was fond of his major, an officer who cared for his men but brooked no misbehaviour.

The men knew Edmond was hot tempered, but always fair. He asked nothing of them that he wouldn't face himself. His discipline was strict, yet, when necessary, he showed understanding and compassion. There was not another officer in the regiment so well liked and respected.

Wilson and Edmond enjoyed an easy relationship, but Wilson knew not to overstep the line drawn between officer and man. His life as a batman—a soldier acting as servant to an officer—was far easier than that of an ordinary soldier.

On returning to the tent, Wilson poured hot water into a canvas bucket, hanging in a wooden tripod in a corner of their tent.

Edmond entered.

'I'll go for your horse while you wash, Major, Sir,' Wilson said.

'Very well, Wilson,' Edmond said, sitting on his bed to remove his boots.

Wilson placed a washcloth, and a towel on a thin rope line, that ran the length of the tent wall. After dropping a bar of evil-smelling army soap into the water, Wilson searched for a clean shirt, waistcoat, jacket and breeches.

Edmond removed his ravaged uniform, and washed the clinging grime from his hair and his body. Three times, Edmond changed the filthy water.

Dirt-free, Edmond's damp hair curled on his forehead.

'Are you still here, Wilson?' he grumbled, as he dried himself with a rough towel.

'I had to clean your boots, Sir,' Wilson said, looking

sidelong at Edmond.

Edmond let out an exaggerated sigh and started dressing.

With his bloody, mud spattered clothes replaced, and his boots polished, he looked more upright, all trace of the battle washed away.

'I've brewed some tea, and put a shot o' rum in it for you, Sir,' Wilson said, handing his Major a battered beaker.

Edmond drank a mouthful of the hot tea.

'Thank you, Wilson. Now *please,* will you make haste and fetch my horse.'

'Yes, sir,' Wilson said, saluting smartly before leaving the tent.

Edmond finished the welcome drink. Yawning, he sat a moment on his camp bed. He stretched and allowing himself a moment's rest, lay on the bed. Weariness engulfed him. He gave in to it and slept.

Wilson set out again. He seemed a different man from the one who, eyes wild with worry, dashed frantically from place to place, searching for Edmond, thinking he had perhaps lost him.

This time, Wilson walked briskly with his head held high. He made his way to the stables, eager to carry out Edmond's orders.

Wilson arrived at the edge of the camp. A series of long tents served as stables where army orderlies looked after the senior officers' horses. Wilson sought out Monahan, Edmond's orderly, who had served as groom to his horses since Edmond's promotion to Captain.

'Good day to you, Wilson. How is Major St Vere?'

'He is well, Monahan. But Jet's gone.'

Monahan's face fell. 'The Major's favourite horse? He was a thoroughbred. The Major brought him back with him when he returned after his father died; told me his father had hunted with Jet. What happened?'

'Shot from under him in the battle on the beach,'

Wilson said, with a weary shake of his head.

'He'll be unhappy about that. Jet served the Major well,' Monahan said, contemplating Edmond's loss.

'Aye, he did. Now he needs another. Onyx might do. But is Warrior fit? I heard he pulled a tendon,' Wilson said.

'Yes, he's well recovered,' Monahan said. 'Next to Jet, the Major has a partiality for Warrior. He's not pure thoroughbred, but he's a dependable animal.'

Monahan went off to retrieve the horse.

Wilson watched him go. He had time to rest, so sat on a bale of hay, his hands on his thighs, his head leaning back on a post, his eyes shut. He wondered where he would find himself next, in a world where war seemed never ending.

Monahan returned leading a big bay.

'Sleeping on the job, Sergeant?' Monahan said, with a grin, as he tethered the horse to the post.

'Inspecting me eyelids, Monahan. Are you sure the horse is fit?'

Monahan ran a hand down Warrior's injured leg.

'Yea, he'll do,' he said over his shoulder, as he went to fetch saddle and harness from the tack area.

Returning, he threw a saddlecloth on Warrior's back, followed by the saddle, and continued to prepare the horse for the Major. Monahan worked in silence, a quiet placidity coming over him, as he saw to the horse.

'There, Wilson,' Monahan said, as he smoothed the horse's neck, and gave Wilson the bridle. 'My compliments to Major St Vere, and my sympathy for Jet's loss.'

Wilson nodded in reply and started walking Warrior back to Edmond.

The men he passed on the way were in sober mood. The majority had been engaged in the fighting and had lost comrades. Wilson passed campfires, acknowledging those he knew. Many, in shock, didn't see him, lost in their thoughts. One man caught him by the arm.

'Dan, did you find Major St Vere? Last I saw you, you

were searching for him,' Davie Southwick said. The two had joined the Army together, so were longstanding comrades.

'I found him, Davie, an' he was messed up proper, but unharmed. He's all scrubbed up now, though. Did you find Josh Makepeace?'

'I did. He ain't too bad, slash on his arm, but he'll mend. Old Josh leads a charmed life, I reckon. Did ya hear about the Colonel, though? Bad business that,' Davie said, shaking his head.

'Yea, I heard all right. The Major was with him when he died. He has to go now, to tell the Colonel's daughter of her loss, so I better get on and bring the horse for him to ride there. Good luck, Davie.'

'Good luck to you, Dan,' Southwick said.

In his tent, lying on his bed, Edmond's breathing quickened. His head moved restlessly on his pillow. Vivid dreams disturbed his sleep.

He is high up on the cliff. The wind whips his hair into disorder and whistles in his ears. He overlooks the beach, where men are awaiting the boats to ferry them to the safety of their ships. A swirling grey mist, enveloping the cliff, clears. As Edmond watches, he sees a swarm of evil-looking enemy troops descending on the unprepared men, who are oblivious to the enemy's approach. Edmond gives a shout of warning, but the wind carries his words away. Silence thunders in his ears. Helpless, he watches the enemy butcher the men below. Blood rises in a dark wave, flooding the beach beneath him.

Suddenly, he is on the beach, in the thick of the carnage. The intense, deafening noise of battle, crashes in on him. Mounted on Jet, Edmond slashes and lunges with his sword. Each sword stroke hacks the enemy to pieces. No matter how badly wounded, they laugh with cruel menace and come at him repeatedly. The more they come, the more Edmond fills with anger. The more furiously his blade flashes, the bloodier the enemy soldiers become. An

15

ear-splitting rifle report … Jet falls. The horse's screams swirl in Edmond's mind….

When Wilson returned, he was pleased to find Edmond sleeping. Wilson was of a mind to let Edmond sleep a while longer, but knew enough not to provoke the Major's annoyance. As he moved towards Edmond, he heard him grunting in his sleep, a crease across his forehead. His head jerked spasmodically, pressing into the pillow. His eyelids flickered, his hands twitched. Wilson realised Edmond was dreaming. He knew he must wake him gently. He caught Edmond's wrists, bent forward, and said softly near Edmond's ear. 'Major, Sir.'

Edmond awoke with a cry, straining his arms in Wilson's grip. Eyes wild, he sat up, looking about, horrified.

His tension relaxed. 'Ah, Wilson, I was dreaming,' he said placing his palms on his forehead. He shook off the tension, letting out a grunt. 'Hah! I was back in the battle….'

He paused a moment, measuring his breathing, gaining composure.

'Have you brought me a horse?'

'Yes, Major. Warrior awaits you,' Wilson said, concern in his eyes.

Edmond's thoughts of his dream receded. Stretching his arms, he yawned, blinking at Wilson.

'Are you pleased now, Wilson? I have rested as you recommended,' he said, amusement in his eyes.

'Not for long enough, Major, but 'tis better than no rest at all,' Wilson said, as he held the tent flap open again.

Edmond stood, eased his stiff shoulders, and went outside to find Warrior tethered to a post. Not as splendid as Jet had been, but a sturdy, reliable mount, which had served him well in the past.

The horse whinnied at sight of Edmond, who ran a hand over the horse's sleek neck before he mounted.

'Should anyone ask for me, Wilson, tell them I am

carrying out Colonel Erdington's orders.'

He wheeled his horse and wove his way through the camp.

Men looked up as he passed, and stood to salute him. Their mood brightened on seeing him; his fresh, impressive appearance gave them heart. He represented the epitome of a British officer, with his straight back; his head held high; seemingly untouched by the ordeal they had recently shared.

He acknowledged their salutes with his own, and nodded when men shouted 'Good luck to you, Major.'

Once clear of the camp, he took the path east towards the road to Membillier.

CHAPTER THREE

Edmond rode with a sorry heart. He studied a land scarred by the recent battle, the scene at odds with the tranquil stillness of early autumn in the air. He breathed the earthy aroma of recent rain.

A gentle breeze ruffled the remaining leaves on trees, wearing their uniform of autumn colours. On either side, they formed a canopy of branches overhanging the path. While he rode under the sheltering boughs, falling leaves fluttered about him.

As Edmond rode on, the dazzling autumn display vanished, where skeletons of once-proud and beautiful trees, lay exposed. Misplaced cannon fire had reduced them to blackened stumps, leaving them standing naked and forlorn.

Edmond reached the road and quickened his pace.

In several places, large craters pitted the terrain, where poorly aimed shot had landed in the fields, charring the earth. The harvest incomplete, here and there a stalk or two of uncut corn stood unharvested. Many seasons would pass before the fields recovered enough to support a crop again.

Edmond shook his head as he passed the ruined trees and fields.

Three years ago, fever had carried off Edmond's father and older brother. Suddenly Edmond found himself heir to the St Vere title, a vast estate—Crawford Lees in Oxfordshire—and, to his astonishment, a considerable fortune.

Edmond had never envisioned himself in such a position. What did a title mean to him? What was he to do with such an estate?

He had returned home for his brother and father's funeral. Vere House in Kensington, where his father and brother had lived, was empty but for the servants. For several days, Edmond rattled around in the vast mansion, with nothing to do.

Then relatives descended on the house like a flock of starlings. Uncles, cousins and aunts, about whose existence he had little or no knowledge, chattering, exchanging news, expressing insincere sympathy for Edmond.

His sister, Perdita, had taken charge, efficiently organising the servants into activity; ensuring everyone was accommodated and fed. His father's steward had organised the funeral arrangements. Everything went forward like clockwork. There was little for Edmond to do.

Edmond de Murville, as the second son of the Marquess of St Vere, had always understood his destiny was a military career. With the death of his father and brother, his status had undergone a momentous change; no longer a second son, but head of the family.

He had become the new Marquess, Lord Edmond St Vere.

As a boy, he had visited Crawford Lees. He was enamoured of its vastness; the villages within it; its plantation; its endless rolling fields; the swift flowing river. Most impressive of all were the tenants, who paid great respect to his father, his brother—and to him.

After the funeral, Edmond consulted with the various bailiffs and agents whom his father employed to ensure the smooth running of his domains.

Edmond had travelled once more to Crawford Lees with his father's agent, Mr Treadwell. He had escorted Edmond over the enormous estate, with great aplomb, rushing him here and there, until his head spun.

On his return to London, as quickly as they had descended on him, Edmond's relatives all departed, having given him the benefit of their opinion. They all agreed. He must resign his commission. "Take up the reins where your father left off", they had said.

'It is your duty as head of the family to do so,' his sister had urged.

He was loath "to do so". His life, so far, was very different from that which his society-loving father and brother's had been. He didn't relish the thought of living as they had.

He eagerly read each new issue of the "London Gazette" for news of battles.

Military activity increased daily. As the aggression escalated, Edmond itched to return to his regiment.

The war beckoned.

He ignored his relative's advice and resumed his military activities.

In the three years that passed since then, he slowly became less devoted to his occupation, giving serious thought to the prospect of resigning. Again, and again, he came to a decision. But always there was something to hold him back.

Today's carnage, particularly the death of Colonel Erdington, gave his thoughts impetus. As he rode, he mused on his growing decision.

Yes, I shall settle on my estate, and enjoy a peaceful life, he thought.

At present, however, he had a hard task before him: breaking the awful news of her father's death to Sophia.

Perturbed, he thought of her.

She is young. What is she? About fourteen?

Edmond had seen Sophia many times when invited by her father to dine with him. Colonel Erdington's French wife, Sophia's mother, had died some years before. The Colonel loved his daughter well. He knew he should send her back to England. Yet, he had no relatives whom he could trust to take care of her, so, he kept her with him wherever he went, housing her far from any fighting.

Full of life, Sophia's large, expressive, brown eyes, danced with fun. Her dark hair tumbled past her shoulders, in unruly curls. She had a tenderness about her which Edmond found appealing; a charming child.

Edmond remembered a conversation he had with his Colonel

'She is a scamp, Edmond, always looking for what she terms "adventures", fearless, reckless, becoming more intrepid, as she gets older,' Colonel Erdington said as he drank port with Edmond after dinner.

'She cannot be that bad, Sir,' Edmond said. 'I found her polite, and most proper.'

'Ah, she was on her best behaviour. Depend upon it; she will be up to her "adventures" as quick as you can blink,' the Colonel said with a nod, and a smile.

Edmond laughed.

Colonel Erdington continued. 'There is no harm in her, though. She is but impulsive, and inquisitive, and has a passion to explore. I love her dearly, and would not be without her.'

Edmond's wife had died in childbirth seven years before. The child had died too.

He wondered what his own daughter would have been like had she lived. He thought John Erdington was a lucky man to have a daughter.

How Sophia will miss her father.

Sophia has no one now.

I must assure her of my support. 'Twould be better for her if I were to take her to England.

The idea fell well within his current plans.

Yes, of course, if I do not act now, resign my commission, I never shall. I shall do so as soon as I may. Today, in fact, and I shall take her home with me.

On this assignment at St Cast, no heavy action had been expected. But Colonel Erdington wanted Sophia safe, just the same.

The Colonel had sent Captain Orpwood to visit the Church at Membillier and ask the padre if he knew of a suitable house, situated several miles from the proposed encampment at St Cast. *Pere Alain* knew of only one, so Orpwood had recommended the Colonel commission it.

The Colonel hadn't envisioned his stay in the area to be long. Having commissioned the house, he had sent Captain

Orpwood once more to consult *Pere Alain* to ask whom he might hire to keep house for Sophia. *Pere Alain* had recommended Clothilde Caron as housekeeper-cook, and her cousin, Berthe, as maid. François Mynatt, he suggested, might serve as stable boy, and anything else that needed the boy's capable hand. They would take up residence in the house, for as long as Sophia was there.

Sophia's governess, Miss Roseberry, hadn't come to Membillier. She disliked the idea of living in France in wartime, so had returned to England.

Edmond arrived at the austere, cheerless-looking house, where Sophia stayed. Once a comfortable farmhouse home, it had lain empty for some years. The whitewashed walls were faded, partially covered in moss, and ivy.

On either side of the path leading to the front door, occasional flowers struggled against abundant weeds.

His heart laden, Edmond slowly dismounted from Warrior, tethering him to the rickety fence surrounding the weed-choked garden. He picked his way over the cracked, broken path.

At the grey-painted door, he removed his hat, and knocked, breathing deeply to dispel his sense of dread.

When the door opened, the housekeeper stood before him. She wore a light grey gown, covered by a white apron, a lace cap on her blonde head. Her grey eyes bright, she looked with enquiry at Edmond.

'May I help you, Monsieur?'

'I am Major St Vere. I have come to have speech with Miss Sophia Erdington,' Edmond said.

'I shall inform Miss Erdington you are here, Monsieur. Will you wait here, if you please?' she said, in heavily accented English. She took Edmond's hat and placed it on the hall table.

Her heels clicked on the red tiled floor of the passage before she disappeared up the stairs.

Edmond heard the murmur of voices, and in a moment, the woman reappeared.

'Miss Erdington will see you, Major. Please follow me, Monsieur.'

She led the way to the stairs.

Edmond caught a glimpse of a large kitchen, spotlessly clean. A welcoming aroma of fresh baked galette wafted from it, into the hall. The housekeeper indicated the staircase to the left, set between two walls. He ascended the stairs, and she followed him.

They arrived at a spacious landing, a colourful rug covering the floor. Several doors led off this landing, the handles on the doors burnished to a brilliant shine. A shaft of light from one door, standing ajar, cast a long beam into the hall. Edmond could hear the crackle of a fire and caught the warm homely smell of beeswax polish.

The housekeeper knocked, and Edmond heard Sophia's voice.

'Come in, Clothilde,' she said.

'Major St Vere, Mam'selle,' Clothilde said, as she held the door for Edmond to enter the room.

Sophia sat on a couch by the fireplace, her feet tucked under her, a book in her hand. The glow from the firelight played in the chestnut highlights of her curling hair, cascading about her shoulders. She dressed simply in a green gown, sprinkled with a cream floral pattern. A yellow shawl rested on her shoulders.

Sophia rose, shoving her white-stockinged feet into her yellow satin slippers set before her chair. She moved towards him, a welcoming smile on her lips, her eyes dancing.

'Major St Vere, I am glad to see you. How good to have your company. I am all on my own as my Father is not here.'

Her eyes searched his face. His bleak expression filled her with apprehension. Her smile faded.

'What is it, Edmond?'

'Sophia …'

He could say no more. A long ill-omened pause hung in the room.

'Edmond, is it my father?' she asked, her voice a mere whisper.

He was silent. His eyes closed. He nodded.

'No, Edmond, no,' she said, a sob in her voice. She caught her lower lip between her teeth. Tears formed in her eyes, her arms hugged her body.

'I am sorry, Sophia,' he said. The words caught in his throat.

She gained control of her voice.

'How did it happen, Edmond?' Her breath shuddered.

Edmond bent his head. He swallowed.

With a supreme effort, he took command of his emotions. Lifting his head, he looked at her with deep compassion.

'There was a battle. He did not survive his wounds, Sophia. I was with him until the end. His last words were of you. He asked me to take care of you.'

Edmond drew her to the couch. Sitting beside her, he took her hand in his. The warmth of his hand comforted her.

Sadness at the loss of his friend filled him, sadness for her too. He knew her loss was far more difficult to bear.

She sat still, hardly breathing.

'Oh, poor Father,' she whispered at last. 'Yesterday morning he was in good spirits.'

Sophia heaved a shuddering sigh.

'He said the camp might be struck today. He said we would travel somewhere else. He said we might go to England. Now I shall never see him again.'

Sophia buried her face in Edmond's coat.

'How can I bear it, Edmond?' she said, her voice muffled, her body shivering.

His hand tightened on hers. She sat quiet for some minutes, thinking, trembling, without crying.

Sophia lifted her head. 'Edmond, what is to become of me? I have nowhere to go.'

'Hush, Sophia. Do not worry, my dear. I promised your father I would care for you, and I shall,' he told her.

She shifted her head to look into his face, a desperate glint in her eyes.

'You will until you are killed, too.'

Her mouth turned down as she stared at him, her eyes angry.

She turned her head away.

'No, Sophia, I shall not be killed, as I have determined to give up fighting. I shall return to England, and take you with me,' he said, his voice low, calm, resolute.

She didn't move for several seconds. Lifting her head, she stared at him, her eyes open wide.

'Do you mean it, Edmond?' she whispered. 'You will take me to England?'

A faint smile appeared on his face.

'Yes, Sophia. I promised your father I would look after you as my own daughter.'

Sophia's eyes lifted to his face.

'You promised that?' She shook her head.

'Oh, how can I ever thank you, Edmond?' she said, placing her hand on his arm. She could hardly breathe for thinking of so many things at once.

Edmond rose from the couch. He stood before her, his face serious.

'We shall go in a day or two, Sophia.'

He bent towards her and took her by the shoulders. Raising her up, he looked intently into her eyes.

'Listen to me now. You must put together anything you want to take with you. I shall send my man to you early tomorrow to bring you to the camp. You and your belongings must be ready.'

His dark eyebrows emphasised his serious expression.

'I am glad you are here, Edmond,' she said, trying to smile.

Edmond wasn't sure whether she was too distracted to pay attention.

'Do you understand what I have said, Sophia?' he asked gently.

'Yes, Edmond. I shall do as you say. I shall have my

belongings ready,' she said.

Edmond nodded.

'Good. Now I must return to the camp. If there are problems, send your stable lad to find me.'

He made for the door, glancing at her before opening it.

Her chin trembled; she was about to cry.

Edmond returned, and took her hands in his, looking at her closely.

'Try to be brave, Sophia. There will be time enough to weep when all is done.'

He put a firm hand on her shoulder.

'I would stay with you, but my absence will be noticed if I am away too long.'

'Go then, Major. I shall do as you say. Being occupied will be good for me.'

She tilted her chin, emphasising her determination.

'Good girl. Adieu, Sophia.'

He had gone.

She was alone.

She would never see her father again. No more would she hear his cheery laugh; no more would he scold her, the while trying not to smile.

She went to the window. In bright sunlight, the view was pleasant. Today, grey clouds, moving swiftly by, cast the picture into gloom, matching her mood.

She had never thought that her father might die.

He was so strong, so capable, so invincible.

Ah, but he was a soldier, and soldiers are killed.

How foolish, never to realise what might happen.

Yet, he had told her that this assignment wasn't dangerous. It was simply an auxiliary force in case of trouble. No one had contemplated a battle.

What went wrong?

Sophia's thoughts turned to Edmond, and the prospect of going to England.

The concept was both exciting and daunting.

'I shall not cry. I shall be strong. I shall do as he bid me,' she murmured to herself, wiping the tears from her cheeks.

She needed company.

She called Clothilde.

When she arrived, Clothilde was all curiosity to know why the Major had come alone to speak to Sophia. She stopped short when she saw Sophia's wan expression.

'What is wrong, Mam'selle?' She asked, anxious for Sophia, hurrying to her side.

'My father, Clothilde. He was wounded. He is dead. Major St Vere came to tell me.'

'*Ah ma pauvre,*' Clothilde said, catching Sophia to her in a close embrace. Again, Sophia struggled with her tears.

Clothilde held Sophia in her arms, crooning soothing sympathy. Sophia clung to her, trembling, her breathing ragged.

Regaining her composure, Sophia stood back from Clothilde, brushing tears from her cheeks.

'I must be strong, Clothilde. I have much to do. I must pack all my belongings. Will you help me, please?'

'*Mais, certainement Mam'selle.* When are you to go?'

'Early tomorrow morning,' Sophia said, pressing her hands together on her chest.

'And, *where* will you go, *ma chérie*?'

'Major St Vere is returning to England, and he will take me with him,' Sophia said, her eyes shining with unshed tears.

Clothilde said nothing, her lips folded.

'He promised my father he would look after me as his own daughter,' Sophia said, oblivious to the woman's disapproving look.

'He and my father were good friends,' she continued. 'He said I must be ready to go early tomorrow. He is sending his man to collect me, and my trunks.'

Clothilde's disapproval still lingered. Nevertheless, if the Colonel trusted the Major, it was none of her business to judge. She put her misgivings aside.

'Come then, Mam'selle Sophie, we must start *immédiatement,*' she said.

CHAPTER FOUR

When Edmond returned to the encampment, he headed towards the administrative sector, situated near the officers' accommodation, in well-appointed tents. Although Edmond and the other officers' quarters were more comfortable than those of the enlisted men, the administrative furnishings were far superior. Well-crafted pieces of furniture, which dismantled for easy transportation, rested in luxury in each tent. Upholstered chairs stood at each compact desk. Beds, as opulent as those in any grand house, were available to each officer of administrative rank. No canvas buckets suspended in tripods here, but proper washstands, accompanied by matching china basins, and ewers. Orderlies assigned to each quarters kept the furnishings spotlessly clean. Hard surfaces were polished to perfection.

On entering the main area, Edmond sought out the adjutant, Captain Jameson.

'Good day, Captain Jameson. I wonder whether I might see a colonel?' Edmond asked, eyeing the Captain's arm, which was in a sling.

'Good day, Major St Vere. Can you tell me what you wish to see him about, Sir?'

Edmond frowned. *So begins the tedious round of being quizzed about my requests.*

'I wish to resign my commission, and take charge of the late Colonel Erdington's daughter, and his possessions,' Edmond said.

Captain Jameson frowned, his mouth open in surprise.

'Resign, Major? You cannot be serious!'

'I am perfectly serious, Charles. Are either of the Colonels free?'

'Yes, I believe Colonel Radford is. But why Sir? You are the most competent major in the regiment.'

'I have my reasons,' Edmond said. 'What happened to

28

your arm?'

'Oh, that? I was on the beach. A bullet; just a graze. I shall go and tell Colonel Radford you are here,' he said, realising Edmond had no intention of divulging his business.

Edmond was left to sit in a comfortable chair in Captain Jameson's office, for over twenty minutes, before the captain returned.

'I am sorry to have kept you waiting, Sir. Colonel Radford will see you now,' he said.

He led Edmond to another tent and announced him.

'Major St Vere to see you, Colonel Radford,' he said, and left Edmond standing before the Colonel.

A lean, redheaded man, with a luxuriant moustache, Colonel Radford sat opposite Edmond behind a campaign desk. The beauty of his slim white hands caught Edmond's eye. Hands remarkably devoid of the grime sustained by men engaged in warfare. When he looked at Radford's long, pale face, a bored expression in his heavy-lidded eyes, Edmond's heart sank. He knew the type well; one who fought from behind a desk.

The Colonel listened to him with stoic indifference.

'Resign your commission? Why?' Colonel Radford said, his chin tilted, his brows drawn together.

'I have business to attend to in England, Sir. I wish to take the late Colonel Erdington's daughter back with me. I promised the Colonel on his deathbed I would look after her. I wish to fulfil my promise,' Edmond said.

Colonel Radford's blasé attitude irritated Edmond. With difficulty, he kept his impatience in check.

'Most noble of you, Major; but surely that does not warrant you resigning? Would not a furlough suffice?' He sat back in his chair, steepling his long fingers before him.

'Would you grant me one, Sir?' Edmond asked, believing it unlikely.

The Colonel took a moment to think. He had to accept a resignation if offered, but he was not obliged to grant leave. Edmond was an efficient officer, an asset—a pity to lose him.

'Under the circumstances, I am sure we can oblige you, Major,' he said, his tone affable, 'How long a leave of absence do you require?'

'Three months, if you please, Sir.'

Colonel Radford took a paper from in front of him and began to write.

Edmond smiled inwardly. *Strange, when it suits them, the Army's strict ruling can bend with such facility.*

'You are most gracious, Sir,' Edmond said with a slight bow of his head, trying to make his words sound genuine. He decided to exploit the situation; go a little further.

'I wonder, Sir, may I request my batman, Sergeant Wilson, accompany me? He is a most reliable man; I would hate to lose him. If I am not here, they will reassign him.'

Edmond held his breath.

'Come now, Major, you are pushing things somewhat,' Radford said. He paused, contemplating, giving Edmond a concentrated stare as he drummed his fingers on the desk.

With decision, he drew forward another sheet of paper. 'Yes, I shall allow it,' he said. 'I appreciate what breaking in a new batman is like.'

He signed the documents with a flourish and was about to place his seal on them when Edmond spoke again.

'I have one more request, Sir.'

Edmond watched the Colonel, who put a hand to his mouth, pinching his lower lip between finger and thumb, narrowing his eyes.

'Go on,' Radford said, with a twist of his hand.

'I need a pass for Colonel Erdington's daughter.'

The Colonel gave Edmond an appraising look, nodded, took another sheet of paper, and started writing.

'Her name?'

'Sophia Erdington.'

'Where is her mother?' Radford asked, casually.

'She died some years ago, Sir.'

Colonel Radford glanced up at Edmond.

'Who was she?'

'Her name was Camille Arouette. I know nothing more of her, Sir.'

Edmond resisted the temptation to adjust the uncomfortable stock at his neck.

'She was French?' the Colonel's chin lifted as he regarded Edmond with suspicion.

'Yes, Sir. Is that a problem?' Edmond inquired, his irritation passing into annoyance.

'Indeed it is, Major. The authorities regard such persons as alien. She may not enter England. If she had a relative to go to, all would be well. But a woman alone with no one to stand surety for her? No,' he said, putting down his pen with care.

'I beg your pardon, Sir; she is a fourteen-year-old child. How can she be regarded as an alien? The same objection would not apply to her returning home with her father,' Edmond said, trying to keep a tight rein on his mounting anger.

'No, of course not, for he would be her guarantor.'

The Colonel waved a languid hand, a false smile on his face.

'I promised Colonel Erdington I would be a father to her. Can I not be her guarantor?' Edmond asked, his smile as false as the Colonel's, whose tone grew belligerent.

'No, Major, you cannot, as your relationship is not certified. There is nothing in writing to say that her father officially put her into your care,' he said, an ugly twist to his mouth.

'But her father *did* put her into my care, Sir.'

Edmond's mouth assumed an unpleasant stiffness. Anger overtook him; his voice rose.

'When he did so, he was on the point of death; therefore, had no time to commit it to writing,' he said, exasperated by the Army's discriminate application of regulations.

The Colonel eyed him with displeasure. He shifted in his seat, all his languor dissipated.

'You are sailing close to the wind, Sir,' he said, running his fingers over his bushy moustache.

With an effort, Edmond reined in his temper.

'I apologise, Colonel,' Edmond said, his voice losing its edge, 'but how can I care for the child under such circumstances? My wish is to remove her from danger, and bring her to the safety of England.'

The germ of an idea flitted through his mind.

'Perhaps if I were to marry her, would that relationship accommodate the Army's requirements?' he said, the idea taking root.

The Colonel shouted in mirthless laughter, 'Ha, Ha, Ha. Is that not a trifle extreme, Major?'

Edmond ignored the Colonel's words. 'Would requirements be fulfilled, Sir?' he asked, warming to the idea of circumventing the Army's inflexible rules.

The Colonel sat back in his seat, one hand stroking his chin.

'Strictly speaking, Major, yes, they would. Banns should be read, but in a wartime situation such as this, well… pfff.'

He leant forward again, one arm lying on his desk, his other hand stroking his chin as he looked at Edmond, his lips pursed, his eyelids drooping languidly.

'But would you be willing to take on a fourteen-year-old bride?' The Colonel said, with a speculative lift of an eyebrow, a lecherous smirk on his face.

Edmond's shoulders shifted. Although incensed by the Colonel's implication, taking a deep breath, he managed to ignore it.

'If that is what it takes to fulfil my obligation, Sir, yes, I am willing.'

He straightened his shoulders, continuing, 'I would be obliged, therefore, if you will supply me with the necessary papers so the marriage may take place.'

Edmond stood rigid, ready to sustain an onslaught. But the Colonel's amusement overrode his ire.

The ugly sneer still on his face, Radford pulled more

paper towards him.

'You have not thought this through, Major,' he said, as he began to write. 'Nonetheless, I shall supply you with a permit. I hope you do not live to regret what you are doing.'

'Sir, it remains to be seen whether I regret a marriage, but I am certain I would regret abandoning this child,' Edmond said, fighting the urge to vent his fury in a slap, to wipe the supercilious expression from Radford's face.

The Colonel continued to write as Edmond spoke, glancing up at Edmond's determined words. Yet, the Colonel said nothing, as he sealed the documents, and handed them to Edmond.

Edmond placed them in his inner pocket and stood to smart attention. He focused his eyes above the Colonel's head, clicked his heels, and bowed his head a moment before turning to leave Radford, without fulfilling his desire to strangle the man.

Outside the tent, Edmond stood, calming the anger boiling inside him. He took several controlled breaths, thinking, trying to decide whether to return to Sophia, to tell her what he had done, or proceed to his tent, to tell Wilson to start packing.

He chose to do the latter, and walked his horse to his own tent.

Once Edmond had left Membillier, Sophia had told the stable lad, Francois, to put her two brassbound trunks in the drawing room. She charged Clothilde with carrying all her possessions there, where Sophia intended to sort them.

While she waited for Francois and Clothilde to complete their tasks, she stood by the window thinking about Edmond.

Sophia's father had often brought the officers, who served under him, to dine at his home. But the most frequent visitor was Major St Vere.

Sophia thought on how she always liked Edmond for his quiet self-assurance. Other officers treated him with respect. She remembered how he spoke little in company. But when he did, he made witty, sharp, and knowledgeable conversation. Occasionally, when one of the younger men spoke injudiciously, she noticed annoyance in his expression, as a glint came to his eyes, but never had she seen him act or comment on what caused him irritation.

I always admired his self-control.

She had said as much to her father, who had also noticed this quality in Edmond. She harked back to her father's answer.

'I have a high regard for him, Sophia. His temper is, indeed, easily aroused, but he keeps himself under control. I commend and admire him for it. You, my girl, are clever to have observed it.'

She recalled how he had ruffled the front of her unruly hair. She sighed at the remembrance of her father's familiar gesture.

She thought of the times when Edmond dined alone with her and her father. How their conversation had fascinated her, as the two men bantered about the Army, politics, religion, and philosophy—all a little above her at the time. But her father, having someone so agreeable to talk to, had pleased her.

CHAPTER FIVE

Wilson was busy in the tent, mending and cleaning Edmond's damaged uniform. He looked up when Edmond entered, putting aside the Major's coat.

'Start packing, Sergeant Wilson,' Edmond said, a gleam in his eye.

'Why, Sir. What's afoot?' Wilson asked, his frown wrinkling his nose.

'I acquired a three-month furlough, Wilson; I am going to England. I have obtained one for you, too, if you wish to come with me,' Edmond said.

Wilson's eyebrows flew up. His mouth opened on a gasp as he stood up.

'Three months, Major? No need to ask if I want to come—o' course, I do. Does your goin' have anythin' to do with Miss Erdington, Sir?'

'Yes, Wilson, it does. She is coming with me to England. I want you to take our things with hers to the port at Marronville tomorrow. You must arrange passage for the three of us. We shall follow, and meet you there at *Le Coq d'Or*. When I return from seeing her, we shall discuss the details.'

'I'll start right away, Major,' Wilson said, gathering his mending.

'Good man,' Edmond said over his shoulder, as he left the tent.

Edmond mounted Warrior, and once again set out for Membillier.

On the way, Edmond thought on the task before him. He was not sure how he would explain the new turn of events to Sophia. Marriage to a man of his age, he felt sure, would be abhorrent to her.

Imperative I assure her I shall regard her and treat her as my daughter.

Remembering Radford's attitude, Edmond's gorge rose. His anger at Radford resurfaced, causing his hand to tighten on the rein, making Warrior toss his head. Edmond slackened his grip, and patted the horse's neck, while once more controlling his unbidden emotion.

Although marriage to a fourteen-year-old was within the law, Edmond could not contemplate it, other than in name only. Yes, Sophia was appealing, but only as the daughter of his friend, and now as his own ward. He was singularly averse to the prospect of anything else.

Edmond mused on how Perdita, his sister, would take the news. He must assure her, too, that his motives were purely altruistic. Besides, he knew she would revel in assisting him in caring for Sophia until the girl was old enough to marry a suitable man.

While lost in thought, Edmond hadn't noticed how far he had come. He was surprised to find himself approaching his destination. The trees thinned out as the dilapidated farmhouse came into sight.

He rode up to the same rickety fence, dismounted, and tethered Warrior to it once more.

Edmond walked up the same broken path and knocked.

Clothilde opened the door. A look of surprise covered her face as she held it open for him.

'Major St Vere. I did not expect you here again so soon. Is anything wrong?' she said, her curiosity aroused. She ushered him into the hall and took his hat, as before, placing it on the hall table.

'No, Clothilde, nothing is wrong. I must talk with Miss Erdington again.'

'Mam'selle Sophie is packing her belongings. I will show you up.'

They walked along the passage to the staircase.

'Mam'selle tells me you are taking her to England, Major.'

'Yes, Clothilde. I am now her guardian,' Edmond said, noting a somewhat critical look in Clothilde's eye. 'My sister will assist me in caring for her,' he added, hoping to allay any qualms the woman had on Sophia's behalf.

Clothilde smiled at him, placated to some degree. She

went before him up the stairs, leading him to the drawing room.

Edmond found Sophia sitting on the floor in the middle of the room. The two large, brassbound trunks stood before her. Clothes and belongings surrounded her. She was sorting through a heap of books, putting those she would take, and those she would discard, in separate piles. The task took a long time, as she frequently stopped to flick through, and read parts of her favourites. Edmond stood in the doorway. He watched her reading, amused, seeing her distracted from her mission.

'I have a well-stocked library, Sophia. Books weigh heavy. Only keep those you love the best,' Edmond said.

She turned at the sound of his voice. Her eyes widened at seeing him again, only a few hours having elapsed since he left. She jumped up.

'Edmond, why are you here?' she asked, dropping her book, a frown creasing her brow.

On his way through the piles of possessions, he picked up the book she had dropped.

'"Five Love Letters from Heloise to a Cavalier", by Sir Roger l'Estrange,' he read, glancing at the spine of the book. 'Have you read this, Sophia?' Edmond asked.

'I read some of it with Miss Roseberry, Sir. I could not understand it. But I want to keep it, as it reminds me of her. Has something happened?' she asked.

'Yes. However, the problem is solved,' he replied, so as not to alarm her when he told her of the Army's intransigence.

She moved a pile of books from the couch.

'Do be seated, Major,' she said.

Edmond sat, the book still in his hand. He turned it over, looking at it, not seeing it. Sophia came to sit next to him, gazing at him, waiting for him to continue.

He moved in his seat, glancing sideways at her, unable to think of soft words to tell her his news. He launched into it bluntly, without preamble.

'Sophia, you have no English relative living. Therefore,

you are not entitled to enter England.'

Sophia stared at him, a hand to her mouth.

He held up his own hand before she spoke.

'The matter is resolved, Sophia; I shall become your relative,' he said, with a reassuring smile.

Her frown deepened. 'How will you do that, Sir?' Her knuckles turned white as she clasped her hands on her chest.

'I have permission to marry you, Sophia.'

He drew the paper from his pocket and held it out to her.

Sophia looked at the paper and raised her eyes to his, as she shook her head. She stared at it for a long moment, unsure of what to do.

Anxiety in her huge eyes, her hand trembling, she took the paper, shooting a frowning glance at him before unfolding it. When she finished reading, she stared at him.

'I do not understand, Major; I am not ready for marriage.'

'Our marriage will be in name only, Sophia,' he said gently. 'The marriage will not be consummated. It will be annulled when necessary,' he explained, his voice low, earnest, steady, hoping she understood.

Her blushing face told him she did not, and was uneasy. Edmond took the paper from her hands and replaced it in his pocket. He didn't know quite what to say to dispel the bemused look on her face.

'Do not worry. I shall do my best to be a faithful guardian to you. I shall not try to replace your father. Nonetheless, I shall treat you as my daughter, although you will officially be my wife.'

He spoke softly, looking into her mournful eyes.

'I cannot get my mind around it, Edmond. I have not yet made my debut into society. How could I marry?'

'You do not need to have made your debut to be married, Sophia. Yet, not many men marry a girl so young.'

Her expression worried him. He didn't want to cause

her upset. He took her hand and spoke gently.

'Believe me, Sophia; I cannot get you safely to England any other way. Please try to understand,' Edmond entreated her.

Her misgivings are understandable. But how can I overcome them?

'Early tomorrow I shall send Wilson with a cart. He will take you to the encampment with your belongings, and add them to ours. When you arrive, we shall go to the chaplain, who will marry us. The day after, we shall journey to Marronville to take ship for England.'

'Edmond,' she said, looking closely at him, 'I cannot take it in—so much is happening. I am to be your wife, but you are to act as my guardian?'

She thought a while, running a hand through the front of her hair.

Father has given me into Edmond's care. Father respected Edmond. He was fond of Edmond. He trusted Edmond.

Major St Vere's face was often serious, and somewhat forbidding, with his long nose, and his black eyebrows. Looking at him now, she saw a tender, caring expression in his dark-green eyes. Soft sympathy shone in his face. His full lips parted in expectation, waiting for her to understand, and agree to do what he said.

I have always liked him. I know him to be a man of integrity. I know he would not harm me or take advantage of me.

She sat up in her chair, her back rigid.

'My father trusted you, Edmond, so I shall do the same. Tomorrow I shall be ready. I promise,' she said, a determined look on her face.

With relief, Edmond said, 'Good girl,' and gave her a wide beaming smile.

'But, for the moment, I must be away again, my dear. I shall see you tomorrow.'

He rose and picked his way to the door again.

She followed him, opening the door for him, giving

him a somewhat uncertain smile.

He put a hand on her shoulder, patting it gently before he left.

She turned back to the room, surveying the chaos. She picked up "Five Love Letters from Heloise to a Cavalier".

'I never did understand you,' she said to the book, 'I am not sure I understand me either.'

When she heard Edmond's horse's hooves galloping away, Sophia hurried to the window for a sight of him. But she only glimpsed a red blur disappearing at the bend in the road.

She shook her head thinking of her father. The truth of his death penetrated her thoughts. Immense sadness filled her, yet she couldn't cry.

To take her mind from her distress, Sophia turned to her task of sorting the things she would take with her.

No more mooning over books she had read; no more reminiscing over this vase or that piece of table wear. She cast aside all her nostalgia, as she began to pack the trunks efficiently. At the end of an hour, she had filled them.

Sophia folded the clothes she no longer wished to keep, and placed them on a wing chair, next to the stacked possessions she intended to discard.

When Clothilde came to tell Sophia her supper was ready, she was pleased to see the progress. But, she also saw dark smudges under Sophia's eyes.

'Clothilde, will you dispose of these things for me, please?' Sophia said, waving a hand at the piles of discarded possessions.

'Do not worry, Mam'selle Sophie, I shall find a good home for them. But now, you must eat. Come, you look exhausted,' Clothilde said.

'I am, indeed, tired, Clothilde.'

Clothilde took Sophia by the hand and led her to the kitchen. There she ladled ragout onto a deep plate.

'A lot has happened to you today *ma chérie.* You are grieving for your father. You are leaving this place too. You have worked hard on your packing. It has all been too much for you,' Clothilde said, and set the plate of ragout on the table. She put her arms around Sophia, hugging her tight. Clothilde kissed Sophia's cheek then let her go.

'But now you must eat!' she said, pulling a chair out for Sophia.

The delicious aroma of herbs, spices, and wine in the dish, tempted Sophia to eat, even though she didn't feel hungry.

Thinking of her father, and the certain knowledge of his death sapped her energy. A dark phantom blurred her mind. She was numb. Her head was light with tiredness. She could think no more. With meagre appetite, Sophia ate a little of what Clothilde had put before her.

'I am sorry Clothilde. I am too tired to eat. I must sleep.'

Clothilde clicked her tongue as she looked at Sophia's drawn face.

'Come, then, Mam'selle Sophie. I will help you to bed.'

They left the kitchen and climbed the stairs together to Sophia's bedroom.

A warming pan stood by the fire. Taking tongs from the hearth, Clothilde removed red embers from the fire. She placed the heated brands in the warming-pan, put the lid on it, and ran it between the bed sheets.

Clothilde left the warming-pan in the bed, and helped Sophia to undress, and to don her nightgown. As she sat at her dressing table, Clothilde brushed Sophia's hair. The brushing soothed Sophia. She drooped in her seat, almost asleep.

'I wish you could come with me, Clothilde,' Sophia said, her voice lazy from her weariness.

'I wish it too, Mam'selle Sophie. My mother is sick, and I cannot leave her. But we can write to each other, yes?' Clothilde said, still brushing Sophia's thick, curling hair.

'Oh, I would like that Clothilde. But I must write to you first, for I do not know where I am going.'

'If you send the letter to *l' église* at Membillier, *Pére*

Alain will give it to me.'

Sophia nodded. Clothilde plaited Sophia's hair, and going to the bed, removed the warming pan. She helped Sophia into the warm bed and tucked her in.

'*Bonne nuit, ma petite fille.* Sleep well,' she said and kissed Sophia's cheek. Picking up the candle from the nightstand, she made for the door.

Sophia was almost asleep when a thought suddenly struck her. She sat up.

'Clothilde!' she called, awake again.

'Yes, *chérie,* what is it?' Clothilde said, a little alarmed.

'I must be up early tomorrow, as Major St Vere's man, Wilson, is coming very early to collect me. Will you make sure I am awake?'

Clothilde put the candle down again and went to the bed.

'Of course I will, Mam'selle Sophie,' she said, tucking Sophia in once more.

Sophia snuggled down in the soft, warm bed, and was asleep before Clothilde closed the door.

CHAPTER SIX

'Good morning, Mam'selle Sophie,' Clothilde said, as she put back the shutters at the window. 'How do you feel today? Did you sleep well?'

'Oh, Clothilde! I did not. I woke many times from *such* disturbing dreams. I feel so sad. I do not think I shall ever be happy again,' Sophia said.

'Ah, do not worry, Sophie. When bad things happen, they often come out in our dreams. But they are only dreams. Remember—soon you will be on your way to England. Is that not a great adventure?'

'Yes, I suppose so, Clothilde. My father always said I was an optimist. Yet, I do not feel optimistic. I shall try to look on the bright side. There is no point in wallowing in my misery, is there?'

'Ah, *Non*! It is futile. Now, let me see you smile ...'

Sophia gave a small laugh, and a smile appeared on her face.

'You see *Ma fillette,* is that not better? Now tell me, what will you wear for your journey? You did not pack everything away, did you?'

Sophia chuckled. 'I almost did, Clothilde. But I kept my blue woollen gown out of the trunk, and my dark blue coat. They should keep me warm. My tan bonnet is in the hall downstairs,' she said.

Clothilde was gratified by Sophia's seeming recovery from her bad dreams.

'Would you like me to arrange your hair, Mam'selle Sophie?'

'Yes please, Clothilde. I never can make it look tidy,' Sophia said.

'I shall come back when I have breakfast ready,' Clothilde said and hurried down to the kitchen.

Sophia poured hot water into the plain, glazed pottery basin, from the pitcher Clothilde had brought. She took a washcloth from beside the washstand and scrubbed at her

43

face then passed the cloth over her neck, and the rest of her body, shivering in the chill morning air. She stood in front of the fire while drying herself. With several petticoats beneath, she dressed in the plain, blue, woollen gown, wishing it were more flattering. She sat to put on her black woollen stockings. Sophia was finishing tying the laces of her stout, brown boots when Clothilde appeared.

'I will do your hair now, Miss Sophie,' she said, sitting her down at the dressing table.

Clothilde brushed Sophia's springy locks firmly off her face, tied her hair at the nape of her neck, twisting it into a neat chignon.

Sophia looked at herself in the mirror. She didn't care for the style. But she didn't have the heart to tell Clothilde.

'Thank you, Clothilde. That is fine,' she said.

With a tilt of her head, Clothilde raised her hand to smooth Sophia's hair.

'It is *un peu* severe, Mam'selle Sophie. All the same, on a journey you must have tidy hair. Now, come down for your breakfast,' Clothilde said, putting Sophia's brushes and combs in a small portmanteau, in which Sophia had packed a number of things she thought necessary for a journey.

Although Sophia wasn't hungry, Clothilde's freshly baked galette couldn't be resisted. She ate some of the buttered flatbread, along with a cup of milk.

Sophia put on the thick, blue coat, retrieved her tan felted-wool bonnet from the hall, and went to the drawing room to await Wilson's arrival with the cart.

She didn't wait long.

Wilson knocked at the door. Clothilde moved to open it in response to Wilson's knock. He quickly removed his hat at the sight of her, holding it before him.

'*Bonjoor*,' he said. He could say no more. It was not simply his lack of vocabulary that made him pause. The sight of Clothilde's pretty, heart shaped face, her clear grey eyes, her sweet red mouth with its full lower lip, made his heart beat faster.

Clothilde blushed. She caught her breath and smiled at the amiable British soldier.

'Ah, you are Weelson, no?' she said, blushing a deeper pink.

His face broke into a crinkling smile when he realised she spoke English.

'I've come for Miss Sophia, and her trunks, *Madamoozel*,' he said, never taking his eyes from her face.

Clothilde took Wilson's hat and, as was her habit, put it on the hall table. Turning to him, she smiled again, dimples peeping in her cheeks.

'Weelson, please, come to the kitchen. You will take a drink while you wait, yes?' Clothilde asked, moving before him down the passage to the kitchen.

Wilson followed her, admiring her trim figure and neat appearance. Her full skirts moved to the sway of her hips, as she walked. His heart beat even faster.

Too soon, they arrived at the kitchen door. Clothilde held it open for Wilson to pass by her into the warmth.

'Sit, Weelson,' she said, pulling forward a chair. 'Would you prefer wine or brandy?'

She stood with her hands folded before her. Her bright eyes danced as she pushed a stray wisp of hair from her forehead.

'Oh, brandy, *sil voos play*, *Madamoozel*,' he said, a wide grin on his face, a twinkle in his eye.

Clothilde moved to a sideboard and stood on tiptoe to retrieve a glass. Bending, she took a bottle from a shelf in a cupboard. Her measured movements made Wilson's heart dance.

She poured a generous quantity slowly into the glass, glancing at Wilson as she did so.

He watched her, his eyes riveted on her. He had never seen a woman so lovely. She handed him the glass. Their fingers touched. They looked into each other's eyes.

Clothilde moved away from him towards the door. Wilson's chest felt it would burst; his eyes couldn't leave her.

'Stay, Weelson, while I go to tell Mam'selle Sophie you are here,' she said, leaving Wilson to sit, and sip from the glass, and fantasise about her. He imagined her on his knee, his arms around her, his lips on hers. Ah, how sweet that could be.

I've never met a woman I could settle down with. I could spend the rest o' me life with this one. Am I too old for her? Maybe I am, and maybe I ain't. But the way she looks at me, whew! Does she like me too? Could I have read her wrong? Maybe it's cos she's French. I never had nothin' to do with French Madamoozels before. Take it easy, Wilson, me boy. You'll probably never see her again after today.

He swirled his brandy in the glass, and held it up to the light, looking at the contents appreciatively. He continued to sip and dream, until Clothilde appeared again, followed by Sophia.

Wilson stood, and nodded to Sophia. 'Good morning, Miss. I'm Wilson, the Major's batman.'

With curiosity, he studied Sophia. *Colonel Erdington's daughter. Poor little thing looks wretched, and no wonder, losing her father and travelling to England, all at once. The Major will see her right, though, or I'm a Dutchman.*

'Good morning, Wilson,' Sophia said, a tight smile on her lips. She felt nervous—apprehensive. Today she would move into an entirely new experience.

Clothilde stood close to Wilson, putting her hand on his arm. He drew a small sharp breath. He held his arm still, not wanting to disturb her hand.

'Weelson,' she said, her eyes dark, as she looked up at him. 'Miss Sophia's trunks are upstairs. They are very heavy, and ....'

'Enough said, *Madamoozel*,' Wilson said, smiling down at her. 'Show me where they are.'

He knocked back the rest of the brandy and followed Clothilde from the kitchen.

Sophia sat on the chair vacated by Wilson. Her stomach churned, her heart fluttered. She wanted to run away and hide.

There is nowhere I could go.

'Look on the bright side,' she muttered to herself. 'Be optimistic.'

What am I afraid of? Edmond is a good man. I am not myself. This stupid fear is not like me.

She breathed slowly to calm her nerves, but could not stop thinking of her father. What would he have said?

"Think of now, do not look to the future, and worry. It is pointless."

He was right. The past is gone. I remember when he said that. It was when we were coming to France. I was worried for our safety. My life with Edmond will be a new beginning.

Sophia's thoughts were interrupted by Wilson's slow, heavy footsteps on the stairs. She watched him carry first one trunk, and then the other, out of the front door.

As the second trunk moved from his strong, broad shoulder to the waiting cart, Sophia saw Clothilde go towards the rickety fence.

Clothilde was still, and quiet. Wilson had taken his handkerchief from his pocket, and wiped the sweat from his brow before he caught sight of Clothilde. He straightened his back and smiled at her over the fence. She looked up at him, returning his smile, but with sad eyes. Sophia watched them together, unaware of the strong, bittersweet emotion between them.

Clothilde's hand gently rose to rest on the fence, as she gazed at him. Wilson hesitated, then covered her hand with his. They both wondered if, after today, they would ever meet again. Both their hearts were full of the magic of love at first sight, and the inevitable parting so soon to take place.

Sophia left the house and walked towards them. Their hands dropped from the fence.

Clothilde turned from Wilson and took Sophia in a warm embrace, tears in her eyes. Still holding her, Clothilde said close to her ear, 'you know I would go with you if I could, Mam'selle Sophie.'

Sophia stood back from her, taking both Clothilde's hands in hers.

'I know, Clothilde. I understand. I shall miss you. You have been very good to me,' Sophia said.

Wilson came through the gate and took Sophia's arm.

'Come, Miss Sophia. Time to go,' he said gently and led her to the cart.

When they reached it, Wilson helped Sophia up onto the flat-board seat at the front.

A breeze caught her skirt and petticoats, and nervously she giggled, as she smoothed them down. With the extra weight of the trunks, the springs of the cart creaked beneath her as she took her seat.

Wilson turned to say goodbye to Clothilde, the woman he had quickly come to believe was the love of his life.

She wasn't there. His heart almost stopped beating. Nearly frantic, he looked about for her.

Clothilde stepped out of the house, holding Wilson's hat. She hurried towards him.

'You forgot this, Weelson,' Clothilde said, as she came to him through the gate.

Wilson breathed a sigh of relief, and with a laugh, he accepted his hat. He allowed their hands to brush as he took it from her.

'Thank you, *Madamoozel*,' he said.

'You are most welcome, Weelson,' Clothilde said warmly. She couldn't take her eyes from his.

A broad grin wrinkled Wilson's face. 'Thank you *Madamoozel*,' he said again, 'And thanks for the drink,' he said, a tender glow in his eyes.

'My name is Clothilde, Weelson, and you are very welcome.'

Her eyes shining, she smiled up at him, cheeks dimpling.

On a whim, Wilson took her hand and kissed it. She bowed her head, blushing.

'Goodbye Clothilde,' Wilson said, moving a little

closer to her again.

'*Au revoir*, Weelson; until we meet again.'

She shyly stood back as Wilson swung himself up onto the cart. He took a long look at her. Then, he blinked hard, sniffed, and hastily snapped the rains.

The horse took off, with Wilson and Sophia in the cart behind him.

Wilson held the reins in one hand, swivelled around, and raised the other hand high in salute to Clothilde.

Clothilde waved to him until the cart came to the bend in the road, and disappeared out of sight.

'Weelson! Oh, Weelson!' Clothilde whispered, her chin trembling. She went into the house, closing the door firmly. Leaning her back against it, she covered her face with her hands, and let her tears flow.

CHAPTER SEVEN

Sophia sat quietly beside Wilson, who was silent, too.

After a while, Sophia sniffed.

'I shall miss Clothilde,' she said, swallowing a lump in her throat.

Wilson looked at Sophia from the corner of his eye.

'She seemed a good woman,' he said, not trusting his voice to say more.

'We lived in that house for only a few weeks. Yet, I feel I have known her forever. She was almost like a mother to me. But we shall write to each other. I am to send my letter to the church in Membillier, and the priest will give it to her.'

Wilson's heart gave an excited lurch. He would write to Clothilde, himself. Someday he might even see her again.

They sat in silence a while, as the horse trotted on.

'I heard tell you had a governess, Miss. Where is she?' Wilson asked, to break the silence.

'Oh, she did not come to Membillier. She felt safe enough when we stayed in Prussia. But when she heard we were to go to France, she went back to England. She offered to take me with her, but I wanted to stay with my father and did not go.'

Sophia stayed quiet once more. Wilson didn't break in on the silence again. He was too busy thinking of Clothilde.

Sophia mused on her situation.

Without Clothilde, I have but one friend in the world: Major Edmond St Vere. I know I can depend on him. I shall be safe with him.

The thought filled her with confidence, and her usual optimism returned. She took off her hat, smoothed her skirt, and made herself as comfortable as she could. She watched the landscape as it passed by, and wondered whether she would ever see France again.

She wondered what England would be like. Sophia had

been there when she was small but remembered very little. Now that the journey had begun, she felt less nervous.

A whinchat's joyful "chir-whee, chir-whit-whee", trilled on the air, as they passed an elm tree. Sophia's spirits lifted.

Sophia saw the same trees that Edmond had seen, with their leaves arrayed in the season's colours. She smelled the rich, earthy smell that Edmond had smelled after the rain. She saw the skeletal, blackened trees and the craters, and felt a renewed sense of desolation.

The cart passed under the canopy of trees just before a clearing, and the camp came into view.

More than a hundred small tents lay before her, arranged in groups of ten, with paths running between them. At the end, nearest her, she heard the sound of horses whickering and whinnying, while the orderlies busied themselves mucking out their stalls.

Towards the middle, she saw the well-appointed administration blocks, and beside them a group of larger tents, where the officer's accommodation lay. She marvelled at the number of men, who seemed to be about a multitude of tasks. It wasn't the first time she had visited an encampment, and memories came flooding back, as her nostrils filled with the smell of the campfires.

'Where is the Major's tent, Wilson?' Sophia asked.

'In the middle, Miss, where it's safest,' he said, as he negotiated the narrow paths that ran between the tents.

They approached the officers' area, where Sophia saw Edmond pacing up and down.

I hope he is not angry; he looks somewhat agitated.

Wilson brought the cart to a halt at the front of the Major's tent. Edmond hurried over to them to lift her from the cart.

'You have made good time, Wilson,' Edmond said, and turned to Sophia, taking her by the arm.

'I do not wish to hurry you, Sophia, but Reverend Slayne is awaiting us. Come, my dear,' he said.

As Sophia and Edmond left, Wilson began to load his

and Edmond's trunks onto the cart beside Sophia's.

The Reverend Cameron Slayne was a quiet, thoughtful, conscientious man. Short in stature, most of the men towered over him. All the men, enlisted and commissioned, were respectful to him. Many believed in God, but Slayne worried about those rough, raucous troops who paid him scant attention. Nevertheless, every man attended Church Parade on Sunday.

Earlier, when Edmond told him of the proposed marriage, the chaplain's eyebrows had settled into a frown. His lips folded in disapproval.

'She is young for marriage, Major,' Slayne had said in his high nasal voice, casting a despondent look at Major St Vere.

'Our marriage will be in name only, Sir,' Edmond said. 'I give you my word. If there were any other way, I would take it.'

'Could you not become betrothed?' Slayne asked, worried, yet sympathetic.

'Betrothal is not regarded as a relationship, Mr Slayne.'

Reverend Slayne wasn't devoid of compassion. Despite his disapproval of the unusual circumstance, he agreed to perform the marriage ceremony.

Upon arrival at the chaplain's tent, Edmond presented Sophia to the Reverend.

'Miss Erdington, do you understand what is about to take place?' Reverend Slayne asked gently.

'Major St Vere promised my father he would look after me,' she said, her voice quiet. 'Army regulations will not permit me to enter England without a relative standing as guarantor for me.'

She paused, looking at Mr Slayne.

'I have no English family, you see. The Major most kindly offered to marry me, so he may become my relative.'

Sophia paused again. Looking the chaplain boldly in

the eye, she continued. 'He assures me he will treat me as his daughter. He was my father's friend. I trust him. I regard him as my guardian.'

She lifted her chin, viewing the chaplain solemnly.

Her answer satisfied Slayne. He put his stole about his neck, picked up his book, stood before Edmond and Sophia and began to read at a somewhat fast pace.

'I require and charge you both, as ye will answer at the dreadful day of judgement, when the secrets of all hearts shall be disclosed, that if either of you know of any impediment, why ye may not be lawfully joined together in Matrimony, ye do now confess it. For be ye well assured, that so many as are coupled together otherwise than God's Word doth allow, are not joined together by God; neither is their matrimony lawful.'

Sophia bowed her head and glanced sideways at Edmond. He stood impassive, eyes fixed in the distance.

The Reverend Slayne looked at them both, turned to Edmond and continued,

'Edmond Alexander Henry, wilt thou have this woman to thy wedded wife, to live together after God's ordinance in the holy estate of matrimony? Wilt thou love her, comfort her, honour, and keep her, in sickness and in health; and, forsaking all other, keep thee only unto her, so long as ye both shall live?'

Slayne looked up from his book at Edmond.

Edmond paused.

'Major?' Slayne said, looking at Edmond over his spectacles.

Edmond nodded and said, 'I will.'

Slayne turned now to Sophia and repeated the same words.

'Sophia Maria, wilt thou have this man to thy wedded husband …

Sophia gave Slayne a concentrated look and gulped. The seriousness of the vows filled her with awe.

'I will,' she said. Looking at the man next to her, she wondered whether he recognised the importance of the

53

vows they were exchanging.

Slayne said, 'Major, you must now take her right hand in yours, and repeat these words after me.'

'I know the words, Mr Slayne,' Edmond said, taking Sophia's right hand in his.

'I, Edmond, take thee, Sophia, to my wedded wife, to have and to hold from this day forward, for better for worse, for richer for poorer, in sickness and in health, to love and to cherish, till death us do part, according to God's holy ordinance; and thereto I plight thee my troth.' He added not a speck of emotion to the words, although he looked into Sophia's eyes as he said them. Sophia withdrew her hand from his.

The Reverend Slayne turned to Sophia and, having invited her to take Edmond's right hand in hers, led her through the same vow.

Slayne said, 'Major, do you have a ring?'

'Ah, yes, I have,' he said, rummaging in his pocket. Sophia was surprised when he produced a small leather bag and spilt a gold signet ring from it.

Yet, again, Edmond knew the words.

'With this ring I thee wed, with my body I thee worship, and with all my worldly goods I thee endow. In the name of the Father, and of the Son, and of the Holy Ghost. Amen.'

Edmond placed the ring on Sophia's finger. It was far too big for her, being his own, which he always kept about him in memory of his father.

The Reverend Slayne continued,

'Let us pray.

'O eternal God, Creator and Preserver of all mankind, Giver of all spiritual grace, the Author of everlasting life. Send thy blessing upon these thy servants, this man and this woman, whom we bless in thy name; that, as Isaac and Rebecca lived faithfully together, so these persons may surely perform and keep the vow and covenant betwixt them made, whereof this ring given and received is a token and pledge, and may ever remain in perfect love and peace together, and live according to thy laws; through Jesus Christ our Lord. Amen.'

During this prayer, Edmond and Sophia bent their heads. Slayne now wrapped the ends of his stole around their joined hands.

'Forasmuch as Edmond and Sophia have consented together in holy wedlock, and have witnessed the same before God, and thereto have given and pledged their troth, each to the other, and have declared the same by giving and receiving of a ring, and by joining of hands; I pronounce that they be man and wife together, in the name of the Father, and of the Son, and of the Holy Ghost. Amen.'

Sophia's hand still rested in Edmond's. He felt it tremble.

'Thank you, Mr Slayne,' Edmond said.

'You are welcome, Major. But we are not finished yet. We must complete the marriage certificate.'

Slayne turned to his desk and drew forward a paper.

'You gave me the information I needed when you came to see me. I have written the entry in my ledger and completed the certificate. It wants but to be signed,' he said.

Sophia made her signature first, then Edmond. Mr Slayne signed the paper in a flowing hand, shook sand on it and gave it to Edmond.

'I pray all will go well with you,' Slayne said.

'My thanks again to you, Mr Slayne,' Edmond replied, and led Sophia away.

As they walked back to his tent, Edmond noticed Sophia's unusual quietness.

'Are you all right, Sophia?' he said.

She looked up at him, with a sad smile. 'Yes, I am. But the words of the service seemed so grand and important. I feel somewhat guilty having said them, not truly meaning them.'

'Ah, Sophia, they were but a formality,' Edmond said.

'We promised things before God, Edmond,' she said in

a small, hushed voice.

'I am sure God understands why we did so, Sophia. Nonetheless, a marriage is not complete 'til it is consummated. That will not happen, so although we are officially married, in fact, we are not.'

They had reached his tent. He opened the flap. She glanced about her as she went inside. The tent was bare apart from two camp beds, and the canvas bucket in its tripod with the ewer next to it. The tent looked empty of life, lonely, cold. She wondered what their quarters looked like when occupied by Edmond and Wilson. Nothing of them remained.

Edmond stood outside a moment, rubbing his chin, thinking on what he had done. He surveyed the encampment. Something important had happened. He tried to dismiss it as a means to an end.

'Where is Wilson?' Sophia asked, coming back out to him.

'He left with the cart for the coast. He found a horse for you so we may ride there tomorrow.'

He took her arm to lead her back inside.

'I have matters I must attend to before I go, Sophia. I do not know how long they will take. If the cart waited 'til I completed my business, we might arrive after nightfall with nowhere to stay, so 'tis better we follow tomorrow.'

He glanced at her, 'I am sorry, but you must sleep here tonight. I hope that does not discomfit you.'

'No, not at all,' she said.

'Are you hungry?'

'Yes, Sir, a little. I could not eat much breakfast,' she said.

Edmond noticed Sophia's face lacked its usual animation. She seemed remote. He went towards her, placing his hand on her arm.

'I am trying hard not to cry, Sir, but I am having great d–difficulty,' she said, pressing her lips together, her chin trembling, her breathing unsteady. She began to cry, tears running down her face. She put a hand out to him, in a pleading gesture, a piteous expression on her face.

Her voice choking with tears, she stammered, 'I miss him so much, Edmond.'

'My poor Little One. Your life is turned upside down, is it not?' Edmond said, looking down at her. The sadness in his heart almost overcame him.

Pity for her led him forward. He enfolded her in his arms, tears in his own eyes.

Sophia's head rested on his chest. Her hands clutched his coat. Heavy sobs wracked her slight body as she gave in to her deep grief.

Outside, the storm broke at last. Rain drummed on the canvas. Lightning lit up the tent. Subsequent thunder clashing overhead, made her cling to him even tighter.

Edmond knew crying was good. He remembered the time when his wife died in childbirth. Later the child died, too. Days had passed before his sorrow overtook him, and he allowed himself to cry for his loss. A heavy weight had lifted from him after that. He knew crying would alleviate the tension in her.

'It is good to cry, Sophia, my dear, it is good to cry,' he whispered.

Edmond held Sophia, stroking her hair, soothing her as he repeated over and over in his head, *Poor dear child. Poor dear child.*

She was lost in desolation, yet his presence penetrated her misery. His strength reminded her of her father. His words, so close in her ear, reassured her. His nearness, his warmth, comforted her. Her trust in him increased. She wasn't alone; she had him to rely on.

Her sobs subsided. He took a handkerchief from his pocket, and lifting her chin, he wiped her tearstained cheeks. He noticed the childlike quality in her face.

Ah! How young she is.

Sophia gulped back the remains of her tears.

'Hush now, Sweetheart; all will be well. I will make it so,' he said, as he smoothed a stray tendril of her hair back into place.

She threw her arms about him, her tears flowing once more.

'How can I ever repay you, Sir, for your kindness? Without you, I have no one,' she said. He felt tears prickle at his eyes. Surprised at the rush of sympathy he felt for her, he held on to her, feeling for her as the daughter he had lost.

CHAPTER EIGHT

The heavy rain subsided to a light patter. The earth hissed, as it absorbed the deluge. A cool, earthy smell rose from the ground.

Edmond disengaged himself from her grasp.

'Come, my dear, it is enough. Dry your tears now. I have much to do,' he said, gently holding her hand, and giving her the handkerchief.

Edmond watched her closely, as Sophia smoothed out the handkerchief, and dried her tears again.

With a start, he remembered tomorrow's trip.

'Ah! Sophia, I did not ask you, can you ride well enough for a three or four-hour journey?'

'I used to ride often, but of late, Father told me not to go far. I am sure I am able enough for such a journey, Sir. I shall do my best. We must pray it be well enough.'

She sighed, sniffed, and almost managed a smile.

'We must hope so. One thing I need you to do for me, though, Sophia,' he added, looking down his long, straight nose at her, his expression stern, yet his eyes smiling.

'What do you want of me, Sir?' she said, her eyes widening.

'Will you please call me Edmond, not "Sir". You are not, after all, one of my men.'

'I shall try to remember, *Edmond,*' she said with a watery smile.

'Good. Now, you must stay in the tent and be quiet, for we must draw as little notice as possible to your being here. I must hand over my duties to Captain Orpwood. When I can, I shall come back with something to eat. Perhaps you can sleep a little, or if you have a mind, there is a book under my pillow. You may amuse yourself with it, if you wish,' he said, taking his hat in his hand. As Edmond stepped through the open tent flap, Sophia saw him put on his hat. Once he dropped the flap, she was alone.

She sat on Edmond's camp bed, looking around at the bare tent walls, at the stained canvas covering on the floor, at the tent flap, which Edmond had tied from the outside. A drip of water in a leaking corner of the tent splashed steadily. Sophia sighed.

How quickly things have changed. Yesterday morning everything was as it has always been, today, nothing is the same.

'Thank you, God, for giving Edmond to me to protect me,' she whispered.

I wonder what God thinks of this marriage? Perhaps Edmond is right. God will not mind, as there was no other way out of my predicament.

She wasn't religious, but her mother had taught her to pray. Her mother had a comforting faith, and Sophia had often seen her kneeling in prayer. In memory of her, she thought about God and prayed to Him often.

Remembering Edmond's mention of the book, she felt under his pillow. She drew out the little book bound in purple velvet, the cover somewhat faded.

Intrigued when she found it was an anthology of verse, she opened it and caught a vague tang of citrus. Where had she smelled that faint aroma before?

Of course, it was Edmond's discreet cologne. The fragrance brought Edmond to her mind's eye.

Sophia stroked the velvet cover. She turned to the first page. Seeing an inscription, she read it.

"To my dearest Edmond.
From your loving wife, Adela."

Beneath the inscription, in a different hand was,

"In memory of my dear wife, died 25th October 1751.
And of my baby daughter, died 28th October 1751."

She looked up from the book, thinking.

So, he was married before, his wife more than seven years dead—he had a daughter too. He knows what grief is.

Although her heart filled with sadness for his loss, she was determined not to allow herself the luxury of more tears. She had cried enough.

Sophia set about reading the poems in the well-thumbed book.

The first she came to, she had read before and liked it: Grey's *Elegy in a Country Churchyard*. His *Ode to Spring* also caught her eye. She smiled over Goldsmith's *Elegy on the Death of a Mad Dog*. Samuel Johnson's *One and Twenty* made her feel uncomfortable, so she quickly passed on to Joseph Warton's *Verses on a Butterfly*.

She put the book down to reflect on the pretty words.

Her eyelids began to droop.

Sophia slept.

CHAPTER NINE

Edmond had spent the past hour handing over his responsibilities to Captain Nathan Orpwood, now promoted to acting Commander. Orpwood seemed to gain stature, as he took in the importance of his duties. Edmond, often abrupt, as he commanded men he expected to obey instantly, was patient with the young, inexpert Nathan, and took time to explain what was required of him.

Nathan was in the same position as Edmond had been. The second son of a peer. A career in the Army had always been his destiny. Of Stocky build, his fair hair always tousled; his face reflected his sunny disposition. Nathan was a jovial young man, full of spirit and dash. Edmond liked him for his bravery and courage. Yet, Edmond worried about him. He wasn't lacking in competence, but it was somewhat erratic. Nathan Orpwood could be hasty, and sometimes rushed in where angels feared to tread.

When Edmond finished detailing all that Nathan needed to know, he added a few words of encouragement.

'You will do well, Nathan, if you think before you act. But when you do, be decisive and do not falter,' Edmond said, placing a friendly hand on the young man's shoulder. 'I have every confidence in you, my lad.'

'I hope I can live up to your confidence in me, Sir,' Nathan said.

'Well, Nathan, you are now in temporary command here; you have a lot of responsibility on your shoulders 'til they find someone to replace me and the Colonel. Do not be overcome by the task. All you have to do is oversee the striking of the camp, and the relocation of the Battalion. Hopefully, you will see no more action.'

Edmond hid his concern regarding Nathan's inexperience as a commander.

'I have been acting Commander before, Sir. I may give the impression of being capricious, but I know how to act responsibly when it is needful. Trust me, Sir,' Nathan said, his expression serious.

Edmond considered Nathan's eager young face. His sincerity was real. Edmond knew that. Edmond sighed and smiled.

'Despite your lack of experience, I do trust you, Nathan. I know you will do your best.'

'Thank you, Sir,' Nathan said, casting a delighted smile on Edmond. 'Perhaps if I do well, they will promote me,' he said.

'Perhaps, Nathan,' Edmond said, hoping the young man would get the opportunity to prove himself.

'One more thing, Orpwood,' he added. 'Will you see that Colonel Erdington receives a decent burial? I should have seen to it, but with everything else, I did not have the time.'

'I'll see to it, Sir,' Nathan said.

'Have him buried in Membillier in the graveyard, and order a headstone. I think that is more fitting than here.'

'Trust me, Major, I shall see to it,' Orpwood said.

'If there is a cost, charge it to me.'

Edmond gave Orpwood a quick nod of thanks and left him to digest all that had been told to him.

Having passed his responsibilities to Orpwood, Edmond's mind was at liberty to concentrate his attention on Sophia.

How strange to think of being her husband, he thought, as he walked towards his tent. *Perhaps Radford was right. I did not think the thing through. Was there another way I could have taken her to England? Anything else would have taken an inordinate amount of time.*

Edmond thought on Sophia's words. "We promised things before God, Edmond." He wouldn't admit it to Sophia, but the words had, for a moment, given him pause, too. He had remembered saying them with Adela.

He gave himself a mental shake.

It is a means to an end. Our intention is annulment. Slayne knew what we did and still went forward. No, I

63

have no real qualms. I have done the right thing.

Having reconciled his doubts satisfactorily, he entered his tent.

He found Sophia curled up on his bed, asleep, the book beside her, open at one of his favourite poems. Edmond smiled at sight of her. One hand under her head, she had taken her hair from the confining chignon, and it spilt about the pillow in curly abundance.

No wife, but a daughter to replace the one I lost, he thought, as he watched her sleep.

I have taken on a big responsibility. Yet, I have done the right thing—I could do nothing else. I promised John. I could not abandon her. Ah, but I have no experience at all with children. Parents learn as they go along—I must learn all at once. It is a challenge. I have faced many challenges before. Surely, Perdita will help me.

He drew the blanket over Sophia. She stirred, and gave a little moan, then settled into the warmth of the blanket. Looking down at her, he was filled with affection for her. The thought of her being a daughter to him gave him pleasure and pride.

Edmond remembered he had promised Sophia food, so he set off towards the officers' mess to obtain some. He was destined for disappointment.

Even though the aroma of cooking lingered in the tent, nothing remained in the pots, which stood on a trestle table amid spillage stains.

Edmond eyed the mess sergeant.

A man of ample proportions with grizzled grey hair, and a harassed look. Apprehensive, he stood stiffly before Edmond.

Edmond spoke in his usual authoritative tone.

'I would appreciate your finding a bowl of food for me, if you please, Sergeant.'

'I'm sorry Major, I can't. It's all been taken,' the Sergeant said and awaited Edmond's fury.

An orderly approached the trestle and with much clatter removed the pots. Edmond watched him in dismay, and frustration.

'I cannot believe you have exhausted all our provisions, Sergeant,' Edmond said, vexed.

Sergeant Olson took a deep breath before explaining his position to Major St Vere.

'No, Sir. But the Mess Captain said we must conserve what we have, which isn't much. We'll strike camp soon, Major. We have to ration, as there won't be any more incoming supplies, Sir,' Sergeant Olsson said, hoping to allay Edmond's wrath. 'I can only offer you bread, Major.'

Edmond saw the futility of remonstration, and let out a grunt. 'Oh very well, give me the bread, and a forage bag to carry it in. Have you any ale?'

'Well, yes, Major, a little, but ...'

'Put some in a flask, *if you please,* Sergeant. I had better have one filled with wine and water, too.'

'Yes, Major,' the Sergeant said. Having disappointed him about the food, Olsson was disinclined to refuse Edmond's request.

With the bag slung over his shoulder, Edmond wandered between the campfires, hoping to find a soldier cooking his own food.

At one campfire, two men, whom he knew, sat eating. A large pot, black from much use, hung on a hook suspended from a bar over their fire. In it simmered a thin stew, consisting of onions, potatoes, turnips, and the occasional morsel of chicken. The men made to stand when Edmond approached them, but with a wave of his hand, Edmond indicated they remain seated.

'Will you sell me a bowl of your stew, Sergeant Parker?' Edmond said, addressing a burly man who seemed to be in charge of the pot.

'Sell you one, Major? You may have it, an' welcome,' Sergeant Parker replied, rummaging for a bowl in his knapsack. He rose, went to the pot and ladled a generous portion of the thin stew into the tin bowl. He searched again in his pack, produced a spoon, wiped it on his breeches and placed it in the soup.

'Will you join us, Major?' the other man said, making room for him on the blanket where he sat.

'Thank you, Trenton,' Edmond said, 'But it is not for me, it is for ...' he paused, wondering how to describe Sophia to the men '... a casualty,' he said.

The men murmured in appreciation of Edmond's generosity.

'Would you like some bread? I have more than I need,' Edmond said, producing the loaf from his bag. Parker handed the bowl to Edmond, took the bread, and pulled his bayonet from the holster at his belt. With a swing of it, he cleaved the loaf in two.

Edmond was gratified to see a little oil left on the bread, which spoke of the fresh cleaning of the recently used bayonet.

'Thank y, Major. That'll go good with me stew,' Parker said, tucking the other half loaf into Edmond's bag.

'Thank *you,* Parker,' Edmond said with a slight bow.

As Edmond walked away, Trenton said to his comrade, Parker, 'There ain't many officers who'd be so considerate of his men.'

'You're right there, Dick. He be a real gentleman, not a jumped-up whippersnapper, wet behind the ears, who cares for nowt but the cut of his uniform.'

Edmond entered his tent in a short while, in time to see Sophia waking. She sat up at sight of him, pushing her hair back from her face, smiling.

He handed her the tin bowl.

'I brought chicken stew for you, Sophia, and some bread. All I could obtain to drink was watered wine unless you would prefer ale?' Edmond said, his voice as cheerful as he could make it.

'Thank you, Edmond,' Sophia said, taking the bowl from him and inspecting its contents.

Edmond retrieved the two flasks from the forage bag and handed the one containing the watered wine to Sophia. He put the one containing ale to his lips and drank it with satisfaction. He handed the half loaf of bread to Sophia.

'You are unused to army food, Sophia; therefore, you may find the stew unpalatable. Calling it *chicken* stew may not be a statement of fact. Nonetheless, it will fill you.'

Edmond took another swig from his flask. He watched Sophia crumble a little of the bread into her stew, and noticed her eyes were puffy, but her ready smile spoke of her brighter mood.

Sophia took a tentative sip from the spoon. 'I have tasted worse,' was her verdict. She crumbled more bread into the stew and continued eating.

After a moment, 'Do you not eat?' she asked.

'No. I had a good breakfast, thanks to Wilson. 'Twould be different if Wilson were here. He always sees I am well provided for,' Edmond said, as he watched her sip from the flask of watered wine. He put his flask to his lips again and took a long swig of his ale.

With interest, Sophia watched him drink.

'What is in *your* flask, Edmond?'

'Ale. Good strong Ale,' Edmond replied and drank more.

Sophia ate more of her stew. She looked at him, her head tilted.

'Edmond,' she said, giving him a glowing smile. 'My father would never allow me to touch strong alcohol. I always wondered what it is like. May I taste yours?'

He chuckled, 'I am sure you will find strong ale not to your liking; but here,' he swapped his flask for hers.

She took a gulp and coughed. Her face screwed up in revulsion.

'Oh, my goodness, Edmond! What a foul brew!' she said and scrubbed at her mouth with her fist.

He laughed at her, 'I knew you would not like ale, Sophia.'

His shoulders shook as he took back his flask, and consumed the rest.

'How can you put such a horrid tasting substance into your stomach?' she said, her face screwed up in disgust.

'Ale quenches one's thirst, Sophia,' he said, chuckling boyishly.

She took her flask, washed the taste of ale from her mouth, and continued eating.

Edmond was pleased to see her eat. Sophia seemed to have become calmer, less unhappy. He knew how she must feel, everything changed from what it had been. Yet, her strength of character overcame her unhappy mood.

She looked up, and seeing him watching her, she smiled. It struck him how disarming her smile was. How her resilience seemed to surmount her despair.

Edmond went to the entrance of the tent and stood a while, surveying the camp, thinking on his decision to leave the Army behind.

Will this be the last time I shall see such a sight? Edmond thought, looking at the efficiently organised encampment. *Shall I miss it? This way of life is satisfying. I am used to it. I now have an aversion to the slaughter I did not experience before. Yet, I shall inevitably have regrets.*

He turned back into the tent to see Sophia running a finger around her bowl.

I might regret leaving the Army, but I shall not regret becoming Sophia's guardian. I shall take pride in caring for her.

As he watched, Sophia wiped her mouth with the back of her hand, the gesture of a child, which amused him.

Sophia glanced at him, frowning.

'I read the inscription in your book, Edmond; I know you were married before. Would it pain you to tell me of her?' she gently asked.

Edmond shrugged a shoulder. 'No, Sophia, it would not pain me. She died so long ago, in another life; yet, I still think of her sometimes,' he said.

'How did she die?' Sophia asked, her voice low.

'In childbirth. My daughter died too, a few days later,' he said, his eyes sad.

Sophia remembered the third inscription in the book.

'The child was early, and a long time coming. They said Adela was losing blood. I knew little of such things—I know little even now—I still remember her pale face when they laid her out.

'The baby was astonishingly small, too small to survive.'

He shook his head, a wan smile crossing his face.

'We were married but two years. I was in the Army, so saw little of her because of the war. When I lost them, to kill my grief I threw myself into my duties—ah, but now I am ready to leave army life,' he said, shaking the dregs of ale from his flask.

'You did not think to marry again?' she asked, her eyes troubled, sympathetic.

He gave a short laugh. 'Ha! I have now, God help me,' he said.

'Do you regret marrying me, Edmond?' she said, sitting back, her eyes round with alarm.

'Not a bit, child; 'twil be an adventure no doubt. My sister will be more than surprised, to be sure,' he said, injecting lightness into his words.

'You have a sister? How old is she?' Sophia asked, inquisitive to know more of him.

'A little older than I. Perdita is her name. She is a widow with one son, Simon—he is about your age—or perhaps somewhat older—I forget. She will love you dearly I am sure. She always wanted a daughter to cosset. Ah, of course, when you are old enough, she may escort you into society. I shall have our marriage annulled before then—but it is all a long way off.'

As he spoke, he turned the pages of his book, laughing when he found an amusing poem.

'Here is one for you, my dear, by Sheridan. Listen.'

"If a daughter you have, she's the plague of your life,
No peace shall you know, tho' you've buried your wife,
At twenty she mocks at the duty you taught her,
O, what a plague is an obstinate daughter.

Sighing and whining,
Dying and pining,
O, what a plague is an obstinate daughter.

When scarce in their teens, they have wit to perplex us,
With letters and lovers forever they vex us,
While each still rejects the fair suitor you've brought
her,
O, what a plague is an obstinate daughter.
Wrangling and jangling,
Flouting and pouting,
O, what a plague is an obstinate daughter."

Edmond closed the book with a snap, putting it in his pocket. He leant forward and looked into her eyes.

'So, my sweet maid, will you be a plague on me, hmm? will you be obstinate? will you 'flout and pout'? Oh! What have I done?' He said, turning swiftly, striking his brow melodramatically in mock horror.

Sophia laughed. 'But, Sir, I am not your daughter; I am your wife,' she said.

Edmond chuckled. 'True, true. However, you are to play the part of my daughter, are you not, Sophia? I pray you do not play your part so well that you become unbiddable,' he said, enjoying the lightness of the moment after the harshness of the past twenty-four hours.

'I promise you, Sir, I shall not,' she said sunnily.

Then, her face serious, Sophia said, 'I owe you too much to cause you pain, Edmond.'

She changed again asking, 'Do no verses tell of wives such as I, who am no wife at all?'

'I doubt it, Sophia, as it is not a common occurrence. You and I are a rare breed, you know,' he said, with a slight bow of his head.

'Ah! Sophia, I almost forgot. May I have my ring back? It was my father's. I would hate to lose it. I always keep it by me, for luck.'

He held out his hand, adding, 'Besides, it does not fit you.'

She slipped the ring from her finger and placed it on his palm.

'You do not mind my taking it from you, do you, Sophia?' he asked, concerned.

'No, Edmond, I cannot wear it anyway, as I am supposed to be your daughter.'

A bright smile lit her eyes, but after a pause, she became curious.

'Will you keep what we have done secret, or is it to be known?' she enquired.

Edmond put the ring in the little leather bag, which he put in his coat pocket. A small frown brought his dark brows together.

'We do nothing to be ashamed of, Sophia. Nevertheless, I do not intend to shout it from the housetops. Society is cruel, in the way it twists the most innocent event into a monstrosity of intrigue. I shall not proffer the information. Nevertheless, if asked, neither shall I deny it. We must pass off our situation, as having been the means to an end.'

'Hmm,' Sophia said, absorbing his words.

As he spoke, Edmond undid the tent flap. 'Come, Sophia, allow me to introduce you to your horse,' he said, holding the flap up for her.

As they walked to the stable area, men watched them with curious looks. Others, knowing who she was, nodded approval of Edmond's care of their dead colonel's daughter.

The news of Edmond's furlough was spreading rapidly, whispered among comrades.

The stables, situated at the end of the camp, consisted of three long narrow tents, with four rectangular tents at right angles, on either side, much like a permanent stable's layout.

Hung along the wall of the long tents, canvas troughs held hay, for the horses.

A little below these, stout ropes served as tethers, to which each horse was tied.

Between each stall, wooden slats were slotted into poles driven into the ground.

As they approached the area, they heard the thump of the farrier's hammer, as he shod a horse. A heap of soiled hay lay behind the stable tent, stinging the air with the familiar smell of horse. Three Orderlies rode up, returning from exercising horses.

'Which tent is my horse in, Edmond?' Sophia asked, eager to see her mount.

'In the middle one, Sophia, not far from mine,' Edmond replied.

They entered the tent, and Edmond led her to the mare's stall.

Going to its head, she gave the horse her hand to nuzzle, stroking its velvety nose.

'What a pretty little mare, Edmond. But, as small and dainty as she is, she is not a military horse, surely?' she said.

'No, she belonged to a lady who left her behind when she went home—as you must do, Sophia; so do not become too fond of her,' Edmond said, strolling off to visit his horses, tethered nearby. He checked his saddlebags, which hung on the wood beside Warrior.

On top of his belongings, he found a packet, and a note from Wilson:

Major,

Some food to tide you over on your journey.
I have also placed Miss Erdington's portmanteau
in her horse's stall.

Sgt D. Wilson.

Edmond smiled.
What a great forager Wilson is! Of course, he would

72

*have known food was rationed, he who always makes sure
I am well fed.*

Sophia continued to stroke the mare, her mood quiet, as
she thought of tomorrow's journey.

*I wonder how far Marronville is from here. I hope I
will be able for the journey. Edmond has finished his
business; why do we not go now?*

'Oh! Edmond!' she called, as the thought took root.

He turned and hurried to her side.

'What is it, Sophia? Have you hurt yourself?'

'No, Edmond, I have had an idea. Why must we wait
'til tomorrow to go to the coast? You have finished all
your business here. Could we not go now? I am sure we
could sleep somewhere tonight, so would not need to
travel so far tomorrow.'

Edmond pulled at his earlobe, looking at her while he
thought on what she said.

A good notion. The child has a head on her shoulders.

He had been aware of the undercurrent, and speculation
of the men, as he passed among them with Sophia. He had
realised what food for scandal it would breed if he and
Sophia slept in the same tent that night. This was a
solution to his misgivings.

'I planned on going tomorrow. I did not think I would
so swiftly accomplish all that I needed to do. But to go
now, and break our journey, rather than try to get to
Marronville in one day, would make sense,' he said,
rubbing his chin, not mentioning his qualms.

Edmond walked out of the stable tent and went to
where orderlies were grooming the horses.

'Monahan!' he called as he went.

In a moment, Monahan appeared. 'Major,' he said,
standing stiffly and saluting.

'Easy, Monahan. Will you prepare Warrior and the
little mare for me, if you please? I am journeying to
Marronville, and thence to England with Miss Erdington. I
shall leave the horses at the farmhouse of one Monsieur
Philippe Simonet. It is a straight hour and a half's ride on

the road to Marronville. There is a sign beside the gate saying *La Ferme de Simonet.* You may collect the horses from there tomorrow,' Edmond said.

'My pleasure, Major,' Monahan said, saluting again. He walked with Edmond to the stall, untethered both horses and took them outside.

'Do you need to collect anything from the tent, Sir?' Sophia asked Edmond.

'No, all I need for the journey is in my saddle bags. They are stored in my horse's stall,' he said, admiring her thinking.

'What of your book?' Sophia asked.

''Tis in my pocket. What of your bonnet?'

She put her hands to her mouth in dismay.

'Oh, my! I left it in the cart.'

'Then we may set off immediately,' he said.

Monahan returned.

'The horses are ready, Major,' he said.

'Thank you, Monahan,' Edmond replied.

Edmond took Sophia's arm and followed Monahan outside with her.

Monahan cupped his hands for Sophia's foot and tossed her up on to the side-saddle. Sophia arranged her skirts about her.

Edmond led the horses out from the stable area. He discreetly walked them to the road behind the stables. There he mounted, and he and Sophia set off at a trot.

'How long will the journey take, Edmond?' Sophia asked,

'About two hours, depending on how fast we ride,' Edmond replied.

'Where will we stay overnight?' she said.

'At a farmhouse,' Edmond answered.

They came to a wider stretch of road and increased the pace to a canter. Conversation ceased as they rode side by side in the autumn sunshine.

A light breeze blew. Sophia's dark hair floated out behind her in a shining cloud.

They came to where a river ran beside the road. Willow trees dipped down to the water.

The breeze blew their branches, making the trees appear to dance, making the leaves rustle and shush.

Sophia slowed her pace to look at the pleasing sight, and listen to the swooshing. Edmond saw her face brighten at the sound.

She glanced at him and said, 'I love the feel of autumn. Do not you, Edmond? Leaves whispering in the wind seem to symbolise its atmosphere,' she said.

Edmond smiled, 'You have a romantic mind, Sophia. You should write poetry.'

'I am not really romantic, Edmond. I am too practical. Yet, I do love natural things. I have *tried* to write poetry. It was disastrous.'

Edmond laughed and felt an inexplicable sense of elation. He was free of worry about his men, free of tiresome army regulations, free of all responsibility. True, he was responsible for Sophia, a different duty, outside his experience. The thought of it troubled him no longer. His previous reservations evaporated.

Their road led through a wooded area. Although rain had fallen, it hadn't soaked far into the hard, dry ground. Yet, enough had fallen to release the pungency of damp grass. The rhythm of the horses' hooves echoed through the trees, accentuating the quiet that enveloped the wood.

They rode a long way in congenial silence. Thinking of their conversations together, Edmond marvelled at how easily they had struck up an amicable rapport.

The road through the wood joined a main thoroughfare, where they made good progress, riding past fields and forested areas.

Sophia's thoughts turned to their journey, and she wondered what would happen if they were lost.

'Do you know the way, Edmond?' she asked, suddenly apprehensive.

Edmond laughed. 'It is my duty to "know the way", Child. However, if I did not, I have a map in my saddle bag.'

He caught her bridle and guided her horse around a deep rut in the road.

'Thank you, Edmond,' Sophia said, 'I did not see it.'

Another thought struck her.

'How do you know if they will take us in at a farmhouse?' Sophia asked anxiously.

Edmond glanced at her. 'I know a place where we are sure of a welcome. Over the past weeks, while awaiting the possible arrival of the troops from St Malo, I explored the countryside hereabouts. Several times, I visited a farmhouse not far from Marronville. I know the farmer and his wife quite well. We may spend the night there. Tomorrow, we shall be at the port in good time to catch the tide.'

Edmond heard her breathe a relieved sigh.

Soon they stopped by the side of the road to eat the provisions Wilson had left for them. When finished, they continued on their way.

The trees were losing their leaves, just as those at St Cast. Yet, the countryside here didn't have the ravaged look of that place. No sad, skeletal, black remains of trees; no craters in the earth here. Although the fields were bare after the harvest.

Across the fields, woodland poplars stood out against a blue sky. A light breeze set their leaves atremble, shining like golden coins, as the sun streamed through them. Quiet autumnal beauty surrounding Edmond and Sophia, enhanced their mood of hope and promise, coupled with some trepidation, as they went forward into the new life before them.

CHAPTER TEN

They saw the farmhouse in the distance.

Behind it, the western sky was streaked with pink and peach. Bands of light spread across low clouds in rippling lines. Steely grey clouds in the East, held the trees in stark silhouette, giving them a vital, magical quality.

They reached the gate of the Simonet farm, where Sophia gratefully let Edmond lift her down from the horse. Sophia looked about her.

The smoky scent of lavender filled the air, from bushes growing along the fence, which guarded a spacious courtyard before the house. In the middle of the courtyard, providing welcoming shade in summer, stood an ancient spreading plane tree.

The grey stone farmhouse was long and low. Its roof was of red-brown pan tiles, with dormer windows set into it. Flanking one side stood a sturdy barn, and on the other side, the stables.

A lad of about eighteen, dressed in a coarse grey homespun shirt, and brown breeches, came from the stables to greet them. His hair was the colour of corn, his country face tanned, and his dark brown eyes twinkled as he greeted Edmond.

'Major, I am glad to see you. And with a different horse. Where is Jet?'

'Ah, good day, Anton. Jet was killed in battle. This is Warrior,' Edmond solemnly told him.

'I am very sorry, Major. Jet was a wonderful horse,' Anton said. He looked at Sophia.

'This is my ward, Sophia. Sophia, may I introduce Anton. The best groom I have ever met,' Edmond said.

A look of prideful pleasure covered Anton's face.

Sophia smiled sleepily at Anton.

'My poor Warrior. He is as weary as we. Look after him well, Anton,' Edmond said, and flipped a coin in Anton's direction. Anton caught the coin, tipped his forehead, and led the horses away.

Edmond took Sophia's arm and steered her towards the door of the large farmhouse, where Evette, the farmer's wife, had come out to greet the visitors.

Her head was bound, peasant style, with a red scarf. A clean white apron, on which she dried her brown hands, covered her grey dress. A smile suffused her face when she saw Edmond. She moved forward with a confident stride.

'Major Edmond, how pleased I am to see you! And who is this?' she said, looking curiously at Sophia.

'Evette, this is my ward, Sophia. We have ridden from St Cast, and she is very tired,' Edmond said.

'Oh, come in, come in,' Evette said, bustling Sophia into the hall, with an arm about her shoulders.

Evette drew Sophia into the parlour and sat her by the fire. She returned to the hall, and called, 'Giselle! Giselle, come to me!'

A slim, auburn-haired girl of about sixteen appeared from the back of the house.

'You called me, *Maman*?' she said, then, seeing Edmond, 'Major Edmond, how do you do?'

'Never mind the Major now, Giselle. Go and fetch a cup of milk and some buttered bread for his ward. Her name is Sophia, and she is sitting in the parlour.'

Giselle bobbed her mother a curtsy and hurried off to the kitchen.

Edmond bent his head and spoke to Evette in a low voice.

'Evette, can you put us up for the night? As you see, Sophia is weary from our journey. A battle took place at St Cast yesterday, and her father was killed.'

Evette put her hands to her mouth, shaking her head.

'*Ah la pauvre petite fille,*' Evette said. Of course you may rest here tonight,' she said.

She went into the parlour, drew Sophia up, and removed her coat. Giselle appeared, bearing the milk and bread. She glanced up at Edmond as she sidled past him to enter the parlour.

The Major was forgotten in the women's eagerness to take care of the young girl.

Edmond was pleased Evette had taken to Sophia. With five daughters of her own, he knew Evette would know how best to look after her. A smile passed across Edmond's face, as he turned into the kitchen to help himself to the farmer's wine.

Edmond relaxed in the warmth of the large kitchen, with its racks of plates on the dresser, the well-scrubbed kitchen table, its black leaded ovens and its big iron range.

The farmer came in from his work to find Edmond in the kitchen, seated by the fire, his long legs stretched before him, a glass of excellent wine to his lips.

'Philippe, pray forgive me for taking liberties with your wine,' Edmond said, making to rise.

'Nonsense, Major—sit, sit. You are welcome to whatever I have means to provide.'

Philippe had a fondness for Edmond. Not only because he paid handsomely each time he visited, but because he was a gracious man, who didn't take liberties with the farmer's daughters, as soldiers were likely to do.

Round and jolly, Philippe was of medium height, with receding, grizzled hair, and a large nose. Time had drawn many lines on his long, brown face. His eyes were intelligent, yet shrewd. A liberal man to those he liked, but sharp and rancorous with those he did not.

His wife was as spare as he was large. Her arms sinewy, made strong by hard work. Yet, her hands were gentle. Her dark-brown eyes dominated her broad, kindly face. Evette came into the kitchen.

'The poor child is exhausted, so I put her to bed. What happened to her father, Major?'

'Men were being re-embarked from the beach at St Cast. Troops came upon them by chance. There was a battle; many were killed. Sophia's father suffered a bayonet wound to his chest. Nothing could be done for him. He died. He was my good friend. He asked me to take care of his daughter, so now I am her guardian.'

He didn't mention his marriage to Sophia, hoping she would have the good sense not to mention it either. He didn't think Philippe and Evette would understand.

Evette busied herself with making supper. She chopped onions and threw them into a large smoking skillet, adding scallops of chicken, with herbs, cream, and a splash of wine, which sizzled. A delicious aroma filled the room. Several bubbling pots stood on the range, which she peered into from time to time, tasting the contents carefully with a long-handled spoon, and adding flavoursome herbs.

'So, where do you go now, Major?' she asked as she tossed the scallops in the pan.

'I am taking her back to England, Evette. She will be safer there, as she belongs not to the French or the English, having had a parent from each side. She speaks both languages with no trace of accent.'

'Where will she live, Major?' Philippe asked.

'With me, on my estate, 'til she is old enough to go into society, at which time I mean to find her a husband. I have an older sister who will, I am sure, be happy to help me with taking care of her,' he explained, suppressing a yawn.

'You own an estate, Monsieur?' Evette said, much impressed.

'I do, Evette, a large one. It is time I took charge of it, instead of fighting battles,' he said, with a smile. 'I inherited it about three years ago when my father and brother died. I should have gone home then, but I am going now, and taking my young ward with me.'

'Ah, but we will miss your visits, Major,' Philippe said, offering to replenish Edmond's glass. Edmond refused the offer, with a smile. 'Philippe, do you want to get me drunk?'

Philippe laughed and put the bottle back on the shelf.

'You are very good to give me your hospitality, Philippe. I fear your life would be in danger if you were caught harbouring the enemy,' Edmond said.

'Ah, pah! Who cares about who wins this war? Who suffers in such times but men like me, who work the land? They may keep their war, and leave us alone!' he said, spitting into the fire.

'When all this fighting is over, Philippe, if ever I return to France, I shall be sure to visit you,' Edmond said, adding, 'I, like Sophia, am weary, my friends, so if you will excuse me, I will take to my bed.'

'You will not eat supper with us, Major?' Evette asked.

'Thank you, Evette, it smells delicious,' Edmond said, glancing at the pots and pans on the hob, 'but I am too tired to eat. I shall break my fast with you in the morning, if I may.'

'You may, monsieur, and welcome,' she said.

Philippe took a candle from a shelf, and putting it in a shining brass *porte-bougie*, led the way up the steep wooden stairs to Edmond's room.

'*Bonne Nuit,* Monsieur Edmond. Sleep well, *mon amie,*' Philippe said, placing the candle on the dresser.

'Good night Philippe. I am so weary, I will, indeed, sleep well,' Edmond replied.

Philippe closed the door, and Edmond heard him descend the stairs.

Edmond yawned widely as he removed his clothes. He went to the bed and pulled back the covers. Climbing into the bed, he pulled the covers around him, sank gratefully into the soft, comfortable, feather bed, and slept immediately.

CHAPTER ELEVEN

The following day, in the first light of morning, Edmond roused from a deep sleep. Evette had tiptoed into the room, to leave a highly-polished copper pitcher of hot water by the washstand. Beside the washstand basin, she laid two snowy towels and a bar of soap.

Edmond lay on his back, his hands linked behind his head, musing.

Delicious smells of cooking wafted into the room, as Evette tiptoed back in with a blue and white patterned flagon of water and a mug. As she put them on a table near his bed, she noticed Edmond was awake.

'Good morning Monsieur. I hope you slept well?'

'Better than I have in many a day, Evette, thank you,' Edmond said.

'*Ah bon!* I shall see you at breakfast,' she said and hurried away.

Edmond yawned and stretched, feeling refreshed from a good night's sleep. Fully awake, he set aside his thoughts and got out of bed.

He found his saddlebags, which Evette had left on a chair by the washstand.

Wilson had packed everything with care, and Edmond retrieved his washing gear from the top of one bag. On the washstand, he laid out his razor, a silver box, containing his tooth powder, and a small sponge, with a larger sponge, with which he would wash.

Fastidious about his hygiene, he undid his plaited cue, and washed his hair, and his body, with Evette's famed herb-scented soap.

He regarded his face in the mirror above the washstand. His hair hung in straggles about his shoulders and curled about his face.

He felt the stubble on his chin.

I look like a vagabond. I wonder, should I grow a beard? Hah, I am half way there already! he reflected.

He brushed his damp hair back from his face, tying it at the nape of his neck with a leather thong. Making a lather from the soap with his sponge, he applied it to his face and shaved.

When he had finished, he looked at himself once more, and let out a sigh of satisfaction, smoothing a hand over his clean face.

'That's better,' he said and opened the silver box.

His tooth powder consisted of a concoction of soot, lemon juice, gin, and ground cloves. Dipping the smaller sponge into the powder, he cleaned his teeth.

He was about to put on his uniform when he remembered his civilian clothes. He chuckled to himself.

What a fool I am, riding around France dressed as a British officer. I should have had the presence of mind to dress in civilian clothes before this.

He went to his saddlebags again and found all he needed, wrapped up in a large square of linen.

Drawers? Ah, yes, there they were, wrapped in his breeches. He put on the drawers.

Unlike the rough cloth of his army shirts, the one provided by Wilson was of soft linen. Fine lace adorned the cuffs. He put the shirt over his head, luxuriating in its comfort.

Edmond held up the coat and breeches, both made of drab green, worsted material. A most elegant suit, the frock coat having gold lace adorning the cuffs. Strips of gold lace ran down the front of the coat, too. He laid it, and the breeches, on the bed, and surveyed them, while he donned a light brown, jacquard waistcoat.

A stock, which did up with a buckle at the back, was his usual army regulation neckwear. It had been a long time since he wore a cravat. He wrapped it around his throat, and carefully tied several knots in it finishing with a soft bow. The fine, white lace at the ends fell in a froth on his chest.

I have not forgotten how to tie the thing, he thought.

Edmond put on his breeches and slid his arms into the

sleeves of the coat. It seemed loose. His uniform jacket fitted him like a glove. This coat, although hugging his shoulders comfortably, was much looser and swung when he walked.

The last items in the parcel were a pair of shining black pumps, accompanied by his stockings, and his dark green tricorn hat. The edges of the hat were adorned with a narrow strip of gold lace, matching that on his coat.

He put on his stockings, but was loath to give up his boots, and wore them with his breeches tucked into the top.

Inside the hat, he found a length of wide, black velvet ribbon. He tied this in a loose bow over the thong, which held his hair in place.

As he picked up his gear from the washstand, he glanced at himself in the mirror.

Instead of a soldier, a well-dressed gentleman peered back at him.

He laughed to himself, amused by the transformation.

Picking up his hat, he started down the stairs to the kitchen. The civilian clothes felt strange to him. It had been a while since he had worn them.

Sophia was already in the kitchen, surrounded by five girls. Mirande, the second eldest daughter of the family, had dressed Sophia's hair in a becoming style, threading red ribbons through the curls. She had given Sophia a red gown, of simple design, with tight bodice and full skirt, divided at the front to show a white underskirt. A white cotton fichu, folded neatly, was tucked decorously into the neckline. The deep red of the woollen material suited Sophia's honey complexion.

When Edmond entered the kitchen, both he and Sophia were surprised to find such a change in each other's appearance.

'Oh, Edmond, how different you are out of uniform. I hardly recognised you,' Sophia said, her eyes round with surprise.

'You are not the tousled little person you were

yesterday, Sophia.'

Edmond waved his hand around for her to turn for his inspection.

'Mirande gave me this dress. Is she not generous?'

'Indeed,' Edmond said, nodding to Mirande who smiled shyly at him.

'Your clothes were somewhat soiled from travelling, Sophia. Did you not think to bring a change of clothes?'

'No, Edmond. I am such a scatterbrain; I put everything in the trunks. This dress is not the style I usually wear. But I like it.'

'The style does not matter. If the dress is warm, then wear it,' Edmond said, with masculine practicality.

Sophia beamed at him.

At the breakfast table, Edmond and Sophia joined Philippe, Evette, and all five daughters, ranging in age from twelve to twenty-two. All the daughters were similar in appearance, with their mother's slim build, and their father's twinkling brown eyes.

Today, Mirande and Giselle were helping their mother serve breakfast.

They placed a variety of blue and white dishes on the table. Being autumn, fruit was abundant: apples, pears and blackberries, plums, cherries and figs. The warm aroma of freshly baked bread rolls filled the air. Evette had made them in honour of Edmond and Sophia. A big wicker basket held the rolls, accompanied by butter and cheese from Evette's own dairy. A large jug of fresh milk stood beside the basket. The rich fragrance of newly ground coffee vied with the smell of bread.

The boisterous good-humoured family welcomed Sophia.

'Sit by me, Sophia,' Dominique insisted.

'Sit here between us,' Collette suggested, moving up to make room for her.

Unused to mixing with girls of her own age, Sophia enjoyed their company immensely.

Laughter and chatter filled the kitchen, as the family

passed dishes and jugs around the table, competing with one another in serving Sophia.

Evette, with a watchful eye, kept order.

'Amandine, fetch *comfiture* for Sophia,' Evette said. 'Mirande, give Sophia more milk.'

Philippe, sitting beside Edmond, turned to him and said quietly, 'Monsieur Edmond, you go to Marronville, *n'est ce pas*?'

'I do, Philippe. I must leave soon. We must get there before noon to catch the tide. The trouble is, my friend,' Edmond lowered his voice, 'I have asked my orderly to collect our horses from your farm today. I am now in a difficult position. I must ride to the port, but the horses will not be here when my orderly comes to collect them....'

Philippe held up a hand. 'Do not worry, Major Edmond, I will drive you to the port in my dogcart,' Philippe said, giving Edmond a cheerful smile.

'Philippe, I do not want to put you to any trouble ....'

Philippe interrupted him. 'Major, please, do not refuse me. You are most welcome. I am pleased to help you and Sophia. You have been an agreeable guest in my house. I will miss you.'

He turned his mouth down at the corners, lifting his shoulders.

'Say no more, Major. The matter is settled. I will tell the boys to harness the cart.'

After the meal, it was time for Edmond and Sophia to go. The five girls fussed around Sophia, kissing and hugging her goodbye.

Evette took Sophia in her arms and embraced her. Putting her hands on Sophia's cheeks, she kissed her forehead.

'*Adieu chérie,*' Evette said, with tears in her eyes. 'I hope you get to England safely and have a happy life there.'

'I am sure I shall, Evette,' Sophia said. She kissed Evette on both cheeks and tried not to cry.

All the girls, plus Evette and Philippe accompanied Sophia and Edmond to the gate, where the cart stood in the road awaiting them, Anton holding the horse's head.

Edmond helped Sophia into the cart and climbed up beside her. Philippe took his seat, and picked up the horse's reins, looking to make sure his passengers were settled. He gave the horse the office to go, and the cart sped off.

The girls ran out into the road to wave to Sophia. A light breeze plucked at their skirts and lifted their aprons. Stray wisps of their hair were caught and floated in the bright sunshine. The crisp air was filled with their lively voices calling goodbye. Sophia turned to wave back enthusiastically.

Evette came to wave, too, then shooed the girls into the house to start on their chores.

'What friendly girls, Edmond,' Sophia said, turning to face front.

Edmond felt a pang of misgiving.

'Sophia, I have few acquaintances in London; certainly, none that have daughters with whom you could form friendships. I hope you will not be lonely.'

'Oh, you need have no qualms on that score, Edmond,' she answered promptly. 'I am used to entertaining myself. I enjoy company, yet am equally happy with or without it.'

Edmond smiled. *What a strange little creature she is,* he thought.

The light cart whipped along at a swift rate. Philippe hummed a soft tune. The horse's clip-clopping hooves accompanied him.

Along the way they passed many farms, their houses set back from the road. Some with water wheels to one side, if the farm had a stream running within its boundaries. One or two windmills stood on the farmers' land. At other farms, great barns for storing crops, stood dwarfing the rest of the buildings.

Philippe called a cheery 'Bonjour Maurice,' to a boy leading cows in for milking. To an old man, leaning over a gate smoking a pipe, Philippe waved a hand.

'You have many good neighbours, Philippe,' Edmond observed.

'I do, Major. We are a close community. We all help each other in troubled times.'

A woman appeared at the side of the road and waved Philippe down.

'I have a surfeit of eggs, Philippe. Will you collect a share on your way back? Evette gave me some of her excellent cheese, so she may have my eggs in return.'

'I will collect them, Madame Perrodin,' he called.

She stepped back, smiling and nodding, and Philippe continued on his way.

The morning sun shone down on them from a brilliant blue sky. Only the chilly wind, and the autumnal character of the trees told them it wasn't early summer.

The farming area seemed to stretch on for miles. At last, they were passing a forest. The road became steeper, and they could smell the sea.

They caught glimpses of it through the trees as they ascended the hill overlooking the bay.

'Oh! There is the sea!' Sophia exclaimed, and inhaled the fresh salty air.

As they drove along the cliff road, far out from the land they sighted several large ships standing at anchor.

'French Men o' War,' Edmond murmured.

Sophia shot him a questioning look.

'I see them,' Philippe said. 'You may have some difficulty sailing, Major.'

'You may have some difficulty explaining why you are transporting enemy English, Philippe,' Edmond said, frowning, worried.

'You would pass for a Frenchman, Major, and Sophia's French is excellent. I do not worry,' Philippe said.

'I do not either, Philippe, 'til they ask for our papers when we try to board a ship. No, I shall not put you at risk, Philippe. Put us down before we enter the town. We shall walk the rest of the way to *Le Coq d'Or*. It is not far.

Philippe made to protest, but Edmond stayed him with a hand on his arm.

'I insist, Philippe,' he said in a voice that brooked no argument.

They caught sight of chimney tops as they descended the hill. The land flattened out on the approach to Marronville.

At the edge of the town, Philippe stopped the cart.

'I do not like this, Major. I feel I am abandoning you,' he said, his lined, brown face unhappy.

Edmond jumped down and helped Sophia from the cart. Philippe leant over to shake Edmond's hand. Edmond put a small leather bag in it.

'What is this, Major?' Philippe said.

'It is a "thank you", Philippe. A *pourboire.*'

'*Mais, non*, Major, it is too much,' he said, weighing the bag in his hand.

'Nonsense, Philippe, I am indebted to you for your help, and for your care of the horses.'

Philippe frowned and shook his head. 'You have paid me well in the past, Major, and I am grateful. But I cannot accept so much from you. I have my pride,' he said, holding out the bag to Edmond.

'Well, Philippe, if you insult me by not accepting it, I will not be a happy man,' Edmond said, his eyebrows drawn together.

Philippe drew a breath and blew out his cheeks, glowering at Edmond.

The two men looked at each other for what seemed a long time.

'Buy a present for Evette,' Edmond said, at last.

Philippe let out a long, growling, 'Ahh,' and put the bag in his pocket, allowing himself to be persuaded.

'I do not wish to part on bad terms, Major, so I will accept it … reluctantly!'

Philippe got down from the cart and held his hand out again. Edmond grasped it warmly.

Philippe looked at Sophia. He stepped forward, and

taking her by the shoulders, kissed her on both cheeks. He went to the horse's head, turned the cart around, and climbed back up on his seat.

Edmond retrieved his saddlebags and Sophia's portmanteau from the back of the cart.

'*Au revoir, bon voyage, et bon chance, mon amie*,' Philippe said. 'I hope someday we may meet again.'

'Perhaps we shall. *Au revoir*, Philippe, and thank you,' Edmond said, stepping back as Philippe shook the reins. The horse set off at a trot, and Edmond's last remembrance of Philippe, was a cheery wave of his arm, as the cart rounded a bend in the road, and was out of sight, speeding back to his farm, his wife and his five daughters.

Sophia watched the cart go. Turning to Edmond, she said, 'What shall we do now, Edmond?' a concerned look on her face.

'We must continue on this road, Sophia, and we shall come to a row of houses. At the end of the row, on the corner, is an inn called *Le Coq d'Or*. It is there I arranged to meet Wilson,' Edmond said. He slung his saddlebags over his shoulder and picked up Sophia's portmanteau.

'I can carry that, Edmond,' she said, wanting to help.

Edmond gave her a sidelong look and set off.

Sophia bowed her head, hiding a smile, and walked beside him.

The road was dusty. The wind caught the dust and blew it in little swirls around their ankles.

Sophia wished it had been possible for Philippe to take them to the Inn.

The town stood back from the sea on a rise, but the road to it was on flat land. Sophia had been looking at the sea with pleasure, but now she couldn't see it. To their right, a dark wood of pine trees created a dismal aspect. Sophia's elation at being near the sea dissipated.

'Are you all right, Sophia, you are very quiet,' Edmond said, glancing down at her.

'I am thinking of those ships. What exactly are they?' she asked.

'They are warships, Sophia, part of the French naval fleet. They are probably there to ward against attack by us English. There have been a number of English raids on busy French ports, of late.'

'Are we in danger, Edmond?'

'We could be, Sophia. If we are careful, however, we shall come through safely,' he said, attempting optimism, yet with no idea how he could board a ship.

Trying to allay her fear, he laughed. 'I thought you enjoyed adventure?'

'Oh, I do,' she said, brightly, ignoring her feelings of unease.

They reached the row of houses and walked to where *Le Coq d'Or* stood, dominating the area.

A low wall surrounded the old two-storey building. A sign in gold lettering over the weathered, dark-wooden door, proclaimed *Le Coq d'Or,* with a picture of a golden cockerel set into the wall above. Mullioned windows sparkled in the bright sunlight. The whitewashed walls of the building dazzled the eye.

Wilson sat on the wall, smoking his pipe, much at his ease.

Edmond walked up to Wilson and dropped the saddlebags and portmanteau on the wall next to him.

'Good day to you, Wilson,' Edmond said, annoyed. 'A fine day is it not? You seem to be enjoying the sunshine.'

Wilson stood, and looked as if he would salute, but caught himself in time.

'Good day, Sir. Have you had a good journey?'

'Yes, Wilson. What have you been doing with yourself whilst you awaited us, hmm? Apart from sitting in the sun. And what, pray, may I ask, are you wearing?'

Wilson looked down at the loose midi jacket he wore over his shirt. A pair of wide white trousers came down to his ankles. On his head, he wore a round, wide brimmed straw hat.

'I'm tryin' to blend in, Sir. I bought these clothes from a sailor,' Wilson said, with a twinkle in his eye, unabashed by Edmond's curt tones.

'Are you aware that there are a number of French Men o' War in the bay? Does that not strike you as a problem?' Edmond said, his irritation rising. 'I presume there is a French naval presence at the dock?'

'There is, Major. The place is crawlin' with 'em,' Wilson said. 'But have no fear, Sir. I managed to book passage for the three of us. Not sure if you'll approve of the crew, Sir, but needs must,' he said.

Wilson tilted his head and gave Edmond a conspiratorial wink.

'What on earth are you talking about, Wilson?' Edmond asked, still annoyed.

'Well, Sir, all the *legal* ships have French naval officers checking the passengers' papers. But I came across a fella in the inn while I was waiting for you, Sir, and his captain is in the … em … "export" business.'

Wilson winked again, and paused for effect, casting a cautious eye at Edmond, whose eyebrows had flown up.

'Go on,' he said, his eyebrows now drawn together.

'We got chatting like—he bein' a Frenchie that speaks English. I told him, me and me comrade, and me comrade's ward was seekin' to get to England. But with the port bein' checked as it is, we was at a bit of a standstill. He said his captain wasn't too particular who his passengers were, as long as they paid well.'

Wilson looked sidelong at Edmond. 'It's either that or wait till the Frenchies clear off, and Gawd knows when that'll be, Sir.'

Edmond rubbed his chin.

'Where is this man's ship anchored, Wilson?' Edmond asked.

'It's on t'other side o' the headland, Sir. Thierry Bonnaire said, he and his mate could row us round to it in a jolly boat. We'll have to walk through the dockyard to get to it. It's sort of "hidden in plain sight". As long as we keep our heads down, we shouldn't have any bother.'

Edmond looked at Sophia. He did not want to put her in

jeopardy. Then he saw her eyes were bright with anticipation.

'It is an *adventure*!' she said. 'You are referring to free traders, are you not Wilson?'

Wilson coughed. 'Them's not words to bandy about, Miss. But you have the gist of it.'

Edmond looked at Sophia sternly.

'You have been reading too many novels, Sophia. Smuggling is a dangerous business … nothing romantic about it at all. If caught, those with them are regarded as equally guilty of criminal activity.'

Sophia tried to look suitably fearful. 'What would happen if we were caught, Edmond?' she asked, frowning, her lips pressed together, eager anticipation in every pore.

'At the very least, they would imprison us, Sophia. You would probably be comparatively safe. But Wilson and I, as British military, would fare badly. They would think we are spies. Along with that, if we got to England it would not be much different. We could all end up in prison.' Edmond paused. Sophia's face, although less animated, still showed excitement. He decided to hammer home to her their predicament, adding, 'But we are even now in danger, Sophia if the French find out who we are. If they catch us, they will treat us none too gently. We could be executed, or at the very least, we could be imprisoned 'til the end of the war.'

Sophia's eyes became big and round, her excitement crumbled. Her hands came up to her mouth.

'Oh, how dreadful! We *must* get away immediately!' she said, looking about, as if for a means of escape.

'We must, indeed. Yet, we must not go half-cocked. We must be cautious, and all will be well. You must follow my instructions, Sophia. Wilson, where is Bonnaire?'

'He's in the inn, Sir. I procured a private room.'

'And where are our trunks, Wilson?' Edmond asked.

Wilson swallowed. 'Er … I had them put aboard Bonnaire's ship, Sir, *L'Oiseau de Paradis,*' he said.

'Thierry rowed out to make sure his captain would take us to England, so I suggested he take the trunks with him.'

'His Captain agreed?' Edmond said, becoming less annoyed, beginning to think perhaps Wilson's arrangements were the best they could hope for.

'More or less, Sir. He wants a lot o' money.'

'Hmm,' Edmond grunted. 'That is not a problem. We had better have words with Monsieur Bonnaire. Come, Sophia,' Edmond said, taking her arm.

Wilson picked up the portmanteau and the saddlebags and led Sophia and Edmond into the inn. Edmond spoke to Sophia in an under voice.

'Sophia, I want you to keep quiet while I speak to this man. Can you do that for me?'

'Yes, Edmond. I shall say not a word. I promise,' she said.

Wilson opened the heavy door and held it for Edmond and Sophia. They walked into the vestibule. Edmond noted that the place was quiet and clean, with polished furniture and a well-swept floor. As they passed the inn's main room, they caught a draft of warmth from the open door and heard a hum of conversation. The innkeeper, swathed in a large white apron, made to approach Edmond. He considered Edmond to be a man of means, worthy of his personal attention.

Edmond placed a coin in the man's hand and waved him away.

Wilson led them down a cool, dark, stone-tiled passage, to the back of the inn. He opened a door on the right, holding it for Edmond and Sophia.

As they entered the long, narrow chamber, their eyes met the broad figure of Thierry Bonnaire. His imposing presence filled the room.

He stood by the open window, smoking a long clay pipe, his red hair drawn back into a queue, his beard neatly trimmed. He wore a voluminous, white-linen shirt, a drab blue waistcoat over it; a red kerchief tied loosely at his neck. Grey wool stockings showed beneath his wide, dark-yellow nankeen trousers that came down to his calves. Silver buckles shone brightly on his shoes of plain, dull brown leather. His battered black tricorn hat lay on a high-backed settle beside the fire. The deep brown of his weather-beaten skin enhanced the bright blue of his piercing, intelligent eyes. He looked at Edmond keenly.

'Monsoor, this is my comrade M—Mr St Vere, and his ward,' Wilson said.

Thierry spoke in heavily accented English.

'I am pleased to make your acquaintance, Monsieur St Vere. Wilson tells me I may be of service to you.'

Edmond spoke to him in French.

'I hope so, Monsieur. I presume you may speak for your Captain?'

'Indeed, Monsieur St Vere. I am what might be called his second in command.'

Edmond nodded in acknowledgement. 'I want to be away as soon as possible. How soon may we leave?'

'We may start right away, Monsieur,' Bonnaire said. 'The jolly boat is moored between two ships, at the end of the quay. The ships do not sail till tomorrow, so no attention will be paid to them.'

Bonnaire looked Edmond up and down.

'My only misgiving is your attire, Monsieur. You present too grand a figure in your gold lace and ruffles.'

Edmond smiled. 'That is easily remedied, Bonnaire,' he said, turning to Wilson. 'Do you have your black-leather jerkin with you, Wilson?'

Wilson's eyes twinkled. 'I do, Sir,' he said. He reached behind the door to retrieve his portmanteau. After rummaging in it, he drew out the jerkin and handed it to Edmond.

Edmond removed his splendid coat and put on Wilson's Jerkin.

Wilson folded Edmond's coat and put it neatly in the portmanteau along with Edmond's hat.

Sliding the leather tie and ribbon from his hair, Edmond ruffled his fingers through his locks, until they fell untidily about his shoulders, and flopped over his eyes.

Grasping the lightly sewn lace at his cuffs, Edmond tore it free. The lace at his cravat suffered the same fate. After stuffing the loose lace into a pocket, he retied the cravat in a simple knot. His transformation was complete.

'Is that better, Bonnaire?' Edmond asked.

Bonnaire gave Edmond a crooked smile. '*Parfait, Monsieur.*'

Bonnaire turned his attention to Sophia. He scanned her up and down with a critical eye.

'Your clothes are simple, Mam'selle. You will do as you are.'

'*Merci, Monsieur,*' she said, shyly smiling at him. She saw Edmond glance at her. Realising she had promised not to speak, her conscience pricked her. She lowered her eyes.

'*Bon,*' Bonnaire said. 'Then we may go.'

Bonnaire picked up his hat and set it at an angle on his head. He led the way down the gloomy passage, and out of the inn. As they passed the innkeeper, Bonnaire murmured to Edmond, 'I have paid the innkeeper.'

'Thank you,' Edmond said.

Bonnaire grunted as he glanced at Edmond. 'You may reimburse me when you pay your passage, Monsieur,' Bonnaire replied.

Edmond's lips twitched. *How very Gallic*, he thought.

Edmond, Sophia and Wilson followed Bonnaire towards the dockyard. Edmond held Sophia's hand in the crook of his arm. Wilson walked behind, carrying Edmond's saddlebags and the two portmanteaux.

CHAPTER TWELVE

Sophia jumped, as a burly sailor shouted to another man on a ship. Orders were yelled between man and man, and from ship to shore. The noise, resounding off the walls of the dock's warehouses, was deafening.

She winced at the booming crashes, as sailors hauled wooden crates from the dock onto a ship.

The clanging of metal rang out as men hefted heavy chains.

Luggage and equipment, of various shapes and sizes, were moved from place to place as the crews prepared the ships for sailing.

The smell of the sea mingled with that of tar, and damp wood. Sophia stepped over ropes, as they stretched, coiled, and snaked everywhere.

As Wilson had said, the dock was crawling with French soldiers. French uniforms wove everywhere through the throng. Sophia looked about her, eyes huge, fearful, yet excited.

They passed French officers standing at the bottom of heavy gangplanks, stopping people to inspect their papers, as they waited to board the ships.

Edmond's hand held Sophia's, with a firm grip, in the crook of his arm. She felt his hand tense on hers when a French officer looked intently at Edmond as he approached them. She looked up at Edmond. His face showed no emotion. The officer passed by, and she felt Edmond's hand relax.

Sophia caught sight of the towering masts of the ships.

'Edmond, how tall those ships are,' she whispered, craning her neck.

'Sophia,' Edmond murmured, 'look straight ahead of you. Do not smile. Do not look frightened. Say not a word, and do not look at me.'

Sophia glanced at him and nodded. She did what she was told. Nevertheless, she remained enthralled by the chaotic bustle of the dock.

They reached *L'Oiseau's* jolly boat, moored as Bonnaire had said, between two ships. Bonnaire's mate, Gaston Travert, sat in the boat waiting for them.

Three French soldiers lounged a few feet away. Sophia drew closer to Edmond. Her eyes darted to the soldiers and then lowered their gaze.

Bonnaire noticed her apprehension. In a low voice, he said, 'They will not approach us, Mam'selle. They are aware of *L'Oiseau's* activities and have been paid well to turn their eyes away.'

Wilson led Edmond and Sophia to an iron rail, curling up over the dock. The rail was attached to a ladder fixed to the dock wall and lead down to the boat.

Wilson passed their luggage to Travert. He swiftly descended into the boat, stood to help Sophia down, and seated her at the stern.

Bonnaire and Edmond climbed down next, Bonnaire sitting beside Travert.

Behind them, Wilson sat by Edmond, who looked at him with narrowed eyes.

'This boat calls for four oarsmen, Wilson, not two,' he observed quietly.

'Yes, Sir,' Wilson said, glancing at him sideways. 'I'm sorry, Sir.'

Edmond let out a low, irritated growl but said nothing, as he took up an oar.

The tide was turning; a stiff breeze ruffled the sea. Little waves lapped at the side of the boat. Further out, the sun sparkled on the crests of the billows. The oars creaked as the men rowed steadily towards the headland. With four strong men rowing, the boat cut swiftly through the waves.

Sophia, sitting in the stern, kept her eyes fixed on the horizon, her hair blowing about her.

She had forgotten her hat again.

They soon reached the headland and turned into the shelter of a quiet bay, where '*L'Oiseau* lay at anchor.

When the jolly boat reached the ship, the crew threw a

line over the side to secure it. A stout rope ladder followed. The two sailors ascended it first, followed by Wilson.

They threw a line over the side for Sophia. The rope had a slipknot at the end, making a loop. Edmond caught the rope.

'Put your foot into the loop Sophia and hold tight to the rope,' Edmond told her.

He expected Sophia to be fearful of being hauled up from the boat into the ship, but hadn't appreciated her capacity for what she termed 'adventure'. She placed her foot in the loop, clung to the rope, gave Edmond a huge excited smile, and soared like a bird into the air. Edmond climbed the ladder and hauled himself over the bulwark onto the deck, where he saw Wilson extracting Sophia's foot from the loop.

'That *was* exciting!' she said, in a low voice to Edmond, when he came to her side.

Bonnaire approached a figure standing in the shadow of the main mast.

'Captain Renaud, these are the passengers I spoke of. Monsieur St Vere, his ward, and Monsieur Daniel Wilson.'

The figure stepped forward.

'Monsieur Wilson, you and your companions seek passage to England, yes?'

All three turned towards the deep voice, noting little trace of an accent. In contrast to the smoothly laid question, they found penetrating, amber eyes locked on them.

Tall and slim, Captain Jean Renaud's short, black hair covered his elegant head in crisp, tight curls. His coat closely fitted his strong shoulders. The dark-red jacquard waistcoat beneath spoke of a good tailor's hand. His breeches, unlike those of his crew, clung sleekly to his well-shaped legs. His suit was deepest black, which enhanced the gleaming whiteness of his shirt, and perfectly tied neck cloth. Boots coming up over his knees, completed his stylish appearance.

'We do *Monsoor*. And as you have accepted our luggage onto your ship, I may assume, may I not, that you will accommodate us?'

Edmond was unused to the authority displayed by his batman. The weight Wilson's words managed to accomplish, gave Edmond pause. He saw Wilson in a new light.

'I merely wish to establish that I am not accommodating criminals,' Renaud replied with haughty displeasure.

Much as Edmond appreciated Wilson's newly discovered ability, he felt it expedient to take control of the conversation and spoke to the Captain himself.

'If it is criminal for a man to be a British officer, then I am guilty of asking you to harbour a fugitive. If, however, you see a man who is dedicated to the protection of an orphaned child, whom I have taken into my charge, then I appeal to your integrity, and ask you to aid a man, intent on doing what he thinks is right.'

Captain Renaud's delicately arched eyebrows flew up. 'A pretty speech, Monsieur,' he said, 'Do you know what business we are in?'

'I assume you deal in contraband,' Edmond said, steadily.

'You are right, Sir. However, transporting fugitives does not sit well with me. The authorities ignore the free trading. Fugitives are a different matter,' the captain said, paying some deference to Edmond's commanding tone.

'I am no spy, Captain. Neither am I a criminal. After a military career spanning twelve years, I intend to resign my commission. I wish to return to England with this child. The French authorities would not give credence to my resolution. My wish is but to see my charge safe.'

'Most commendable, Sir,' the Captain said, echoing Colonel Radford's words.

Edmond spoke with quiet resolve.

'I am a man of means, Captain. I shall pay whatever you require. I am determined to bring my charge to safety.'

Edmond's eloquent words impressed Renaud. He realised he was dealing with an educated man of authority.

'You must not be a problem to us, monsieur. Although the French authorities ignore our activities, those on the English coast are more troublesome. Our destination is Weymouth.'

'Drop us wherever you think fit, Captain. We shall shift for ourselves wherever you set us down.'

'I will transport you, Sir. We sail with the tide. Thierry will show you to your accommodation,' Captain Renaud said, and nodded a courteous bow to Edmond, before moving away to consult the boatswain.

Bonnaire turned to them. 'Follow me please,' he said, in his guttural English.

He led them along the deck towards the stern, and down a steep companionway to a low and gloomy corridor. The men stooped as they walked along it to the end.

Bonnaire opened a door and indicated the cabin inside.

'This will be your accommodation 'till we reach the English coast,' he said. 'If there is anything you need, I will be happy to provide it.'

'Thank you, Bonnaire,' Edmond said.

Bonnaire nodded and retreated.

Edmond and Wilson stood back to allow Sophia to enter the cabin.

Amazement at the gloom and small size of it made Sophia frown.

Tucked under the porthole were a strong, compact wooden table, and a stout chair. Two narrow bunks, one above the other, protruded from the opposite wall. A white, canvas hammock hung at right angles to them, behind the door. Once inside the cabin, they had little room to move.

Wilson opened the door again. 'I mean to speak to Bonnaire, Sir. When we arrive in Weymouth, we must locate an inn and a means of transport, to take us to

London. I will ask Bonnaire about it, and find out what food I can get hold of, too, Sir.'

'Thank you, Wilson. Yes, go. See whether you can discover more about Renaud's activities, as well,' Edmond said. Wilson nodded and left the cabin.

'Why is there so little space? This is ridiculously small,' Sophia said, standing on tiptoe to peer out of the porthole.

Edmond laughed, at which she turned inquiring eyes on him.

'Sophia, the cabin is large compared to some of those Wilson and I have occupied. Why, sailors all sleep in hammocks like this,' Edmond said, pointing to the one in the space behind the door. 'On a Naval ship, they are permitted but fourteen inches, at most, for each sailor to sleep in,' he told her, still laughing.

'How do you know, Edmond?' she asked.

'Well, my dear, Wilson and I are seasoned travellers. Wars have taken us to many far-flung places—India and America, for example.

'Goodness!' breathed Sophia, her eyes wide with wonder. 'My father was away from home a lot while my mother was alive. I suppose he travelled far, too.'

'He did Sophia. After my promotion to Captain, I was on his staff. It takes months to get to some faraway places. Wilson, your father, and I, became accustomed to life at sea.'

Sophia went to the hammock to inspect it. She pushed it, watching it swing from side to side.

'How do they sleep in this?' she asked.

'It is an art, Sophia. You shall use the bunk if you need rest,' he said, once more amused by her inquisitive attitude to everything with which she came in contact.

'Although our journey today will only take a matter of hours, it is best to have a cabin to rest in, or in case the sea is rough, in which circumstance, we must stay below, out of the way. Come, let us go on deck, and watch as we set sail,' Edmond said, as he led Sophia from the cabin.

Once on deck again, Sophia took in the unfamiliar surroundings with eager interest.

She noted boats stored, one on top of the other, lashed to the side of the ship.

'What are those boats for, Edmond?'

'If the ship is in danger of sinking, they are the lifeboats which carry the crew to safety. Although, I expect they are used on this ship to transport contraband to the shore,' Edmond told her.

Gazing up at the enormous sails, as the crew prepared to unfurl them, amazement filled her at the sight of the men, high in the rigging, managing the ropes.

'Edmond, how do those men stay working at such a height without falling?' she asked, her head back as she watched.

'They walk on the footropes under the yard,' he said, happy to inform her interest.

'What is the yard?' she asked, glancing sideways at him.

'The yard is the long shaft of wood to which the sails are attached,' Edmond said pointing it out to her. 'In turn, the yards are attached to the three masts. The masts are the long shafts rising from the deck. You are looking at the mainmast,' he said.

'Hmm, so the masts hold up the sails?'

'Exactly so,' Edmond said. 'The crew are used to climbing and balancing, too. It is not often they fall.' Edmond watched her animated face, as she gazed up, still amazed by their skill. Her amazement amused him.

'I have climbed trees, and enjoyed the exhilaration of seeing so far from so high, but I could never have worked as they do—I always clung tightly to the branches, for fear of falling.'

She drew in an awed breath, when a large square sail billowed, as it was unfurled.

'Whoo, how magnificent.'

'Unfurling a sail is easy. Harder to furl them, especially in a storm when hands and feet are wet and freezing, and the wind is like to blow you off your perch,' Edmond said, staring up into the rigging.

Sophia watched the crew going about their business. They worked methodically. Every one performing their tasks, with practised efficiency.

She watched as four men turned the capstan to haul up the anchor. Others cleared the decks of clutter.

Before she could enquire about them, Edmond, puzzled, asked, 'Where and when did you climb trees, Sophia?'

Sophia took a mischievous look at Edmond, her eyes bright. She blushed, smiling.

'I was quite young; it was before my mother died. We were billeted once, on the edge of a forest in Prussia. I thought if I mastered the art of climbing trees, were the enemy to come too close, hiding up a tree would be safe. My father discovered me doing so, and scolded me—but I still think it was a good notion,' she said, with a defiant little tilt to her chin.

Edmond laughed. 'It *is* a good notion. King Charles, God rest him, did just that in an oak tree in Boscobel Wood, thus escaping capture.'

Edmond looked at Sophia, curiosity lurking in his eyes. 'Did you climb in your skirts? Surely they must have hampered you?' he said.

Sophia gave him a roguish smile.

'I borrowed breeches from a stable boy. I do not know which aggrieved my father the most, the climbing, or my wearing of the breeches. I found them most comfortable, to be sure,' she said, defiantly.

'I can see I shall have my hands full with you, Sophia,' Edmond said.

Sophia immediately looked repentant. 'Oh, indeed, Edmond, you will not, for I mean to behave exactly how you would wish. I promise,' she said, with determination.

'Ah, Sophia, I did but jest. I am sure you will be a model of propriety,' he said, laying a fatherly hand on her shoulder.

'I will try to be, I promise, Sir,' she said, somewhat abashed. Then her mood changed, as the big ship began to move. She rushed to the bulwark and stepped up on the rail. Edmond laughed quietly, 'So much for propriety,' he said under his breath, as he moved to where she was. He stood behind her, in case she slipped. He couldn't decide whether he should admonish her for her foolhardy action but was spared the need, as he caught sight of Captain Renaud himself, bearing down on them.

'I would be obliged if the girl does *not* climb on the bulwark,' he said, a smile belying the curtness of his words.

Edmond lifted Sophia down, saying, 'Forgive us, Captain Bonnaire. Excitement has taken hold of my ward. We shall retire to our cabin, so that we may not be in the way of the crew.'

'Thank you, Monsieur,' Renaud said, and moved away to the bridge.

'Is the captain angry with me?' Sophia asked.

'No, my dear, he is angry with me for allowing you to climb on the bulwark. It is best if we go below again.'

Once in their cabin, Sophia said, 'I am sorry, Edmond. My intention was to be good, yet immediately I did something bad!'

She bit her lip as she viewed him, with soulful eyes.

Edmond laughed. 'Indeed, Sophia, most unfortunate. But you did not know, so I shall not scold you,' he said.

In the cabin, after sitting on the edge of the lower bunk, for a while, Sophia said, with a mournful face, 'Edmond, my head is in a different place to where it should be. And my stomach is unwell.'

'Ah, you are suffering from *mal de mer*—sea sickness. I am subject to it when first the ship starts moving. If the sea is not too rough, and the captain does not object, once we are well underway, and the crew's activities lessen, I shall ask him whether we may remain on deck. I find I am less affected when I can see the horizon. If you do the same, you may feel better. The fresh breeze will be good for you too, for it is somewhat airless in the cabin.'

Once the ship had sailed past the headland, and away from land, Edmond went to the Captain for permission to take Sophia on deck.

'My ward is suffering from sea sickness. She might benefit from being on deck, for a while, if you please, Captain Renaud,' Edmond said.

'I would prefer you stay out of the way, Monsieur St Vere.'

Edmond hid his irritation. 'Whilst serving in the Army, I have spent a great deal of time on ships, sailing to various lands around the world. I know my way about a ship. I promise to keep Sophia close by me. Will you allow it?'

'You must keep her under strict control, Monsieur. If either of you becomes a nuisance, you will be asked to go below. Is that clear?' Renaud said, a commanding note in his voice.

Edmond didn't like the man's tone, but couldn't afford to antagonise him by commenting on it.

'Perfectly clear, Captain,' he replied, with a curt nod.

'Ah, Monsieur St Vere, forgive my harshness. I am unused to carrying passengers. However, I am aware of the difficulties they cause. I am sure you will be careful.'

Edmond, still annoyed at being spoken to in so high flown a manner, acknowledged the apology with a graceful inclination of his head, and went below.

Sophia remained sitting on her bunk, where Edmond found her, wearing a mournful face, her hands pressed to her stomach.

'The captain has said we may go on deck, Sophia. But he has warned me to keep you close, and not leave my side. So, you must remember not to climb on bulwarks, or anything else. Will you do that for me?'

Sophia swallowed. 'I will do anything to be rid of this terrible malaise, Edmond. I feel that I want to vomit,' she said.

'I know, Sophia. Where is your hat?'

'I do not know, Edmond. Please, may we go? This cabin is so stuffy. I am sure I will feel better on deck,' Sophia wailed, almost in tears.

'Come then,' Edmond said, and let her go before him to the deck.

The bracing wind whipped Sophia's hair out behind her. Her cheeks turned pink.

'Come, let us go to the bow,' Edmond said.

'Is the bow the front of the ship?' she said.

'It is, Sophia. But never let a sailor hear you call it that,' Edmond said, with a quizzical smile.

Soon they had walked as far as they could go. They turned, and walked back towards the stern.

Sophia looked up at the Great Cabin. A wide ladder led up to it.

'What is up there, Edmond?' she asked.

'It is the Great Cabin, Sophia; strictly the domain of the Captain. On a British ship of the line, it is used as a day cabin, office, and meeting room. No one may enter without the Captain's permission. It is also used as a dining room, where officers are invited to eat at the captain's table. The captain's sleeping quarters are to the starboard side of it. It looks as if this was once a French or English Naval ship,' Edmond said. As he spoke, the ship dipped into a trough and rose again causing spray from the waves to blow in their direction.

Sophia made to climb on the bulwark, to see the waves.

'No, Sophia, do not!' Edmond, anxious for her safety, said, in a commanding voice.

Sophia immediately came back to his side, 'I wanted to look at the waves,' Sophia said, and frowned. Her mouth opened on a gasp, as she saw Captain Renaud descending from his cabin.

'Oh Edmond,' she said, 'what a blessing you stopped me! I would not wish to incur his wrath again.'

'I have an idea, Sophia. Come,' Edmond said, guiding her towards the Captain.

'Captain Renaud, I wonder, would you indulge me? My

ward desires to look at the waves, and what better place than from the stern. May I accompany her there?'

Renaud surveyed Sophia through narrowed eyes.

'Is this the first time the girl has been aboard a ship?'

'How old were you when you were last on a ship, Sophia?' Edmond asked.

'I was eight, Edmond. I do not remember it very well.'

She treated the Captain to her most engaging smile.

'Then, Mam'selle, it is my pleasure to allow you on my poop deck. You may enjoy the sight of the setting sun,' he said and bestowed on her a gracious bow.

Her smile widened, and she sighed with pleasure. 'Thank you, Captain,' she said and looked happily up at Edmond.

They climbed up to the quarterdeck, and from there to the poop deck. A few steps took them to the taffrail, from where Sophia could see the wake of the ship.

Sophia and Edmond stood side by side and watched the sun, low in the sky, sink slowly until it seemed to float on the horizon. Its rays tinted the low, grey clouds with crimson, orange, and pink.

The sky darkened to a dull grey. Rippling clouds spread across the sky, tinged with myriad shades of red, from deepest carmine to dusty pink.

The sight took Sophia's breath away. She glanced at Edmond.

'Edmond, it is so wonderful, it hurts here,' she said, putting her hand over her heart.

Edmond, despite being a hardened soldier, still had an eye for the loveliness of nature.

'It is magnificent, Sophia, I agree.'

The sun sank lower. They continued to watch as the clouds slowly darkened, until all that they saw, was an orange line. This rapidly changed to purple, and soon disappeared.

Sophia had seen sunsets before, but never so awe inspiring, as the whole of the sky was overtaken by the spectacle of the setting sun.

Twilight gave way to deep blue-black darkness, as night descended.

Sophia looked up at Edmond's face, hardly visible in silhouette, as he stared up at the stars. His chiselled profile, perfect in outline, strong and dependable, filled her with confidence. Her dark eyes shone like jewels, as her heart filled with gratitude. Her father couldn't have chosen a better person to care for her.

Edmond glanced down at her. 'A northerly wind blows, Sophia; the crossing will not take long,' he said.

The crew lit lanterns, hanging them at intervals about the deck. One crewman offered Edmond a lantern. By its light, Edmond helped Sophia to pick her way to the companionway. They descended to the cabin again, and were glad of the light, as the passage to the cabin was in darkness.

When they entered, they found Wilson asleep in the hammock, quietly snoring.

Edmond hung the lantern above the table.

By its light, they saw Wilson had left a tin plate, piled up with bread and cheese. Two wide, heavy-glass conical carafes, one of ale, the other water, stood with two dull-grey pewter mugs. From where Wilson had procured it all, Edmond had no idea. He marvelled at his batman's resourcefulness.

'How are you?' Edmond asked Sophia.

'Still feeling strange, Edmond, but not as I did,' she said, trying to smile.

'If you eat some food, it will do you good.'

'I will, Edmond,' she said, 'I am hungry.'

Edmond sat on the chair. Sophia made herself comfortable on the lower bunk. They were both hungrier than they thought and gratefully ate and drank their fill.

'Are you tired, Sophia?' Edmond asked,

'Yes, Edmond, I think the sea air has made me drowsy,' she said, yawning.

'Sleep then, child,' he said, 'in another hour or two, the voyage will be over.'

109

She lay back on the bunk and pulled the blanket up over her shoulders. Shortly, Sophia's breathing became more measured. Edmond turned to look at her, to make sure she was asleep.

Sitting in the chair, he took his little book of poems from his pocket. It slipped from his hand and dropped to the floor. As he picked it up, the dedication caught his attention.

A ragged gasp escaped him. He remembered the baby girl, so perfect, as he cradled her in his arms. He remembered the tiny hand, so fragile, as she gripped his finger.

He looked at Sophia, so vulnerable and innocent.

'The daughter I never knew,' he whispered. 'I promise you, my Little One, I will care for you, cherish you, and when the time comes, I will find you a husband who will do the same.'

Edmond took his handkerchief from his pocket. He passed it over his eyes and slipped out silently to go up on deck.

Edmond leant on the bulwark amidships, looking down into the dark waves, frothing about the side of the ship, his mind awash with unformed thoughts.

A hand touched Edmond's shoulder.

Edmond gave a start.

'A lovely night, Monsieur St Vere,' a well-modulated voice said.

Edmond turned to see Renaud beside him.

'Is your charge asleep, Sir?' Renaud asked.

'She is, Captain,' Edmond said.

'I wonder, perhaps you would bear me company in my cabin. It is not often I converse with a man of obvious culture, such as you,' Renaud said, his mood much softened.

'You flatter me, Renaud.'

'I think not, Sir. What rank are you?' Renaud asked, giving Edmond a scrutinising stare.

Edmond gave Renaud back look for look.

'Ah, you need not tell me. I am but curious. I myself was a Captain in the French Navy. I committed several unforgivable misdemeanours, including lying with a commodore's wife. I was not willing to accept punishment for my crimes, so I … left. I now make a tidy profit captaining my own ship. Most of my crew are ex-naval men.'

Edmond smiled. The man was a rogue. Nevertheless, his personality seemed amiable. Edmond decided to trust him.

'I have become unenamoured of war, Monsieur. I have not yet resigned, but am about to do so. My rank is Major.'

'We may be of equal rank. I was *Capitaine de frigate,* which I think is equal to Major.'

'What made you turn to free trading?' Edmond asked.

'I am also disenchanted with war. You could say I have turned pacifist, monsieur and—ha! That is not true, but it suffices to placate my conscience.' He chuckled. 'But come, drink with me, and we may share our experiences.'

'Renaud, I will drink with you. As to sharing experiences, perhaps not, since you may still be loyal to your king. I cannot tell.'

'Very wise, Major St Vere. And you may be a spy or a customs official. We must deal with each other with circumspect deference, yes?'

Edmond laughed, his dour mood lightening as he followed the Captain up to his cabin. They spent the next several hours drinking the Captain's contraband brandy and discussing everything but the war. The captain stopped mid-sentence, raising his head, as they heard the call of the look-out at the mast top.

'Ahoy des terres.'

'They have sighted land, Major,' Renaud said, putting down his glass.

'I have enjoyed your company, but our conversation must now end. My work begins.'

He stood to put on a capacious greatcoat and bicorn hat. 'You will stay in your cabin, if you please, Monsieur, 'til it is safe for you to disembark.'

'As you wish, Captain,' Edmond said, with a nod.

They exited the Captain's cabin together.

As Renaud made for his bridge, Edmond quickly moved towards the companionway, leading to his cabin. He turned his head at Renaud's shout to a crewman, who hauled down the French white flag, bearing yellow Fleur de Lis. In its place, the Red Ensign was hoisted, proclaiming the ship to be British.

Edmond frowned. They had escaped danger in France. There would be equal danger if the British authorities caught them on a ship unloading contraband while sailing under false colours.

CHAPTER THIRTEEN

Edmond entered the cabin on Wilson's heels.

Sophia, now awake, turned, all curiosity.

'Wilson, where have you been? What have you found out?' she asked.

'Yes, Wilson. What news?' Edmond said.

'I found out quite a bit, Miss,' Wilson said, grinning at her.

He faced Edmond; his smile replaced with seriousness.

'For a start, Major, Sir, the contraband won't be dropped off on the beach. It'll be put in the boats, and rowed beneath the cliff, to an inlet that can't be seen from the land.

Wilson moved to his hammock, perched himself on it, and continued.

'There's a small beach, leading to an entrance to caves, running inland. The caves lead towards Melcombe, which is very near Weymouth.'

Wilson paused, easing himself more comfortably on the edge of the hammock. Edmond sat on the chair, leaning forward, listening keenly.

'Go on, Wilson.'

'An inn near the road at Melcombe has a hidden passage, hewn out o' the rock, descending from the inn to the caves. So, the inlet caves connect to the inn.'

Edmond looked at Wilson, with raised brows, digesting his words.

'Who told you all this, Wilson?'

'Thierry Bonnaire. While you was talkin to the Captain, I was talkin to Bonnaire.'

He glanced sideways at his Major. 'He wanted me to join 'em,' he said, a fleeting twinkle in his eye.

Sophia gasped and covered her mouth with her fingers.

Edmond rose from the chair and gave Wilson a menacing stare, his eyebrows drawn together. 'I hope you have not agreed to do so, Wilson!'

Wilson chuckled. 'Course not, Major! I didn't commit meself either way. If I said 'no' straight off, he wouldn't o' told me nothing.'

Edmond shook his head, a wry smile flitting across his face. 'Wilson, you should be a spy; or if not a spy, an interrogator.'

Wilson rubbed the tip of his nose with his forefinger. 'Funny, ain't it? People always tell me things. It must be me honest eyes,' he said, winking at Sophia, who giggled.

Wilson, serious once more, continued, 'Anyway, all Thierry and his mates have to do, is drop the cargo off in the inlet. and the villagers do the rest. Thierry said there's over fifty men waitin' in the caves to carry the barrels and bails up to the inn.'

Edmond stiffened. 'And what of us, Wilson? Are we to go up to the inn through the caves, too?' he said, glancing at Sophia, a hint of displeasure in his sarcastic words.

'Ah, bless ya, no, Major,' Wilson said, shaking his head, a gentle look in his eyes.

'Once the cargo's safely landed, Captain Renaud'll sail the ship, a little way east, along the coast to Melcombe. He's known at the inn. We're to put up there for the night. Bonnaire says it's a coaching inn, so we'll be able to hire transport.'

Edmond's stiff posture relaxed. 'You seem to have everything under control, Wilson. Well done,' Edmond said, pleased.

'That's me job, Major, lookin' after you,' he said, with his broad grin.

'You are an excellent man, Wilson,' Edmond said, not for the first time thanking his stars that he had Wilson in his service.

'What do we do in the meantime?' Sophia asked.

Edmond looked down at her. 'We must wait here until they have unloaded their cargo, Sophia. If any customs men should appear, we must simply say we knew nothing of the crew's activities, and hope they believe us,' Edmond said, his expression confident, not wishing to alarm her.

114

'Tis better if we are not visible,' Edmond added.

Wilson stretched.

'If you don't mind, Major, Sir, I shall take a little rest,' he said, as he swung his feet up onto his hammock, lying back, his hands behind his head.

'Not at all, Wilson. I shall do the same,' Edmond replied, hoisting himself on to the upper bunk.

Sophia sighed. 'Is it not strange,' she said, 'one moment we are pitched into adventurous activity, the next we are without anything to do at all.'

Sophia went to the porthole, and watched the little that she could see of the sailor's activities. She heard movement on the deck above her head, and saw, one by one, the men row jolly boats to the side of the ship, to be loaded with crates. She was amazed how swiftly the men worked. She saw hooks, attached to the ropes which bound the crates, and heard more scrabbling, as the men above her lowered them to their mates below. Sophia could just see the crates stowed neatly in the boats. As the sixth boat took off, the first boat returned to be filled again. Sophia surmised the inlet mustn't be far away. She pictured the villagers, unloading them with the same efficiency.

After a while, Edmond broke the silence. 'We should be in London, in a few days, Sophia.'

Sophia turned from the porthole. 'London? Do we go to London?' she said, excited. 'I have heard much about London from my governess; good things and bad. Are we to live there, Edmond?' she asked.

'We shall, Sophia. Well, just outside London, in Kensington, at Vere House, until my house at Crawford Lees, in Oxfordshire, is refurbished. It is in a run-down state. I mean to renovate it as I wish to live there— eventually.'

'Crawford Lees? In Oxfordshire? Is that in the country?'

'It is my estate, Sophia. Indeed, Oxfordshire *is* in the country.'

'Oh, Edmond, I would love to live in the country,

although, I *am* looking forward to seeing London.'

Sophia wiggled her shoulders in delight.

'You will see London, Sophia, but as I said, Vere House is in Kensington, close to London.'

Edmond hoped Sophia wouldn't be disappointed when she realised she wouldn't reside in the most fashionable area.

A knock at the door interrupted their conversation. Edmond unwound himself from the bunk, to open the door. Captain Renaud stood on the threshold.

'We have completed our task,' Renaud said, as he advanced into the small cabin to address Edmond.

Have you been told about the Inn at Melcombe, where you are to stay?' Renaud asked.

'Yes, Renaud. Are you sure it is safe?' Edmond said.

'Oh, it is safer than any other inn in the area. I often stay there. The innkeeper is a woman, and she is … ah … a very good friend.'

'Hmm,' Edmond murmured. 'Do you not find the locals are suspicious, you being French?'

'Not at all, Monsieur. We are their chief source of income. They buy the contraband from us and sell it on at a profit. For the customers, the price is lower than it would otherwise be. Everyone is happy.'

'What is so wrong in that?' Sophia asked, her lively curiosity getting the better of her.

'The government charges duty—a tax—on things imported into the country, Sophia. The people who deal with Captain Renaud, avoid this, by buying from him and cutting out the tax payment. It is against the law, particularly now, as the tax on imports pays for the war,' Edmond explained.

'I advise you to stay below for a short while longer,' Renaud said. 'Once we have cleared Weymouth, you may come on deck, and prepare to board my launch. I trust Bonnaire has acquainted you with the details?'

'He has, Captain, and I thank you for your care of us. I have my reservations about this inn, however. The authorities must know, it is a place frequented by smugglers,' Edmond said, unable to dismiss his misgivings.

'They probably have their suspicions, Monsieur. Do not worry. If they should come to the inn, there is nothing to connect you with me.'

'I would prefer not to test that theory, Monsieur,' Edmond's said, with his wry smile.

'Come, Major. Where is your sense of adventure?' Renaud said, laughing, a hand on Edmond's shoulder.

'I have had enough adventure to last me a lifetime, Renaud. Yet, I am not anxious for myself. It is for my ward I worry.'

'I promise you, she will be safe,' Renaud said, in a softer tone.

He raised his head, listening, as the boatswain called for the crew to weigh anchor.

'Ah, Messieurs, our run to Melcombe will take less than half an hour, and then I shall escort you to *The Traveller's Rest*—an apt name, would you not agree? You will lie there tonight, and tomorrow you may be on your way.'

Edmond was still uneasy but held his peace.

Renaud led them to his launch, which was suspended on davits over the deck. It was larger than the jolly boats, and not as precarious.

Before attaching the launch to the davits, the crew had heaved their passenger's trunks into the space in the stern, behind the seats.

The captain, himself, gave Sophia his hand to help her into the boat. Edmond Wilson and Bonnaire joined her, followed by the six sailors who would row them. The Captain took up position in the stern.

Crewmen on deck swung the launch out over the water. Sophia clung tightly to the arm of her seat as the boat swayed. Sailors manned the ropes, lowering the boat safely into the water.

Sophia sat spellbound, watching this manoeuvre.

The launch hit the water with a splash. It rocked ominously, and Sophia wondered whether they would all be pitched into the swell. In a moment, it steadied. Yet, in the choppy sea, it continued to roll with the waves. The oarsmen fiddled with the rowlocks, padding them with strips of cloth.

'What are they doing, Edmond?' Sophia whispered.

'They are muffling the oars, Sophia. Normally, as the oars scrape in the rowlocks with each pull, they make noise. With cloth between the oars and the metal of the rowlocks, the noise is much reduced,' Edmond whispered. 'Be quiet now, my dear. Renaud will be giving orders to his crew. Speech between us might cause confusion,' he added.

The captain, in a low voice, gave the oarsmen a series of staccato orders. They moved as one at each order, taking up their oars, attaching them to the rowlocks, splashing them into the waves and pausing, ready to take off.

Captain Renaud stood in the stern, with a dark lantern in his hand. He pointed the lantern towards the land, opened the shutter twice, waited three beats, and opened it twice more.

An answering light twinkled in the distance.

'*Allez!*' he said, his voice soft, but clear.

The boat lurched as the oarsmen began rowing. The precision with which they dipped and raised the oars in unison impressed Sophia. She longed to comment on it to Edmond, but dared not. The tide was coming in, which helped the little craft move more swiftly. The boat rose and fell, as each wave rolled towards the beach. The experienced oarsmen rowed with the waves. Renaud set down the lantern, and took the rudder in his hands, guiding the launch towards the shore.

As they sped through the water, the twinkling light from the shore flashed at five-second intervals and grew brighter as they drew closer to the land.

The sound of waves, breaking on the beach, covered the slight noise from the oars. In the moonlight, Sophia clung tightly to Edmond's arm. She tasted salt on her lips, as a stiff breeze blew spray from the oars, over the occupants of the launch. Sophia was pleased she had found her bonnet in her portmanteau, where Wilson had put it. It now shielded her from the worst of the wind-borne, misty spray.

Gusting winds drove pale purple-tinged clouds across the face of the full moon, sitting high in the sky. By its light, Sophia saw the shadow of a low jetty, come into view.

The Oarsmen lifted their oars and stowed them in the boat. Renaud tied a rope, from the stern of the launch to a ring on the jetty. One of the oarsmen climbed onto the jetty and tied another rope from the prow.

The Captain stepped onto the jetty and moved off in the direction of the twinkling lantern light. Although he crept with the stealth of a cat, his boots echoed softly on the planks of the jetty.

Edmond alighted and gave Sophia his hand. Bonnaire and Wilson followed.

Bonnaire paused Wilson with a hand on his arm.

'Wait till the Captain gives the signal. If there is a problem, we must take off immediately,' he whispered.

Sophia cowered beside Edmond, pressing herself closer to him. He put an arm around her shoulders and felt her shivering.

'It is simply a precaution, Sophia, I am sure all is well,' he murmured.

'I hope so, Edmond,' she whispered.

Wilson and Edmond were accustomed to moments like this, having waited silently, with baited breath, in patient alert, before an attack.

Wilson moved to Edmond's side. 'Brings back memories, don't it, Major?' he whispered.

Edmond nodded, his teeth gleaming in a broad smile.

Halfway along the jetty, the Captain was met by an old

man, in a greasy black hat and a grey smock. It was he who held the guiding lantern.

When Renaud approached, the man removed his hat, clutching it to his chest. In the moonlight, his pale face seemed like a ghostly apparition.

'Is all clear, Mr Taverner?' Renaud asked, his voice barely audible.

'Aye, it is, Sir,' the old man said, his voice equally low.

Renaud waved an arm. Two sailors left their seats to haul the trunks onto the jetty. Their task completed, they undid the rope's, fore and aft, and returned to their companions in the launch to await the Captain's orders.

Sophia watched their activities. She knew how heavy their trunks were, and marvelled at the ease with which the men had handled them.

They must be very strong, she thought.

At another wave of the captain's hand, the men replaced the oars in the rowlocks and dipped them into the water. At a word from one, they began to row in unison, making hardly a sound as the oars rose and fell in the water. Soon, Sophia couldn't hear the splashing of the oars, above the steady beat of the waves, breaking on the beach.

As the launch moved farther and farther away, Sophia noticed it was painted black. The rower's clothes were black, too. The farther away they moved, the harder it became to see them; a mere shadow, which disappeared as they rowed nearer to their ship.

Taverner held his lantern open. Its light guided the little group, as they set off noiselessly, following Taverner on a well-worn path, leading to *The Travellers Rest*, looming on a raise.

'Come, Major,' Renaud murmured. 'Mind your footing; the path is not smooth.'

Wilson set out first after Renaud. Edmond took a firm grip on Sophia's arm, and followed, while Bonnaire brought up the rear. A fresh breeze whistled in the long marram grass, growing on either side of the path.

'Are you all right, Sophia?' Edmond whispered.

'The sea breeze is sharp, Edmond, and I am cold. I hope the inn is warm,' Sophia replied.

Bonnaire was close behind them.

'The inn is well appointed, Mam'selle,' he said softly. 'Madame will see to your every comfort. Quiet now, we must not be detected. I shall take my leave of you, but I shall see you in the morning,' he said, turning to one side, and disappearing into the darkness.

Just then the moon appeared from behind the clouds. Its light illuminated the inn; a tall, high-roofed, three-storey building, imposing itself on the landscape. Trees on either side cast ominous shadows around it. All the downstairs windows and several of those upstairs were lit. Despite its dominating appearance, the lights gave it a welcoming quality.

As they approached the inn, the door opened.

The shape of a tall woman filled the doorway, casting a long shadow into the night.

At the sight of the slender figure, Renaud quickened his pace. The uneven track gave way to a carefully laid path. Renaud's boots crunched on the gravel, as he hurried towards the inn, his head up, his gaze fixed on the woman. Renaud paused for a moment before taking her in his arms. Some distance behind Renaud, Edmond, Sophia, and Wilson watched, as Renaud and the woman merged in silhouette, against the warm yellow light streaming from the doorway.

Focusing on the reunion before them, the travellers on the path didn't see the shadowy figure, moving in the trees near the outer wall of the inn. The figure scurried away as the party neared the door of the inn.

Renaud smiled at them. He moved to one side of the woman, keeping his arm about her waist. Her body still merged with Renaud's, her hand resting lightly on his chest.

Tall, slim, dark haired and beautiful, dressed simply, but with elegance, Mrs Maitland disengaged herself from

Renaud and stood back to allow the party to enter her inn. When safely inside the spacious vestibule, Mrs Maitland closed the door and shot the bolts.

'May I make known to you, Mrs Maitland, the innkeeper?' Renaud said.

'Welcome to my inn, gentlemen,' she said, and catching sight of Sophia, added, 'May I welcome you too, Mam'selle.'

'Thank you, Mrs Maitland,' Sophia said. 'I am happy to be on dry land. I do believe I am not a very good sailor.' Sophia gave Mrs Maitland a beaming smile.

'You are English, Miss?' Mrs Maitland said, her curiosity aroused.

'She is, *ma chérie*,' Renaud said.

'My mother was French, Ma'am,' Sophia said.

'Oh, my dear! So was mine!' Mrs Maitland said, and kissed Sophia on both cheeks.

A large chandelier lit the space. A tasteful, expensive rug lay on the tiled floor. Several tapestry hangings covered the walls. The place spoke of sophisticated style.

Mrs Maitland took Sophia's arm and led her along the wide passage, well-lit by candles in sconces on the wall. Paintings hung between them; paintings of obvious quality.

Mrs Maitland opened a door.

'Do come into the parlour. There is no one there. They are all busy—elsewhere,' she said and led Sophia into the room. The men followed.

The large, comfortable parlour exuded the same air of quiet charm found in the vestibule.

Opposite the door, providing warmth to the room, a fire burned in a magnificent steel grate, surrounded by a large, stone fireplace.

At one end of the parlour, polished wooden settles and tables formed cosy booths. At the other, were ten cushioned easy chairs, upholstered in heavy, red velvet, and arranged in groups around low tables.

A well-knit man with sharp, intelligent, grey eyes,

followed them into the room. He wore a simple brown coat and breeches, smart and unassuming. His soft voice gave nothing away, yet he had an air of strength about him.

'Ah, there you are, Gregory. Gentlemen, this is my steward,' Mrs Maitland said.

Gregory closed the door and turned to bow to the gentlemen before him.

'I came to tell you, Madame. The boys have brought the passengers' trunks up from the jetty. Shall we put them in their rooms?'

'Yes, if you please, Gregory, and will you tell Matilda to bring refreshments?'

Gregory nodded and went to do his employer's bidding.

'Perhaps now we may continue with our introductions, Jean?' Mrs Maitland suggested.

Captain Renaud turned to Edmond, 'I hardly know how to introduce you, Sir. You have several titles. Perhaps you might introduce yourself. You can trust Nicole with any secrets you may have. She is the soul of discretion.'

'In that case, Madam, I am Lord Edmond St Vere, at your service. I am also Major St Vere of the second of foot,' Edmond declared with an elegant bow.

Mrs Maitland curtsied and rose, saying, 'This is the first time I have entertained a peer, my Lord. You are most welcome. And this is your daughter?'

'No, Madam, this is my ward, Sophia. Her father has… she has recently lost her father. I am escorting her to England, where my sister will look after her,' Edmond said.

'How long will you be staying with us, my Lord?'

'Just one night, Ma'am. We travel on towards London tomorrow,' Edmond replied.

Mrs Maitland turned to Wilson. 'And who are you, Sir?' she asked.

'I am the Major's batman, Madam, Daniel Wilson, at your service.'

The maid, Matilda, entered carrying a heavy tray.

The sleeves of her black dress were long and tightly

123

fitting; the front buttoned high at her neck. A lace-edged, white pinafore covered her full skirt. Under a small white cap, her dark hair curled on her forehead.

She put the tray down on a low table.

'Will that be all, Ma'am?' she asked Mrs Maitland.

'Yes, Matilda. We shall dine in an hour if you please.'

'Very good, Ma'am. I will tell cook,' she said, bobbing a curtsey before hurrying away.

Mrs Maitland smiled. 'Well, Gentlemen, now that we all know who we are, pray, make yourselves comfortable,' she said, indicating the seats.

Sophia and Wilson sat in easy chairs, while Renaud joined Edmond by the fireplace. Mrs Maitland took her place by the tea tray, opposite Sophia.

'I have brandy, if you prefer it to tea, Major,' Mrs Maitland offered, as she spooned tea into the warmed pot.

'Thank you, ma'am,' Edmond said.

When Mrs Maitland finished pouring boiling water on the tea from an ornate kettle, she rose, and went to a cabinet, from where she produced a bottle and three glasses.

'I presume you would prefer brandy, too, Wilson?' she said.

'I would, ma'am. Thank you,' Wilson said, grinning.

Mrs Maitland poured a measure into each glass, and waved a hand for the men to take up their drinks. Renaud took one glass, and handed another to Edmond. Wilson rose, and picked up the other. Silently they raised their glasses in salute to Mrs Maitland, and savoured the expensive French brandy.

'Would it be rude of me to inquire of you why you travelled on *L'Oiseau*?' she asked.

'Not at all, Ma'am. The port of Marronville was crowded with French Soldiers, checking papers. Mine say I am a British officer,' Edmond explained.

'And I took pity on them, and transported them to England,' Renaud added.

Mrs Maitland gave him a warm look.

'Jean, you are all consideration.'

Mrs Maitland sat down gracefully, smoothing her skirt before reaching for the teapot. With practised, elegant poise, she poured tea for herself and Sophia.

'Milk and sugar, Sophia?' she asked.

Heavy pounding at the front door interrupted Sophia's reply. No one moved.

Mrs Maitland was the first to react. She quickly stepped to the end wall. Grasping the corner of a wall hanging, she turned it back to reveal a door.

'Quickly, all of you, in here!' she commanded, her manner brisk, her expression alert.

Without hesitation, Renaud grabbed Edmond's arm, and steered him swiftly into the small dark space. Wilson joined them. Sophia made to follow.

'Not you, Sophia. Can you play a part? You are my niece. You are visiting me.'

Sophia wasn't sure why she should, but said, 'Yes, Ma'am.'

Mrs Maitland silently closed the door behind the men. She locked it with a small key, which she tucked into her cleavage, and dropped the curtain back into place.

Gregory and Matilda entered the room.

'What shall we do, Madam?' Matilda asked.

'Take up those glasses and the brandy, and place them back in the cupboard, Matilda,' Mrs Maitland told her.

Swiftly, Matilda did so, while Mrs Maitland took her former seat.

The banging repeated on the front door.

Gregory's eyes were bright and alert as he looked at his mistress.

'Madam?' he questioned, his chin high, his body poised.

'Answer the door, Gregory. Whoever it is, show them in here,' Mrs Maitland said, her voice calm, her expression cool.

'Are you sure, Madam?'

'Good God, Gregory. We have had "visitors" before

this. Let them in before they knock a hole in the door.'

Gregory nodded, and departed with Matilda.

Mrs Maitland gestured to the seat opposite to her.

'Sit, Sophia.'

Sophia sat.

'Can you keep a cool head, Sophia?' Mrs Maitland asked.

'I think so, Ma'am,' Sophia said, her eyes bright with anticipation of what she thought was going to be another adventure.

'Then say not a word. Let me do the talking,' and in a louder voice she asked, 'Milk and sugar in your tea, Sophia?'

'Both, if you please, Aunt Nicole,' Sophia said, adopting the role of family member as two men, dressed in black uniforms, entered the room.

Mrs Maitland willed her hand not to shake, as it paused before putting down the milk jug. Her heart pounded in her chest, as she slowly turned to look the men up and down.

'Good evening, Mr Cartwright, Mr Bloom. May I offer you some refreshment on this cold night?' Mrs Maitland coolly asked, as she allowed a smile to dawn on her face.

'Thank you, no, Mrs Maitland. We are here on business,' Bloom replied, adjusting the stiff stock at his neck.

'Business? What sort of business?'

'Excise business, Ma'am. Three men were seen entering your inn. Where are they?'

'I do have three guests, Mr Bloom. I assume they are in their rooms, changing for dinner. They will be down shortly,' she replied, unruffled. 'I can assure you, Mr Bloom, they are respectable men, as you may ascertain when they arrive,' she said, taking up a bell from the tea tray, and ringing it.

Within seconds, Matilda appeared.

'You rang, Madam?' she asked, never looking at the men.

'Yes, Matilda. Will you take a message to my three

guests? Tell them they are wanted in the parlour, as soon as they are ready.'

Sophia glanced at Mrs Maitland, but lowered her gaze to hide her surprise.

'Yes, Ma'am,' Matilda said, and went quietly from the room.

She raced upstairs, and almost fell over Gregory, who stood at the top, peering over the balustrade.

'They're riding officers, Gregory!' she said, her quiet manner deserting her.

'I know, Matty. And there's four more of them outside with their horses,' Gregory said, smiling at her.

'What are you smiling at, you fool. Where are Captain Renaud and the other two?'

Gregory smiled mischievously at Matilda.

'In one of the guest bedchambers, changing their clothes,' he said.

CHAPTER FOURTEEN

When Wilson and Edmond were bundled into the unlit passage behind the hanging, Renaud whispered, 'A stair is just by us, gentlemen. It leads to one of the guest bedrooms. Put your hand on my coat, and follow me.'

In complete darkness, Edmond put his hand forward, until he felt the soft fabric of Renaud's coat, and clutched it.

'Take hold of my coat, Wilson,' Edmond whispered.

Wilson grunted as he reached for Edmond. He caught the end of Edmond's coat and held on to it.

In the dark, musty passage, Edmond felt disorientated. He took a firmer grip on Renaud's coat.

'Softly now, Gentlemen, we must make no sound,' Renaud whispered. Edmond heard Renaud's hand sweeping the wall, as he slowly crept up the narrow, steep stairs. Edmond and Wilson carefully felt the stairs with their feet, before placing them on each step. Edmond almost lost his footing on an uneven step and reached out his free hand to steady himself against the wall. The stone was cold and damp.

Reaching the top, Edmond heard a click, as Renaud released the catch of a door, which opened into a cupboard.

The three stepped from the stair into the cupboard, and from there into a large bedroom, where a leaping fire burned in the grate. The room enveloped them in its warmth, after the cold dank passage.

Renaud crept to the window and peered through the shutters.

'It is as I feared; riding officers.'

He caught up a tinderbox from the mantelshelf, and striking the flint, lit one candle. The gloom lessened.

He blew out his cheeks, as he looked around the room.

'If they recognise me, I am done for. Because you are with me, you are in danger, too.'

Edmond put his hand to his face and rubbed his chin.

Wilson caught sight of a trunk, set against the wall, between the two windows. Edmond's saddlebags were on top of it, accompanied by Wilson's portmanteau.

'I have it, Sir!' he said.

'Then spit it out, man. Do not keep it to yourself,' Edmond urged him.

Wilson went to the trunk, undid the straps, and rifled through the contents. He pulled out a red soldier's jacket, held it up, and grinned at the other two men.

Dressed in British Army uniforms, the three men stood in the room, regarding each other.

'We need a name for Renaud, Wilson. Wearing your uniform, he has to be a sergeant. But sergeant what?' Edmond asked, frowning, thinking.

'What about Sergeant Fox, Sir? His name reminds me of Reynard the Fox in the children's story,' Wilson said, his eyes twinkling.

Edmond slapped the side of his leg. 'Excellent, Wilson!' He turned to Renaud.

'Do you mind being called Sergeant Fox, Renaud?'

'Not at all, Major,' Renaud replied, with a laugh.

Matilda appeared. Her eyes rounded at the sight before her.

She bobbed a curtsey to Captain Renaud. 'Excuse me, Sir,' she said, tentatively.

'Yes, Matilda, what is it?' Renaud answered, still smiling. He was enjoying the frivolity of the moment; all care for his safety abandoned.

'Mrs Maitland said she wants you in the parlour.'

'Then, Gentlemen,' Renaud said with a flourish of his hand, 'may I suggest we descend to the parlour?'

The three intended a spectacular entrance, to put the riding officers off their guard, so made a lot of noise descending the stairs. Edmond rattled his sword against the banisters, and all three deliberately stomped, in their heavy boots, laughing and joking all the way.

129

Edmond knocked on the parlour door.

'Come in,' Mrs Maitland's voice called. Edmond entered, and exaggeratedly pulled up short, at sight of the riding officers. Wilson and Renaud came into the room behind him.

'More guests for dinner, Mrs Maitland?' Edmond asked, his eyebrows flown up, a smile hovering at the corners of his mouth.

Mrs Maitland laughed. 'No, Major, the funniest thing. Mr Cartwright and Mr Bloom were informed that three men were seen entering my inn. They think you are dealing in contraband. Do you not think that hilarious?'

Edmond's rich laughter filled the room.

'That is the funniest thing I have heard in a long time, to be sure. Sergeant Wilson, Sergeant Fox, do you not think it most amusing?'

Wilson and Renaud joined Edmond in his laughter.

Cartwright coughed and drew himself up to his full height.

'We're only doing our duty, Sir. May I ask you what you are doing in the area?'

'Ah, yes, Bloom, is it?' Edmond asked.

'Cartwright, Sir,' he said.

'Cartwright, Bloom, it makes no odds,' Edmond drawled. 'Yes, you must indeed do your duty, of course. I am on my way home, Mr Cartwright. I am on leave. I managed to book passage on a merchant ship, which dropped me here. Would you like to see my papers?' Edmond said, drawing them from the inside pocket of his coat, and holding them out to Cartwright.

Cartwright shook his head and waved them away.

Bloom took hold of them, and read them.

'Do you want to see my sergeants' papers, too, Mr Bloom?' Edmond asked, snapping his fingers at Wilson, and holding out his hand.

'Ah, no, Major. If you vouch for them, then I am content. We are sorry to have bothered you, Sir. Goodnight,' he said.

The two men saluted.

Edmond acknowledged their salute, and they departed.

As they left, Edmond's laughter died, as he glanced with troubled eyes towards Sophia.

Letting out a sharp breath, Mrs Maitland collapsed in her chair. Renaud sat in another chair, his head down, his shoulders shaking. He lifted his head, and let his laughter sound forth.

Wilson glanced at him, and grinned widely.

Sophia looked from one to the other, her mouth open, her eyes shining.

'What an adventure,' she said. 'Edmond, you are a consummate actor, you know. Although my heart is pounding with fear, I have not had so much fun in a long time.'

Edmond's grim expression softened. He smiled.

Mrs Maitland shook her head. 'I found it much too close for my liking,' she said.

She rose, went to the cupboard, and took out the brandy bottle again. Handing the men their glasses, she withdrew one for herself, poured the brandy, and lifted her glass.

'To continued luck,' she said.

The men knocked back the brandy. Mrs Maitland took a generous gulp, before moving to sit back in her seat. She glanced, one by one, at the three "British" officers. She gazed at Renaud, thinking how well the red coat suited him.

'I must say, you all look very grand. What an excellent idea, to be sure,' Mrs Maitland remarked.

'It was Wilson's notion,' Renaud said. 'He thought if the riding officers were presented with two soldiers and a civilian, they would question the civilian. If three soldiers stood before them, then they were less likely to pick on one of them.'

'I wonder who it was who reported seeing us?' Edmond pondered, a crease above his nose.

'Gregory said he saw a stranger skulking in the wood at sunset. Do not worry. We shall see to it. I am sure our people will deal with whoever it was,' Mrs Maitland reassured him.

'What of your merchandise, Captain? Will you risk moving it, with the riding officers sniffing about?' Edmond asked.

'You are right, Major. The men must keep the merchandise in the caves, for a day or two,' Renaud said.

'How often do you make a drop, Captain?' Edmond asked.

'We vary it, Major. If we worked with regularity, we would be more easily caught.'

A knock sounded.

'Come in,' Mrs Maitland said.

Gregory entered, barely hiding a grin.

'Dinner is served, Mrs Maitland,' he said, eyeing the three "soldiers".

CHAPTER FIFTEEN

Edmond planned to set forth on their journey, early the following morning. They would stay two nights at inns along the way. Before they departed, they breakfasted together in Mrs Maitland's beautiful dining room.

On entering the room the night before, the grandeur of it had impressed Sophia. She had never seen such splendid décor. It was beautiful by candlelight.

In daylight, it was even more impressive.

As everyone bid each other good morning, Sophia gazed out of the East facing windows, overlooking the bay. She admired the midnight-blue velvet curtains, gathered to the sides of the windows in swags. She marvelled at how light the room was, with the sun streaming in, shining on the pale primrose walls and the white plaster mouldings, edging the ceiling. More light reflected from the peer glasses, between the windows, and at intervals along the walls.

Looking up, she was delighted to see a magnificent chandelier, hanging from the high ceiling, its crystal pendants twinkling in the morning sunlight, and casting rainbows above them.

She moved near the ornate limestone fireplace, where large logs burned in the broad, polished steel grate, flames dancing upwards into the high chimney. A mantelshelf stretched along the length of the fireplace. Impressed by the ornaments on the shelf, she let out a soft 'Ohhh.' An ormolu garniture, consisting of a clock and two side urns, in *Bleu du Roi* and painted with country scenes in the Sevres style, was accompanied by four matching candelabra, two on either side. Crystal pendants hung from their branches. Over the mantel, a vast mirror, surrounded by gilt plasterwork, stretched up to the ceiling.

Sophia's gaze wandered to the floor. A primrose pattern flowed over a deep-pile carpet of the same blue as the ornaments. Sophia wanted to take off her shoes and bury her toes in it.

In contrast to the ornate opulence, the cabinets, which stood against the walls, and the long, highly-polished table with matching chairs, were of modest design, yet still spoke of French elegance.

Bright conversation filled the room, as the party partook of a simple French breakfast; a variety of breads and fruit, accompanied by coffee or chocolate.

Having eaten, they prepared to bid their farewells.

'We must keep in contact, Major,' Renaud said. He patted his mouth with his napkin and placed it beside his plate. 'If I can be of further service to you, you must communicate with Mrs Maitland.'

'Likewise, Renaud. I must give you my direction,' Edmond replied.

'No need, Major. I have already given Bonnaire the address of Vere House,' Wilson informed him, sitting back in his chair, one hand on his full stomach.

'Why would you do that, Wilson?' Edmond asked.

'French Brandy, my Lord,' Wilson said, with his usual twinkle.

Edmond frowned. 'French Brandy, Wilson?'

Wilson tapped his nose. 'Probably best you don't know Major. Let's just say, you will never want for it,' Wilson said, glancing at Bonnaire, who gave him a wink.

Edmond coughed. 'Foraging expeditions, Wilson?'

'Exactly, Sir!' Wilson replied.

Sophia leant towards Mrs Maitland. 'Do you know what they are talking about, Ma'am?'

'I have a vague notion, my dear. I do not think we need concern ourselves,' Mrs Maitland murmured.

Edmond pushed back his chair, and rose, straightening his waistcoat.

'I think we must be on our way, if we are to arrive before nightfall, at the inn you have recommended.'

The others rose from their seats.

'It has been a pleasure to accommodate you, Major,' Mrs Maitland said, proffering her hand.

Edmond gently brushed it with his lips as he bowed.

'It has been an, er—interesting experience, Mrs Maitland,' Edmond said, smiling. 'And I must thank you for the loan of your carriage and horses.'

'You are most welcome, my Lord.'

Edmond's eye caught Renaud's.

'I must thank you, too, Renaud, for all your help. Without you, I do not know what would have become of us.'

Renaud bowed his head graciously.

'I have enjoyed your company, Major.'

He turned to Sophia. 'I must bid you *adieu*, Mam'selle Sophia. I hope you will be happy in your new home, and that you have many adventures!'

'Thank you, Monsieur. I hope so, too,' Sophia replied curtsying and bestowing her sweetest smile on him.

As Edmond and Renaud left the room, Mrs Maitland caught Sophia's hands and bent to kiss her cheeks.

'You are a brave girl, Sophia. You acted just as you should when the riding officers came. Courage in the face of danger is a virtue, you know.'

'If I am to have any more such adventures, I will need my courage, Ma'am. I am pleased to have met you. Thank you for your hospitality in your beautiful inn, and…'

'Come, Sophia,' Edmond called from the hallway.

Nicole and Sophia followed the men, and the four descended the stairs.

Wilson and Bonnaire stood by a window in the dining room, discussing the prospects of Wilson purchasing various items of contraband.

'Wilson!'

Edmond's deep voice interrupted their deliberations.

'Oi-oi, I'd better get goin', Bonnaire. Don't want to upset him.'

He quickly shook Bonnaire's hand and left the room.

'Comin' Major, Sir,' he called, as he hurried down the stairs.

Mrs Maitland's plain, black coach stood in the road

before the entrance to the inn, with four black horses harnessed to it. Servants had strapped their luggage into the boot at the back of the coach.

Mounted on the front nearside horse, a postilion, liveried in black and red, waited for the off.

Gregory sat on the box in the driver's seat. Wilson climbed up beside him.

The postilion would drive the coach to the first stop so that the horses might be returned quickly to Mrs Maitland. For the next stage of their journey, Edmond would hire fresh horses.

Edmond hurried down the steps and entered the coach. Sophia followed, and he drew her up next to him.

As the coach moved off, Sophia waved to Mrs Maitland, who stood in the doorway of the inn, with Renaud beside her.

Renaud lifted his arm in a parting gesture, as his other arm slid around Mrs Maitland's waist.

Sophia wondered quite what their relationship was, and thought to ask Edmond. She would have had no problem asking her father, but she suspected it might embarrass Edmond. She didn't enquire.

She leant back on the dark green squab-cushioned velvet, which lined the coach.

Although the morning was bright, it was frosty. The interior of the coach, however, was warm. Hot bricks had been placed under the fur rug, which covered the floor.

'I am looking forward to seeing England, Edmond. When I was here before, we did not travel much. I only remember fragments of things I saw.'

'I might be biased, Sophia, but I think England has the most beautiful countryside in the whole of Europe. Autumn is not the best time of year to see it. But in summer, it is like a green jewel. I do believe Shakespeare likened it to a jewel. When it snows in winter, it is—ah, words fail me,' Edmond said. A feeling of eager anticipation of seeing his home again stole over him.

'Magical?' Sophia supplied.

'Ah yes, Sophia. I told you that you are a poetess!'

'I read it in a book, Edmond, so I cannot claim the credit,' she said.

The coach took the cliff road, which brought them high above the sea. White capped waves rode the sea in the spellbinding panorama presented to them. The bright sun rose higher in the sky. Fluffy clouds, driven by a westerly wind, took on fascinating shapes, which then melted away. Sophia, silent for a while, watched the sea, the sky, and a headland in the distance. She breathed a contented sigh.

'I think I have fallen in love with the sea, Edmond.'

The cliff path merged with the main thoroughfare and dipped into a wooded area. Sophia settled into her seat. Edmond leant his head against the cushioned wall behind him, and closed his eyes, thinking about what the future might hold.

Sophia watched him and smiled to herself.

How lucky I am. Edmond is such a good man. Yet, I still miss my father. Edmond is somewhat stern sometimes, but it is always for a good reason. I wonder what his sister is like? I hope I get on well with her.

She turned her face back to the window, as the coach took a bend in the road. They were passing through a forest of dark trees.

Edmond opened his eyes when light flooded into the coach, as it broke free of the forest.

'Were you asleep Edmond?' Sophia asked.

'I am not sure, Sophia. I think perhaps I was.'

He took out his watch.

'In a short while, we shall stop at an inn. The horses can only go a couple of hours before they need rest. We can stay in the coach, or seek easement in the inn.'

Sophia jumped when the sharp blast of a horn sounded.

'What was that, Edmond?' she asked in alarm.

'The coachman's horn. He blows it to alert the inn that a coach approaches,' Edmond told her.

The inn yard was alive with activity. Two other coaches were having their horses changed, and a stagecoach, piled high with passengers, was just leaving. Servants and ostlers darted here and there, as people passed in and out of the inn.

'I think I will stay where I am, Edmond,' Sophia said. 'I would not wish to be jostled about in the crowds.'

'It does seem inordinately busy,' Edmond mused.

A servant approached their coach with a tray of drinks.

'Mulled wine, Sir, to keep you warm while you're waiting?' he asked.

Edmond pulled a coin from his pocket, giving it to the servant. Leaning out of the window, he took two cups from the proffered tray.

'Why so busy, Lad?' Edmond asked him.

'There's a boxing match in the village in a short while, Sir. Nothing like a boxing match to stir up business,' he replied, offering Edmond change from the shilling he had been given.

'Keep it, Lad,' Edmond said, smiling at the boy, whom he judged to be no more than twelve years old.

The boy's eyes widened. '*Thank* you, Sir,' he said, gazing at the money in his hand.

Edmond sat back in his seat and handed a cup to Sophia.

'Here is your chance to drink strong alcohol, Sophia. I think you will like it better than ale,' Edmond suggested, as he wrapped his hands around the cup, and sipped the sweet, hot, spicy liquid.

Sophia took a tentative sip.

'Edmond, it is delicious!' she said.

'Sip it slowly, Sophia. You will soon feel a warm glow.'

The courtyard gradually cleared of people. At last, their horses were changed. The boy came to the window of the coach to retrieve the empty cups.

'Is there anythin' else I can do for you, Sir?' the boy asked eagerly.

'Thank you, no, my boy,' Edmond said, knowing he was a canny soul, who hoped for another tip.

Riding on one, and leading another of Mrs Maitland's horses, Gregory came to the window of the coach.

'Adieu, my Lord, Miss Sophia,' he said, with a bow. 'It has been a pleasure to serve you. I hope the inn's horses are reliable. We go now to return her horses to Mrs Maitland, so I will take my leave of you.'

'Goodbye, Gregory. Tell Mrs Maitland I shall return her coach when we reach London. A safe journey,' Edmond said.

Gregory tipped his hat and took off, followed by the postilion on another horse, leading the forth.

The ostlers harnessed fresh horses to the black coach. Wilson climbed into the driver's seat.

The coach sped along, stopping from time to time, at toll gates along the way. Sophia watched bare fields go by, crows rising at the sound of the passing coach. The soporific effect of the mulled wine took hold of her. She leant her head against the soft wall beside the window and dozed.

She missed the next change of horse, waking when the horn blew at the second.

Used to long journeys, Edmond was lost in thought and half-asleep. He shifted in his seat when he saw Sophia wake.

'Goodness, how long was I asleep Edmond?'

'About two hours. The mulled wine is most relaxing. I dozed a bit myself. Are you all right?'

Sophia yawned, 'Oh, yes, I feel exceedingly rested. Is it much farther?' she asked.

'About another three or four hours. Are you hungry?

'I am, yes, a little,' Sophia said.

'We shall stop at the next inn for something to eat,' Edmond said.

Although it wasn't usual for a servant to accompany his master while dining, Edmond invited Wilson to join them in the inn parlour. He had dispensed with his sailor's garb and now presented a more respectable image.

'It's good of you to invite me, Major. Bread and cheese

would be all I'd get if I ate with the rest of the help,' he said, making good progress with his bowl of soup. Roast chicken, boiled potatoes and baked vegetables followed the soup.

'Do not become too familiar with the practice, Wilson. My servants at Vere House are sticklers for protocol. Well, they were three years ago. The Butler, Furlong, is most conscientious regarding etiquette. I doubt anything has changed, so do not take liberties with them,' Edmond told him, trying to keep a serious expression.

'Ah, Major! You know I knows me place. I don't overstep the mark with you, Sir, now do I? Not often, anyways.'

'You are a paragon of convention, Wilson,' Edmond said, suppressing his laughter.

'I think Wilson has looked after us very well, Edmond. But for him, we would never have found out about L'Oiseau,' Sophia said, coming to Wilson's defence.

'I agree, Sophia. I would be lost without you, Wilson,' Edmond said, inclining his head towards his batman.

The meal finished, Edmond paid the tariff and led Sophia back to the coach.

They stopped one more time for a change of horse. The next stop was *The Bull Inn.*

Mrs Maitland had sent a messenger ahead to reserve rooms for them.

When Edmond and Sophia alighted from the coach to enter the inn, the innkeeper greeted them deferentially. His bald head shone in the candlelight. His round belly wobbled as he ushered them to the Parlour, overjoyed to be entertaining a lord in his inn.

The Bull was welcoming and warm. The innkeeper, Thomas Claypool, served them supper himself. Edmond, once again, invited Wilson to eat with them.

The sumptuous meal laid out before them included ham, beef and chicken, accompanied by a rich variety of sauces and gravies. Boiled, buttered potatoes, beans, peas and preserved summer vegetables complimented the rest.

The quality of the food impressed the three, particularly Wilson.

'This beats army food, hands down, don't it Major?'

'You produce some creditable concoctions yourself at times, Wilson,' Edmond said, as he started on a syllabub.

'Practice makes perfect, Sir, and anyways, I know what you like, Major.'

'You will be spared the task of cooking for me at Vere House, Wilson, as I doubt Mrs Cribb will let you set foot in her kitchen,' Edmond said.

'Who is Mrs Cribb?' Sophia asked.

'She is the cook at Vere House. A very fine cook she is, too,' Edmond said, patting his mouth with his napkin. 'No more foraging for you, Wilson,' Edmond added.

'"foraging"? What exactly is that,' Sophia asked.

Wilson coughed, and Edmond hid a smile.

'It's finding food when the Major needs a decent meal, Miss,' Wilson said and changed the subject.

'This inn is a bit full, Sir. It's well we had rooms reserved for us,' he said.

'Indeed, Wilson,' Edmond agreed, as the host entered.

'I hope the food was to your liking, my Lord?' Claypool said, as he cleared the covers, and offered them fruit.

'Yes, Mr Claypool. I have never eaten so well at an inn. And I think I speak for my companions,' Edmond responded amiably.

Sophia, who was very tired, smiled sleepily.

Mr Claypool turned to Sophia. 'I'll get one of the maids to show you to your room, Miss, and see to your comfort.'

Sophia stifled a yawn. 'Thank you, Mr Claypool.'

'And I will show you and your companion to your rooms myself, my Lord,' he said bowing and smiling.

When the maid arrived, she and Claypool escorted them upstairs.

Sophia had a room to herself. Edmond and Wilson occupied adjoining rooms.

The maid ran a warming pan between the sheets. She

assisted Sophia in undressing, helped her into her nightgown, then under the covers.

Sophia snuggled down, anticipating a good night's sleep.

She was destined for disappointment.

The inn received more guests after the three retired. The atmosphere became very noisy. All night, the people in the taproom caroused, sometimes singing, sometimes shouting drunkenly. Sophia heard at least four brawls break out, with much crashing of furniture, followed by women screaming. She slept little.

The following morning, when she entered the dining-room, she found Wilson and Edmond had arrived before her.

'Good morning Sophia,' Edmond greeted her, 'I hope you slept well?

'I slept hardly at all, Edmond. Do they make that much noise in all the inns? Mrs Maitland's inn was not like that. I slept well there. I am exhausted,' she grumbled, yawning to prove it.

'I did not notice it, Sophia. We shall try to find a quieter inn tonight. Perhaps, if you lie on the seat of the coach, you may sleep a little on the journey.

Wilson stood and went to fill a plate with coddled eggs and buttered bread for her, accompanied by a cup of hot chocolate.

When Sophia and Edmond entered the coach, he pulled a pillow from the rack above their heads. From a basket under the seat, he produced a blanket.

As the coach set off, Sophia lay on the seat. In a little while, she dozed, waking each time they stopped to change the horses, and settling again when they set off.

At the last stopping place, *The Black Bear*, Edmond gave Wilson instructions to enquire whether there was a quiet inn nearby.

Before ascending the box, Wilson spoke to Edmond.

'One of the ostlers said he has a cousin, who works as a

stable hand in a small Inn, about five miles away. They're a bit out o' the way, so they're always quiet.'

'Excellent, Wilson. Did he give you directions?' Edmond asked.

'Yes Sir, I wrote 'em down,' Wilson replied.

Edmond climbed into the coach. Wilson folded up the steps and shut the door, before climbing onto the box.

Sophia was still asleep. Edmond soon dozed himself.

It seemed minutes later that Wilson opened the coach door.

'We're here, Major, Sir,' he told Edmond, who was instantly awake.

Sophia roused, too, and peered about her.

As she alighted, she looked up at the thatched roof of the inn. Ivy grew up one wall, giving the place a charming appeal. The walls were painted white, as was the picket fence, which ran along the front.

'What a lovely house, Edmond. I am sure it will be much quieter than the noisy *Bull Inn*. Oh, look, the sign says it is called *The Roses*, and those bushes at the sides are rose bushes. It must look wonderful in summer.'

'It certainly has a pleasant aspect, Sophia,' Edmond remarked.

Wilson climbed down from the box, as a stable lad appeared, and took charge of the coach and horses.

Edmond laid a hand on Sophia's elbow and guided her towards the front door.

Wilson knocked.

He stood back from the door, awaiting an answer. Moments passed, so Wilson knocked again.

A diminutive creature, of indeterminate age opened the door, and gazed at them with beady, black eyes. A mob cap trimmed with bedraggled lace sat low on her forehead. Her grey gown was wilted and creased while her white apron drowned her.

'Yes?' she asked, curtly.

Before Wilson could speak, Edmond stepped forward.

'Good evening,' he said, with authority. 'We are

seeking accommodation for the night. Have you any rooms free?' he asked.

'Hmm,' she said, looking Edmond up and down, 'we always have rooms free. I'll fetch Mrs Coombes,' she said, with a sniff, disappearing along a gloomy passage.

Edmond, Sophia, and Wilson stepped into the hallway, and Wilson closed the door. While they waited, Wilson stretched his back. Sophia gazed about the hall. Its only furnishing was a small table and two high-backed wooden chairs. Edmond impatiently took several steps in the direction the maid had gone. He stopped, when a tall woman soundlessly appeared, from the depths of the passage.

The vertical stripes of the woman's shapeless gown accentuated her height. The cotton material clung to her skeletal frame. The woman's face was narrow, her forehead high. Her pale blue eyes seemed weary. Iron grey hair pulled back into a tight chignon, offered nothing to alleviate her stark appearance.

'Jessy informs me you seek accommodation,' the woman said, her voice rough and toneless. Her thin lips attempted a brittle smile, which didn't reach her eyes.

'We do, Madam. We would also like supper if you have the means to provide it,' Edmond replied.

'Walter!' the woman boomed, keeping her eyes fixed on Edmond.

A sullen, stooping porter, with straggly hair and an unshaven chin appeared.

'Yes?' he grunted.

'Tell cook we have three guests, who require supper. But first, show them up to the best front rooms. Then you can get their baggage from the coach. Don't forget to make sure Will has seen to their carriage and horses.'

'Yes, 'um,' the man replied, and gave out a wheezing cough.

'Follow me,' he mumbled and led the three up the stairs. On the landing, he paused for breath, wheezing again.

144

He opened three doors, 'There's y'r rooms,' he panted, and retreated down the stairs, his gait proclaiming stiffened joints.

Edmond gave Wilson a questioning look.

'I'll go and get our bags, Sir,' Wilson said, in reply to the look.

A meagre fire burned in the grate of Sophia's room, barely taking the chill out of the air. Sophia decided to wash her face. She found the water in the cracked ewer was cold. When she had dried with the rough towel, she found hanging by the washstand, she looked at her face in the mottled mirror above it. The rough fibre of the towel had made her cheeks pink.

Jessy came into her room without knocking. She deposited Sophia's portmanteau on the bed, and, wordlessly, she left the room.

Sophia took her hairbrush from her portmanteau. As she tidied her hair, she wondered at the seeming rudeness of the people employed at the inn.

She inspected the sagging bed. Pulling back the patchwork covers, she discovered that the ancient looking sheets were damp. The only redeeming feature was the plump feather pillows at the head of the bed.

With an impatient groan, she looked about the room. Cobwebs festooned every corner. A mouldy odour hung in the air. She wondered when the room had last been inhabited.

This will not do. I must have a word with Edmond.

Sophia left her room and descended the stairs.

The door to the dining room was open. She saw Edmond and Wilson standing by the fire, speaking in low tones.

'Edmond,' she said, as she entered the room. 'This place is practically uninhabitable. Can we go somewhere else?'

'I doubt if we would find another inn at this time of night, Sophia. You must make the best of it,' he said, adding, 'I am sorry.'

'At least this room has a good fire,' Sophia remarked, 'the one in my room is very small, and the place is freezing.'

She looked around at the plain, serviceable furniture, the patched curtains, and the worn rug on the floor.

'The interior of this house does not match the pretty picture presented on the outside, does it, Edmond?' she asked.

'No, Sophia, but it is better than nothing. I suspect this was once a farmhouse.'

'Yes, it was, Major. I got talking to Will, the stable lad. Him as is the ostler's cousin in *The Black Bear*. He was tellin' me, the tall woman used to be the farmer's wife. The farmer died and left her in debt. She sold off the farm and opened the house as an inn. Jessy was her dairy maid, and the porter is Mrs Coombes's brother. They just about make ends meet, he was sayin'.'

Edmond turned surprised eyes on Wilson.

'How is it, Wilson, that you always manage to glean so much information?'

'I don't know, Major. It just happens. I says a few words to 'em, and they open to me like a book.'

Before Edmond could reply, Jessy entered carrying a large covered dish, which she placed in the centre of the table. Mrs Coombes followed her, bearing a plate, piled high with slices of freshly baked bread. Jessy took three deep plates from the sideboard, plus three spoons and put them on the table.

'I'm sorry it's plain fare, Sir, but without notice, it's all we have,' Mrs Coombes explained.

'Do not apologise, Mrs Coombes,' Edmond soothed. 'We are soldiers, Ma'am. Whatever you have produced will be a feast after army food.'

Mrs Coombes managed a smile and left them to their supper.

Wilson went to the table and lifted the lid from the serving dish. He inhaled.

'I believe it's mutton stew, Major. There's onions and

other vegetables in it, too. Come and sit down, and I'll serve you, Sir.'

Edmond and Sophia came to the table. Wilson placed the threadbare napkins on their laps and ladled the stew onto their plates. He took up the plate of bread, and with one hand behind his back, offered it to them.

'My goodness, Wilson,' Sophia remarked, 'You act like a real footman.'

'Well, Miss Sophia, I'm a man of many talents. A batman has to be, so he can look after his officer,' Wilson said, as he sat down, filled his own plate, and helped himself to bread.

After tasting the stew, Sophia said, 'It is not like the sumptuous meals we had at Mrs Maitland's inn, but it is warming. Ha! Edmond, it is better than the chicken stew you gave me at the camp. But that would not be difficult to achieve.'

'I'll have you know, Sophia, that I had to beg that chicken stew from a sergeant,' Edmond informed her. He placed a hand on his chest, and added, 'you wound me, Sophia!'

Sophia giggled.

Jessy came to clear away the table.

'I've put a warming pan in your bed, Miss, and added some more wood to the fire. Would you like me to come up and help you into bed?' she asked.

'No, I can manage, thank you,' Sophia replied.

Jessy took three candles, in candlesticks, from on top of a dresser. She lit them and handed one to each of the guests.

'Goodnight, then,' she said. Bobbing a curtsy, she left them to find their way back to their rooms.

When they reached the top of the stairs, Wilson bid Edmond and Sophia goodnight and went to his room.

'I hope you sleep better tonight, Sophia. At least this inn is quiet,' Edmond said.

'My only qualm was when I inspected the sheets, I found they were damp. The warming pan will have

147

rectified that. Goodnight Edmond,' she said and entered her room.

Once inside, Sophia removed her clothes. She took her nightgown from her portmanteau, put it on, and slid between the warmed sheets.

How blissfully quiet this inn is, in comparison to the last. I am sure to get a good night's sleep tonight, she thought, as she drifted into slumber.

Peace was forgotten when a flash of lightning, followed by a roll of ear-splitting thunder, woke Sophia with a jolt. The inn rocked with the impact.

Sophia lay still, holding her breath. Another flash of lightning, and peal of thunder had her burying her head beneath the covers.

A gusting wind whistled eerily at the window, rattling the frame. Rain, driven by the wind, dashed against the pane.

Sophia lay curled up in the bed, wondering when the storm would abate.

It reminded her of the storm, which broke over Edmond's tent in the camp when she had cried for the loss of her father. The memory brought tears to her eyes. She sniffed and tried not to cry.

For what seemed like hours, the wind continued to spatter rain against the glass. The doors of the inn shook noisily, intermittently covering the sound of a drip somewhere. Sophia longed for the warmth of the clamorous inn of the previous night.

As Sophia awoke the following morning, she wondered how long she had slept. She rose from the bed, opened the shutters, and looked out at a dark cloudy sky. Rain still poured, but the howling wind had ceased.

The doorknob rattled, as Jessy fought to open the door. She entered, carrying a pitcher of hot water, which she placed beside the washstand. As was her wont, she retreated without saying a word.

Sophia was pleased to find the water hot and set about washing herself before the dwindling fire. She dressed

148

once more in Mirande's red gown, before brushing her hair.

Sophia gladly left her room. As she descended the stairs to the dining room, a faint, and not unpleasant aroma of fish, met her.

'Good morning Miss Sophia,' Wilson said, in salutation.

'Good morning Wilson. Do you think we shall have fish for breakfast? I can distinctly smell fish.'

'Yes, Miss. Knowing the Major's liking for kedgeree, which he first tasted when we were in India, I told the cook how to make it. I thought to surprise you, Sir,' Wilson explained.

'Very thoughtful of you, Wilson,' Edmond replied.

Jessy arrived. She placed the same covered dish in the centre of the table and silently retreated.

When they were seated, Edmond remarked, 'I hope you slept better last night, Sophia.'

As Sophia spread her napkin on her lap, she voiced her woes to Edmond.

'I slept not a wink, Edmond. The storm and the noise of the wind howling around the house kept me awake.'

'I am sorry, Sophia. Was there a storm? I did not hear it. I slept well. Did you not, Wilson.'

'I did, Sir, yes,' Wilson said.

Sophia was unimpressed. She frowned, glaring at Edmond and Wilson.

'You are seasoned soldiers, used to sleeping in camp in unfavourable conditions. I am not a complete innocent where bad conditions are concerned, but this place is quite outside my experience,' she said, her lack of sleep making her grumpy.

Edmond raised his eyebrows, inclined his head, took a breath as if to say something and thought better of it.

Wilson, also thinking it best to hold his peace, quietly served Sophia and Edmond,

'Thank you, Wilson,' Edmond said and began to eat his kedgeree.

For the rest of the meal, Sophia was quiet, while Edmond and Wilson tactfully discussed the inclement weather.

'You will get very wet driving the horses, Wilson,' Edmond remarked.

'Oh, don't worry, Major, Sir. Me coat and hat are thick, and I reckon the rain'll stop soon.'

Mrs Coombes entered the room and hovered by the sideboard.

'How much do I owe you, ma'am?' Edmond asked.

The woman came to life and turned a smiling face towards him.

'Now, em, let me see …' she said, counting on her fingers.

'Will a guinea be enough?' Edmond asked, producing the coin from his pocket.

The woman's eyebrows rose almost into her hair.

'Indeed, Sir. Thank you, Sir,' she said, dipping curtsies all the way to the door.

Having settled the tariff, Edmond walked out into the rain, grateful the coach stood close to the inn.

Edmond handed Sophia into the coach, climbing in himself.

Wilson, swathed in his large army greatcoat, a wide-brimmed hat on his head to protect him from the rain, climbed onto the box.

Sophia was, indeed, exhausted. Edmond settled her once more on the seat opposite him, with a cushion beneath her head. She came to herself each time the coach stopped to change horses and fully woke to the noise of the teeming London streets.

'Where are we, Edmond?' she enquired.

'We are in London, Sophia. This particular area is not the most wholesome. Shortly, we shall be in Kensington, which is far less crowded and noisy.

Sophia looked out of the window of the slow-moving coach, impeded by the volume of traffic, and press of pedestrians spilling into the road. Represented among the throng were all levels of society, from the poorest beggar to the occasional high-ranking gentleman. She saw scantily clad women, making strange gestures, to passing men. Appalled by their provocative behaviour, Sophia turned her face away.

'Why are those women behaving so strangely, Edmond?'

'They are prostitutes plying their trade, Sophia,' Edmond said, embarrassed for her discomfort.

Sophia frowned. 'I do not understand, Edmond,' she said.

'They are women of easy virtue, Sophia, and sell themselves to pleasure men,' Edmond said, an uncomfortable heat rising to his face.

Sophia continued to frown, then gasped. 'Ohh!' she said, shocked.

'So this is London?' she remarked, her cheeks burning.

'Yes, Sophia. This is Covent Garden, a place notorious for its degeneracy. Unfortunately, it is the quickest route to our destination,' Edmond said. He leant over and pulled down the blinds on the windows.

'There, Little One. That will spare your blushes,' he said gently, adding 'Do not judge all of London by what you see here. Some parts are quite beautiful.'

Sophia sat quietly in her corner. She smiled timidly at Edmond, in the gloom of the airless coach, and hoped the journey wouldn't be much longer.

Edmond, meanwhile, became more and more eager to see his home once more, after three years' absence. He had failed to send word of his arrival to his staff. He pictured the flustered servants, when he arrived unexpectedly, falling over themselves to prepare the house for his occupation. He regretted his omission, yet knew he would derive amusement from the reception he would receive. As he settled more comfortably in his seat, the thought made him smile,

Sophia glanced at him.

'What has amused you, Edmond?' she asked.

'I am thinking of Vere House and am looking forward to seeing it again,' he said, his voice warm and contented.

CHAPTER SIXTEEN

Vere House stood in two hundred acres of Land. Built the century before, of red brick and sandstone, it offered an imposing presence.

The main building was three storeys high.

In the centre, tall sandstone pillars supported a portico, capable of accommodating even the largest carriage. It protected the alighting passengers in inclement weather. A flight of ten shallow steps led up to the black painted double front doors.

On either side of the portico, rounded bay windows spoke of large rooms inside. Six more windows, on either side, completed the lower storey. Above the portico, a long, narrow, perpendicular window covered the frontage, stretching up to the crenelated roof. To the right and left of this, eight windows of the same design as the lower storey's windows, and eight more above them gave a pleasing aspect to the observer. A dark grey slate roof rose steeply above the crenelations, topped off by a variety of chimney pots.

On either side of the main building, two-storey wings sprouted incongruously, obviously later additions.

Before the house was an oval, well-manicured lawn, bisected by a wide, bricked path, and surrounded by the sweep of the gravel drive.

When Edmond saw the gatehouse with its black iron gates, he couldn't hide his elation.

'We have arrived, Sophia,' he exclaimed.

The gatekeeper came to the gate.

'There is no one in residence,' he called to Wilson.

'No, gatekeeper, we know. Major St Vere is within the coach, and requires admittance,' Wilson replied, and took great pleasure in seeing the gatekeepers changed expression, from careless unconcern to alert surprise.

He was aware that Wilson's words could be a ruse. He disappeared back into the gatehouse and returned in a moment carrying a bunch of keys. The gatekeeper didn't open the main gate, but appeared at a smaller gate to the side.

'What is happening, Edmond?' Sophia asked, peering out of the window, craning her neck to see what was going on.

'I am pleased to say that my gatekeeper is coming to ascertain that it is indeed me who craves admittance, Sophia. He will not allow entrance to unknown, dubious characters,' Edmond told her. 'It is cruel of me, but I shall gain much amusement from seeing my people skittering about in confusion. The gatekeeper is the first.'

'Why will they be confused?' Sophia asked.

'In all that was going on, Sophia, I did not remember to inform them of my arrival.'

Sophia smiled, 'You are wicked to enjoy their discomfort, Edmond.'

The gatekeeper appeared.

Edmond opened the window and put out his head.

A look of horror covered the gatekeeper's face.

'My Lord!' he exclaimed, rooted to the spot.

'Good day to you, Harman. Will you open the gate, if you please?' Edmond said his face serious.

'Oh, er … yes, my Lord. Of course, my Lord,' he spluttered, and went back in by the side gate.

Edmond saw a young boy hare off up the beech-lined avenue, which led from the gate to the main house, and surmised Harman had sent him to inform the house of their master's arrival.

The gatekeeper appeared again, opened the ornate main gates, and pushed them to either side. As the coach passed him, he touched his forehead. Edmond acknowledged him with a bow, as he drew his head back in, smiling at Sophia.

The coach bowled along the tree lined avenue, rounded the drive, and stopped under the portico.

Edmond alighted, and helped Sophia from the carriage.

He stood at the bottom of the steps, looking about him.

'Ah, Sophia, 'tis good to be home,' he said, with a wide smile.

The front door opened. A tall, thin man, dressed neatly in black, and wearing a powdered wig, descended the steps. Behind him, Edmond caught sight of several maids, busily lighting candles in the enormous marble hall.

Furlong, the butler, a man who rarely showed any emotion, managed to hide his astonishment at his master's arrival.

'My Lord, welcome. I apologise my Lord. We did not know you were coming. Most of the house is shut up,' Furlong said, as he let down the steps of the carriage.

'Thank you, Furlong. It is I who must apologise to you. Circumstances prevented me from informing you. We shall wait in the library, while you do whatever needs doing,' Edmond said. He alighted from the coach, and having helped Sophia down, they ascended the steps together.

A groom appeared from nowhere, and Wilson relinquished the reins to him, before climbing down from the box. He walked up the steps, and stood in the doorway, unsure of where he was to go.

'Come in, Wilson,' Edmond said, stripping off his gloves, which Furlong was quick to take. He placed them on the hall table and moved to close the door, eyeing Wilson with hostility.

'Wilson is my erstwhile batman, Furlong. He will now serve as my valet. See to it that a bed is made up in one of the anterooms to my suite. Tomorrow we shall decide where his permanent accommodation will be. Will you also see that he is fed, if you please,' Edmond said.

'Very good, my Lord,' Furlong replied, glancing down his nose at Wilson, and helping Edmond off with his coat.

'I should inform you, Furlong, this is Miss Erdington. She is my ward, and will be staying with me,' Edmond said, standing back a little so that Furlong could see Sophia.

'Allow me to welcome you, Miss Erdington,' Furlong said, with a deferential inclination of his head. The movement of his eyes was almost imperceptible, as he appraised Sophia's appearance.

Sophia didn't know quite how to take such an exalted personage as Furlong. She felt she should say something, so contented herself with a brief, 'Thank you, Furlong,' and gave him her best smile.

The grandeur of the building outside had impressed her. The inside took her breath away.

With dozens of candles now lit, a soft yellow light shone off the pale, honey-coloured marble floor and staircase, which rose from the middle of the vast round hall. It branched to either side, leading up to a gallery running around the upper floor, enclosed by a gold painted iron railing. Many doors opened onto this gallery. Another staircase ascended to the second floor from the middle of the gallery. The second gallery mirrored the one on the floor below. Sophia had never seen anything so astonishing.

She looked up at Edmond, who laughed quietly at the awe-stricken look on her face.

'It is somewhat overpowering at first sight, Sophia, I know. An ancestor, with a large ego, and enough money to indulge it, built Vere House,' he told her, adding, 'the library is this way.'

Edmond took Sophia's elbow and walked several steps before he turned back to Furlong.

'You may serve us with light refreshment, Furlong, when you can,' Edmond said and continued shepherding Sophia towards the library, situated behind the stairs.

'Follow me, Mr Wilson,' Furlong said, swanning to the other side of the hall, where the back stairs led down to the kitchen, and other rooms used by the servants.

At the bottom of the lower stairs, an important looking woman stood in a doorway to the right. Dressed in grey, her hair was hidden under a white, lace trimmed cap. She wore a chatelaine at her waist.

'Well, Furlong, and what are we to do? I have sent the maids to remove the Holland covers from the drawing room, and more to make ready my Lord's bedchamber. Mrs Cribb is preparing dinner for him. It is unlike Lord Edmond not to inform us of his arrival. He is usually more considerate,' she said, frowning.

'Circumstances prevented him, Mrs Narrowby,' Furlong said to the housekeeper.

'Where is he now?' she asked, standing back, as three maids rushed past them, with armfuls of bedding.

'In the library, with the young lady,' Furlong informed her.

'Young lady? What young lady?' Mrs Narrowby's mouth opened, her eyes wide with curiosity.

'Her name is Miss Erdington. Lord Edmond informs me she is his ward,' Furlong said, pausing to observe Mrs Narrowby's surprise.

'Goodness me!' Mrs Narrowby's eyebrows flew up. She caught sight of Wilson.

'Who is this, Mr Furlong?' she asked, looking Wilson up and down.

Before Furlong could reply, Wilson stepped forward.

'I'm Daniel Wilson, Ma'am. I've been serving Major St Vere as batman for the past seven years or so,' he said, the ever-present twinkle in his eye.

Mrs Narrowby pressed her lips together, and looked at Furlong, then back to Wilson.

'I hardly think my Lord needs a batman here, Mr Wilson,' she said, her mouth tight, her eyebrows frowning.

'No, ma'am. I am to serve as his valet while we are here,' Wilson replied, undaunted by the formidable woman.

'Lord Edmond requested that we feed Mr Wilson, Mrs Narrowby,' Furlong said, giving Wilson a disapproving glance. 'My Lord ordered light refreshment be brought to him in the library. I am about to see to that myself, so may I ask you to show Mr Wilson to the kitchen?'

'As if I haven't enough to do,' she said, to Furlong's

157

back, as he disappeared into his pantry.

'Come with me, Wilson. We have already eaten dinner, but we shall see what is left over. You may eat it here in the servant's hall,' she said, as she opened a door on a long narrow room. A large table, with twenty or more chairs around it, filled most of the space in the room.

Dirty plates, with the remains of the servant's dinners, were still on the table.

'My Lord arrived just as we were finishing,' Mrs Narrowby explained. She lifted lids on the dishes that stood in the middle of the table.

'There is plenty left over, so help yourself. You will find clean plates and cutlery in the sideboard,' she said and left him to himself.

Wilson paused before the table, looking at the mess.

'Hey-Ho. Best show willing I suppose,' he said to himself and started to clear the table.

He found a large tray resting beside the sideboard and piled the dirty plates and cutlery on it. Finding an empty, covered dish, he scraped the leftovers into it, leaving the loaded tray at the end of the table. He found himself a plate and piled it with potatoes, vegetables, and beef stew, all barely warm. He was hungry, so that didn't matter. Wilson sat back in his seat, easing his stiff back. Full of dinner, he began to feel more cheerful. He rose and went to the door. On opening it, he saw Furlong, disappearing into a room at the end of the corridor. Wilson followed him and peered into the room.

The Kitchen was warm and inviting. Everyone was intent on their tasks, rushing here and there, to get dinner ready for "my Lord" as quickly as possible.

Wilson heard Furlong's voice.

'How long, Mrs Cribb?'

Wilson saw a well-proportioned woman, rolling out pastry, on a clean-scrubbed table. At sight of Furlong entering her kitchen, she drew in an audible breath, her lips forming a thin line.

'It'll be ready when it's ready, Furlong,' Mrs Cribb

replied, holding her rolling pin menacingly in one hand.

No love lost between them two, Wilson thought.

'I am about to deliver light refreshment to Lord Edmond, and the young lady, Mrs Cribb. I would like to inform him how long his dinner will be,' Furlong said, in a wounded tone.

'Young Lady?' Mrs Cribb said, echoing Mrs Narrowby's words.

'His ward. Did Mrs Narrowby not inform you?' Furlong said, laying aside his antagonism, as he enjoyed Mrs Cribb's discomfort.

'No, Furlong, she hasn't been near the kitchen. So, I'm cooking for two, not one?' she said.

'I'm afraid so, Mrs Cribb. I am sorry you were not informed.'

'It's all right, Mr Furlong. Such things happen in times like these. I'll manage. It'll be ready in about half an hour. Now go away and let me get on, there's a good man' she said. Looking up from her pastry, Mrs Cribb caught sight of one of the kitchen maids coming from the larder.

'NO-NO-NO! Not the mutton, the chicken. Do you want them to wait all night for their food?' she shouted at the girl, who hurried back to the larder with the offending mutton leg.

Furlong slid from the room and bumped into Wilson.

'What are you about, skulking there in the hall?' Furlong said, scowling.

'I ain't skulkin', Mr Furlong. I've cleared the table in the servant's dining room, and I were wonderin' where to put the dirty dishes. I were thinkin' o' washin' them up, seein' as I'm at a loose end, and everyone else is so busy.'

'You may take them to the scullery. Just a moment.' Furlong disappeared back into the kitchen.

He returned with a little dab of a scullery maid in tow.

'Now, Brigit, this is Mr Wilson, Lord Edmond's valet. He has offered to wash up the dishes from our dining room. Will you show him to your scullery?' Furlong said, and with great self-possession, walked away to his pantry.

Wilson towered over Brigit, who looked up at him in awe.

'Hello, Brigit, me dear. Just let me fetch the tray, and you can show me where to go,' he said, grinning at her. Moments later, Brigit appeared in the kitchen, followed by Wilson. Everyone stopped to stare at Brigit, with the big stranger carrying the heavy tray-load of dishes following her.

When Mrs Cribb recovered her voice, 'Tell Brigit to come here to me, this minute,' she bellowed.

Upon Brigit telling her who Wilson was, and what he was doing, Mrs Cribb was astounded. Ever after, Wilson had a special place in the kitchen staff's hearts, having been good enough to help in a time of crisis.

In his pantry, Furlong picked up the tray he had prepared to take to Edmond and made his way up the back stairs.

As he reached the hall, he observed two maids, coming downstairs from the drawing room, with armfuls of Holland covers, which they had removed from the furniture.

'Is a fire lit in the drawing room, Dora?' Furlong asked one of the maids.

Dora bobbed a curtsy. 'Yes, Mr Furlong, and I placed a bowl of potpourri on the mantle, in case the room is musty,' she told him with a questioning look.

'Good,' was all Furlong said, and ascended the stairs to the drawing room.

Dora breathed a sigh of relief. 'I wasn't sure he would approve of the potpourri, Meg,' she remarked to her companion, 'it being of French origin, you know.'

Furlong set down his tray and disposed of its burden on two low tables, beside two couches either side of the fire. He placed a glass and a jug of lemonade, for Sophia, with a plate of cake and macaroon biscuits, on one table. A glass, and a decanter of Madeira, and another assortment of sweetmeats for Lord Edmond, on the other.

As he descended the stairs to the library, he passed two

footmen, carrying the traveller's trunks to their rooms.

Furlong knocked, and entered the library.

'You will, I hope, forgive our tardiness in preparing your dinner, my Lord. Mrs Cribb assures me, it will be ready within half an hour,' Furlong intoned solemnly, with an apologetic look at his master.

'Nonsense, Furlong, I gave you no notice at all, so you need have no qualms about preparation. Why, if necessary, we could repair to the kitchen, and sup on soup with bread,' Edmond said, and turned to Sophia, 'We would be happy, would we not, Sophia?' Edmond smiled in his own charming way.

Sophia, still unsure of how to address Furlong, smiled too.

'Oh, my Lord!' Furlong protested, scandalised by Edmond's expressing a wish to do such a thing. 'Why, the drawing room is now ready to receive you. I have laid out your refreshments there.'

So saying, he went to the door and opened it for them.

With great dignity, he led the way up the stairs to the drawing room and held the door for them again.

'I shall inform you when dinner is served, my Lord, Miss.' He bowed deeply and retreated.

Edmond sat on a couch beside the brightly burning fire, crackling in the fireplace. He leant back in the comfortable seat, with a sigh, and gazed about the familiar room.

There stood the Sèvres clock on the mantle shelf, a painting of his father above it; the soft green velvet curtains at the windows; the Sheraton satinwood cabinets, either side of the door; the matching glass fronted cabinet and escritoire; the green patterned Turkey carpet. Everything was as he remembered.

Sophia went to inspect the ornaments in the glass-fronted cabinet.

'These things are beautiful, Edmond,' Sophia observed.

Edmond turned his head towards her, 'Indeed, they are. Most of them are very old; been in the family forever. Would you like some lemonade, Sophia?' Edmond asked.

'Thank you, Edmond,' Sophia replied.

Edmond rose from his chair to pour lemonade for her. He poured himself a glass of wine, stood with his back to the fire, and drank it with pleasure while Sophia sipped her lemonade.

'Your house is exceedingly grand, Edmond, as are your servants. Why, I am quite in awe of Furlong,' she confided.

Edmond chuckled. 'He is a pussycat compared to Mrs Narrowby, the housekeeper,' he said, sitting down again. 'She is so fierce, she frightens me at times ... well, she used to when I was a boy ... perhaps she has mellowed with age.'

He took a sip of his wine.

'Or, perhaps now I am unlikely to get into scrapes—like breaking windows, or disturbing the washing—she may not regard me as an imp sent from hell to torment her.'

He leant forward, looking seriously at Sophia. 'Do not fall foul of her, Sophia. I swear, her tongue is as sharp as a whip.'

He refilled his glass, looking at Sophia with twinkling eyes.

'I hope dinner will not be too long, for, although I am hungry, I am tired, too. Are not you, Sophia?'

'I am not hungry at all, Edmond. I would prefer to go straight to my bed,' she said.

'You cannot, Sophia; they must prepare our rooms. The reason they are insisting on serving dinner is to keep us occupied while they do that, I'll be bound.'

'I would never have thought of that. When we lived in billets, Father and I never had above two or three servants. They were never as deferential as yours,' she said, nibbling on a biscuit.

Edmond saw, that despite her protestations regarding her lack of appetite half the biscuits had disappeared.

'Sophia, do not eat too many of those, as you *must* eat your dinner, since they will be put out if you do not,'

Edmond said, gravely.

'Gracious me, Edmond, do servants run their employers' lives?'

Edmond considered a moment.

'Well, no, Sophia,' he replied. 'It is all to do with consideration. I always find people in one's employ, or those merely supervised, are far more likely to serve one better if one treats them with consideration. I behaved this way towards my men in the Army, and have found it to be so.'

'Edmond, how wise you are,' she said, eying the biscuits, and resisting the temptation to choose another.

'If wisdom is mine, Sophia, I have acquired it in a hard school. Controlling men is like walking a tightrope. Too lenient, and they take advantage, too strict, and they dig in their heels. A light touch with consideration and respect goes a long way.'

They sat in silence for a while, gazing lazily into the fire leaping, and crackling in the hearth.

I hope her surroundings and the servants will not overwhelm Sophia. Yet, from what I have seen of her, it would take a lot to daunt her. I must write to Perdita tomorrow and invite her and Simon to visit.

Sophia's thoughts were optimistic.

I like this house. It is magnificent. I would never have dreamed of living in such a vast mansion. I must get to know the servants. I am sure they cannot be as aloof as they seem.

Furlong's return interrupted their reveries.

'Dinner is served, my Lord,' he announced, in melancholic tones.

'Come, Sophia. Let us discover what miracles Mrs Cribb has concocted for us, at such short notice.'

Edmond led Sophia to the dining room, situated on the other side of the gallery.

On the table, in crystal and silver splendour, two place settings sat at either end of a long table, covered in a crisp, white damask tablecloth. Matching napkins rolled up in silver holders, lay on the plates. Candelabra, six candles in each, set forward from each place setting, provided the main light in the room.

Furlong pulled out a chair for Edmond and seated him.

He made to go to the other end of the table to pull out Sophia's chair, too.

'Miss Erdington will sit next to me, Furlong,' Edmond said.

'Yes, my Lord.' Furlong bowed, pulled out a chair for Sophia, and seated her carefully. He placed a napkin on her lap, shifted the cover from the other end of the table, and laid it out before her. Lastly, he moved the candelabra to a position nearer to her.

'The Cook apologises, my Lord, for there being only one course served. However, she has prepared a dessert of baked fruit with *Crème Française*, if my Lord will find that acceptable,' Furlong said.

'Most acceptable, Furlong. Please send my compliments to Mrs Cribb, with my apologies for putting her to so much trouble. You may go now, Furlong. We shall serve ourselves. Thank you.'

'Thank you, my Lord,' Furlong said. He moved the covered dishes from the sideboard to the table and stepped quietly from the room.

The dinner consisted of a fricassee of white chicken, accompanied by a raised game pie, pureed cauliflower, honeyed green beans, and boiled potatoes smothered in butter. Edmond and Sophia ate well; they were hungrier than they thought. The fruit and *Crème Française* completed a most creditable meal.

'If the cook can accomplish such as this in half an hour, Edmond, her usual creations must be wonderful. She must be greatly skilled,' Sophia said, sitting back in her chair, replete.

'Oh, she is. She has cooked for seventy people without turning a hair. She is most proficient—all the servants are. My father liked to have competent people about him. I expect they are pleased we are here, as they will be able to

164

practise their skills again,' Edmond said, patting his mouth with his napkin.

'I only spent some five months here, and at Crawford Lees, when my father died three years ago. I came home once or twice for a short furlough, in the meantime. But since then, the servants have been doing goodness-knows-what, to keep themselves occupied.'

'Who is in charge while you are away?'

'Furlong and Mrs Narrowby look after this house. In Oxfordshire, my estate's manager and my accountant oversee all my business. However, when last I was in Crawford Lees, the house was uninhabitable. I had to put up at the lodge.'

He took a sip of wine, thinking on the experience, as he gazed into the distance.

'My father and brother never lived there, preferring to be here, near London.'

He rose, and going to a cabinet, he took out a bottle of brandy.

'Things have not changed,' Edmond muttered, glad to find the brandy in its usual place. He chose a large brandy glass from another cabinet and poured himself a measure.

Edmond stood with his back to the fire, warming the glass between his hands, feeling more at home in this house than he ever had done before.

'By rights, you know, Sophia, you should now retire to the drawing room and leave me to my port or brandy. As there is no one here to observe our indecorum, you may stay,' Edmond said.

'Father used to make me retire at dinner parties. I often wondered what gentlemen do when ladies retire,' Sophia said.

'They smoke, and talk on subjects, which you would find boring, Sophia,' Edmond said and mused a moment.

'As I was saying, I intend to bring Crawford Lees up to a good standard, rebuilding parts of it. I also wish to make better use of the land, making sure the tenants' houses are in good order. I hear that on many estates when one leaves the running of a place to a manager, they have not the tenants' welfare in mind. If there are wrongs, I mean to set them right; run it more profitably.'

'It sounds rather dull, Edmond,' Sophia said, stifling a yawn.

'Ah yes, my dear, you would think so, but to me, it is stimulating.'

Edmond sat at the table again, put his glass down, and leant forward, looking at Sophia intently.

'For you, I mean to hire the best of tutors to complete your education. I know you have an intelligent head on your shoulders. I want you to be well instructed,' he said.

'I doubt you will find anyone as good as Miss Roseberry,' Sophia said, with a rueful smile.

'I would like to continue learning Latin. And perhaps Italian. Miss Roseberry said I would be good at Italian since I already speak French and with my Latin, she said Italian would be easy,' Sophia said.

'What else would you like to learn, Sophia?'

'I enjoyed geography and history. I don't know much about England. We always concentrated on the countries in which we were living. Perhaps I could learn a bit more about England. And music.'

She sat up straight and gave Edmond a hard look.

'I hope you do not expect me to paint or sew. I cannot paint for love, and although I can sew, I see no point at all in producing samplers and chair covers,' Sophia said, looking at him warily to judge his reaction.

'To speak truth, Sophia, neither do I, where sewing is concerned. But to produce a competent picture must be satisfying, surely?' Edmond said.

'Indeed, Edmond, but I am not proficient at all. Pray, do not make me do it.'

'Very well, my dear, if the thought fills you with such disgust, I will not.'

Sophia straightened her shoulders, but her eyelids drooped.

'Now, Sophia, I can see you are tired. I, too, am in need

of sleep, so I suggest we retire,' he said. He rose from his chair, stretched languidly, and pulled the bell rope.

'I *am* tired, Edmond. Will you please show me where I am to sleep?' she said, carefully placing her napkin beside her plate.

'I have rung for someone to show you to your room, Sophia. I am not sure which one they have assigned to you,' Edmond said.

A moment later, Furlong appeared.

'Ah, Furlong. Ask Mrs Narrowby to show Miss Sophia to her room, if you please,' Edmond said.

Furlong bowed and went to find Mrs Narrowby.

'I am a little apprehensive about meeting your housekeeper, Edmond,' Sophia said, chewing the side of her lower lip.

'She won't eat you,' Edmond said, with a chuckle.

He led Sophia to the top of the stairs, where Mrs Narrowby was waiting for her.

'Good evening, Mrs Narrowby,' Edmond said.

'Good evening, my Lord. It is a pleasure to have you home,' Mrs Narrowby said, with a smile.

'If you will follow me, Miss Sophia, I will show you your room.'

'Thank you, Mrs Narrowby,' Sophia said, and turned to Edmond.

'Goodnight, Edmond.'

'Goodnight, Sophia. I hope you sleep better tonight than you have on the journey.'

'I am sure I shall, Edmond. There will be no brawling or noisy singing, and no storm will encroach on my windows, I am sure.'

Mrs Narrowby walked along the gallery, to the left. As she followed her, Sophia looked at the pale green walls around the gallery, with their white ornate plasterwork, surrounding large portraits of St Vere ancestors hanging on the walls.

Edmond took a turn to the right of the gallery, and Sophia heard his receding footsteps, echoing in the large marble space, as he made his way to where his rooms were located.

Edmond's suite was once occupied by his father. When he had stayed here before, Edmond had used them. This had brought home to him, with daunting force, the circumstance of his being head of the household. Tonight, he found comfort in his position.

Before retiring to his bed, Edmond decided to look in on Wilson.

Several anterooms adjoined the main bedroom. At the second room he looked into, Edmond found Wilson, sitting in an easy-chair by the fire, snoring, his boots off, his feet stretched before him; a half-finished tankard of ale in his hand.

Edmond smiled to himself. Fondness for Wilson touched him.

He removed the tankard from Wilson's grasp and placed it on a table.

Pulling a cover from the bed, he draped it over Wilson.

Edmond stood looking at him for a moment.

A dependable man. I cannot imagine my life without Wilson. I have come to rely on him greatly.

Edmond closed the door gently and went to his own room.

Wilson had laid out a nightshirt for him on the bed. Edmond smiled again in appreciation. He removed his clothes, put on the nightshirt, and slid gratefully into his own bed, luxuriating in the perfumed sheets, the plump pillows yielding gently to his head. Warm comfort enfolded him.

'How good it is to be home,' he whispered, as he drifted into sleep.

Mrs Narrowby opened the door to Sophia's room. A maid stepped forward and bobbed a curtsy.

'This is Dora, Miss Sophia,' she said. 'She will see to your needs. Goodnight, Miss,' she said, and hurried from the room.

'I've unpacked your things, Miss, and laid out your nightgown. Your clothes are sadly crushed, so if you are agreeable, I will have them seen to,' Dora said, giving Sophia a tight smile.

'Thank you, Dora. Please do whatever you think best with my clothes. They are more practical than fashionable, and they all need cleaning,' Sophia said, a little embarrassed.

'Don't worry, Miss, I'll work on them myself. Would you like me to brush your hair?'

'Thank you, Dora, but I am so very tired, I just want to sleep. Will you brush it for me tomorrow?' Sophia said, with a yawn.

'Of course, Miss,' Dora said and helped Sophia out of her clothes. She slipped the nightgown over Sophia's head and folded back the covers.

When Sophia slid into the warmth, Dora pulled the curtains around her bed, before silently leaving the room.

Sophia snuggled into the blissfully comfortable bed. She yawned, and tried to think over all that had happened in the last few days. She couldn't concentrate and began to drift on a tide of drowsiness. Her last thoughts, before she descended into sleep, were of Edmond. The most kind, generous, perfect man she had met.

CHAPTER SEVENTEEN

It took some days before Edmond's letter arrived with his sister, and longer for her to organise her journey to Kensington. Nevertheless, within two weeks of Edmond and Sophia's arrival at Vere House, Perdita descended upon them, with her son in tow.

'Edmond,' she said, as she accepted a kiss on her cheek from her brother, 'who is this child with whom you have encumbered yourself, pray?'

Edmond knew Perdita disliked sitting with the light shining on her face.

Four years older than Edmond, Perdita worried about her fading looks

He led Perdita to a couch, with her back to the window.

'I am not encumbered, Perdy. I told you in my letter, I promised her father, on his deathbed, I would care for her, and that is precisely what I mean to do, with your help, I hope.'

'But, my dearest brother, you mentioned you had married the girl,' she said, disposing herself on the couch.

Although Perdita had lost her first bloom of youth, she was still an attractive woman. Her hair was, even now, a shining golden blond. With dress-sense as impeccable as ever, her style, of late, accommodated her more voluptuous figure.

'Ah, yes, I did. But, Perdy, 'twas but for the sake of expediency I took her to wife. Our marriage is in name only, and when the time is right, I mean to have it dissolved,' Edmond said, and pulled the bell rope.

'I am indeed gratified to hear it. Although such a marriage would be legal, Edmond, I would not think you to be so foolhardy as to encumber yourself, with what is practically a child bride.'

A woman of decided opinions, Edmond knew he must tread carefully with Perdita if he was to persuade her to help him look after Sophia. He must not allow himself to be annoyed with her.

'No, my dear, in truth, I have not. I employed the measure only to obtain a pass for her to enter the country. She regards me as her protector, and I regard her as … as the daughter I never knew,' he said, lowering his eyes.

'Ah, if only Adela had not died,' Perdita said, with a sigh.

Edmond looked up. 'Do not dwell on it, Perdy. I do not. I am happy to care for Sophia, for as long as she needs me.'

Edmond was about to embark on his plea for Perdita to come and live at Vere House, with himself and Sophia, when a knock sounded. A boy entered the room.

His large, brown eyes dominated his pale, lean face. His straight, dark hair flopped on his forehead. His tall frame stooped, as if in an effort to hide his height, yet his thin body accentuated it.

He stood inside the door. Dressed in a dark grey suit of clothes, which hung on him loosely, his hands plucked at his ruffled, white cuffs. In their black shoes, adorned with sparkling silver buckles, his feet shuffled restlessly.

'Simon, do come and sit down, and stop fidgeting by the door,' Perdita said to her son.

Simon walked to a seat opposite his mamma and sat on the edge of it.

'Do you not think him grown prodigiously, since you last encountered him, Edmond?' Perdita said, regarding her son.

Simon hung his head and gave her a tight-lipped glance.

Edmond viewed the boy, who scanned his uncle evasively, a worried expression on his face.

'Indeed, Perdy, I should be most surprised if he had not, as three years have elapsed since then,' Edmond said, with a jovial snort. 'How old are you now, Simon?'

'I shall be sixteen next month, Sir,' Simon said, his voice quiet, his hands in two tight fists, resting on his knees. Edmond noticed his discomfiture and wondered why the boy was so ill at ease.

'You are of an age with Sophia, Simon,' Edmond said.

'Sophia, Sir?' Simon's huge eyes looked at Edmond, with what could only be described as anxiety.

'I told you, Simon, she is the girl, whom your uncle brought with him from France. She is under his care,' Perdita said, giving her son an admonishing frown.

'Oh, of course, yes … I … I do remember,' Simon stammered.

Furlong knocked, and entered the room.

'My Lord?'

'Ah, yes, Furlong, will you please fetch refreshment for my sister,' Edmond said.

Furlong came near to smiling at Perdita.

'Negus, Mrs Luxton?' he asked, unbending his usual stiff pose.

'Thank you, Furlong, I have need of it after my journey,' Perdita said.

Furlong bowed low to Perdita and departed.

In the servant's hall, rumour had it, Mrs Luxton would come to live at Vere House. A welcome prospect to Furlong. Furlong rather despaired of Edmond's easy-going attitude. As long as everything ran smoothly, Edmond cared little for the niceties, to which Furlong devoted his attention. Furlong liked times to be precise. He thought it proper for Edmond to consult with the housekeeper, with gardeners, and with Cook.

'Do not bother me with details, Furlong. Tell Mrs Cribb, we shall eat whatever she puts before us. I trust her completely,' Lord Edmond had told him.

And Wilson—a rough and ready soldier, if ever Furlong had seen one, to be Lord Edmond's Valet— monstrous! All the other servants adored Wilson, to Furlong's constant chagrin. Yes, Mrs Luxton would soon bring order to what, to Furlong, seemed chaos.

'I hope, while you are here, Simon, you and she may

172

become acquainted. She needs companionship from one more of her own age,' Edmond said.

'Yes, Sir.'

Simon didn't appear at all enthusiastic.

Furlong returned. He lovingly placed a tray next to Perdita.

'I have brought you Ratafia biscuits, too, Mrs Luxton. I remember your liking for them in the past,' Furlong said.

'How good of you to remember, Furlong, thank you,' Perdita said, reaching for an expensive, sparkling cut-glass goblet, enjoying the attention.

'Will that be all, my Lord?' Furlong said, with an inclination of his head towards Edmond.

'Yes, Furlong. Except, could you tell me the whereabouts of Miss Sophia, if you please?'

Furlong paused to think.

'Yes, my Lord. I believe she is in the garden, or more precisely, by the lake,' Furlong replied, and with a further inclination of his head, he retired.

'Perhaps you might go and introduce yourself to her, Simon. I am sure you can find your way to the lake.'

'Yes, Sir,' Simon said, glad to escape.

Simon went through the French windows, and onto the terrace. He descended the grey, Portland-stone steps, which led to a formal evergreen avenue. Carefully clipped holly, laurel, privet, box and yew grew on either side of a rolled gravel path. In contrast, pleached hornbeams wore no leaves. Covered in delicate light green foliage in summer, they would form a canopy of shade. Simon passed swiftly along the avenue. The formality of it offended him. From the avenue, a lawn sloped down to the ornamental lake.

Simon walked towards the lake but didn't see Sophia. After skirting the water, he found her sitting beneath an elm tree on a hillock, a little way beyond the lake. He moved up behind her.

'Good afternoon, Miss Sophia,' he said, in his soft, gentle voice.

173

Sophia jumped up to look at him.

'Who are you?' she asked, her eyes wide in surprise.

'I am Simon Luxton, Lord St Vere's nephew. He sent me to find you,' Simon replied.

'Oh, you have arrived!' Sophia moved towards him, her hand outstretched. 'I have been looking forward to meeting you.'

Simon took her hand, bowing over it. Sophia made a small curtsey. Simon smiled at her, the apprehension in his eyes clearing.

'Do you want to go into the house, Simon? Or would you like to walk for a little by the lake?' Sophia asked, 'I am told, spending time in fresh air, after a long journey, makes for better comfort.'

'Indeed, Miss Sophia, I will walk with you, if you wish.'

'No, no, Simon, only if *you* wish. Perhaps, if you prefer, we shall return to the house.'

'Thank you. I would like to walk by the lake. I remember it from when I was here before, and I thought the trees beautiful then.'

His face became animated.

'One particular willow tree dipped its branches to the water, and a stand of cedars grew a little farther back from it. In spring, a patch of bluebells covered the ground under them and—Oh, pray forgive me, I do not mean to bore you,' he said, breaking off his reminiscences, and blushing.

'You do not bore me at all, Simon.'

Sophia patted his arm. 'I know the trees you mean, and I, too, think they are beautiful, although the poor Willow is lacking her leaves. The cedar trees are not, though, and, when spring comes, we may feast our eyes on your patch of bluebells together.'

Simon's expressive eyes shone with pleasure.

'I hope mother and I are still here then. She thinks, perhaps, uncle Edmond means for us to stay with him,' he said.

174

'Edmond would like you both to live with us,' Sophia informed him.

'Would he? I would like that. Although I love my home, and the countryside, London would provide more opportunity for what I want to do,' Simon said, his expression wistful.

'What is it you want to do, Simon?' Sophia enquired, impulsively taking Simon's arm, as they walked towards the lake.

'Ah, Miss Sophia, it is an impossible dream.'

Simon sighed, and scuffled his feet in the fallen leaves littering their path. They looked up at a lone blackbird, singing its last song of the season, in a branch above their heads.

Simon steered the conversation away from his dreams.

'How long have you been in England, Miss Sophia?' he asked.

'Nearly three weeks,' Sophia replied.

'You travelled from France?'

'We did. We sailed in a ship carrying contraband. It was quite an adventure,' Sophia told him, her eyes shining.

Simon's eyebrows raised. 'Were you not afraid?' he asked.

'I must admit to a little fear. Mostly I found it exciting,' Sophia confided. 'The best part of our journey was the voyage. The sea is magnificent.'

'Yes, the sea is truly inspiring,' he said and lowered his head.

An unhappy cloud seemed to descend on Simon's face.

Sophia glanced at him.

'What makes you look so sad, Simon,' she inquired, frowning.

'Mother thinks love of nature is unmanly. She thinks I should follow more masculine pursuits.'

His expression changed again to impassioned seriousness. 'I do not think appreciating the beauties of nature is unmanly. One can still be a man and care for loveliness.'

His eyes took on an angry light, as he focused them on hers.

'Do you not think so, Miss Sophia?' he said, his breath quickening.

Sophia caught his mood. 'Oh, Simon, yes I do. The sunset on the sea, when we sailed from France, was magnificent—so wonderful it hurt. Edmond and I stood watching till the sun disappeared below the horizon.'

Her face glowed with enthusiasm.

'Edmond? He watched the sunset with you?' Simon said, frowning, and looking at her sideways, eyes narrowed, sceptical.

'Indeed, yes. Edmond has great sensibility,' Sophia said, with a sage nod.

'Then, perhaps, he may understand my position, after all,' Simon mused, his eyes wide now with hopeful anticipation.

'Your position, Simon? What is that?' Sophia asked.

'I have feared our visit, Sophia, as my mother intends to ask Edmond to buy me a commission. She thinks if I join a regiment, it will "make a man of me", as she puts it. My father was an officer, killed in battle—one would think such a circumstance might dissuade her from a wish for her son to be put in a position of danger, too—but no, she took this notion into her head, and I am powerless to remonstrate with her. She is sure Edmond will agree with her.' His worried expression returned, as he shook his head. 'I thought, perhaps, he would take her side,' he said.

He paused and watched a duck bobbing in the lake. A chilly breeze blew across the water, making the surface resemble dark rippling satin.

Simon's mood changed from dark to light again.

'If Edmond is a man of sensibility, perhaps he will not,' he said, his eyes bright, as he glanced at Sophia. 'To tell you true, Sophia, I always feared Edmond a little. He seemed stern and aloof.'

After another reflective pause, Simon continued.

'I was but twelve when last I met him. It was at his father's funeral. I suppose, at such a time, anyone would seem stern.'

'His face *is* stern sometimes, but he is not aloof at all,' Sophia said. 'I do not think he would force you into the Army, if you truly do not wish to go, Simon. Perhaps you should speak to him alone, and explain how you feel,' she suggested.

Their walk, having taken them some way around the lake, they came to the favoured willow tree. Simon lifted his head and gazed up into its branches.

'I do not think myself capable of facing him alone, Sophia,' he said, shaking his head, and added, 'This tree has grown much bigger since last I was here. It has such majesty now—in spring she will be a queen reigning over the lake.'

He turned to Sophia,

'I tell my mother continually I am no coward—perhaps I should prove I am not, and be less in awe of Edmond—face him alone, and be done. Shall we go in now?'

Edmond and Perdita heard Simon and Sophia's voices in conversation, as they climbed the steps to the terrace.

Perdita smiled at Edmond. 'He seems to have found her, at last,' she said.

The two-young people brought the soft autumn scents of windswept leaves, and fresh air, floating into the room.

Edmond stood as they entered, and drew Sophia forward.

'Perdita, may I make known to you, Miss Sophia Erdington. Sophia, my sister, Mrs Perdita Luxton.'

Sophia bowed her head and curtsied. Perdita didn't rise but nodded towards Sophia.

'Come here. Let me look at you, Child,' she said.

Sophia went to stand before Perdita.

'Edmond, how old did you say she is? Did you not say fourteen?'

The fire crackled in the grate, as Perdita scrutinised

Sophia from head to foot.

'I would not have credited it. Why, Child, you look older,' she said, shaking her head, as if it were a fault.

Far from being perplexed or annoyed, Sophia said, 'I am tall for my age, ma'am. So, I seem older. But, I assure you, I *am* fourteen.'

Perdita sat back in her chair and pursed her lips.

'And not afraid to speak up for yourself, either. Come here and kiss me, Sophia.'

Sophia dutifully went nearer to Perdita and bent her head to kiss the woman's cheek.

'What am I to call you, Ma'am?' she said, as she straightened, and smiled sweetly at Perdita.

'You may call me Perdita, my dear. As we are in no way related, Aunt would be inappropriate,' she said, with a somewhat condescending smile.

'It seems disrespectful to do so, Ma'am, but I call Edmond, "Edmond". I suppose, calling you Perdita, is a similar thing. I am pleased to meet you, Perdita.'

'As I am you, Sophia,' Perdita said, and patted the seat beside her. Sophia sat by her and folded her hands decorously in her lap.

Edmond watched the exchange, pleased to see Perdita liked Sophia. Perdita didn't intimidate Sophia, and Sophia even used her particularly charming smile on Perdita. Edmond knew this smile already. It was the one Sophia used when she wanted her own way. He couldn't hide his amusement or quell the sparkle in his eye.

Simon, on the other hand, regarded Sophia in awe. His mother was putty in Sophia's hands. If only he could be … what was the word? Was duplicitous too strong? Wheedling was too deprecating. The only fitting word was charming. Simon knew he couldn't charm his mother, as Sophia did. He looked at Edmond and saw she charmed him, too. More than that, Edmond was amused.

Simon watched his mother talking with Sophia. He looked at Edmond again. As he looked, he realised Edmond regarded *him*.

Simon took a deep breath, his determination strong.

'Uncle, I wonder whether I might have a word with you?' he said, and hoped the ground would open and swallow him, so apprehensive was he.

'Of course, you may, Simon, what is it you want to say?'

To him, the boy looked anxious and had done so since his arrival.

Simon swallowed, and glanced at his mother.

'In private, if you please, Sir,' Simon said, almost inaudibly.

'Certainly—When? Now?'

'If you please, Sir, if it is not inconvenient.'

Simon lowered his head, glanced at his mother, then flicked his eyes back to Edmond.

'Perdita, will you excuse us? I need Simon in my study. We shall return shortly,' Edmond said, and before Perdita could object, Edmond opened the door for Simon, and they went out.

He led Simon to his study at the back of the hall, next to the library. Edmond indicated a chair by the window. Simon sat. Edmond stood leaning against the window frame, arms folded, at ease.

'What do you want to say to me, Simon?'

'Sir, I do not wish to join the Army,' Simon said, in a rush.

Edmond shifted his position and scrutinised Simon for a moment.

'Well, Simon, the Army is not to everyone's taste. I respect your sentiment, but why are you telling me of it?' Edmond said, his chin tilted up, his eyes narrowed.

Simon's hands were sweaty, his throat dry. Edmond's quizzing expression did nothing to calm Simon's nerves.

'Because of my mother, Sir. She desires that I become a soldier, and means to enlist your help in achieving her ambition.'

Simon swallowed, and bravely looked Edmond in the eye.

'If you please, Uncle,' he continued, 'I would be much obliged to you if you did not aid her in her endeavour.'

There, I have done it. I have said it, and whatever storm might break over my head for it, I will take it like a man. Like the man I am, Simon thought, proud of having faced his fear.

Again, Edmond paused before he spoke, prolonging Simon's agony.

'Simon, I would never try to force anyone to do something against their will. Not unless they were under my command, and I had given them a direct order,' Edmond said, raising an eyebrow and smiling crookedly.

'I am aware my sister is a strong-willed woman and does not enjoy being thwarted. Were she insisting on your obeying a tutor, or learning some new accomplishment, then I would be in agreement with her. However, dictating what career you should follow—well, to some extent, I would say she should guide you, but to cajole and force you into something, which is clearly abhorrent to you, no, I would not encourage that.'

Edmond leant his head back, regarding Simon. Simon closed his eyes, and breathed out a long slow sigh, as his great burden lifted.

'Uncle, oh, you cannot appreciate how relieved I am. To be sure, I was convinced you would side with her, and not me. She would listen to none of my objections, saying her course would be the best to take. My father was a soldier; you are a soldier, and she desires I should follow in both your footsteps ...'

Edmond broke in on him.

'What do you wish to do with your life, Simon?'

'I want to be an artist, Sir,' Simon said, without hesitation, 'I want to paint.'

Taken aback, Edmond stood straight, his eyebrows raised.

'You amaze me, Simon!' Edmond said. 'What experience do you have, my boy?'

'I have always drawn what I see, Sir,' Simon began,

'One of my tutors introduced me to painting the pictures I had drawn. He said I showed talent. The last time we came to London, I visited exhibitions of painting—Hogarth, Reynolds, and Gainsborough's work in particular, at the foundling hospital—I knew I wanted to create images.'

He paused, and his look of unhappiness returned.

'When Mamma discovered my ambition, she was horrified.'

His animation dwindled, as he mentioned his mother.

'I have had to hide my canvases and equipment from her, for fear she will dispose of them.'

Edmond was seeing a new side to Simon.

'I can make no judgement until I see your work, Simon. If you show talent, I shall do all in my power to help you. However, I am no expert. Your work would need to be seen by a professional artist. I would then be sure of your abilities,' Edmond said and went to a cabinet to pour himself brandy.

Simon looked at Edmond with nothing short of awe.

'I am astonished you take me seriously, Sir. I must thank you. If canvas and paint could be procured, I would paint a likeness of ...' he thought a moment. 'Sophia,' he said, with delight. 'Except, my mother must not know, Sir.' His enthusiasm curbed again.

'Let me think on it, Lad. I am sure we shall come to some arrangement. Now, we must return to your mother; she will wonder what plots we are hatching,' Edmond said, and patted Simon's shoulder.

They found Perdita and Sophia on the terrace, admiring the garden. Edmond and Simon overheard the tail of their conversation.

'Of course, Sophia, my dear, I had a sylph-like figure then, and a constant stream of beaux in attendance,' she said, reminiscence painting her face with nostalgia.

'And was Mr Luxton one of those beaux?' Sophia asked.

'Indeed he was, my dear, and for both of us it was love at first sight.'

She turned when she realised Edmond and Simon had entered the drawing room.

'What, pray tell, have you been discussing for so long, Edmond?' she asked as she and Sophia took their seats, once again, on the sofa.

'Simon and I were speaking of the possibility of his joining the Army,' Edmond replied.

Simon shot him a horrified look.

'I am not in favour of a military career for Simon. I have persuaded him otherwise. In a few years, when he is a little older, he may consider it, but not now. I am convinced I was too young when I bought my commission. I am of the opinion he should acquire a little more education first.'

Simon breathed an inward sigh of relief.

What a cunning fox Edmond is, he thought.

Simon looked at his mother and saw her frown.

'Indeed, Edmond, if that is your opinion, who am I to disagree with a seasoned soldier, such as you?' Perdita said. She took up her glass, and sipped from it, casting a suspicious eye on her son.

CHAPTER EIGHTEEN

'I need to speak to you, Perdy,' Edmond said when she joined him one morning at the breakfast table. He had finished his oatmeal with sweet cream. Swithun, the new footman, came forward.

A tall, well-built young man, Edmond had noticed him for his quiet efficiency. Furlong had taken him under his wing.

He served Edmond his grilled trout with white butter sauce. Knowing his penchant for fish, Mrs Cribb always made sure it was on the breakfast menu.

Perdita took her seat across the table from Edmond. The ever-vigilant Furlong appeared.

He placed a napkin on her lap and offered her a soft, hot roll from a silver bread basket. When she had chosen her roll, Furlong glided to a cabinet to pour her hot chocolate.

'What is it you wish to say to me, Edmond?' she said as she delicately broke bread from her roll.

Edmond swallowed what he was eating, then cleared his throat.

'What do you think of Sophia's appearance?'

Perdita gave Edmond a measured look.

'I do not wish to criticise or interfere, you understand,' she said and took a sip of her chocolate.

'Since you ask, Edmond, I must remark, I have noticed a certain inelegance about her.'

She slowly shook her head.

'Do you think I should provide her with a suitable wardrobe?' Edmond said, pausing over his fish.

'Yes, Edmond, I think you should. The only dress she has, which is in any way presentable is the red wool. The rest are a disgrace.'

'Indeed, Perdy. Some of her clothes are more patch than original and those that are not are démodé.'

'*Trés démodé*!' Perdita said with a disdainful lift to her

shoulder.

Edmond made a wry face and tried to reclaim something positive.

'Her shoes are practical.'

'Yes, Edmond. But she cannot be happy with them. I have never seen a girl of her age wear such ugly shoes. And does she possess only the one bonnet?'

Edmond looked unhappy.

'I fear so. Tis a drab affair, is it not?'

Edmond put down his fork and rubbed his chin. He glanced at his sister, who now attacked her boiled egg and dipped a fragment of bread in the yolk.

Edmond inhaled deeply.

'I am ignorant of such things, Perdy, and I wondered…'

'You wondered, Brother if I would take her in hand?' Perdita smiled and chuckled.

'How astute you are, Sister-mine.'

Edmond shifted an eyebrow, 'Are you willing?'

Perdita's eyes brightened with anticipation.

'Willing, Edmond? I have been here a week and itched to do so, ever since I clapped sight on her.'

Edmond smiled, relieved.

'Thank you, Perdy. I thought you would be of help to me. You may start tomorrow, and do not consider the cost.'

He rose, and began to pace as he spoke.

'I want her to look the thing,' he raised an admonishing finger, 'but not too forward, you understand. I want her to wear clothes suitable to her age. But also, suitable for a girl who is my ward.'

Glad to have broached the subject at last, a smile hovered on his lips as his uneasiness cleared.

'Leave her in my hands, Edmond. I will trick her out in a way to make you proud.'

She sat up, rearranging her skirts.

'I think her hair needs attention, too, would you not agree? All those curls running riot over her head and down her back—it appears 'twere cut with a knife! Depend upon it; I shall set my dresser to put her in order.'

She leant back in her chair with a satisfied sigh.

Edmond resumed his seat, frowning at his sister.

'Perdy, is her hair so bad? I always thought it spectacular. Indeed, I have never met anyone with so much. I like her hair.'

'Indeed, *so much* comes to my mind. *Too much* would be more apt. Edmond, my dear, your perception is out of line, and it is because you are a man who has had scant contact with women.'

Edmond shifted in his seat and flicked a glance at her.

'You possess little knowledge of how a woman should look. You are aware only of her difference, but you do not realise, difference is not always attractive.'

Edmond sat back with a shrug.

'When I have finished you will not recognise her, I promise you,' Perdita said, her eyelashes flickering, her chin high.

Edmond balked. He sat up.

'Ah, Perdy, do not go too far. It is but her clothes I want to amend, not her whole person.'

Perdy shook her head and waved a dismissive hand.

Edmond continued, 'And, if she objects to anything you do, you must not force her. I will not have her upset. She has been upset enough of late,' he said, assuming an air of military authority.

'Oh, poof, Edmond,' Perdita said, not in the least cowed. 'I do not think anyone could force that young miss into something with which she was not happy. She has spirit and a forceful character, which I admire in her. However, she is not wilful. She is obliging and eager to please. I also applaud that. I am becoming quite fond of her, you know,' Perdita said, her expression soft and wistful, never having had a daughter of her own.

'I would still prefer to be able to recognise her, Perdy. Just do not go too far.'

His tone was dubious.

Perdita arose from her chair.

'I think I will go and find her. I expect she will be in her favourite haunt by the lake, and no doubt Simon with her. I am gratified to find they enjoy each other's company.'

She glided from the room through the French doors, leaving Edmond to ponder. He began regretting having asked for her help, but in the absence of any other female on whom to rely, he resigned himself to Perdita's ministrations.

His thoughts turned to Simon.

Edmond had already enquired concerning a suitable assessor of Simon's work and obtained the name of an artist, employed as a drapery painter by many of the best masters in London.

He made an appointment to see the man, setting off one morning without telling anyone where he went, for fear Perdita might hear of it. He didn't think Simon could produce a painting in secret at Vere House. Edmond's plan was for Simon to go to Mr Peter Toms's studio and work on a piece so that the man could assess him.

Edmond arrived at Rathbone Place and enquired of Mr Toms. A surly porter directed him to a studio at the top of the house. The building was old and dilapidated and the stairs rickety.

They creaked as Edmond climbed them cautiously. When he knocked at the door, the unkempt man who opened it appeared to be drunk.

'I beg pardon, Sir. I wish to speak to Mr Peter Toms. Do you know his whereabouts?' Edmond said, trying not to inhale. A dank, musty and unidentifiable odour emanated from the room.

'You're looking at him, Sir,' the man said gruffly.

Alarmed by this reply, Edmond toyed with the idea of leaving.

Toms's face had an unhealthy, jaundiced hue. His cheeks were covered in purplish thread-veins. To describe his appearance as dishevelled would be to compliment him. He wore a scruffy wig—askew—a coat darned, patched, and stained with paint and food. His breeches, once white, an indeterminate colour, the end of his shirt inexpertly stuffed into them, and he wore no waistcoat. He opened the door wider for Edmond to enter.

'You are Lord St Vere: I take it.'

The tone was sullen, the voice gravelly.

'I am, Mr Toms. How do you do?'

Edmond removed his hat but kept his gloves on as the room was in terrible disorder, and needed cleaning. Piles of crockery and laundry rested on every conceivable surface. Articles of clothing hung everywhere.

'Hmm, much you care how I do. What do you want of me?'

Toms finished off his wine and poured another generous measure into the dirty glass.

'My nephew wants to become an artist, Sir. I am willing to finance his apprenticeship. Before I do, I want to be sure of his talent. What I want from you is an assessment of his ability.'

Edmond resisted the temptation to hold his handkerchief to his nose.

'Well then, will you show me some of his work?' Toms removed a pile of papers from a chair, which he dusted off with a rag and held his hand towards it in invitation for Edmond to sit. Not wishing to insult him, Edmond took the seat.

'Unfortunately, Mr Toms, I cannot,' Edmond said. 'His mother is averse to his following such a profession. His works and equipment are stored in secret at his home in the country.'

Edmond glanced around the room. An easel with drapery over a half-finished picture stood in pride of place. Sketches littered the floor. On a table, a collection of paint, brushes and stretching canvases lay in confusion.

Edmond continued.

'I propose he comes here and works on a piece, so you

may judge whether he shows promise.'

Edmond glanced around the room again. Lit by windows let into the sloping roof, a shaft of sunlight highlighted an unmade bed in one corner. Edmond thought the place most unsuitable for Simon to frequent.

Toms gulped at another glass of wine.

'Ah, and will you pay me, Sir?' Toms said, bringing Edmond's thoughts back to Simon's assessment.

'Of course, I will pay you, Sir. Name your price.'

Toms rubbed the stubble on his face and peered at Edmond out of one bleary eye.

'It would probably be best if he does not come here, Sir.'

Edmond inwardly breathed a sigh of relief and listened to what Toms proposed.

'This is not the best of areas but is all I can afford. I would need to hire a studio for a week, maybe two. Then there would be the cost of materials, and, of course, my time. While I am occupied with your nephew, I will not be pursuing my usual occupation, you see.'

He scratched his head—further unsettling his wig—and looked up at the ceiling, then back at Edmond.

'Shall we say one hundred guineas?' he proposed, screwing up his eyes.

Edmond's eyebrows flew up. He blew out his cheeks and came to an impulsive decision.

'Very well, Sir. When would it be convenient to start?' Edmond said, with a cordial inclination of his head.

Toms made an effort to hide his surprise and coughed.

'I will contact you, Sir, when I have obtained a studio and the materials. Next week perhaps?'

'Excellent.'

Edmond stood, fished a card case from his waistcoat pocket, and handed his card to Toms.

'I look forward to hearing from you, Mr Toms. Good day to you.'

Toms bowed and opened the door for Edmond.

'Good day to you, my Lord,' he said.

Edmond carefully descended the ramshackle stairs. When he reached the street, he was glad to inhale comparatively fresh air. He wondered whether allowing Simon to associate with such a disreputable-looking character was appropriate. But popular opinion of artists seemed to be that they were all of them unconventional, and Toms had been highly recommended.

Edmond walked to Percy Mews to retrieve his horse. As he rode home, he pondered on possible ways to facilitate Simon's visits to Toms without arousing Perdita's suspicions.

He was loath to confront her, and would only do so if Simon did indeed exhibit an aptitude for his passion.

On one morning of the following week, while Edmond sat thinking of Simon, the boy entered the room from the terrace. He had seen an opportunity to speak to Edmond when his mother whisked Sophia off to discuss her wardrobe's transformation.

'Uncle Edmond, Sir, have you had word from Mr Toms?' he asked his face eager and worried all at once.

'No, Simon, but the post has not yet been collected. Today might bring a letter from him.'

Edmond put a genial hand on Simon's shoulder.

'Concerning your visits to Toms without your mother's knowledge, Simon, I thought of two possibilities. One is to tell Perdita outright what we do.'

Simon's face took on a paler hue as he shook his head vigorously. Edmond laughed, continuing.

'The other is for me to take you and Sophia to see the sights of London each day. I would indeed take Sophia sightseeing, but you would go to Toms while I do so. Knowing how your mother's awful wrath would turn my peaceful life into turmoil, I recoil at the former and embrace the latter. What think you?'

Relieved, Simon said, 'I live in dread of ever telling mother, Sir. I prefer the latter choice, too. But would not Sophia become uninterested after so many days junketing about London?'

'Perhaps, if it were all we do, she might object. However, if I have learned anything of our Sophia, she will take enormous pleasure in the intrigue and join us willingly in the conspiracy. We shall collect you at the end of each day when you may show her your work; then we shall all return here together. Depend upon it; she will delight in helping you,' Edmond said, patting Simon's shoulder again.

A knock sounded, and Swithun entered.

'My Lord, your mail has been placed in your study.'

'Thank you, Swithun,' Edmond said. 'Come, Simon. Let us see whether a letter from Mr Toms is among my correspondence,' Edmond said and led Simon to his study.

Both fearful and delighted when Edmond held up the awaited letter, Simon couldn't contain his anticipation. Edmond opened it and read, his expression grave, his heavy eyebrows knit in concentration. Such a look made Simon apprehensive. His agitation overcame him.

'Sir, what does he say?'

'Hmm?' Edmond glanced up absently. 'Oh, yes, he rented a studio and purchased all that is needful, and you must present yourself on Monday next.'

'Uncle!' Simon gripped the back of a chair to steady himself. 'But your face tells me something is wrong. What is amiss?'

'Ah, nothing to concern you, boy, all is well.'

Edmond folded the letter and put it in his desk drawer.

He had correctly anticipated Toms's request for more money. His employment would last a few weeks only. Edmond supposed Toms to be taking advantage of the little time he had to fleece as much as possible from a rich Lord. Edmond would have abandoned the project and told Toms to go to the devil but decided to swallow his ire and proceed, not wishing to disappoint Simon.

Over the next few days, Edmond and Simon saw little of Perdita and Sophia. Each morning after breakfast, they departed for London in a carriage, returning late in the afternoon.

On the fourth morning, Sophia appeared in the morning room wearing a simple day-dress of cream satin with no adornments. The plain skirt billowed fashionably; the bodice was well-fitting, and the neckline demurely cut higher than current mode dictated. A pale-blue fichu was tucked into this and rested delicately about her neck. The sleeves were tight, widening from the elbows in a lace-edged flounce. Most notable was her hair. Clipped, brushed into submission and piled up becomingly, a few stray ringlets bobbed on her shoulders.

'Good morning, Edmond,' Sophia said, her eyes shining.

'Good morning, Sophia.'

Edmond glanced up from his newspaper for a moment, then swiftly lifted his head to look again. He sat back in his seat. A frown creased his forehead. Sophia's expression changed to disappointment.

'Oh, you do not like it!' She lowered her head, and her shoulders drooped.

'No, no, Sophia, you are … charming. I am surprised at so remarkable a transformation. Turn around. Let me look at you.'

Edmond rose and walked around the table towards her. Sophia's smile returned, as she pirouetted, then curtsied.

'Perdita has so much good taste, Edmond. When she said she would "take me in hand", I was quite fearful, as I do not wish to be turned out like a painted doll, all frills and ribbons. But she had no intention at all of doing so, and everything we ordered and purchased is exactly what I wanted …' She twirled again then looked up at him. 'You do not think it is a little *too* plain, do you, Edmond?'

He surveyed her, standing with his feet apart, his arms folded, a hint of a smile on his lips. Her eagerness for his approval amused and touched him. Taking her hands, he smiled down at her.

'Sophia, it is perfect. You are right, frills and bows would not suit you at all. I have one objection, however,' he said, his face serious.

'Oh, what is it? Tell me, please.'

She put a hand to her throat.

'Your hair, Sophia.'

Her hand went to her hair, and she shook her head.

'I am fearful of ruffling it, as I sometimes do, as I should ruin it,' he said and chuckled.

'Oh!' she said and laughed.

'And one other thing, Miss—which I would have mentioned had you been about for me to do so,' he said, trying once more to be serious. 'Were you not half-way up a tree a few days ago, hmm?'

She pouted. 'I was not half-way up, I only climbed onto one branch. I wanted to go higher, but Simon was afraid I would fall and was so agitated, I came down again,' she said, her voice gruff.

'But why did you want to climb the tree at all, Sophia?' Edmond asked, genuinely curious.

She gave him her sweetest smile. 'I wanted to look at an old bird's nest.'

'Well, Sophia, you must know, do you not? You cannot climb trees dressed like *that*.'

He was unsure whether he shouldn't speak to her more sternly.

'Oh, do not worry, Edmond. If I feel a need to climb a tree again, I shall change into my old clothes, or perhaps borrow Simon's breeches.'

Her eyes sparkled.

'Sophia?' Edmond's eyes narrowed.

She laughed.

'I am funning you, Edmond. Of course I will not do so again; I did it only to tease Simon. He offered to go up, but I said I wanted to. He begged me not to, but it is so easy to dupe him; I could not resist provoking him. I like him a lot, but he is prodigious serious.'

While she spoke, she served herself kippers and sat to eat them.

Edmond resumed his seat. He decided not to comment

on her disclosure, unsure whether he wanted to know what other escapades she might have indulged in. *She should have been born a boy*, he thought and changed the subject.

'Speaking of Simon, Sophia, we are plotting together, he and I, and want your help to carry out our plans,' Edmond said.

Sophia gasped, her face alive with eagerness.

'Edmond! How exciting. Do tell me. What is it?'

'Has Simon told you of his ambition to be an artist?' Edmond asked.

'Indeed, yes.'

She took a sip of her tea. 'Simon told me you were to have his work assessed by a proper artist, and you awaited a letter from the man to confirm when it is to be.'

'The letter arrived a few days ago. Simon is to visit Mr Toms on Monday morning to begin painting a piece for assessment,' Edmond said.

'Oh, Simon must be pleased. He did not tell me. But there, being out with Perdita so often, I have not seen him as much as usual. What is this plot you speak of, Sir?'

Her fork hovered over her plate, her food forgotten.

'We decided, since Perdita is averse to Simon's artistic activities, we would not tell her where he is going.'

Sophia listened, eager to help, as Edmond explained the planned escapade.

'I am not sure when we shall be finished with my wardrobe, Edmond. Perhaps, as Perdita and I are out most of the day, she will not notice if you and Simon are not here either. On the days when we are not out, I can go "sightseeing" with you. Is that not even better?'

'Yes, Sophia,' Edmond said, placing a finger to his lips. 'Hush now, if Perdy should enter the room, we must not be found talking of it.'

CHAPTER NINETEEN

On Monday, when Sophia and Perdita left the house, Edmond and Simon took horse for London and arrived in St Martin's Lane.

They rode to the mews at the back of the building where a groom took charge of their horses.

On their way to the front door, Edmond said, 'Toms informed me this building is owned by William Hogarth.'

'Is it?' Simon said.

'Toms also informs me that he often works for Hogarth.'

'Does he?' Simon said.

'Yes. Toms said when he told Hogarth of your plight, Hogarth offered his studio for rent.'

'Did he?' Simon said.

Edmond glanced at Simon, about to admonish him for answering in monosyllables. Simon's face was even more pale than usual. His hand shook when he pushed a lock of hair from his forehead. Realising Simon's nervous state, Edmond ceased trying to make conversation and walked in silence beside the lad.

At the front door, Edmond knocked.

'May I help you?' a smartly dressed servant asked when he opened the door. Edmond produced his card.

'We are here by appointment to see Mr Toms,' Edmond informed him.

The servant looked at the card.

'You are expected, my Lord,' the servant said.

Ushering them into the hall, he took their riding crops, hats, coats and gloves.

Looking about him, Edmond noted the order and cleanliness of the place.

The servant showed them up to the room Toms had rented.

'This is a vast improvement on the ramshackle muddle

194

that was Toms's studio,' Edmond remarked to Simon in an under voice.

Simon said nothing. He stared around the room, his eyes wide with wonder.

Edmond noticed the artist's equipment was neatly arranged. Slight disarray was visible but exhibited a certain charm rather than a clutter of unsavoury rubbish.

He was pleasantly surprised at the vast change in Peter Toms, too. Clean, sober, wearing a new wig and dressed a la mode, he greeted them with an ostentatious bow, his sullen attitude replaced by affability. Edmond wondered whether he was the same man.

Toms smiled at Simon.

'This is the boy whose talents we are to explore?'

'Yes, Mr Toms. May I present to you Mr Simon Luxton,' Edmond said.

Simon, tongue-tied, made a formal bow to Mr Toms who came forward to shake Simon's hand.

'Are you shy, Mr Luxton? Well, we shall soon overcome that. Once we get started on our work, all else will matter not a whit to you.'

'Thank you, Sir. I am sure you are right,' Simon said colour creeping into his pale cheeks.

Toms turned to Edmond.

'I hope this location pleases you, my Lord?' he said as he ushered them to a sofa. A table stood before it, where Toms had laid out refreshments. He sat opposite Edmond and Simon on a high-backed chair.

'Indeed, Mr Toms, it is good of Mr Hogarth to rent it to you,' Edmond said, sitting back, at ease.

Simon wasn't easy. He sat on the edge of his seat, his eyes lowered.

'May I offer you refreshment, gentlemen?' Toms said, picking up a carafe of wine from the table.

'Thank you, Mr Toms,' Edmond said.

Simon glanced at Toms and nodded. Toms poured wine for them, but not for himself.

'You are not drinking, Mr Toms?' Edmond asked.

'Never when I am working, my Lord,' Toms replied.

Impressed, Edmond raised an eyebrow without comment.

Toms turned his attention to Simon.

'I stretched several canvases for your use, Simon, not wishing to waste time. Do you normally stretch your own?'

'I do, Mr Toms,' Simon said, colouring again. He took a gulp of wine.

'Excellent news. Now tell me, have you a subject in mind?'

Toms sat forward, his elbows on his knees, his hands loosely clasped between them, listening intently to the boy.

Simon came to life.

'My first thought was of my... er ...' He glanced at Edmond, wondering how to describe Sophia. 'My cousin, Sophia. That was when I thought of working at Vere House. I like to paint portraits. Landscapes are also stimulating—but perhaps you could make a suggestion, Sir?'

Edmond was pleased to see Simon less timid.

'Yes, Simon,' Toms said, straightening his posture, and looking indulgently at Simon. 'I composed a still life for you, first to draw and then to paint. I will take note of all you do ...'

Simon frowned and bit his lip.

'Oh, do not look nonplussed, my boy. I must consider your work so that I may make an honest assessment of your ability. Your uncle has paid me for that purpose.'

Toms glanced at Edmond who sucked in a slow breath.

Mr Toms hung his coat over a chair then produced two smocks from a cupboard, handed one to Simon, putting on the other himself.

'I shall leave you to your efforts, gentlemen,' Edmond said and rose.

'You are welcome to stay if you wish, my Lord.'

Edmond had intended to stay, but seeing the

196

transformation of Mr Toms, he decided to leave them to become acquainted.

'No, I thank you, Mr Toms; 'tis better I go. I do not wish to distract Simon. At what time shall I return?'

'The light will begin to fade by four o'clock; come after that, my Lord. Allow me to show you out.'

At the door, Edmond glanced back at Simon and smiled to himself. Simon had donned his smock and stood gazing rapturously at the paint and brushes laid out on the table.

At the street door, Edmond turned to Toms and took a small leather bag from his pocket.

'I presume you received the first payment I sent you, Mr Toms?' Edmond said, his brows drawn together. Toms looked at him, unabashed.

'I did, my Lord, and I thank you. I hope you perceive I put it to good use. I spent almost all—paint and brushes are not cheap, you understand—and I took the liberty of buying new clothes in order to make a better impression,' Toms said with a tight smile.

'I appreciate your effort, Mr Toms. Here, take this— twice the additional sum you requested.'

Edmond handed Toms the bag. 'But I do not expect to be asked for more. I hope *you* understand.'

'Sir, you are extremely generous. I guarantee I will ask for nothing more. Thank you, my Lord.'

Edmond inclined his head and left.

Edmond was in half a mind to return to Vere House, but if Perdita returned and Simon was not there, all would need telling.

He walked to the mews. While he waited for his horse, he thought of riding in the park.

Yes, a ride will refresh me.

He remembered his club.

I have not mixed with my own kind in weeks. I will pay the club a visit. After that, what shall I do?

He mounted the horse and guided it into the main thoroughfare.

Oh, I am sure I can find something else with which to

amuse myself in town, he thought as he took off for St James's Park.

The morning was fresh. The chill of winter was setting in. The number of people in the park had dwindled. To 'see and be seen' was a great attraction to London society. But not in the cold.

He rode at speed on a track through the trees, making a full circuit of the park.

The ride was exhilarating. It was in exuberant mood Edmond entered the portals of the Horatio Club in St James's Street, a favourite haunt of infantry officers.

The Porter didn't recognise Edmond.

'Are you a member, Sir?' he asked.

Remembering it had been some years since his last visit, Edmond hid his frustration and produced his card. The porter checked in the register and placed the card on a rack.

'You may go up, my Lord,' the porter said.

Edmond looked about him as he ascended the stairs. The place hadn't changed. Dark mahogany cabinets and chairs furnished the hall. The black and white chequered tiles on the floor dazzled the eye, as always. Ancient portraits of long dead officers adorned the wall beside the stairs. The Banister on the marble staircase was just as highly polished. At the top of the stairs, the large double doors to the library stood open. The hum of conversation, with the occasional loud guffaw, spilt out and enfolded Edmond in its familiarity.

Edmond entered the library and stood to look about him. He recognised many faces, one of whom disengaged himself from a group of men and limped over to him.

'St Vere? How do you do!'

'Orpwood, what do you here? Did I not hand my duties over to you but a few weeks past?' Edmond shook the young man's outstretched hand.

'You did. I was wounded and sent home to recuperate.'

'My God! Where were you hit?'

'Right leg; bullet lodged in the bone. Devilish painful,

but they managed to remove it, so my leg mends.'

'But how did it happen, Orpwood? What action did you see?' Edmond asked.

'Ah, nothing of any great moment,' Orpwood said, blushing. 'A man on guard duty came across two French soldiers. He alerted his comrades. They tied up the Frenchmen and came to report the matter to me. I decided to interrogate the prisoners. Before I got to them, one broke free, got hold of a gun, and as soon as he saw me, he used it,' Orpwood said, rubbing the side of his leg.

'Turned out the scoundrels were deserters,' Orpwood added and pressed his lips together.

'Damned bad luck, Orpwood. When are you going back?' Edmond asked.

'Won't be going back for a few months yet,' Orpwood said.

Edmond caught the eye of a passing waiter and motioned for him to fetch a bottle to a nearby table.

'I am not returning,' Edmond said. 'I mean to resign my commission and settle on my estate in Oxfordshire. I have had my fill of warfare.'

Orpwood nodded.

'I must admit I am considering it myself. It is likely they will put me to work in an administrative capacity. I could not bear that. I am thinking of marriage—have a girl in mind too—but it is a big step. Did you not marry Erdington's girl?'

Edmond steered Orpwood to the table before he answered.

'I did, Nathan. But our marriage is not common knowledge, and I would not want gossip, you understand. The marriage is in name only. She needed a guarantor to get her into the country and marriage was the only way I could achieve it.'

'Indeed, my friend—very young—in name only. I will not breathe a word.'

Orpwood tapped the side of his nose.

'But tell me, will you not be encumbered by your

current nuptial status if you were to meet a woman you wished to marry? I assume you want to father an heir.'

Orpwood poured Cognac into two glasses—the waiter having discreetly deposited a bottle and glasses before them.

'Indeed, but in three or four years the marriage will be annulled. I shall then find a wife whom I hope will produce many children. I mean to be a respectable country gentleman!'

Edmond lifted his glass in a toast to his friend.

'I heard you had a wife once. She died, did she not?' Nathan said.

'Yes, you have it right, in childbirth.'

Orpwood looked suitably commiserating.

'What is she like, this new daughter of yours?'

Edmond gave a short laugh as he thought of his mischievous Sophia.

'She is like a breath of fresh air in my life.'

He looked into the distance as he described her.

'She is tall, with dark eyes, a mop of unruly brown curls and a capacity for getting into scrapes; constantly looking for what she terms "Adventure".'

He took a sip from his glass and put it down.

'At present, my sister has taken her in hand. She is composing Sophia's wardrobe. I, unbeknownst to her, am helping her son gain an apprenticeship to an artist.'

'An artist? How old is *he*?'

'He is almost sixteen with a passion for painting. So you see, my dear Nathan, my life is not, at the present time, dull in the least.'

Orpwood smiled.

'You do not miss the Army?'

'No, I do not.' He shrugged. 'I have only been gone for three weeks.'

Orpwood frowned and looked thoughtful.

'Three weeks? And not yet resigned?'

'I am too busy to go to headquarters to do so. Time enough.'

Edmond refilled Orpwood's glass, and then his own.

'Time enough? Edmond, your furlough was for three weeks.'

'Three months, my friend,' Edmond said taking another sip of his brandy.

'No, no, Edmond. When I dealt with your papers, they most certainly stated the duration of your furlough was three weeks.'

Edmond looked at Orpwood, the implications of the matter dawning on him.

'If that is so, I am in trouble.'

Edmond drained the rest of his drink and hastily rose from his chair.

'I must pay them a visit right away and make sure of my position.'

'Do you want company? Shall I go with you?' Orpwood said, also rising.

'Yes, Nathan. I would like someone with me as witness to their incompetence. I would not be surprised if Radford wrote three months on my paper and recorded it as three weeks. I must send a note to Wilson to retrieve the papers and carry them to headquarters.'

Edmond struck his forehead and opened his mouth in horror.

'Good God! Wilson! He is in the same predicament—but 'twill be worse for him. They will treat him as a deserter!'

'In that case, Edmond, I will go to your home, ask Wilson to give me the papers and I will bring them to you.'

'Nathan, you are a friend indeed. Here is my card. Is your leg well enough for you to ride?'

'Oh, yes. Riding is fine. Tis walking gives me difficulty.'

'Thank you, Nathan. I must go immediately. Do you know Kensington?'

Orpwood looked at Edmond's card.

'Yes, Sir. My sister lives in Drayton Square. I know

where Vere House is,' Orpwood said.

'Good. Come to me at Head Quarters with the papers and bring Wilson with you.'

'I will, Major,' Orpwood called after him as Edmond ran down the stairs and hurried from the club. Orpwood followed at a slower pace.

Edmond retrieved his horse from the mews and rode as fast as the thronging streets would allow.

CHAPTER TWENTY

On arrival at his regiment's headquarters, not far from St James's Palace, Edmond was left to kick his heels in an outer office for half an hour.

Such delay was typical of army administration. Slow and ponderous for no good reason.

The room he sat in was sparsely furnished. The walls panelled in grey painted wood; the chairs hard and uncomfortable. A copy of the *public ledger* lay on a table by the window. Edmond read it with little interest and finally threw it back down on the table to pace the room.

A pimply young cornet appeared.

'Will you follow me, please, Major?' he said.

The cornet escorted him to an adjutant's office.

Adjutant Jepson knew Edmond by reputation and was slightly in awe of him.

Edmond explained the situation. Jepson pursed his lips.

'I did not hear mention of your error, Major,' he said. 'You may wait here if you please, while I enquire.'

He left the room and returned ten minutes later.

'Colonel Courtney will see you, Major. Follow me if you please.'

They arrived at Lieutenant Beaumont's office.

'Major St Vere to see Colonel Courtney, Sir,' Jepson said and left Edmond in the lieutenant's capable hands.

Beaumont was a neat young man. Edmond surmised he was in his mid-twenties. Of medium height and slim build, he wore his fair, curly hair short.

'Good morning, Major. Sorry to keep you waiting,' he said with a cheerful smile. He came around his desk and opened the door to the adjoining office; a large room where a colonel sat behind an enormous desk.

'Major St Vere to see you, Colonel.'

Not being in uniform, Edmond felt at a disadvantage. He marched smartly forward, stood to attention and saluted.

'Y'r Major St Vere?' drawled Colonel Aubrey Courtney.

'Yes, Sir,' Edmond said.

'Some sort of error regarding y'r furlough, I'm told, Major?'

'Yes, Sir.'

'Would you care to explain the situation t' me?'

'Yes, Sir.'

Edmond cleared his throat.

'A circumstance arose where I was obliged to return to England. I was not sure how long the matter would take. I, therefore, requested a furlough of three months, which Colonel Radford graciously granted me, Sir.'

Edmond glanced at the Colonel. He sat at ease behind his desk; his head tilted to one side. His heavy eyelids drooped as, with a resigned expression, he regarded Edmond.

Edmond wondered whether the Colonel was listening; his face gave nothing away.

Edmond continued.

'I also requested my batman, Sergeant Wilson, be granted a similar leave of absence.'

Edmond waited for some response from the Colonel. None was forthcoming, so he went on.

'On meeting Captain Nathan Orpwood today, he informed me he was under the impression the period of my furlough was three weeks, not three months. Therefore, I considered the best course of action was to come here to discover where the error lay.'

Colonel Courtney sat still, surveying a spot above Edmond's head.

Is he trying to put me off guard? Edmond thought. *Has he heard a word I said?*

The Colonel eased himself in his seat.

'Hmm,' he finally said, clasping his hands on his stomach, twiddling his thumbs. The Colonel allowed his eyes to travel up-and-down Edmond from head to toe and back again. He inhaled a long breath through his nose.

'Officially, Major, ya should be in uniform. Y'r three-week furlough ended yesterday.'

Edmond made to reply. The Colonel forestalled him with a raised palm.

'Officially, ya should not be here at all; ya should be in France commanding y'r men.'

Edmond frowned, irritated by the Colonel's apparent indolence.

'Officially, I should discipline ya with a fitting punishment for dereliction of duty.'

Edmond inwardly fumed.

Another bloody ineffectual good-for-nothing, he thought. In an effort not to show his thoughts, he lowered his gaze.

The Colonel pursed his lips. He knew Edmond for a competent officer. He decided to bait him no further.

'Have you y'r release papers stating the length of y'r furlough?' he said, in a less apathetic tone.

Edmond regarded Courtney with narrowed eyes.

'Yes, Sir, at my home. Captain Orpwood went to retrieve them for me.'

'Hmm,' Courtney said again and rang a bell on his desk.

Lieutenant Beaumont appeared.

'Sir,' he said.

'Yes, Beaumont, find whether a Captain Orpwood is somewhere in the building, will you?'

Courtney's voice sounded weary, his heavy-lidded eyes bored.

Beaumont clicked his heels and left.

The Colonel waved a languid hand towards a chair to one side of the desk.

'Sit, Major.'

Edmond sat.

'I do find this sort of thing extremely tedious,' Courtney complained casually.

'I do not think for a moment y'r at fault, St Vere. Some clerk somewhere miscopied the word. Sloppy. Any reports written by ya have always been impeccable. I'm inclined, therefore, to believe ya. Nevertheless, we must follow the correct procedure. Ya know how it is.'

'Yes, Sir, I do,' Edmond said, nodding in agreement. Perhaps the Colonel wasn't a good-for-nothing, after all.

Edmond wondered whether he should make polite conversation while they waited.

He was spared this ordeal, as Lieutenant Beaumont opened the door for Orpwood to enter. Pausing at the door, Orpwood surveyed the room. Edmond thought him ill at ease.

Orpwood limped to the desk and saluted.

'Captain Orpwood?' Colonel Courtney asked.

'I am, Sir,' Orpwood replied.

'And ya have Major St Vere's orders?'

Orpwood glanced at Edmond, paused, and swallowed.

'I am sorry to say, I do not, Sir.'

Edmond, puzzled and alarmed, sprang from the chair, moving towards Orpwood.

'Did Wilson not give them to you, Nathan?'

'Wilson was not there, Edmond. He was arrested and carted off this morning by a group of soldiers.'

'What!' Edmond cried, his voice strident. He gave the Colonel a contrite glance and moved his gaze back to Orpwood.

'Why?' he asked, in a quieter tone.

'Desertion,' Orpwood said, apology in his eyes. 'No one else in the house knew where your papers might be kept.'

'Where is Wilson now?' Edmond asked.

'He's probably imprisoned, Major,' the Colonel said stoically. 'There are cells in the basement of this building. He may be there.'

Edmond stood still and upright. His mind ran riot as he thought on what he must do to rescue Wilson.

The Colonel continued.

'I would think his court-martial will take place tomorrow, and if found guilty, his execution will follow. I think ya must go yourself to retrieve the papers to secure his release.'

Edmond nodded slowly, his eyes alert, his thoughts still racing.

The Colonel rang his bell again. Beaumont appeared.

'Beaumont, find out where a Sergeant Wilson is held. He was arrested this morning for desertion.'

Beaumont nodded curtly and left.

'Y'r fortunate, St Vere, that I know you through y'r reports, and am persuaded to help ya. I shall write an order staying any hand from sentencing y'r sergeant until ya can procure the necessary evidence proving no crime has been committed.'

Edmond breathed a sigh of relief.

'Thank you, Colonel.'

'Y'r welcome, St Vere. Go now, and return to me with the papers as soon as ya can. Oh, and since y'r officially on duty, may I suggest ya return in uniform?'

'Yes, Sir, I will. And thank you again, Colonel. I am much obliged to you.'

Colonel Courtney adjusted his position. He leant back in his chair, his hands gripping its arms. An enigmatic look appeared in the Colonel's eyes as he painstakingly addressed Edmond.

'Major St Vere, ya can have no conception of how tedious this job is. Since ma injury, I am unable to return to active duty. I must sit behind a desk each day dealing with unbelievably petty matters, presented to me by unimaginative and unintelligent individuals. You cause me a small diversion. It is I who thank you,' he said, a curl to the corner of his mouth.

Beaumont returned.

'Colonel, Sergeant Wilson is imprisoned in a cell located in the lower basement.'

Edmond's eyes widened at the news. He frowned. He had to see Wilson for himself.

'May I go to him, Colonel,' he asked, urgency in his voice. 'No doubt he must be in fear for his life. He is a good man and I would like to reassure him.'

Colonel Courtney's rare smile appeared.

'A good commander always cares for the welfare of those under him, Major. I'm pleased ya exhibit such a quality. Yes, ya may go to reassure him. Beaumont, go with him and tell anyone who tries to impede him it is at my command he visits the prisoner. Is that clear?'

'Yes, Sir.'

Beaumont clicked his heels, and, turning, opened the door for Edmond and Orpwood.

'Ah, wait,' the Colonel called before the door closed.

'Beaumont, ya may have Wilson released into the Major's care and bring him here.'

'Yes, sir,' Beaumont said and closed the door.

Outside in the hall, Edmond gave out a long breath.

'A close shave, would you not say, Nathan?'

'Indeed, Sir,' Orpwood said, equally relieved.

'Shall I accompany you to the cells, Sir?'

'No, Nathan. I want you to carry a message for me.'

Edmond put his hand in his pocket. He drew out a pencil and his card case, wrote on a card, and turned to Nathan.

'My nephew, Simon, is at this address with Mr Toms. I am due there at four. Please tell Simon what has happened and escort him home to Vere House if I am not there by then,' Edmond said as he placed a hand on Orpwood's shoulder. 'Lord, but I am glad I met with you today,' he added.

'Pleased to be of service, St Vere. Doubtless, I shall see you at Vere House in due course. I think, under the circumstances, my friend, you owe me dinner,' he said with a wide grin.

'Of course, Nathan,' Edmond said patting Orpwood's shoulder. 'I shall tell them at the house there will be one more to dine.'

Orpwood nodded, smiled and walked down the corridor to the front of the building.

Edmond watched him go then turned to Beaumont.

'Well, Lieutenant, where is this basement dungeon?'

'Follow me, Sir.'

Beaumont walked in the opposite direction to Orpwood. They came to a small, winding, iron staircase and descended into a stuffy hallway. From here, they walked a little way to another similarly ill-lit winding staircase.

They arrived in a dark, musty-smelling passage. Passing strong metal doors on either side, they walked towards a light. It shone into the darkness from a room at the end of the narrow corridor.

As they approached the room, a large, hard-nosed sergeant moved into the doorway, blocking much of the light.

'Sergeant Yately. Where are you holding Sergeant Wilson?' Beaumont asked, his voice hushed in the gloomy place.

'He's in cell number five, Sir,' Yately said looking down at Beaumont's slight figure.

'Take us to him,' Beaumont said, his chin held high in an effort to exert his authority.

'Not sure I can do that, Sir,' Yately said. 'He's a deserter, so can't see no one,' Yately said with a derisive sniff, an unpleasant sneer on his face.

Edmond stepped from behind Beaumont.

'You will take us to him, or you will be on a charge yourself, Yately,' Edmond barked.

'Who the hell ...?

'We are on orders from Colonel Courtney. Do as he says,' Beaumont said more forcefully, taking his cue from Edmond.

Muttering to himself, the Sergeant went into his room, emerging with a large bunch of keys. He rumbled along the passage, fumbled with the keys and opened the door to cell number five.

Edmond covered his mouth and nose as stale, foetid airlessness, redolent of mould, wafted over him.

Edmond looked in.

209

It took time for his eyes to adjust to the near darkness. After a moment, Edmond made out the figure of Wilson, his elbows on his knees, his head in his hands. He sat on a narrow bench attached to the slimy wall. His ankles and wrists were manacled. Looking up when the door opened, he peered to see in the gloom.

Edmond removed his hand from his face, straightened his shoulders and walked forward.

'Wilson, what the devil are you doing here?' he said, making his voice sound jovial.

Wilson jumped up and moved towards Edmond, as fast as his chains would allow.

The Sergeant saw his authority undermined. Wilson was *his* prisoner. He stood between Edmond and Wilson.

'I am Major St Vere of the second of foot. Stand aside, Sergeant Yately,' Edmond ordered.

The Sergeant recognised the voice of higher authority.

He stood to attention.

'Beg pardon, Major,' he mumbled and moved to a position outside the door.

A relieved Wilson did his best to smile.

'Major, Sir, I've never been more pleased to see anyone in me life, and that's the truth. How did you find me?'

'I met Captain Orpwood by chance. When he pointed out the discrepancy between my papers and the records, I realised we both might be in trouble.'

Edmond put a hand on Wilson's shoulder.

'I am all right. They might give me a reprimand and a fine. You, old lad, could be executed. Colonel Courtney dealt with me, fortunately. I doubt anyone else would be so obliging. Come now. Let's get you out of here.'

He turned towards the door, once more mustering his authoritative tone.

'Sergeant Yately!' he called.

Yately stepped into the cell.

'Sir,' he said, saluting.

'My sergeant is released into my care. I am to take him to Colonel Courtney. Kindly remove his fetters.'

The Sergeant, bemused, looked to Beaumont for support.

'You heard the Major, Sergeant. Do as you are told and be quick about it.'

The Sergeant gave them each a hostile stare. Slowly he took a bunch of keys from his belt, located the one that fitted Wilson's shackles, and removed them.

Wilson rubbed his wrists where the manacles had chaffed his skin. He gave Yately a sullen look before following Edmond and Beaumont into the corridor.

'I don't know how to thank you, Major, Sir. I was sure I were a gonner,' Wilson said, wearing a worried frown.

'I couldn't let them execute you, Wilson. Who would polish my boots?'

Wilson grinned.

The three made their way back to Colonel Courtney's office.

'So, this is Wilson?' the Colonel said, giving him an appraising look.

'Yes, Colonel,' Edmond said and decided to try his luck.

'In view of his having had a shocking experience, Colonel, may he go with me?'

'Indeed, he may not; I have not seen y'r orders yet, Major. Wilson may wait in ma outer office under the watchful eyes of Beaumont here. When you return, he may go, assuming, of course, that y'r papers are in order.'

The whole incident had caused the Colonel some diversion. His mouth remained severe. His eyes amused.

'Very good, Colonel,' Edmond said, noting the Colonel's wry humour. He performed an exquisite attention and salute before marching out into the hall.

Edmond retrieved his horse from the stables and rode swiftly home.

Once there, he deposited his horse, Pandora, with Greer, the head groom.

'Saddle Warrior, if you please Greer. I will not be long; I must return to London urgently.'

Warrior had been transported from France earlier in the week.

Edmond walked from the stables to the kitchen garden, entering the house from the rear. He ascended the back stairs, heading for his study.

Once there, he rifled through a pile of papers in his desk drawer.

Finding what he was looking for, he let out a satisfied 'Ah.'

Inspecting his and Wilson's orders, Edmond was relieved when he read "three months".

He folded the papers, placing them in his inner pocket.

To Furlong's surprise, Edmond met him in the hall.

'I did not see you return, my Lord. Is all well?'

'It will be, Furlong,' Edmond said, making for the back of the hall. Remembering Nathan, he turned.

'Furlong. My friend, Captain Nathan Orpwood, will arrive later. If I am not returned before he comes, attend to his comfort. Tell Mrs Cribb there will be one more for dinner.'

'Yes, my Lord,' Furlong said to Edmond's retreating form.

Edmond went to the stables. About to mount Warrior, he remembered his uniform.

'Damnation,' he said under his breath and approached the groom.

'Greer, I have forgotten something. Will you please take the horse to the front and wait with him?'

'Of course, my Lord,' Greer said, as he watched Edmond hurry off.

Arriving in the hall again, Edmond dashed up the stairs to his dressing room.

He ran a hand through the front of his hair, wondering where Wilson could have stored his uniforms.

He noticed four trunks standing against the wall. Opening the first, he delved into it but found no sign of a uniform. He did the same with the second and then the third.

Despairing, he started to fling the clothes out of the forth. At the bottom of the trunk, he came across a parcel wrapped in linen.

Undoing the string tying it, with relief, he unfolded the red coat.

'Confound the thing,' he hissed when he saw it was his dress uniform.

'I cannot go riding through the streets of London in this.'

He could think of no other place to look.

The uniform was a magnificent affair covered in frogging and gold braid. White breeches of the softest calfskin; boots, mirror-bright, with real-gold tassels. He scratched his chin, furrowing his brow. He began undressing.

'Nothing for it, but to wear it,' he muttered.

He put it on as fast as he could and looked at himself in the mirror.

'It will have to do,' he said to his reflection, and put on his tricorn hat.

Retrieving the papers from his cast-off coat, he dashed downstairs.

Furlong hid his bewilderment on seeing Edmond in his dress uniform charging down the stairs. He frowned as he watched Edmond disappear through the front door, a blur of red and gold.

When the groom saw Edmond, he walked the horse to him.

'Your horse, my Lord,' Greer said, and handed Edmond the bridle.

'Thank you, Greer,' Edmond said as he swiftly mounted.

He rode off at a gallop, leaving Greer scratching his head.

Frustration filled Edmond as he rode as fast as he could through the London traffic.

At last, he arrived at regimental headquarters, hot,

sweaty, out of breath, his hair, beneath his hat, unkempt. He took his horse to the stables and, now that he knew the way, set off along the maze of passages that led to Colonel Courtney's outer office.

All who beheld him took a second glance. No one dared impede his progress. Without knocking, Edmond entered Beaumont's office.

'Lieutenant Beaumont. Will you please inform the Colonel I am here?'

Beaumont glanced discreetly at Edmond, saying not a word before going to Colonel Courtney.

Once alone with Wilson, Edmond turned to him.

'Where the devil do you keep my uniform?' Edmond growled.

'Most of your trunks are in the attic, Sir,' Wilson said. 'I haven't got round to putting the last of em up, Sir.'

Edmond glowered at Wilson, then laughed.

'Oh, I suppose there is no harm done, Wilson. I feel somewhat conspicuous wearing this, though. Yet, 'tis better than no uniform at all.'

'Yes, Sir,' Wilson said with his irrepressible grin.

Beaumont opened the door to Courtney's office.

'The Colonel will see you now, Major,' he said, holding the door open for him.

Edmond walked into the Colonel's office, whipped off his hat, placing it under his arm, and stood to attention.

Courtney greeted Edmond with a smile.

'Apart from y'r hair, Major, y'r exceptionally smart. The papers, if you please,' Courtney said, holding out his hand.

Edmond took the papers from his pocket. He passed them to Colonel Courtney who read them thoroughly.

While he waited, Edmond tried to gain composure. He ran his fingers through the front of his unruly locks, straightened his stock, and pulled at the front of his jacket.

Courtney folded the papers together. He looked up at Edmond.

'They seem to be in order, Major. Ya may take y'r

sergeant and go. And good luck to ya.'

'Thank you, Colonel. I am obliged,' he said with an elegant inclination of his head.

'If there is ever anything else I can do for ya, St Vere, do come to me. I have enjoyed our little encounter,' he said as he rose, holding his hand out to Edmond.

Edmond shook the outstretched hand.

'Thank you, Colonel. I shall bear your words in mind,' he said.

He formally saluted and smartly retreated from the room.

CHAPTER TWENTY-ONE

Outside the building, Edmond handed Wilson his furlough order.

'Here, keep this in your pocket, Wilson,' Edmond said. 'Can you make your own way home?'

'Of course, I can, Sir. I'll hire a jobbing horse and take the animal back tomorrow,' Wilson said, relief painting a wide grin on his face.

'I think we can do better than that,' Edmond said. He brought Wilson to the stables behind the building.

Edmond looked about him. He spotted a young orderly rubbing down a horse.

·'Ho there, you lad, come here,' Edmond called.

'Yes, Major?' Private Karisdale hurried up to Edmond. He saluted, regarding Edmond's dress uniform in awe, wondering what occasioned the Major to be wearing it.

'I am in need of a horse. Can you help me?' Edmond asked in the commanding tone he hadn't used in weeks.

'I would be happy to saddle one for you, Major,' Karisdale said. He cleared his throat and glanced at Edmond.

'I trust you will not take offence, Sir. I need you to sign the record book,' he said, hoping the Major wasn't the sort of officer who thought they were above army regulations.

'Of course, lad. We have to keep the records straight, do we not? I am glad to see you are so conscientious,' Edmond said.

Karisdale blushed. 'Thank you, Major. Will you come to the office? You may sign the book while I saddle your horse.'

Edmond followed Karisdale into the office.

Karisdale found the right book, opened it at the correct page and handed Edmond a pen.

'I will be back with your horse shortly, Major,' he said, nodded, and left the office.

When Edmond had signed the book, he went to join

Wilson in the stable yard.

Wilson smiled.

'That lad'll go far. Respectful, yet stickin' to the rules.' Wilson smiled and winked.

'You may be right, Wilson.'

Edmond looked about before he spoke again.

'You may take Warrior, Wilson,' he said softly. 'You will find him in the stables behind this. I had better ride the one I am about to borrow in case you are stopped and arrested for horse stealing. I would not like to go through the motions of breaking you out of prison again.'

'Very good, Major,' Wilson said. He tipped his forehead in the hint of a salute and was off towards the other stables.

The trooper returned leading a beautiful, black stallion, whose eyes flashed as he tossed his magnificent head. Edmond eyed him appreciatively.

'What is your name, Lad? Edmond asked.

'Private Karisdale, Sir,' the boy said.

'Well, Karisdale, thank you for your prompt attention. I have signed your book. I shall have the horse brought back to you tomorrow,' Edmond assured him.

'Beg pardon, Major,' Karisdale said, glancing at Edmond before he spoke.

'What is it, Karisdale?' he asked.

The horse shook his head, pawing the ground. Edmond kept a good hold on the bridle and ran a hand down the horse's neck.

'You might find him a bit restive, Sir; he is in need of exercise. The only other horses available were not up to your standard. I thought you would prefer Midnight. He will soon settle down after a good run.'

'Thank you for telling me, Karisdale.'

Edmond mounted Midnight. The horse, eager to be off, sidled while Edmond struggled to hold him in.

'Ha! I see what you mean, lad. I enjoy a challenge. Good day to you.'

Edmond let Midnight have his head. He shot out of the

stables as if chased by devils.

Karisdale watched him go.

Private Pawson came out of the office carrying the record book. He walked over to Karisdale.

'You know who that was, don't you, Karisdale?' he remarked.

'A major. I didn't catch his name,' Karisdale replied.

'Look,' Pawson said, holding out the open book.

'*Major Lord Edmond St Vere*, Karisdale read. 'Pawson, I've heard of him! They say he is one of the best officers in our regiment. Oh-my!'

Edmond took off along the road towards St Martins Lane.

Ladies stared at the handsome major in full-dress uniform riding the magnificent black stallion.

The streets were busy at this time of day. Carriages of every size and description moved at a slow pace. Riders tried to weave their way between them. Midnight strained, wanting to gallop at full tilt. Edmond had difficulty holding him.

'Easy, boy,' Edmond said many times, patting the horse's neck.

When he reached the studio, Edmond rained in Midnight, much to the horse's chagrin. He sidled and tossed his head. Edmond didn't dare dismount.

Seeing a young street urchin sitting on the other side of the road in a doorway, Edmond called to him.

'Ho there, Lad. Come here if you please.'

'You want me to hold the horse, Mister?' the boy said, eager to earn a penny or two.

Edmond laughed. 'No, boy, he would have you for breakfast. Go to that house with the green painted door. Knock on it, for me, if you please. Here, catch,' he added, throwing a silver sixpence to the boy.

The boy caught the coin. When he looked at it, his eyes widened.

'Thanks, Mister!' the boy cried and knocked.

After a moment, a young footman came to the door. He

stared up, astounded at the marvellous sight before him.

'Will you tell Mr Toms that

Major St Vere is here awaiting Mr Luxton and Captain Orpwood,' Edmond called to him.

A small crowd of onlookers gathered on the other side of the road. At sight of them, the horse whinnied, shaking his head. Edmond patted his neck. Midnight pawed the ground, not happy standing still.

The footman left the door open. Edmond watched him racing up the stairs.

Moments later, Edmond heard a clattering. The boy descended again, followed by Simon.

He gazed at Edmond, disbelieving his eyes.

'Uncle, what do you here? Where did you get that horse? My, you look superb!'

Nathan, perforce, descended the stairs more slowly.

'What is causing such a commotion, Simon?' He asked. He caught sight of Edmond.

'Edmond, Good Gad! What a figure you cut! Why the dress uniform? Is that horse yours, he is magnificent!'

Mr Toms joined them in the street. He too was astonished at the sight before him, wondering who the officer was.

Realisation dawned.

'My Lord! I did not recognise you,' he called.

At the noise of their excited voices, the horse reared and showed signs of bolting.

The three men, plus the footman and the urchin pressed their backs against the wall, fearing a trampling.

Edmond expertly held midnight together.

At the sight of the rearing horse, the onlookers on the other side of the road let out oo's and ah's with a general air of enthusiasm. Midnight became further agitated.

'Go. Get your horses. I cannot hold him for long. He is impatient to be off again,' Edmond called as the excited horse wheeled while Edmond fought to control him.

Simon and Nathan hurried off to the Mews for their horses. Mr Toms sent the footman to fetch canvas and charcoal. When Simon and Nathan returned, they found Toms furiously sketching Edmond and the horse.

'Good day, Mr Toms. We will see you tomorrow,' Edmond called. He gave the horse its head. Midnight took off like a bolt of black lightening.

Nathan and Simon followed, doing their best to keep up.

Through the streets, Edmond and the stallion caused mayhem as people assumed Midnight was bolting.

Other riders pulled up their own mounts, moving to the side of the road. Pedestrians pressed themselves into doorways and shop fronts. Occasionally women screamed. Several men shouted in protest. Hearing the commotion, coach drivers guided their carriages out of the way.

Edmond was aware of the dangers that might befall in the crowded streets, yet he enjoyed the exhilaration of the flight. He rose in the stirrups and continued riding along the middle of the road at a thundering gallop.

With Simon and Nathan following close behind, some speculated Edmond was a miscreant, the authorities giving chase. Others concluded that Edmond was the innocent party, chased by footpads.

The incident was fuel for rumour and conjecture, livening up riders and pedestrians alike on a dreary, windswept afternoon.

Reaching Hyde Park, the horse continued to gallop, but now in a safer environment.

They emerged from the park in Kensington, where the streets were more easily negotiable. Midnight, calmer now having enjoyed a good gallop, trotted in a better-behaved manner.

'What a strange afternoon this has turned out to be, Uncle,' Simon said as he rode on one side of Edmond.

'A strange sort of day altogether, Simon,' Edmond remarked. 'I take it you found the studio with no trouble, Nathan?' he asked Orpwood who rode on his other side.

'I did, Sir,' Nathan replied. 'You found Wilson's furlough papers?'

'Yes, Nathan, I did,' Edmond said.

'If I may be so bold, Sir, why the dress uniform?' Nathan tentatively enquired.

'Colonel Courtney insisted I return in uniform. This was the only one I could find.'

'Was Wilson released?' Nathan asked.

Edmond smiled. 'Yes, and I have never seen a man so relieved. I lent him my horse and borrowed this from the stables behind Head Quarters,' he said.

Vere House came into view.

At the gatehouse, Edmond called the gatekeeper.

'Have Miss Sophia and Mrs Luxton returned yet, Harman?' Edmond asked.

'No, my Lord, not yet,' Harman said.

'Good. I have reason to delay their arrival at the house. Please close the gates and lock them,' Edmond instructed.

'I will, my Lord,' Harman replied.

With a frown on his face, Harmon watched the three men ride along the avenue towards the house.

'I'll never understand the goings on o' the gentry,' he said to himself, scratching his head.

'Why did you ask Harman to delay Sophia and my mother, Uncle?' Simon asked, puzzled.

'Because, my dear Simon, I would be hard put to it to account for having you with me while I am wearing my dress uniform, riding a strange horse,' Edmond explained.

'Oh yes, of course, Uncle,' Simon said, nodding vigorously.

As they rode along the gravel drive, they saw Wilson on the lookout for them.

Edmond dismounted handing Wilson the reins.

'A fine lookin' animal they lent you, Major, Sir,' Wilson remarked.

'And a fine handful too, Wilson,' Edmond declared. 'His name is Midnight. When I first mounted him, he was like a demon from Hades. The trooper told me he was restive, not having been exercised. Restive? He was positively manic!'

'He seems to have galloped off his fidgets now, Major,' Wilson said.

'He is placid enough now, Wilson,' Simon said. 'You should have seen the chaos he caused galloping through London. The whole town clamoured to get out of his way.'

'I wish I *had* seen it,' Wilson said, his eyes twinkling.

'I will admit, there were moments I feared for my life,' Edmond said 'I enjoyed the ride, just the same,' he added. He pressed his lips together in an uncertain smile.

Wilson took charge of Nathan and Simon's horses. He led them with Midnight towards the stables, chuckling to himself.

The three entered the hall where they were met by Swithun.

'Will you require refreshments, my Lord?' he asked.

'We will, Swithun. In the drawing room, if you please.'

'Yes, my Lord,' he said, eyeing Edmond's uniform. He made a mental note to ask Wilson about it. He and Wilson had struck up a friendship, Swithun's father having been a sergeant in the infantry.

Edmond showed Orpwood into the drawing room.

'Simon, will you entertain Captain Orpwood while I go to my rooms to change? You will excuse me, Nathan. I do not want Perdita to see me dressed in this. As I said, the fuss and explanations would cause much unpleasantness. I shall be with you shortly.'

Edmond left them, hurrying to his rooms.

He was gratified to find Wilson had tidied away the muddle. Wilson had also left his clothes ready for him to put on. Edmond removed the dress uniform, washed, put on his everyday clothes, and tidied his hair.

Within twenty minutes he returned to the drawing room where Simon and Nathan were conversing amicably over tea and Ratafia biscuits.

'May I offer you brandy, Nathan?' Edmond asked.

'Thank you, Major. Yes, if you please,' Nathan replied.

Edmond poured brandy into two glasses and was about to hand one to Nathan when Perdita and Sophia entered the room.

Edmond turned to them. 'Have you had a pleasant day, Perdita, Sophia?' Edmond asked sipping his brandy.

'Indeed, Edmond. Most gratifying,' Perdita said, making for the couch facing away from the window. Sophia joined her.

'The strangest thing, Edmond. When we arrived at the gatehouse, the gate was locked. It took Peter Coachman an age to get Harman to open them. We must have been waiting a full ten minutes. Do you know anything about it?'

Edmond shrugged. 'I expect Harman was asleep. He is getting on, you know,' Edmond said, looking mystified. Skirting the subject, he said,

'Perdita, may I make known to you to my friend, Captain Nathan Orpwood. Nathan, my sister, Mrs Luxton.'

Nathan rose, going to Perdita who stretched out her hand.

Nathan bowed elegantly over it.

'How do you do, Mrs Luxton. I am pleased to make your acquaintance,' he said.

Perdita smiled.

'There is no need to introduce *me,* Edmond, I recognise Captain Orpwood,' Sophia said. 'Were you not on my Father's staff, Captain?' she asked.

'Yes, Miss Erdington, I was. How good of you to remember me.'

'Are you on leave too, Sir?

'No, Miss Erdington, I am recuperating from a wound,' Nathan said bowing his head to her.

'Oh, I am sorry to hear it, Captain. How did it happen?'

'Sheer accident, Miss Erdington. It mends,' Nathan said modestly.

Swithun came to announce dinner.

'Thank you, Swithun,' Edmond said.

As usual, Perdita, stuck to protocol, rising when dinner came to an end. She motioned Sophia to join her in the drawing room. The men remained in the dining room to drink port.

'Simon, you may come with us, if you please,' Perdita said.

Edmond intervened. 'Perdita, in such a small gathering, I do not think we need be strict regarding social niceties. Simon is more man than boy. He may stay with us.'

Perdita drew breath, about to remonstrate.

Edmond gave her a stern look, at which Perdita realised he would brook no argument.

'As you wish,' she said. With a swish of her skirts, she left for the drawing room with Sophia.

When they had gone, Edmond turned to Nathan.

'You will wonder, Nathan, why I did not want Perdita to know of our exploits this afternoon,' he began.

'I must say, Major, I am somewhat curious,' Nathan said.

Edmond continued. 'I told you about Simon wanting to be an artist. Do you know he is creating paintings, so his work may be assessed?'

'Yes, Sir. I saw some of his work this afternoon.'

'My sister knows nothing of this. She is not in favour of Simon becoming an artist. If I were to tell her the full story of our exploits, the likelihood is Simon's activities would become evident. I deemed it best to say nothing at all.'

'I see, Sir. Surely she will have to know if Simon succeeds in gaining an apprenticeship.'

'Of course, Nathan. Until such time, we must keep her in the dark.'

'Well I, for one, wish you luck, Simon. Your work is magnificent. I am sure you will succeed. A toast to you, lad,' Nathan said and raised his glass. 'To Simon!'

Raising his Glass, 'To Simon,' Edmond said.

CHAPTER TWENTY TWO

As Edmond adjusted his cravat, he glanced at Wilson in the mirror.

'I am sorry for yesterday's debacle, Wilson.'

Wilson, a grim look on his face, avoided Edmond's gaze.

Edmond sat in a straight-backed chair by the mirror to put on his stockings.

'If I had not met Orpwood yesterday, I do not dare think what might have happened.'

'Sir, I don't want to be reminded of it. Let be,' Wilson said, his normally sunny disposition replaced by dour discomfort, as he bent to help Edmond into his boots.

Edmond decided to change the subject to something more positive.

'I mean to resign my commission, Wilson. Do you wish to stay in the Army or leave?' he said, pushing his other foot into his boot.

Wilson looked up into Edmond's face.

'To leave, Major, but what can I do? *I* can't resign. I must return in two months. What happens after that, I haven't a notion.'

'So, you do not wish to stay in the Army, Wilson?' Edmond studied his man, to make sure he understood Wilson's intentions.

Wilson paused, waistcoat in hand, before he replied.

'I have two choices, Sir, serve you or serve the Army. My experience of military life has been both good and bad. From me experience with you, I'd prefer to serve you, Major. How can I leave the Army, though, Sir, without mortal consequences?'

'I think I can buy you out, Wilson,' Edmond said, slipping his arms into the waistcoat Wilson held out for him.

Wilson stood, impassive, reluctant to hope what Edmond said was possible.

Edmond continued, 'I will do my best, Wilson. You have served me well, and I do not want to lose you.'

Edmond did up his buttons.

Wilson gave him a rueful smile and handed Edmond his coat.

'The Army has a way of presenting a body with surprises, Sir. You may not find it possible. But I'd be grateful if you'd try, Sir.'

Wilson looked at Edmond sidelong, assessing Edmond's expression.

'Leave it with me, Wilson, as I said, I will do my best,' Edmond promised.

He put on his coat, then patted Wilson's shoulder. Hat in hand he left to escort Simon on another visit to Mr Toms, leaving Wilson to ponder on the possibility of leaving the Army.

A few days later, Edmond sat behind his desk in his study. He opened a package sent to him by Beaumont. Spreading the papers on his desk, he read them carefully. Edmond smiled with satisfaction. He went to his dressing room where he knew he would find Wilson.

'Wilson, do you know what this is?' he asked, waving the sheaf of papers at him.

Wilson turned to see what Edmond had in his hand.

'I haven't a notion, Major.'

Wilson frowned, wrinkling his nose.

'They are your release papers, Wilson,' Edmond said, a note of triumph in his voice.

Wilson's eyes lit up. For a moment he couldn't speak.

'Major, Sir, I can't thank you enough,' he said when he found his voice.

'I can't repay you, Sir, but I promise I'll serve you for as long as you want me.'

A broad smile covered Wilson's face.

'How did you manage it, Sir?' he asked.

'It was not difficult, Wilson. I thought of contacting Colonel Courtney again, so went to see Beaumont.

'Beaumont told me there was no need to bother the Colonel with a little thing like that. He said he would see to it himself. This morning I received a package from him containing these papers.'

Wilson gave Edmond a knowing wink. 'That lad's a miracle worker, Major, Sir,' Wilson said. 'When I were waiting in his office for you to come back with the furlough orders, he were tellin' me such tales. The people he knows and the strings he can pull are nobody's business.'

'I do believe you are right, Wilson. He has a calm demeanour. He plays his cards close to his chest and makes himself inconspicuous. He would make a good spy if he could speak good French,' Edmond said, glad he had been able to make use of Beaumont's expertise.

Edmond hadn't yet resigned. He thought the Army so perverse, they would somehow foil his intentions if they correlated his resignation with Wilson's release.

He had written that Wilson was now a liability. Although he was eager to serve, Wilson was too old and infirm to be of use to the Army. Out of concern for a conscientious veteran, Edmond was willing to pay for his release. Beaumont had smiled when he read this.

'Excellent, Major. We should have no trouble since you have put the case so eloquently. I will set the wheels in motion, adding a few words of my own. We should hear within the week.'

'Thank you, Beaumont,' Edmond said. 'If there is ever anything I can do for you, do not hesitate to ask.'

Graciously bowing his head, Beaumont replied, 'I shall bear that in mind, Major.'

Beaumont was right. Those in charge of such matters had readily agreed.

Edmond derived great pleasure from Wilson's delight in being free of the Army. On more than one occasion, Wilson had bemoaned never being able to taste civilian life. Edmond wondered whether now he had his freedom, he might lose Wilson anyway. He might find a woman to marry.

It was Edmond's intention to leave the matter of his own resignation for another month, then put in his papers. He would visit Colonel Courtney again.

He realised his first impressions of the man had been mistaken. He thought the Colonel must have been an excellent officer. He could understand his frustration in dealing with tedious paperwork instead of leading men. Edmond now found himself pleasurably anticipating another meeting with Courtney.

On the other hand, the matter of resignation was proving a source of unease the closer it came.

Civilian life seemed alien to him.

Indeed, Sophia occupied his thoughts, but as Perdita had taken over her care, Edmond wondered whether he would have enough to do.

Simon had provided him with an interesting enterprise, but that wouldn't last long.

When he had made up his mind to come home, and take up the cudgels of running his estate, the prospect seemed enticing. Now he felt misgivings. Would he find enough occupation in Crawford Lees to replace his responsibilities as a leader of men? Would he become disillusioned with life, like Colonel Courtney?

Thoughts of Simon jogged his memory. He must speak to Mr Toms regarding Simon's future.

When Edmond and Simon next arrived at the studio, he drew Toms aside.

'Mr Toms, Simon's time with you will soon be at an end. What impression have you formed of his work?'

'He certainly has talent, my Lord,' Toms said. 'I have approached Mr Reynolds to ask whether he will take him on as apprentice. Mr Reynolds was impressed with what Simon has achieved so far. But, he requires Simon to produce more pieces for assessment before he will make a final decision. It will mean that I must hire the studio for another week.'

Edmond eyed Toms with a raised eyebrow.

'Ah, no, my Lord. Do not look at me askance. I do not mean to ask you for more money. You have provided me with more than enough to cover another week's rent,' he said.

Edmond inclined his head. 'I am gratified to hear it, Mr Toms. One more week, you say?'

'Yes, my Lord. I have every confidence Mr Reynolds will accept him.'

'Thank you, Mr Toms. I will inform Simon later today. I am sure he will be more than pleased. Good day to you, Mr Toms.'

'Good day, my Lord,' Toms said, going back into the studio.

Edmond returned at four o'clock to accompany Simon home. They rode west through Hyde Park towards Kensington.

On their way, Edmond broached the subject of Simon's apprenticeship.

'Simon, I must tell you something,' Edmond said as they progressed through the park.

'What is it, Uncle?' Simon asked, worry in his eyes.

'Do not be pessimistic, Simon, it is good news,' Edmond said, amused by the look of apprehension on Simon's face.

Simon immediately brightened. 'Is it about my work, Uncle?'

'It is Simon. Mr Toms has approached Joshua Reynolds about an apprenticeship with him.'

Simon's eyes widened and his lips parted in an enraptured gasp.

'Apparently, Mr Reynolds was impressed by what you have already produced. He would like you to paint more pieces for his appraisal,' Edmond informed him.

So ecstatic was Simon, Edmond feared he would fall from his horse. He caught the bridle when Simon dropped the reins.

'Uncle Edmond, is it true? Does he think so well of my work? Oh, I am in transports! To be apprenticed to one so accomplished and famed as Mr Reynolds! It is beyond my wildest dreams.'

His face glowed with radiant joy. He clutched his hands together on his breast, gazing up into the sky. Edmond wished he hadn't mentioned the subject until Simon had dismounted, safe in the stables.

'Have a care, boy. Take control of your mount, if you please.'

'What?' Simon said, lost in his "transports".

'Oh yes, of course. I am sorry, Uncle,' he said, taking the reins in his hands.

'You must understand, Uncle. This is what I have dreamed of for I-do-not-know how long.'

Abruptly Simon's mood changed.

'Uncle, how are we to tell my mother? She will be averse to my becoming apprenticed—oh, what shall I do?'

Edmond was somewhat irritated by Simon's mercurial mood changes.

'Leave your mother to me, Simon. I will convince her of the advantages of your apprenticeship to Mr Reynolds,' Edmond said, with assurance, but felt anything but assured of Perdita's acquiescence.

Simon was right. It would be difficult to sway her from her antipathy regarding Simon's wish to be an artist.

When Edmond returned with Simon, he left him to wait in the library. Going to Perdita's room, he scratched on the door.

'Come in,' Perdita's low and lazy voice answered.

Edmond entered.

'Good afternoon, Perdita. Are you busy?'

'Not at all, Edmond,' she said, somewhat distracted.

Edmond looked about at the comfortable furnishings, themed in blue and gold.

Perdita had taken possession of the room next to her

anteroom, which she had turned into a boudoir. She spent many afternoons here, sewing or reading or writing letters.

Today, Edmond found her sitting on her blue, velvet-covered daybed. Her eyes inspecting an array of modish gowns hanging on the doors of cupboards or draped on the many chairs dotted about the room.

She turned doleful eyes on her brother.

'Ah, Edmond,' she said, 'I am contemplating my new gowns, and wondering whether the time has come to choose clothes more befitting my age.'

Edmond hid a smile.

'Perdita, you are no more than four years older than I, and *I* am not about to take to a bath chair and wear an old man's hat. Come, my dear, what brought this mournful mood upon you?' He sat beside her on the daybed, taking her hand in his.

'Sophia reminds me of when I was her age—still a child, yet ready to become a woman—our mother bought me a new wardrobe, just as I have for Sophia. I thought on how the years have passed. How, in but four years, she will come out and enter society, and I shall be almost forty. Oh, what an unhappy prospect, Brother, to be sure,' she said, pressing a wisp of handkerchief to her nose.

Edmond patted her hand.

'What nonsense, Perdy. You have many years before you. Why of all the women I know of your age, you are the most handsome, and most youthful.'

That Edmond paid scant attention to any women of *any* age eluded Perdita, and she turned affectionate eyes on him.

'Oh, Edmond, how prettily you speak at times. Thank you. I will not send back the gowns after all, but enjoy wearing them while I may.'

'I think you should, Perdy. After all, if you are to cultivate friendships, you will need to dress fashionably.'

Perdita's eyebrows rose as she smiled with delight at the prospect.

'Why, you may even be invited to a dinner or two or

maybe a route party. You will need to dress well on such occasions,' Edmond said.

'You are right, Edmond. Oh, you have made me feel much more comfortable.'

Still gazing at the gauzy creations, Perdita said, 'Was there a particular reason you came to me?'

'Yes, Perdy. It concerns Simon.'

Edmond tried to keep his tone light.

'Simon?' Perdita said, sitting up straight and alert, a worried frown on her face, her clasped hands resting on her bosom.

'Do not look alarmed, my dear, it is news of good fortune,' Edmond said.

'Good fortune? Oh, Edmond, have you bought him a commission after all?'

Edmond coughed. He realised she still did not perceive Simon's unsuitability for military life.

'Perdita, I must be blunt with you. Simon is a boy of great sensibility. He would never prosper in the Army.' Edmond looked at her intently, a firm jut to his jaw.

'Army life will make a man of him, Edmond. I love him dearly, but how is he to prosper in life if he continues to be shy and retiring?'

She made use of her handkerchief again, shaking her head.

Perdita continued, 'He has a silly notion in his head and wants to be a painter. Now tell me, Edmond, what good is that? How can he make a living from painting?'

'Well, Perdita, I am sorry for being underhanded. I have had his work assessed, and he has great talent, I am told.'

Edmond held his breath, ready for the onslaught he knew was about to come.

Perdita stiffened, dropped her handkerchief, and turned her head slowly towards him.

Her voice deepened an octave, her eyes widened, incredulous.

'You did *what*, Edmond?'

232

'I hired an artist, and a studio, where he went each day. He produced a number of excellent, well-executed pieces. The artist, Mr Peter Toms, is an associate of Mr Joshua Reynolds, of whom I assume you must have heard. Toms suggests Simon take up an apprenticeship with Reynolds.'

Perdita sat still and silent. She regarded Edmond, blinking in disbelief, her mouth open, her head stiffly erect.

'Why did you not inform me?' she said, her voice even, pregnant with wrath.

'I knew you would not allow it,' Edmond said, smiling sweetly.

'You were right!' She rose from her daybed and began to pace.

'If Simon had shown no talent, I would have suggested he do something else—not soldiering,' Edmond added, hastily.

Perdita glared at him.

Edmond's ire rose. He stood up and went to Perdita, towering over her. When he spoke, his voice was deep, quiet, yet powerful.

'Do you know anything of the hardships a soldier endures? We go hungry at times, other times we have no sleep at all. We witness appalling sights during and after a battle, seeing men's blood and guts; the stench of dead bodies is appalling. Army life is harsh and demanding, and no romantic occupation. Do you want to expose your gentle son to such crude brutality? It would not make him, Madam; it would break him!'

Perdita put her hands over her ears.

'Enough! Enough! I do not wish to hear more.'

She bent her head and screwed her eyes tight shut. Edmond leant towards her and pulled her hands from her ears.

'But you must, Perdita; for I want to remove the notion of Simon's becoming a soldier out of your head. He shows great talent and has a passion for becoming an artist.'

Edmond released Perdita's hands. His voice softened.

'Give him a year. If he impresses Reynolds and continues improving, I suggest you allow him to follow his heart. If, after the year, the outcome is not favourable, we will think again.'

Perdita looked up at him and heaved an impassioned sigh.

'Oh,' she breathed, scowling at him. 'I wish you had not deceived me, Edmond.'

Edmond gently took her hand and led her to the daybed. They sat side by side, her hand in his.

'Simon was loath to deceive you, Perdy. Nevertheless, I could think of no other way of doing it.'

She turned her face away from him.

'My dear, I understand you better than he does and I knew you would never agree to it. He told me he tried to dissuade you from wanting him to become a soldier, but you would have none of it. Now, tell me true, would you not be proud of a son who was a famous artist? Hmm?'

Perdita sat still. She sniffed. Turning to Edmond, she took a hard look at him.

'A year you say?'

'A year. Then we assess the situation,' he said gently.

Edmond inwardly breathed a sigh of relief. The battle was won with no casualties.

'May I see his work?' she asked tentatively.

'Of course, you may, dearest,' Edmond said as he rose and went to pull the bell rope.

'Come to the studio with us tomorrow. You will meet Mr Toms, who will sing Simon's praises to you,' Edmond said, and thought, *this is progress indeed.*

In answer to the bell, Swithun knocked at the door.

'Come in,' Edmond said.

Swithun entered.

'My Lord?' he said.

'Yes, Swithun. You will find Master Simon in the library. Escort him here, if you please. When you have done that, fetch Negus for Mrs Luxton, and wine for

Master Simon and me.'

'Yes, my Lord,' Swithun said, and left.

'Simon will be delighted to know you wish to see his work, Perdy. He very much disliked deceiving you, you know. He will be vastly more comfortable now that you know what he has been doing,' Edmond said.

'Hmm,' was all Perdita could say. Her eyes were still stormy, her lips a thin line.

Simon knocked before entering the room. His face white, his eyes enormous, his jaws clamped together; he glanced from his mother to his uncle.

Edmond's tone was light and friendly.

'I have informed your mother of your success with Mr Toms, Simon.'

Simon took a step backwards, his hands clenched by his sides as he looked fixedly at his mother. He swallowed hard before he spoke.

'I am sorry for deceiving you, Mother, but it seems I do have talent and …'

On her dignity, her face imperious, Perdita cut him short.

'Yes, yes, Simon, your uncle informed me of the whole. I shall come with you tomorrow to meet this Toms person and to see your work. I cannot say I approved of the methods used to produce it,'—she shot a disapproving glance at Edmond—'But what is done is done. I have agreed on a year's trial to prove yourself,' she said.

'Oh, Mother! Oh, thank you!' Simon rushed to her and hugged her to his spare frame.

She returned his embrace, patted his back, then put him from her.

'Is there a cost to the apprenticeship?' Perdita asked Edmond.

'Yes, Perdy, but I will take care of that. The cost will probably be less than a commission—I believe you intended to ask me to purchase one?' Edmond's eyes sparkled mischievously.

Silently, she gave him a look that spoke volumes.

'I shall leave the two of you alone to talk.' Edmond said, as he left the room, pleased at the outcome of his machinations.

CHAPTER TWENTY THREE

Edmond wondered with what he would next occupy his time. What of Crawford Lees? The rebuilding of part of it and the refurbishment of the rest would be something to keep him busy.

He decided to explore the matter. He went to his study to write to his agent, Henry Lambert, who would understand better than he what needed to be done. He also wished to inspect the land.

Edmond remembered his astonishment at the estate's vastness. On his previous visit, after the death of his father, he hadn't the time to inspect it. Now he had lots of time. The more he thought, the more he remembered what his initial intention had been.

'I need to organise myself. I must know what needs to be done. I must make plans,' he murmured to himself.

Perdita and Simon were now permanent residents in Vere House, about which Edmond had no qualms. Perdita irritated him occasionally. Most women did, he realised. Simon, he found amusing and was glad to help him.

If he were to go to Crawford Lees, he intended a long stay. Simon and Perdita couldn't come, as Simon's painting necessitated his living near London.

Should I take Sophia with me?

He enjoyed her company. She was interested in everything she saw, and he thought she would take delight in exploring Crawford Lees.

Yes, an excellent plan, he thought

Having come to a decision, he went in search of her.

As usual, he found Sophia by the lake. She wore one of her new gowns, a pale pink satin affair. Pink ribbons mingled with her curls, which flowed down her back.

Edmond smiled. She looked charming when first he saw her with her hair arranged by Perdita's dresser. Today she was more like her old self. She was poking about with a stick at the edge of the lake.

'Sophia!' he called to her as he approached.

She turned, dropped the stick and ran to him, grasping his hand.

'Edmond, there are a lot of tiny frogs. I have met big ones, of course, but never ones so tiny. They are fascinating—come and see!'

She pulled him towards the lake.

His smile widened, and he allowed her to drag him to the water's edge. She bent to scoop water in her hand and caught two little frogs.

'Look at them, Edmond. Are they not beautiful? So tiny, yet so perfect.'

Edmond crouching beside her, and inspected the little creatures. He had to admit he had never seen them in the same light as Sophia did.

Edmond gently tapped one with his finger.

'They are splendid specimens, Sophia. But do you know the ducks will eat them? Some will survive, but most will serve as food.'

'Oh, Edmond, no!' Sophia was horrified.

She put her other hand over the frogs to protect them.

'Is there nothing we can do to save them?'

'Sophia, it is nature. We eat sheep and sometimes lambs. We also eat chickens and ducks. Ducks eat baby frogs.'

He straightening up, dusting off his hands.

'The only thing we might do is take some and put them in a bowl. But you must feed them, and I am not sure what they eat.'

He noticed the hem of her dress was wet and muddy. Her shoes were the same.

'Nature is cruel, is it not?' Sophia said. 'I suppose I must let it take its course.'

She gently placed the small frogs back into the water and ran her hands down the sides of her skirt to dry them.

'Sophia,' Edmond said, hesitantly, 'I am not admonishing you, my dear, but have you seen the state you are in? Your hem is muddy, your shoes are soiled, and now you have left dirty marks on your skirt. For myself, I do not mind, but will not Perdita be annoyed at your treatment of the clothes she chose for you?'

Sophia regarded her spoiled clothes. Her mouth turned down at the corners, and she frowned.

'Oh dear, how thoughtless of me. I must remember to wear my old clothes when I go exploring in your garden, Edmond. I am sorry,' she said, looking up at him with penitent eyes.

Edmond thought her on the verge of tears and quickly changed the subject.

'I left Simon and Perdita discussing Simon's future as an artist,' he said.

A shocked look replaced the penitent one.

'You told her, Edmond?'

'I did. And how astonished I was when she expressed a wish to visit the studio tomorrow.'

'No! Truly?' Sophia laughed, 'I think she must realise what a forlorn hope trying to make a soldier of Simon was. He must be pleased.'

'He is,' Edmond said, glancing at her.

'There is something else I must tell you. When I resign my commission, I plan to go to Crawford Lees to assess what needs to be done.'

Sophia straightened her back. She looked at him solemnly, her head tilted to one side. A habit she had that always reminded him of a little bird.

'How long will you be gone?' she asked. He saw tears gathering in her eyes.

'Several months, at least. A lot of work needs to be done, as I remember.'

He paused, looking at her sad face.

'I wondered whether you would like to come with me?' he asked.

Her face brightened immediately. She rushed forward and threw her arms around him, hugging him tightly.

'I would miss you so dreadfully if you went away for such a long time. May I really come with you?'

Edmond was taken aback by this sudden and almost aggressive display of affection. He stood with his hands outstretched a little, not knowing quite what to do. Then he embraced her. As he did so, warm regard for her came over him.

How dear this daughter has become to me.

'Well, my dear,' he said as he let her go. 'When finished, it will be your home, too. You may have some say in what is done. Besides, there is a lot for you to explore. You have a passion for exploring, have you not?'

'When I was with my father, I was closely confined with no freedom at all to look at anything. I revel in the freedom I now have. But I thought you had already resigned your commission?'

'No, not yet. I shall wait another few weeks. They will have forgotten about my buying Wilson out by then.'

'Be sure you do resign, Edmond. I do not want them to cart you off to war again. I lost one father; I do not wish to lose another.'

'No fear of that, my dear, I am done with war and fighting. It is strange to me, no longer being in the Army, and thinking of not going back. If I work on making Crawford Lees habitable again, it will keep my feet from itching to be with the regiment.'

'Do you miss the regiment so much, Edmond?'

'I have to admit, sometimes I do, Sophia. It is natural to do so since I have been soldiering for more than twelve years. I shall adapt in time, no doubt.'

'You left because of me, I think, Edmond.'

Tears formed again in her eyes.

'No, Sophia, I decided when your father...after your father died, I had enough of it. You made the decision easier to realise. Never blame yourself for my resignation. I wanted to do so for a while before we ... before we married.'

The conversation was becoming difficult. He never mentioned her father or their marriage to her. Now he had mentioned both.

'Sophia, are you still uncomfortable about our marriage?' he asked, putting a hand on her shoulder.

'Oh, no, Edmond. You are not at all husbandly. I could not wish for a more thoughtful and generous guardian. I could never survive without you.'

I believe without her, neither would I survive outside the Army.

'Then I am content. Now come. You must remove those soiled clothes before Perdita sees you. She will not be in a pleasant mood, having lost her battle regarding Simon becoming a soldier, and she will give you a set down for the state of your clothes.'

'I shall race you to the house, Edmond! But you must give me a head start.'

Gathering up her skirts in a most unseemly way, she bounded off.

'Hoyden,' he murmured to himself as he ran after her.

CHAPTER TWENTY FOUR

'You miss it, don't you, Sir?' Wilson asked.

'I do, Wilson, some of it,' Edmond replied, as he put on his coat. It smelled fresh and clean. His breeches and waistcoat seemed whiter than ever before, too.

Wilson had retrieved Edmond's regular uniform from the trunk in the attic. He had cleaned and pressed the red coat, white waistcoat and breeches, polished his boots, and oiled his leathers.

Edmond caught the whiff of oil when he secured his leathers, bringing memories of days soon to be left behind.

Adjusting his lariat, Edmond regarded himself in the mirror. He shook his head and smiled ruefully at Wilson.

'I miss the edge, the wound-up nerves before a battle. I am not sure I miss the fighting, although I miss the exhilaration of first engagement. I miss having my men about me, looking after their welfare and keeping them in order.'

Having let a month pass, Edmond was preparing to go to his Regimental Headquarters again. He stood straight and tugged at his stock, then looked back at Wilson.

'Still, I do not miss the carnage left in the aftermath of battle.

He expression became serious.

'The death of Colonel Erdington was beyond endurance.'

Edmond paused, gazing into the distance, thinking of his friend.

'I saw comrades killed before and was moved by their loss. Somehow, John's passing was the worst blow I have ever experienced—worse even than when my father died.'

Wilson's voice was quiet.

'I know, Sir.'

There's nothin' I can do to soften this mood of his. Today is goin' to be a difficult time for him, resignin', Wilson thought.

'Can't say I miss any of it, Sir,' Wilson said with a sniff and put Edmond's boots before him. 'I only joined 'cos I had no other means of employment. I learned quick to keep m'yead down and not get into no trouble. It were a step up for me when they put me to serve you, Sir. So, I'm happy to be out o' the Army an' happy to serve you here instead o' there—if you understand me, Sir.'

'I do, Wilson,' Edmond said, trying to shake off his restiveness.

'And a good job you make of looking after me. Why, I can almost see my face in these boots.'

Edmond worked his feet into the boots and turned once more to the mirror.

'Will I do, Wilson? This is probably the last time I shall ever wear it, you know.'

'You'll do, Sir. I pride meself on turning you out well. An' I made a special effort today. You're a fine figure of a man, an' no mistake.'

Tears came to Wilson's eyes. He took out his handkerchief and blew his nose.

'Stop that now, Wilson, or you will have me blubbering, too.'

Edmond picked up his white calfskin gloves and his hat. Leaving Wilson in the dressing room, he made his way to the stairs.

Having finished breakfasting together, Sophia and Perdita emerged from the morning room. Seeing Edmond walking slowly down the stairs, dressed in his uniform, they stopped to regard him.

'La, Edmond, I do not think I have ever seen you look so handsome,' Perdita remarked, looking with pride at her younger brother. 'You are the picture of importance.'

Perdita stepped back, looking Edmond up and down, taking in every detail. She walked around him unhurriedly, the better to inspect him.

Sophia found pleasure in seeing Edmond dressed in a way familiar to her. While serving in the Army in wartime, civilian clothes were rarely worn.

'I have often seen you looking like that, Edmond, when you came to dinner at our billet. I had forgotten how good you look in your uniform.'

Edmond chuckled.

'Between Wilson and the pair of you, I shall not be able to get my hat on my head—it will be so swollen with pride. Perhaps, with so many compliments, I should not resign at all. Perhaps I should simply walk up to the enemy and dazzle them into submission.'

Sophia laughed, imagining Edmond, tall and straight, brandishing his sword at a fleeing army.

Possessively, Perdita brushed an imaginary speck of dust from Edmond's sleeve.

Furlong arrived in the hall from the kitchen, carrying a tray under his arm, on his way to the morning room. Sophia waylaid him.

'Furlong, do you not think Edmond is beautiful?' she asked.

Furlong stopped and viewed Edmond from head to toe. He cleared his throat.

'Beautiful is not a word I would use to describe his Lordship. However, I shall say, he looks very grand. He is the epitome of a British officer, Miss Sophia.'

Allowing the hint of a smile to touch his lips, Furlong bowed his head to each of them, before continuing to the morning room.

'That, I think, is the longest speech I have ever heard him utter,' Edmond said, his shoulders shaking as he tried to suppress his laughter. 'I am highly honoured.'

The banter helped to lighten his mood.

'I must take my leave of you, Ladies,' he said as he bent to kiss Perdita's cheek.

'I shall walk with you to the stables, Edmond,' Sophia said, threading her arm through his.

They left by the front door, walking along the gravel path to the end of the house.

'You will no longer be 'Major' when you return, will you, Edmond?' Sophia remarked.

'No, Sophia. Although it will take a day or two to process my papers,' Edmond explained.

Sophia looked at him in alarm.

'They cannot make you go to war in those few days, can they Edmond?' She bit her lower lip.

'No Sophia. They cannot. Stop worrying, my dear,' Edmond counselled as he put his hand over hers, gripping it tightly. The firm touch of his hand reassured her.

The stable block lay some fifty yards from the house. A long low brick structure, two wings at right angles to each other.

One wing accommodated thirteen horses. Eight carriage horses, three more for Edmond's own use, and another two for Sophia and Simon.

From this wing, a strong smell of horse permeated the air as three young stable lads mucked out the stalls.

Ten stable hands' quarters stood above the other wing. Four coaches were housed below. A large room at the end of the building stored equipment, including that of the blacksmith. His shelter abutted the end wall. This served the purpose of a small forge.

Edmond and Sophia heard the clang of hammer on anvil as the blacksmith worked at fashioning a shoe for the carriage horse patiently waiting nearby to be shod.

'Ho, Greer!' Edmond called when they reached the stables.

A small, wiry man, a deal older than Edmond, walked from a stall.

'Is Pandora ready?' Edmond asked.

'Yes, my Lord. I'll lead her out to you in a moment,' he said, wiping his hands on a towel.

'Why is your mare called Pandora, Edmond?' Sophia asked as they waited in the yard.

'Have you not heard the Greek legend, Sophia?'

Sophia shook her head.

'Ah, then I must tell it to you. Briefly, the legend goes that Pandora was told dire consequences would ensue if she opened a particular box. Being inquisitive, the woman did not heed the warning. When she lifted the lid, all the ills that plague mankind were released,' Edmond declared with relish.

'Gracious me!' Sophia exclaimed.

'Yes, indeed. When I discovered that my mare was exceedingly inquisitive, I named her accordingly,' Edmond informed her.

'Do you always name your horses appropriately?' Sophia asked.

'Invariably,' Edmond replied.

Greer led the mare out and checked the girth.

'What will you do with yourself today, Sophia?' Edmond asked.

'I have nothing planned, Edmond. Perdita is to pay some morning calls. I did not want to go. It is such a fine day. I thought it a shame to waste it. Simon, of course, is off to the studio this afternoon,' Sophia replied.

'Do you notice a difference in Simon, Sophia? He seems to be losing much of his shyness.'

'Indeed he is, Edmond. He is in his element and can talk of nothing but his experiences with Mr Reynolds. I am very happy for him,' Sophia said, smiling.

Greer gave Edmond the reins.

'Thank you, Greer,' Edmond said.

'A pleasure, my Lord,' Greer replied. He walked back into the stables, calling for the stable lads to hurry with their chores.

Edmond mounted.

'Adieu, Sophia. I hope you enjoy your day.'

Sophia laid her hand on Edmond's booted leg. She put her head back to look up at him, her face serious, her eyes big with concern.

'All will be well, will it not, Edmond? I suddenly feel uneasy. There is no chance they will not allow you to resign, is there?'

He leant down and put his hand under her chin.

'No, my Little One, no chance at all. I have no intention of going to war again, so do not fear. I shall probably be back for luncheon. Then you may pack your bags, and we will be off to Crawford Lees as soon as we may.'

'Adieu Edmond,' Sophia said, doing her best to smile.

Edmond put his hand on the bridle and Sophia stepped back as he spurred the mare.

She watched him ride along the gravel drive towards the gatehouse.

When she could see him no more, she whispered,

'Dear God, please keep him safe. Let nothing untoward happen.'

Edmond enjoyed his ride through the park from Kensington to London.

Arriving at the outskirts of the city, he slowed to a leisurely pace. Once at his Headquarters, he rode to the stables and left his horse with an orderly. Walking to the main entrance, he made his way along the now familiar maze of corridors straight to Beaumont's office.

Edmond removed his hat and ran his hand over his hair before knocking.

Beaumont's voice bid him enter.

'Good morning, Lieutenant Beaumont. Will you ask Colonel Courtney if I may speak with him?'

'Certainly, Major St Vere. I am sure he will see you. If you will wait a moment, I'll ask him,' Beaumont replied.

He left his desk, heading for the Colonel's office.

Alone, on the brink of a life-changing deed, the enormity of the step he was taking gave Edmond a momentary jolt. His face became serious.

He looked out of the window. A blustering breeze drove rain from a passing shower spattering against the pane.

Feeling despondent he turned from the window. He glanced about Beaumont's room. The neatness of the lieutenant's desk caught Edmond's eye. The ticking of a clock measured the passing seconds. Edmond wondered how long he would have to wait.

As he thought of the career he was about to abandon, an aching unease covered his mind, smothering his resolve. Sick apprehension gripped him.

'It is not too late to turn back,' a voice whispered in his mind.

Ah, I have made my decision. I cannot turn back now, he thought in response. He took several measured breaths in an attempt to pull himself together.

Before he could contemplate further, Beaumont returned.

'The Colonel will see you now, Major,' he said, holding the door open for Edmond to enter.

Colonel Courtney stood before his desk. Both men bowed their heads in greeting. Edmond gripped the hand Colonel Courtney held out to him.

Unlike the first time Edmond saw him, the Colonel's face was wreathed in smiles, his attitude jovial.

As he smiled, the Colonel thought,

I shall take pleasure in sharing some of my morning with a man with whom I feel comfortable.

'Good morning, Major St Vere. Do not tell me y'r sergeant has been arrested again?' he asked as he took his seat behind his desk.

Edmond smiled.

'No, Sir, I am here to inform you I wish to resign my commission. I should probably go through other channels, but you dealt with me with such effectiveness the last time, I thought perhaps I would come to you again.'

The Colonel sat back in his chair, at his ease.

'I enjoyed our last encounter, Major. I thought when Beaumont said ya wanted to see me, I was to uncoil another calamity. Tell me, why d'you wish to resign? Had enough, eh? What is it, twelve years' service?'

Edmond nodded.

'Yes, Sir. Twelve years. There are a number of reasons for my decision. Basically, I want no more of blood and killing. The death of Colonel Erdington moved me more than I can say.'

Edmond lowered his eyes.

The Colonel leant forward.

'Ya will miss the action, St Vere. Civilian life can be tedious compared to life in the Army.'

Edmond lifted his chin.

'I know, Sir. I find the adjustment is taking time. Yet, I feel it is the path I must follow.'

Edmond's words *sounded* positive. Now that the moment had come, his thoughts were a different matter. They shifted from elation to regret and back again.

Colonel Courtney looked Edmond steadily in the eyes.

'I understand y've a fourteen-year-old wife, Major.' The Colonel said, shifting in his chair.

Edmond coloured and gave him back look for look.

'Do you also know why I married her, Sir?'

'I dare not imagine, Major.'

The Colonel eased his position again, eyes narrowing. He paused. He had taken Edmond for a man of integrity. Marrying a fourteen-year-old girl seemed at odds with his character.

'Ya may tell me if ya wish. Take a seat.'

The Colonel gestured to the chair beside his desk.

Edmond nodded and sat, ill at ease. His mouth stiffened. He knew exactly what Colonel Courtney was thinking. Glad of the opportunity to explain the matter, he took a breath and began,

'Briefly, Colonel, before her father died, he gave her into my care. She had no English relatives, and so was not permitted to enter the country. Hence, I married her and brought her home. I hasten to add, our marriage is in name only. My Sister has come to live with us and has taken charge of her.'

'Ah …' the Colonel said, lifting his chin, his tension lessening. 'Now I understand. A most commendable arrangement, Major.'

Edmond sat back in his seat, his stiff posture eased. His mouth curved into a smile.

The Colonel cleared his throat.

'Are ya sure ya need to resign? Surely, this sister of yours can take care of the girl in y'r absence? We are at war, ya know, and y'r one of our most experienced officers. Perhaps, if we offered ya the position of Lieutenant Colonel, would that tempt ya not to resign?'

Edmond tilted his head to one side, a smile on his face as he glanced at Courtney. His hand gripped the arm of his chair. He paused, gathering his thoughts.

If only Colonel Courtney knew of the struggle I suddenly find myself going through. Why do I have misgivings? I decided on this months ago. I must be more resolute, he thought.

When he spoke, his voice gave away nothing of his unease.

'I knew promotion was a probability, Colonel. But I think not, Sir. My mind is made up. Nevertheless, I appreciate the offer. I promised Colonel Erdington I would care for his daughter, and I mean to be true to my word,' Edmond explained.

He shifted forward in his seat, explaining further.

'My deep responsibility to Colonel Erdington and his daughter is the main reason I shall not change my mind. I have confidence in the rightness of my decision.'

Voicing his resolve dispelled the last of his misgivings.

The twisted knot in his stomach evaporated. His hand gripping the chair relaxed.

'Y'r indeed a man of integrity, St Vere. I shall grant y'r request. If I had a choice in the matter, I would not.'

Edmond held his breath. His jaw tightened as a small frown gathering.

Seeing Edmond tense, the Colonel smiled.

'Do not fear, Sir, I shall not stand in y'r way,' he said with empathy.

Edmond breathed again as the Colonel rang his bell.

Beaumont entered.

'Colonel?' he questioned.

'Fetch me whatever papers are necessary in the case of an officer wishing to resign, Beaumont.'

Beaumont, his face impassive, glanced at Edmond.

'Yes, Colonel,' he said, taking a longer look at Edmond before he left the room.

'Ya say y'r having difficulty adjusting, Major?'

'Yes, Colonel. It is only to be expected. I have known no other life for the past twelve years.'

'What will ya do with y'r self?' The Colonel asked, frowning.

'My estate in Oxfordshire is somewhat run down. I mean to bring it back to what it once was. That should keep me occupied,' Edmond explained.

'Ya could always attend parliament, ya know. That is what I'd do in y'r shoes.'

'Oh, I think not, Colonel. If I thought I would make a difference, I might. I doubt I would,' Edmond said, even as he found himself considering the Colonel's suggestion.

Beaumont returned with the necessary papers, halting further discussion on the subject.

The papers were drawn up in advance, with gaps left to fill in name, rank and any other pertinent information to be written in.

Colonel Courtney signed the papers with a flourish and handed them to Edmond.

'You must sign below the Colonel's signature, Major. I will fill in all the details, and send your copy to you within a few days. Other papers must be completed, hence the slight delay. When you receive it, your resignation will take effect,' Beaumont explained.

'Thank you, Beaumont,' Edmond said, regarding the documents a moment before he signed.

The signatures emphasised the finality of his action. There was no going back. Calm acceptance filled him.

So ends my military career, Edmond thought.

'May I offer ya refreshment before ya go, St Vere?' Colonel Courtney offered.

Colonel Courtney's words broke in on Edmond's musings. He didn't have the heart to refuse and nodded his assent.

251

Beaumont produced a bottle and glasses from a cabinet. The Colonel poured two generous measures of Cognac as Beaumont left the room.

'So, Edmond, y'r now, in effect, a civilian,' the Colonel observed.

Edmond chuckled. 'Is it permitted that a civilian wear an officer's uniform?'

'No, Major. I did say *in effect*. As Beaumont told you, y'r still a major until ya receive y'r papers.'

Edmond took a sip of his brandy.

'I explained this to Sophia before leaving this morning. She worries in case they call me off to war in the meantime. Poor child. She misses her father and feels I have replaced him. She is afraid she will lose me, too,' Edmond explained.

'I shall make it ma business to ensure they do not,' the Colonel promised.

'I did not tell Sophia, but it is something which the powers that be are perfectly capable of doing,' Edmond remarked.

'It is so, Edmond. A necessary evil, I'm sorry to say. There is a job to be done. Nothing must stand in its way,' the Colonel said.

'Oh yes,' Edmond granted with regret, 'Rules must be upheld at all costs. Yet, when it suits them, the rules can be bent, or completely ignored, with facility. I am sorry, Colonel, I am somewhat disillusioned with the Army and its uncompromising regulations.'

Edmond finished his brandy. The Colonel replenished his glass.

'I take y'r point, Edmond. This attitude within the Army is what makes ma occupation even more tedious.'

The Colonel sighed as he poured more brandy into his own glass.

Edmond continued.

'In the field, they insist on sticking to stratagems that in modern times are obsolete, Colonel. Time and time again one comes against stubborn pride in the most senior

252

officers who will not listen to reason.'

Edmond warmed to his subject, glad to get his grievances off his chest.

The Colonel shook his head. He regarded Edmond with even more respect. Most certainly a man after his own heart.

'Everything has to go through slow and laborious channels. By the time they have done so, opportunities are missed,' the Colonel lamented.

'Exactly, Sir,' Edmond agreed with enthusiasm. 'Not only that. One never knows where one is with government policy. Between you and me, Sir, I believe corruption is rife in the government,' Edmond said, an angry glint in his eye.

'Undoubtedly! Yet, not all politicians are corrupt. I come across good men at times.'

The Colonel looked at Edmond with a thoughtful frown.

'Of course, ya could do something about the corruption y'r self, St Vere,' the Colonel suggested with a nod and a smile as he refilled their glasses again.

Edmond gave a short laugh.

'I, Colonel? How so?'

'Y'r a peer of the realm, entitled to sit in The House,' Colonel Courtney stated.

He sipped his brandy, looking at the reflected light glinting on the glass as he rolled it between his palms.

'I think not, Sir,' Edmond repeated.

Nevertheless, his face wore a contemplative expression. He had never been interested in politics, apart from where it effected the Army. Would he make a difference? He frowned and took more brandy.

'Think on it, Edmond. It would do no harm, and ya might do some good,' The Colonel suggested.

The brandy decreased in the bottle as Edmond and Courtney, in convivial mood, continued to converse.

Looking at his pocket watch the Colonel realised he was hungry.

'Will ya have luncheon with me, St Vere?' he asked.

'I will, Colonel, with the greatest of pleasure,' Edmond, full of bonhomie and good brandy, agreed.

'Then let us go to ma rooms where we may be more comfortable, Major,' Courtney invited.

He left his desk and went to Beaumont's office in the next room. Edmond rose from his seat. He adjusted his waistcoat and putting on his hat, followed the Colonel.

Beaumont stood, looking to the Colonel for instructions.

'We are going to ma rooms for luncheon, Beaumont. I'm sure there will be nothing of any great importance that will warrant disturbing us. There never is.'

CHAPTER TWENTY FIVE

While Edmond and Colonel Courtney conversed over luncheon in the Colonel's private quarters, eight burly soldiers, led by a sergeant, marched smartly in file around the perimeter of the parade ground towards the officer's quarters.

'Halt!' the Sergeant commanded. The group of soldiers ceased marching with a stamp of their booted feet as they stood to attention.

'At ease, men,' the Sergeant called.

The soldiers stood with hands behind their backs, their feet apart.

'Remember what we agreed, lads. Stay here 'til I come out. If we've no luck with Colonel Courtney, we'll all stand here 'til we do, no matter what the cost. Are you all still with me?'

'Sergeant!' the eight soldiers chorused in affirmation.

The large, barrel-chested sergeant walked briskly up the steps, through the door and into the lobby of the officer's quarters.

A staircase rose from the middle of the sparsely furnished lobby.

Two chairs stood to the right of the staircase, a desk to the left.

Behind this desk sat a youthful soldier.

'I want to speak to Colonel Courtney on a matter life-n-death,' the Sergeant stated.

The fresh-faced Cornet Longley looked at the Sergeant in some confusion. He was temporarily standing in for the duty officer, who had been called away to attend a disturbance at the main gate.

'He is not available at the moment, Sergeant. You must make an appointment,' Longley said, nervously eyeing the determined-looking infantryman.

The Sergeant's lip curled, a menacing gleam in his eye.

'I don't want no appointment. I told you, it's a matter

o' life-n-death. I want to see 'im now,' he demanded, slapping his palm on the desk.

'Well … Well … You can't,' Cornet Longley said, belligerently. He rose, coming around the desk to face the Sergeant, who towered over him.

'Where are his rooms?' the Sergeant asked, leaning threateningly close to Longley.

'I can't tell you that!' the cornet squeaked.

The Sergeant glared into Longley's eyes.

'Bah!' he exclaimed, pushing Longley out of the way. The Sergeant walked around the desk where several large books lay open. He looked carefully at each one. Plucking up a register, he was pleased to see a list of the occupants of the building on the front page. Although his reading ability wasn't great, he made out the name "Courtney", and beside it the room number.

'Put that down. You have no right …' Longley spluttered as he blocked the Sergeant's path to the stairs.

'Ah, ya bloody fool, stand aside,' the Sergeant snarled, barging past the now terrified youth.

'I'll call out the guard!' Longley shouted.

Half-way up the stairs, the Sergeant paused. He turned towards Longley.

'By all means. But I think you'll find they're otherwise engaged at the main gate,' the Sergeant stated, baring his teeth in a knowing smile.

Turning back, the Sergeant bounded up the rest of the stairs.

At the top, he found himself in a quiet corridor smelling pungently of polish. He walked slowly along the corridor, reading off the numbers on each door.

He came to number twelve and knocked.

'Enter,' Colonel Courtney's voice invited.

The Sergeant opened the door and saw two men seated at a table; empty plates pushed to one side. A bottle of port stood before them.

The Sergeant chose to speak to the officer in the Colonel's uniform.

'Am I addressing Colonel Courtney?' the Sergeant asked, breathing heavily.

'Ya are. May I ask to whom I am speaking?' the Colonel enquired, astonished to see an enlisted man in officer's quarters.

'Sergeant Sam Hargreaves, Colonel. I've come here to seek justice, Sir.'

'May I ask how ya got in here, Sergeant?'

'I'm sorry Colonel. That's not important now. I'm here on a matter of life-n-death.'

The Colonel gave Hargreaves a questioning stare. Casually picking up his port, he slowly sipped before speaking.

'Are ya, Sergeant Hargreaves? Indeed!'

The Colonel shifted his position.

'Have ya not thought, perhaps bursting in on me like this might prejudice y'r cause? Why do ya not go through the proper channels?'

The Sergeant nodded, his mouth bitter.

'We tried that, Sir, but had no success. As a last resort, we asked to speak to you, Sir. We've heard you're a fair man. But they wouldn't let us see you, so we thought to do it this way.'

Edmond looked sharply at Hargreaves.

'We? Who is "we", Sergeant?' Edmond asked.

'Me and eight privates waiting outside, Sir.

Edmond rose and went to the window. Glancing out, he saw the eight soldiers in two ranks standing below.

Edmond turned, moving towards Hargreaves.

'Sergeant, will you please tell us exactly what this is about?' Edmond asked, his face impassive.

'It's about Corporal Benson, Sir. He's bin found guilty o' murder, Sir, and is to be executed tomorrow. But we all knows he didn't do it, Major, Sir.'

The Colonel and Edmond glanced at each other.

'He was tried by court-martial?' Colonel Courtney asked.

'Yes, Sir. An' we think it were fixed, Sir.'

Edmond's chin came up, his eyes narrowed.

'Oh? And why do you think that, Sergeant?' he enquired.

Hargreaves expression was grave.

'Because, Major, the chief witness was the one who done the girl in, and him bein' an officer, he were believed,' he replied, his eyes moving between the two officers.

'We never got a chance to speak. Ned was with us the whole evening. We was all together in the barracks, Sir, waitin' to go back to our regiment, so we knows he din't do it. Anderson always had it in for Ned and …'

Edmond gave him a swift glance and interrupted.

'Do you, by chance, speak of Captain Jason Anderson?'

'Yes, Sir, I do,' Hargreaves said, surprised.

Edmond turned to Courtney. 'The man is known to me, Sir,' Edmond stated, his mouth stiff, his eyes angry.

The Colonel shot a look at the tight-lipped Edmond. He rose, turning to Sergeant Hargreaves.

'I understand y'r concern, Sergeant. If an injustice has been done, I pledge ya ma word, I shall get to the bottom of it,' the Colonel promised him.

Hargreaves cleared his throat.

'Beg pardon, Colonel, but Corporal Benson is due to be executed tomorrow, Sir,' Sergeant Hargreaves said with urgency.

'Then I shall order a stay of execution,' Colonel Courtney assured him.

A knock at the door heralded the entrance of Lieutenant Beaumont and Cornet Longley. Beaumont frowned.

'Do you want this man removed, Colonel?' Beaumont asked, eyeing Hargreaves with suspicion.

'All is well, Beaumont. He means no harm. He has come to me to see justice done,' the Colonel said, turning to Hargreaves.

'I suggest ya go back to y'r barracks. When I discover more of this matter, I shall send for ya. I shall give

Benson's case ma full attention.'

'Beg pardon, Colonel, but could you come and tell the men that. They feel strong about Ned. They won't be fobbed off,' Sergeant Hargreaves stated, his mouth stern, his eyes boring into Courtney.

'I will go, Colonel,' Edmond offered. 'Lead the way, Sergeant.'

Beaumont shot a questioning look at the Colonel who nodded his assent.

Cornet Longley watched the episode, awe-struck at being in the exalted company of a colonel, a major and Lieutenant Beaumont, who was well known to everyone as a man who "got things done".

Edmond followed Sergeant Hargreaves along the corridor, down the stairs and out to the parade ground.

He stood at the top of the steps to observe the group of men, standing at ease before him.

One of the men caught sight of Edmond.

'Ere, boys, it's Major St Vere!' he exclaimed.

All eyes turned on Edmond who regarded them with a stony stare.

The men's hands dropped to their sides, and with a loud stamp of feet, they stood to attention as one.

Sergeant Hargreaves addressed his companions.

'Colonel Courtney's agreed to look into Ned's case, lads. He says he'll give it his full attention.'

The men looked dubious, glancing at each other.

Edmond sensed their misgivings.

'You may trust Colonel Courtney, and you may also trust me. I shall give him my best assistance,' Edmond stated in a clear, commanding voice.

The men's faces brightened as they nodded to each other.

'Thank you, Major,' Sergeant Hargreaves said, standing to attention and saluting.

Edmond watched as the Sergeant took charge of his men, marching them off the parade ground, back to their barracks.

Edmond returned to Colonel Courtney's cosy dining room.

He found the Colonel standing by the window smoking a cheroot as he watched Sergeant Hargreaves, on the other side of the parade ground, marching off with his men in the direction of their barracks.

'Is all well, Major?' The Colonel asked when Edmond entered the room.

'I believe it is, Sir,' Edmond answered.

The two men resumed their seats. The Colonel poured port for each of them.

'Ah, St Vere, it appears every time ya visit me, ma boredom is alleviated. Ya say Anderson is known to you?' Colonel Courtney asked.

'Yes, Sir. I served with him some years ago, and a worse swine I have yet to meet.'

Edmond put his clasped hands before him on the table.

'He treated the men under him with brutality and took pleasure in doing so. He is perfectly capable of murdering a woman. His uncle is Major General Anderson, who has pulled strings in the past to get his nephew out of hot water. I would not be surprised if such has happened in this case.'

Edmond picked up his glass, taking a grateful drink of his port.

The Colonel inhaled a long breath and shook his head.

'This sort of thing disgusts me, St Vere. The Army has too many like them. Far too many. Fighting the enemy calls for a certain amount of dispassionate brutality. But brutality towards one's own? Ah! It sickens me. So does corruption,' he said, grimacing.

'There was little I could do to stop him as he outranked me at the time. Even had I been a major then, anything I did would invariably have been quashed,' Edmond said.

'I am not without friends in high places, ma self,' the Colonel confided. 'I shall contact General Greengate. He is a man of integrity. He will see justice done. If he is not in the country, I can call upon others.'

The Colonel picked up his wineglass, sat back and

drained it.

'We must get back to ma office, St Vere where we can get our teeth into this. I shall enjoy having something concrete to do, other than the tedious paperwork I am saddled with,' he said.

Their chairs scraped as the two men rose. Going from the room to the corridor, they made their way down the stairs and into the open.

They strolled across the barrack square in companionable conversation, both with hands behind their backs.

'So, St Vere, is it tedious being tied to this young ward of yours?' the Colonel asked, intrigued by Edmond's situation.

'Not at all, Colonel. I have had little contact with young people of her age. Yet, I find her refreshing. She is a mischievous young thing, very bright and inquisitive. My own daughter died at birth. I have often regretted not knowing her. Sophia gives me some insight into what being a father entails.'

'I never married ma self. Sometimes I wish I had. I'm probably too old and set in ma ways by now,' Colonel Courtney said, looking into the distance.

'Ah, Colonel, do not say so. One never knows what the future holds. This time last year I would never have believed I would be in the situation I am in now.'

The Colonel shrugged.

'What will be will be, Edmond.'

CHAPTER TWENTY SIX

When they arrive at the administrative building, on their way to his office, Colonel Courtney turned to Edmond.

'One thing ya must do for me, St Vere. It is likely the prisoner is held here. I want ya to visit him and ask him what happened—best from the horse's mouth, eh? One of ma lieutenants will help you.'

Beaumont rose from his seat when the Colonel entered his office.

'Beaumont,' the Colonel said, 'will ya find Lieutenants Roswell and Sherlund. Tell them I must see them in ma office immediately, if you please.'

'Of course, Colonel, at once, Sir,' Beaumont said, with the usual click of his heels. He left his office to instruct one of his minions to find the two lieutenants.

'I think Beaumont heard a good deal of what this is about, St Vere. Will you tell him what we propose when he comes back?' Courtney asked.

'I will, Colonel,' Edmond replied.

When he returned, Edmond gave Beaumont the details of the situation.

'We are not sure whether Benson is being held here, Beaumont,' Edmond said as he finished explaining.

'I shall make enquiries about that, Major,' Beaumont said. He went to the door and called for Corporal Browning, who came hurrying at Beaumont's command.

'Go to the basement and ask whether a Corporal Benson is imprisoned there, Browning,' Beaumont told him.

As Browning left, Lieutenant Roswell arrived.

Beaumont showed him into Colonel Courtney's office.

Edmond sat beside Beaumont's desk, impressed by the young lieutenant's quiet efficiency.

While they waited, Browning returned with the news that Benson was imprisoned in the basement.

The Colonel's little bell rang, at which sound,

Beaumont rose and entered the Colonel's office. He returned moments later.

'Lieutenant Roswell will go with you to where Benson is held, Major St Vere,' he said.

Accompanied by Roswell, Edmond made the same trip to the basement as he had done when Wilson was under arrest.

The same sullen sergeant came out of his room to see who was approaching.

He recognised Edmond.

'What can I do for you, Major?' he asked, with no sign of his former insolence.

'You may show me to Corporal Benson's cell, Yately,' Edmond told him.

Yately ushered Edmond to the same cell which Wilson had occupied.

Corporal Benson was in a far worse state than Wilson had been.

He sat on the floor, his knees drawn up to his chest, his arms hugging his body, his hair tumbling about his face, head lowered.

Edmond went into the cell. The same dank odour assailed his nostril; the same foetid air assaulted his lungs.

'Release this man, and bring him to your room, Sergeant,' Edmond demanded.

This time Yately didn't demure. Undoing Benson's fetters, Yately hauled him up, leading him along the dim corridor to his small room.

Edmond regarded Benson closely before turning to the Sergeant.

'You may leave us, Sergeant,' Edmond said.

Yately looked at Roswell for support.

Edmond noticed the look. He turned to Roswell.

'Lieutenant Roswell, I shall not need you, so you may go back to Colonel Courtney.'

'Are you sure, Sir? This man is a murderer,' Roswell said, looking darkly at Benson's rough disorder.

Yately nodded in agreement.

'It is quite possible that he is not, Roswell. His guilt is uncertain. Thank you, Roswell, you may go.' Edmond's tone permitted no argument.

'Sir,' the lieutenant said, and, indicating to the Sergeant with a shift of his head, they both left.

Edmond closed the door and turned to Benson.

'Sit down, Benson,' Edmond said.

A giant of a man, Benson was now reduced to a blubbering wreck. His powerful frame drooped. His eyes were red from crying, his face swollen. His hands shook. His breathing was rough. Benson shuffled forward and sat on a chair next to a table.

Edmond sat on the edge of the table, one foot on the floor. He folded his arms and surveyed Benson.

'Benson, I am Major St Vere. Your comrades came to Colonel Courtney to plead your case. He assigned me to interview you. Tell me exactly what happened.' Edmond's voice was quiet, calming.

Benson pressed his temple, his eyes bemused. Stiffening, he swallowed and looked at Edmond.

'I'm not entirely sure, Major, Sir. All I know is my Annie's dead, and I am found guilty of her murder.'

He bent his head, choking back his tears. As his head came up, he ran his hand through his hair and stared at Edmond.

'At least nine men say you did not. So why do you think Anderson said you are guilty?' Edmond asked; pity for Benson growing in him.

'Because he wanted her, Sir,' Benson said through gritted teeth.

He passed a hand over his eyes before he continued.

'I went to visit her the day before she was murdered. Anderson was there, trying to force himself on her against her will. I used my fists on him, and he left. Next thing I know, the following day, I hear she's discovered dead, and he says he found me with a knife in me hand, kneeling by the body.'

Benson ran the back of his hand under his nose as he

sniffed.

'I loved her, Major, and I wanted to marry her. I'm sure he did it because she refused him and I chased him away.'

He pressed his hands over his eyes. Edmond saw his body heaving with silent, convulsive sobs.

Benson felt the pressure of Edmond's hand gripping his shoulder. He drew in several shuddering breaths.

Turning his eyes on Edmond, he spoke.

'You needn't try for me release, Major. Without Annie, I don't want to live.'

His lips formed a thin line as he nodded his head.

'How old are you, lad?' Edmond asked gently.

'Twenty, Sir,'

'How long have you been in the Army?'

'Since I were sixteen, Sir.'

'And have you a speciality?'

Benson turned his arm to show Edmond the insignia on his sleeve.

'Yes sir, I'm trained as a farrier.'

Edmond nodded. He released his grip on Benson's shoulder moving to stand before him.

'Now listen to me, Benson. I joined the Army when I was eighteen. I lost my wife in childbed when I was twenty-three. I understand your desolation, losing the woman you love and in such abominable circumstances as this. Nevertheless, if you give up, lad, Anderson wins. He killed Annie, and effectively will kill you.'

Benson looked up at Edmond.

'Major, I'm a condemned man. I'm reconciled to me fate.'

Edmond ran a hand across his chin. He wouldn't assent to Benson's morbid acceptance of defeat.

'Colonel Courtney and I are doing all we can to help you. He will order a stay of your execution while he makes further enquiries. Corruption is involved. We are both sure of it,' Edmond told him.

Benson frowned in disbelief, staring at Edmond with wide eyes.

'Benson, do not give up. There is an old saying. "Where there's life, there's hope". Have you eaten?'

'No, Sir, I couldn't,' Benson said, bowing his head again.

'Then get a meal inside you. You will feel better. I shall go now to the Colonel and return when I have more news for you.'

Benson almost smiled and rubbed his cheek where a tear trickled.

'Thank you, Major, you've given me some hope. Do your best for me, Sir, if you please, so my Annie can be avenged.'

'That's the spirit, lad. Never fear, with Colonel Courtney on your side, I am sure in a week or two you will be a free man.'

Edmond opened the door to find Yately slouching against the wall outside.

Edmond's voice took on its commanding tone once more.

'Yately!'

The Sergeant turned to see Edmond exiting the room with Benson following him.

'You may put Benson back in his cell now, Sergeant Yately,' Edmond directed. 'Fetch him a hot meal and do not fetter him. Do not think I shall not check on you.'

'Yes, Sir,' Yately said, saluting.

Edmond returned to Colonel Courtney's office, where Beaumont was with him.

'Ah, St Vere,' Colonel Courtney said. 'What did Benson say for himself?'

'He told me Annie was his girl. When Anderson tried to bed her against her will, Benson bested him, for which Anderson bore a grudge, Sir.' Edmond scowled, 'With Anderson that would be enough for him to kill the girl out of resentment, and accuse Benson of it.'

Colonel Courtney shook his head.

'Beaumont, is there news of the whereabouts of

Anderson?'

'Not yet, Colonel, but I have a man on it.'

The Colonel nodded. He turned to Edmond. 'Beaumont has given me a list of the men who sat on the court martial.'

Turning once more to Beaumont, the Colonel said, 'I really do not know how ya manage to provide me with such things so easily.'

'I have a lot of contacts, Sir. I enjoy acquiring information,' Beaumont said, blushing a smile.

'It is strange, Edmond, everyone knows if ya want something, Beaumont is y'r man. He is a miracle. I am most fortunate to have him. Ya know, he gets me the best port I have ever tasted, and he won't tell me where it comes from.'

'Probably the same place as Wilson gets my brandy, Colonel,' Edmond said, stifling a smile as he glanced at Beaumont.

Beaumont coughed and shuffled papers on the Colonel's desk.

The Colonel, oblivious, handed Edmond the list.

'Two of the men on this are known to me, St Vere. I have sent for them, but they have not yet contacted me. I also sent several men to talk to the people who live in the same street as the murdered girl.

'Beaumont, speaking of port, fetch me a bottle if ya please,' Courtney added.

Beaumont went to the cabinet. He produced port and two glasses.

'What of the stay of execution, Colonel?' Edmond asked, not looking at Beaumont.

'We have seen to that, have we not, Beaumont?' Courtney said.

'Yes, we have, Colonel,' Beaumont agreed, smiling again. He poured the port and handed a glass to the Colonel and to Edmond before retreating to his own office.

'This is more satisfying than y'r problems were, St Vere. Let us hope the outcome will be as felicitous,'

Courtney said, as he raised his glass.

'Indeed, Colonel.'

Edmond raised his own glass in reply.

The day drew on with no word heard from the men who sat on the court martial. Edmond and the Colonel began to despair of anything happening that day.

So, they were relieved when Lieutenant Sherlund appeared, accompanied by Major Dunbar, one of the thirteen officers making up the court martial.

Beaumont followed them and lit the candles on the mantelshelf in the Colonel's office, and then departed.

'You wanted to speak to me, Colonel?' Dunbar said.

'Yes, Major Dunbar. Be seated if you please. It is about Benson's court martial. A matter of not following correct procedure, in ma opinion.'

Dunbar's face reddened. Frowning, he looked at the Colonel in surprise.

'In what way, Colonel?'

'To start with, nine witnesses attest to Benson being in his barracks at the time of the murder, yet none were called.'

Dunbar stiffened.

'It was thought unnecessary, Sir. Captain Anderson found Benson with a knife in his hand kneeling by the body of the girl. An open-and-shut case, we were led to believe.'

'An open-and-shut case? And who led ya to believe that, eh, Dunbar?' Colonel Courtney demanded. He leant forward, his eyes fixed on Dunbar.

Dunbar tried hard not to withdraw his gaze from that of the Colonel.

'The Presiding Officer, Colonel Hastings, Sir. He was eager to get the thing out of the way. His argument seemed reasonable. We went along with him, Sir.'

Dunbar cleared his throat.

His eyes shifted to the window. The sky was darkening as evening approached. He looked back at the Colonel.

'Who defended Benson?' Edmond asked.

'Captain Scotney, Sir.'

'Scotney!' Edmond slapped his hand on the desk. 'Colonel, he is one of Anderson's cronies. Dunbar, did Scotney present Benson's case well?'

'He declared him innocent,' Dunbar admitted. He paused before adding, 'But then he said the girl was Benson's sweetheart, and known to be seeing other men.'

He frowned and glanced at Edmond and Colonel Courtney.

'I must say, that piece of information was most damning,' Dunbar muttered.

'Hmm,' Colonel Courtney said, drumming his fingers on the desk.

'Was Benson called to give evidence?' Edmond asked, lifting his chin and narrowing his eyes.

'No Sir.' Dunbar blinked. 'But he continually interrupted. Colonel Hastings told him to keep silent.'

Colonel Courtney stopped drumming his fingers, put both hands flat on his desk, and leant back in his chair.

'Justice has not been done towards Benson. The whole affair stinks of corruption. I would bet any sum you care to mention; Hastings is on Major-General Anderson's staff.'

'He is, Sir,' Dunbar declared. 'As were at least half the officers present.'

Colonel Courtney clapped slowly in triumph. 'Thank you, Dunbar, ya confirm our suspicions. Ya may go now, but ya may be needed to give evidence before another court-martial, so please hold y'r self in readiness.'

Dunbar frowned and nodded.

'I shall, Sir. Goodnight, Sir.'

He rose from his seat and straightened his coat. Nodding to the Colonel and to Edmond, he went to the door.

When the door closed on Dunbar, Colonel Courtney thumped his fist into his palm.

'We have them, St Vere. We have them!' The Colonel proclaimed with satisfaction.

'Tomorrow I shall hand this over to the Judge Advocate

General, and let him deal with it. We have started the ball rolling. Ha, all this intrigue makes me hungry. I shall be glad of ma dinner.'

'Indeed, Colonel, I am of the same mind. Would you care to accompany me to my home and have dinner with us? You would honour me by accepting my invitation.'

'Damme, St Vere, I believe I shall. I am curious to see this child bride of yours.'

Edmond's face clouded.

'It is not common knowledge, Colonel, so I would be obliged if you would not allude to it in company. As I told you, we are married in name only; I look upon her as my daughter and in no wise my wife.'

'Forgive me, St Vere. I spoke without thinking. I shall not mention it again.'

'Thank you, Sir,' Edmond said.

After a pause, the silence between them growing, Edmond said quietly,

'I would be pleased to introduce you to Sophia—and to my sister and nephew, Colonel.'

'I would like that, St Vere. Thank ya,' Colonel Courtney said.

CHAPTER TWENTY SEVEN

Sophia's feeling of apprehension clung to her. She couldn't dispel the idea that Edmond might be made to stay in the Army, be made to go back to fighting the war. She feared he could be killed. She felt she was on the brink of losing another father.

The picture of misery, she walked back from the stables to the house, eyes downcast, her mouth turned down, and shoulders drooping.

Simon saw her enter the house as he descended the stairs.

'What ails you, Sophia? Why your gloomy countenance?'

'I am uneasy, Simon,' Sophia murmured, her face unhappy.

Simon went to her, putting his arm around her shoulders.

'Why, my dear? What causes you to feel so?' he said, his quiet voice soothing.

Glancing up at him, she held out a trembling hand.

'I fear for Edmond's safety, Simon.'

'Edmond can take care of himself, Sophia.'

He took her hand, leading her to the drawing room. Sitting beside her on a couch, he asked,

'Where did he go?'

'To regimental headquarters to resign his commission. An awful idea is in my head. What if they do not accept it? What if they send him back to fight in the war again?'

She fought back tears.

Simon patted her hand.

'They will not, Sophia. They must accept a resignation, whether at war or not.'

Sophia brightened a little, giving him a wan smile.

'He said he would be back by luncheon.'

'Then do not worry, Sophia. If he says he will be here for luncheon, he will be here. Come, let us walk by the lake. I do believe the bluebell's shoots may be visible.'

Sophia went with him. Indeed, little green spears were peeping through the earth under the cedar trees. Her spirits lifted.

'When they bloom, I shall pick some and put them in my room. Their scent is not strong, but it is very pleasing,' she said.

Sophia and Simon wandered down to the lake.

Buds burgeoned on the willow.

'It will not be long before she is dressed in all her finery,' Simon observed.

Together by the lakeside, they watched the wildfowl searching for food.

From the lake, Simon led her to the Orchard. The trees were bare.

'In Spring, when the trees are in blossom, the orchard is a lovely sight. When the wind blows, the blossoms drift like a snowstorm,' Simon said, trying to lift her mood.

'I look forward to seeing it,' Sophia answered, her usual fervour for the wonders of nature was not as keen as usual.

Their long walk took them to the edge of Vere land then back to where they had started.

Heading towards the house, they met Swithun walking towards them down the sloping lawn.

'Luncheon is served, Miss Sophia, Master Simon,' he informed them.

'Thank you, Swithun. Has Lord Edmond returned?' Sophia enquired, eager to be told he had.

'Not yet, Miss.'

Sophia's face fell. 'Is there any word from him?' she asked.

'No, Miss. There is not,' Swithun replied.

Sophia's unease returned.

'We shall be there shortly, Swithun. Thank you,' Simon said.

Swithun bowed and returned the way he had come.

Sophia turned sad eyes on Simon.

'I told you, Simon, I know something has happened to

him.'

'Sophia, he has probably forgotten his luncheon. I would say he has met an acquaintance and is lunching with them.'

'I hope you are right, Simon,' Sophia said as they entered the house and went to the dining room.

Perdita, already there, stood by the window awaiting them. She looked up when Sophia and Simon arrived, noticing at once Sophia's sad expression.

'What is wrong with you, Sophia, why do you look so unhappy?' she asked, allowing Swithun to seat her and place her napkin on her lap.

'Sophia's thoughts are uneasy regarding Edmond, Mamma,' Simon supplied, seating himself next to his mother.

'What in the name of heaven would give you "uneasy thoughts", Sophia? He has only gone to resign his commission. What danger do you think can befall him doing that?'

'Perhaps they will not accept it Perdita. Perhaps they will send him to war again,' Sophia murmured.

Perdita cast an admonishing look towards Sophia.

'Yes, I am being foolish,' Sophia acknowledged.

Yet, by her sad face and drooping posture Perdita could see Sophia's dejection persisted.

'If I should lose him, too, I do not know what I would do.'

Perdita prided herself on her practicality.

'If anything should happen to him, Simon would inherit, and we would all continue to live here.'

Sophia's heart gave a jolt. Her eyes widened in fear. Her mouth opened in a silent O.

Simon was appalled at his mother's lack of tact.

'Nothing will happen to Edmond. Set your mind at rest, Sophia. They will undoubtedly accept his resignation.'

He turned a reproachful frown on his mother.

'Mamma, have you no regard for Sophia's sensibility?'

Turning again to Sophia, he soothed, 'She does but jest,

Sophia. Come, now, all is well, I am sure.'

Simon had gained a new confidence in himself since his apprenticeship to Reynolds. Perdita was pleased he behaved less timidly. Yet, she could not but harbour a tinge of regret. She could no longer manage him as she used to. Instead, he showed a tendency to manage her. He occasionally criticised her in his gentle way, as he did now.

His manner reminds me of his father. Perhaps Edmond's view of Simon not making a career of the Army is correct. He is indeed a gentle, sympathetic soul.

She smiled indulgently at him.

'Simon is right, Sophia,' Perdita said. 'Edmond has probably gone to his club and is socialising with his cronies. Doubtless, he forgot he said he would be home in time for Luncheon.'

Sophia could only pick at her meal. She continually glanced at Edmond's empty chair, her ears alert to every sound in the house in case it was Edmond arriving home.

Luncheon over, Simon took his leave of them to go to his studio.

'I have a lot to do this afternoon, Sophia. But if I can, I shall return to keep you company. I am sure Edmond will be back soon.'

He took Sophia's hand and gripped it reassuringly.

'Thank you, Simon. I hope you are right,' Sophia said with a pale smile.

Perdita had an appointment to spend the afternoon with Lady Malcolm, with whom she had become friendly.

'You are welcome to accompany me, Sophia. I am sure Susanna would not mind,' Perdita stated. She was becoming somewhat irritated by Sophia's unhappy mood.

'Thank you, Perdita. You are very kind. But I would worry more if I were not here. He might send word about his delay, you see.'

'I cannot understand your concern, Sophia. But there, you must do whatever you wish. I am sure I do not want to upset you further.'

When Sophia heard the front door close and Perdita's carriage wheels crunch on the drive, she felt perhaps she should have gone with her. Yet, Perdita and Lady Malcolm's conversation would hold no interest for her, and Lady Malcolm's daughters were much older than herself.

'I would feel like a waterless fish,' she told herself and went to the library.

She browsed the books for half an hour, each sound of movement in the hall bringing her to the library door to see if it was Edmond.

As the afternoon wore on, Sophia became more anxious.

She felt drawn to visit Edmond's rooms.

Wilson was busy in the anteroom, cleaning Edmond's second-best boots. He was surprised to see her.

'Good afternoon, Miss Sophia. What can I do for you?' Wilson asked.

Sophia sat on the upright, wooden chair beside the mirror. She viewed Wilson dejectedly.

'I am worried about Edmond, Wilson. He should be home by now. Ever since he left, I have had uneasy feelings, growing worse the longer he is away.'

Wilson looked keenly at her. He had never seen her so wan. Her mood seemed to match Edmond's tension.

The polishing cloth in Wilson's blackened hand paused over the boots.

'Ah, Miss, I think your thoughts may be because his Lordship is takin' a big step today, resignin' his commission.'

He swapped the cloth for a brush.

'His way of life is army, Miss. A born soldier he is, to be sure. Made for command. Don't fret, Miss, he decided on quitting after the last battle. Although he may be nostalgic for the good times, I'm certain as can be he's had enough o' the bad times.'

Wilson began to work his brush briskly over the boot.

'I feel something may have happened to obstruct his

resignation, Wilson.'

Wilson paused his polishing again.

'No, Miss, no chance. He would o' sent word. We would o' heard. If I know my master, he'll be home for his dinner and no mistake, mark my words.

'What you've got hold of is his mood, Miss. I felt it in him this mornin. He was despondent. You've caught on to his frame of mind, turned it into somethin' bad. But it ain't bad. A phase of his life is endin', that's all. Things end. Just part o' life, Miss.'

'Wilson, how wise you are. I am sure you are right. I did notice his tension. My apprehensions must be built on that. Thank you. I shall not worry—but if he should not return tonight …?'

'He will return, Miss, depend upon it,' Wilson said, nodding sagely.

He considered her, his chin tilted, his frown making his nose wrinkle.

'You're very close to him, ain't you, Miss?' he observed, an unfamiliar softness to his usually gruff voice.

'Oh, yes, Wilson. I have come to love him almost as much as I loved my father. Poor father never had time to care for me as Edmond does. I do not blame my father. He had a job to do, and did it well.'

The boot forgotten for the moment in Wilson's lap, he said, 'He cares greatly for you too, Miss. He's forever saying you're the daughter he never knew. I think it's good. God bless the two o' you, Miss.'

'I wish I had come to talk with you earlier, Wilson. I have been worried all day. You put my mind at rest.'

She rose to go to the door and turned back again.

'But, if he does not return for his dinner, I think I shall worry again.'

'That won't happen, Miss. In the unlikely chance it does, I'll go to town and search for him meself,' Wilson said, winking at her.

She smiled.

'Thank you, again, Wilson.'

Sophia left, closing the door behind her.

Wilson's eyes filled with tears. Sophia's words had touched him. For the second time that day, he took out his handkerchief and blew his nose.

Perdita returned from her visit to Lady Malcolm at six thirty.

'Has Edmond not yet returned?' she asked Sophia who had come into the hall when she heard the front door open.

'No, Perdita. And he has sent no word. However, Wilson assures me he will be here for dinner.

'Oh, how tiresome,' Perdita complained, clicking her tongue as she stripped off her gloves. 'I shall go to my room and change. Mrs Cribb will undoubtedly hold dinner for him. I hope he is here by the time I come down.'

She swept from the room, with an angry swish.

Ten minutes later, Simon arrived. Seeing that Edmond had not yet returned, he was all concern for Sophia.

'Are you all right, Sophia?' he asked.

'Yes, Simon. I spoke with Wilson who was most sympathetic and is sure Edmond will be here for dinner.'

Simon smiled, pleased that Wilson had dispelled Sophia's fears.

Perdita returned to the drawing room, arrayed in a different gown. Seeing Edmond still absent, she glared at the clock.

'It wants five minutes to the hour,' she announced, her mouth pouting. 'I really think it is too bad of Edmond. He shows a decided lack of consideration. Does he not know that we must all wait dinner for him?'

Simon glanced at Sophia. Unlike her earlier manner, she showed no sign of worry. Instead, she was put out by Perdita's criticism of Edmond. She jumped to his defence.

'He is not inconsiderate in the least, Perdita. I have always found him to be a most caring person. Depend upon it; he will have a very good reason for being late.'

At a quarter past seven, Edmond returned, bringing Colonel Courtney with him.

'I am sorry to have kept you all waiting. We were unavoidably detained,' Edmond explained. 'I shall tell you all about it over dinner. But first I must introduce you.'

He turned to Colonel Courtney.

'Colonel, may I make known to you my sister, Mrs Perdita Luxton. Perdita, Colonel Aubrey Courtney,' Edmond said.

Perdita made a small curtsy holding out her hand. The Colonel took it in his, bowing graciously over it.

'Y'r servant, Mrs Luxton,' he said, smiling into her eyes.

'How do you do, Colonel Courtney,' Perdita replied.

'This is Mr Simon Luxton, Colonel, Mrs Luxton's son,' Edmond said.

The Colonel and Simon bowed their heads elegantly.

'And who is this young lady?' Colonel Courtney asked.

'This "young lady", Colonel, is my ward, Miss Sophia Erdington.'

Sophia regarded Edmond's friend with interest.

'I am delighted to meet ya, Miss Erdington.'

The Colonel smiled warmly.

Sophia curtsied, returning the Colonel's smile.

'Shall we go in to dinner?' Perdita asked. Her previous annoyance at being kept waiting abandoned.

Edmond led the way. Colonel Courtney gave Perdita his arm and followed Edmond. Sophia and Simon exchanged looks, amused by the unaccustomed formality which they knew would delight Perdita.

When they were all seated, Furlong served soup.

Colonel Courtney turned to Sophia.

'Miss Erdington, y'r father was known to me, and a finer officer I have yet to meet,' he stated, adding gently, 'I am sorry for your loss.'

'Thank you, Sir,' she answered quietly, glancing at him. A puzzled expression appeared on her face.

'Sir, you are the same rank as my father. May I ask you, please, what you would like me to call you?'

The Colonel leant back in his seat.

'Ya have a choice, ma dear. Ya may call me Colonel Courtney or plain Colonel. Ya may call me Sir Aubrey or ya may simply call me Aubrey.'

'May I call you Aubrey? That is much friendlier. As you are Edmond's friend, I hope we shall be friends, too,' she said and began to eat her soup.

Edmond passed his napkin over his mouth to hide his smile. By the expression on Colonel Courtney's face, her charm had won him, just as she won all others she encountered. The thought came to his mind, as so often it did concerning Sophia, shy she was not.

As they commenced the second course, Perdita turned to Edmond.

'May we know what delayed you so long, Edmond? Sophia was beside herself with worry when you did not return for Luncheon as you had promised.'

'I was worried in case they would not accept your resignation, Edmond,' Sophia said, giving Perdita a disapproving look.

'My resignation was accepted, Sophia, and will come into effect as soon as I receive the papers,' Edmond told her. 'As to what detained me …' Edmond glanced at the Colonel. 'Is it permitted I disclose what is an ongoing matter, Sir?' Edmond asked.

'Probably not, Edmond,' Colonel Courtney replied, and looking around the table, he began to explain.

'Briefly, a corporal was wrongly found guilty of murder. Together with ma staff, Edmond and I have set the wheels in motion to put the record straight and see the man released. The real murderer will then be tried and punished.'

'Is that all?' Perdita asked.

'We had to act swiftly, Perdy, as the corporal was due to be executed tomorrow morning. His comrades came to us to speak for the man. I went to interview him. The murdered girl was his fiancée. I can say no more than that,' Edmond explained.

Aubrey changed the subject.

'Edmond, the more I consider it, the more I think twould be good to follow y'r example and resign ma commission,' he announced.

Edmond raised his eyebrows in surprise.

The Colonel continued.

'Ma usual duties are remarkably tedious, and to be free of them would be a relief. Yet, what would I do with ma self? How would I occupy ma self?'

'Find yourself a wife and settle on your estate, Sir,' Edmond suggested.

Aubrey leant back in his chair, watching Edmond and rubbing his lower lip with a finger.

'Marry? Aye, I often thought I should marry. Where would I find a wife? I am a man not much in the company of women.'

Perdita had listened with interest to their words.

'You must go into society, Sir, where most people find suitable partners,' she stated. 'I, myself, have not socialised of late. For Sophia's sake, I have begun to renew old acquaintances. You see, we have decided when Sophia is eighteen, I shall supervise her coming out. One must have friends to be a success in society.'

She glanced at Edmond, who kept his eyes on his plate.

'Of course, she will not be eighteen for four years. Yet, one cannot let the grass grow under one's feet. By the time she comes out, we shall have a reasonable circle of acquaintance.'

She straightened herself in her chair, her eyes bright. The prospect of playing matchmaker appealed to her greatly. Already she was mentally running through her growing circle of connections for a suitable match for the Colonel.

'It might be amusing to host a dinner party now and again, though,' Edmond mused.

Sophia's eyes rounded with pleasure as she beamed at him.

'A dinner party! Oh, Edmond, just like when father and I invited you and the other officers to dinner. I did so enjoy those dinners.'

'Sophia, you are too young to attend dinner parties. In a year or two perhaps, but you are a schoolroom miss, and it is improper for you to dine in company,' Perdita said, shaking her head in disapproval.

Sophia, undaunted by Perdita's words, laughed.

'Oh, Perdita. Over the years, I enjoyed dozens of 'em. I know how to behave, do I not, Edmond? Why, I even oversaw menus. You would not stop me from attending, would you Edmond?' she said, her most engaging smile aimed at him.

'Indeed, I would not, Sophia. Yet, have you forgotten? We are off to Crawford Lees in a day or two, so any ideas of dinner parties must wait until we return.'

Sophia looked crestfallen but brightened when she realised it would be something to look forward to while she was away.

Furlong, accompanied by Swithun, entered to clear the table.

'Come Sophia. It is time for us to withdraw,' Perdita announced.

She motioned to Furlong who moved her chair for her to rise.

Swithun did the same for Sophia.

Sophia thought this practice of "leaving the men to their port" unnecessary. She was sure their conversation became more interesting when ladies weren't present. Yet, Perdita insisted they conform to protocol, particularly if they had guests, she wouldn't be moved on the matter.

'What do you think of Edmond's adventure, saving an innocent man from execution?' Sophia said with excitement when she and Perdita reached the drawing room.

'I cannot see why they have to be so secretive about it. Who would *we* tell of it?'

'Oh, they have to be discreet when a case is ongoing. I am sure Edmond will tell us all about it when it is resolved. At least we know that Edmond was not being inconsiderate when he did not appear for luncheon,' Sophia said, and inwardly winced. She hadn't meant to sound accusing. She didn't look at Perdita and was glad when the remark seemed to go over Perdita's head.

'You should have come with me to Lady Malcolm. Her eldest daughter is visiting. She has her three children with her. I am sure you would have enjoyed them more than I. They are rather boisterous.'

'Ah, I am sure I would have. Yet, my afternoon was not wasted. I had a long talk with Wilson. He put my mind at rest,' Sophia said.

'You should not be too familiar with servants, Sophia. It is not quite the thing.'

Sophia said nothing. She didn't want to have cross words with Perdita. Although Perdita irritated her at times, she behaved so kindly towards her, Sophia was loth to upset her.

Perdita itched to bring up the subject of Sophia's attendance at dinner parties. She resisted the temptation, knowing she stood no chance of persuading Sophia, or Edmond, to change their minds when they agreed on a thing. Their stance on various issues often vexed Perdita. Being too indolent, she didn't pursue forlorn hopes.

Simon wondered whether he should stay with the men, as he had done when Captain Orpwood had come to dinner. He hoped his mother wouldn't embarrass him by making him go with her. On all other evenings, he, being the only other male for Edmond to converse with over port, stayed with Edmond in the dining room, drank a small glass with him, discussing his progress as Mr Reynolds's apprentice. On this particular evening, with the Colonel as a guest, Simon thought matters might be different.

As he stood near the door, unsure of his position, Edmond noticed him.

'Join us, Simon,' Edmond said, and pushed the bottle of port in his direction.

Aubrey, interested in Simon's career, plied him with many questions.

Simon happily answered them.

'What caused ya to take up painting, Simon?' Aubrey asked.

'I am not sure, Sir. Perhaps it is because I discovered it is something I am good at. I lose myself in my work when I draw or paint.'

'He is exceptionally good, Aubrey,' Edmond declared. 'Even his mother, who was adamantly against his making art his career, has to admit to his having great talent.'

'I would like to see some of y'r work sometime, Simon,' Aubrey said.

'You may, Sir. At the end of each year, Mr Reynolds stages a private exhibition of his students work. Admittance is by invitation only. If you wish I shall send an invitation to you,' Simon offered.

'I would appreciate it, ma boy. But tell me, what subjects do ya paint?' Aubrey asked. 'What of "life drawing" for instance? I hear they hire prostitutes to sit for students of the human form,' Aubrey commented.

Simon reddened, and Edmond coughed.

'We do not speak of such things for fear Perdita might discover it, Aubrey. She might try to prohibit Simon taking part in such activities,' Edmond told him.

'Oh, so ya *do* practise drawing the nude female form?' Aubrey said, his eyebrows raised.

'The practice is not as disreputable as is supposed, Sir,' Simon said, and gave Aubrey an embarrassed smile.

'Mr Reynolds is most discreet in his choice of females. He does not go to common brothels to hire them. He finds them in the less reprehensible places frequented by such women. They are usually independent women, rarely under the protection of a bawd.'

Simon fiddled with the lace at his cuffs.

'Mr Hogarth is the most concerned for their welfare. He has painted a series of six pictures, called, *The Harlot's Progress*, telling the story of how an innocent girl is enticed into a dishonourable way of life.'

Edmond had observed that Simon remained silent through most of the dinner. Amused, he now noted, when speaking of his occupation, he became animated, his reserve forgotten.

Aubrey's expression became more serious.

'Are y'r models paid, Simon?' he asked.

'Oh, indeed, they are, Sir. Mr Reynolds pays them handsomely. He says his payments mean they will have food enough for a while, so they may live without practising harlotry.'

Aubrey rose. Shaking his head, he tutted.

'While men lust after women, a demand for the means to satisfy their appetite will always be available.'

'Shall we join the ladies?' Edmond proposed, a trifle uncomfortable.

Simon opened the door and went before them, glad to be released from the subject. Edmond caught Aubrey's arm.

'Now, Aubrey, remember, not a word of this to them.'

'Of course not, Edmond, what do ya take me for? I would never discuss such things with women,' Aubrey said, frowning.

'I meant the life drawing, Sir, not the rest,' Edmond said, with an apologetic look.

They repaired to the drawing room where they found Perdita and Sophia sipping tea, deep in conversation.

'Ah, there you are, Gentlemen,' Perdita cried.

'What were you discussing that took you so long?' she asked.

Simon turned his head away to hide the awkwardness that rose within him. He hoped Aubrey and his uncle would not elaborate too greatly on what had been said.

'We were discussing Mr Hogarth and his altruism, Perdy,' Edmond said. 'He is a great philanthropist. His foundling hospital is much to be admired.'

'We were also discussing Simon's progress,' Aubrey added. 'He has promised to procure an invitation for me to see his work in an exhibition.'

'I have seen very little of his work,' Perdita said, somewhat miffed that he had not asked her if she would like to go.

'But you have seen many of his sketches, Perdita,' Sophia reminded her.

'May I come to your exhibition, Simon,' Sophia asked.

'Of course, you may, Sophia,' Simon said. 'And you must come too, mother if you do not think you would find it tedious.'

Mollified by Simon's invitation, belated as it might be, Perdita smiled.

'I do believe I would *not* find it tedious to see your work Simon,' she said.

They conversed over this and that for a while until Simon stifled a yawn.

'I must make my apologies, to you all. I worked hard this afternoon and need my sleep. If you will excuse me, I shall retire,' Simon said.

'Of course, Simon. I hope you have enjoyed a pleasant evening,' Edmond said

'Yes, indeed, Uncle,' Simon replied.

'I shall retire, too, Edmond. Such a day I have had, I am developing a headache,' Perdita complained, placing her fingers to her temple. 'Goodnight Colonel. It has been a pleasure meeting you. I hope you will come to us again.'

Aubrey inclined his head elegantly. 'Be sure I shall. Goodnight Ma'am,' he said.

'Come Sophia. I cannot think you are not tired, too,' Perdita declared, making for the door.

Sophia glanced at Edmond, hoping to be allowed to stay.

'Goodnight to you both,' Edmond said with a particular look at Sophia.

Sophia knew not to question his authority when Edmond used such a look and, nodding to Edmond and Aubrey, she left in Perdita's wake.

When the door shut behind Simon and the ladies,

Aubrey turned to Edmond.

'Well, Edmond, I hate to forego the opportunity to converse with ya further, but I too am ready for ma bed. I seem to have had a good deal to drink today, what with one thing and another. I am somewhat the worse for wear. I must take my leave of you, Sir.'

'Aubrey, have you not heard the rain lashing against the windows? This is not a night for riding home. Please, allow me the honour of offering you a bed for the night.'

'I feel I am imposing on ya, Edmond. However, it is a dirty night, so I accept y'r kind invitation,' Aubrey said.

Edmond pulled the bell rope.

'It will probably take them a little while to prepare your room, Aubrey,' Edmond apologised.

Swithun appeared in reply to the bell.

'My Lord?' he said.

'Yes, Swithun. Colonel Courtney is to lie here tonight. Is there a room ready, or will we have to wait?'

'There is a room prepared for visitors, My Lord. If the Colonel would care to follow me, I will show him to it,' Swithun said.

'There, Aubrey. It is as if they knew, my friend.'

'Thank ya, Edmond, Goodnight,' Aubrey said and followed Swithun out.

Edmond went to the library and lit up a cheroot.

He sat in his favourite chair by the fire, thinking over the happenings of the day.

The smoke drifted in lazy curls above his head.

Strange that I developed qualms about resigning, and now I am quite contented. And through it all, I have acquired a new acquaintance. I can see Aubrey and me becoming good friends, he mused.

He flicked the stub of his cheroot into the fire, wandered to the hall and up the stairs.

As Swithun went to the library to snuff the candles, he heard Edmond murmur to himself,

'All in all, a most productive day.'

CHAPTER TWENTY EIGHT

'Colonel Courtney!' Edmond said with a smile when Aubrey was shown into his study.

Several weeks had passed since their last meeting.

'How good to see you again. To what do I owe the pleasure of your visit?'

'I bring news, Edmond. Good news,' Aubrey announced.

'Do not delay, Sir. Tell me, your news.'

Courtney smiled broadly.

'I heard yesterday, Edmond. Corporal Benson has been exonerated, all charges overthrown,' he said.

'Excellent, Sir,' Edmond said, indicating a chair to Aubrey.

'What of Anderson?' he asked, resuming his own seat.

'Cashiered,' Aubrey said and cleared his throat. 'He should hang by rights, but he pleaded not guilty to murder, saying she came at him with a knife. He tried to disarm her. In the ensuing struggle, the knife lodged in her chest.'

Edmond's eyebrows flew up. 'They believed him?' he asked, pausing in taking a bottle and glasses from a cupboard in his desk.

'They did,' Aubrey affirmed. With a derisory curl to his lip, he added, 'He was on oath.'

Edmond was too angry to comment. 'Bah!' he grunted.

He passed Aubrey a glass.

'His punishment is exile. It is rumoured he is to be sent to India as a clerk.'

Edmond poured brandy into the two glasses.

'The main thing, in truth, Aubrey, is that Benson is free,' Edmond said.

'Indeed. A bird returns to its nest, Edmond. I am sure Anderson's sins will catch up with him eventually. To Benson,' he said and raised his glass.

'Yes, Aubrey, to Benson.'

'I say, this is excellent Brandy. Where did ya get it?' Aubrey asked, delightedly holding his glass up to the light.

The rich tawny liquid glowed in the sunlight.

Edmond laughed quietly.

'Do not ask me, my friend. My erstwhile batman, Wilson, "finds" it for me from time to time. Much as Beaumont supplies you with port,' Edmond added chuckling.

Aubrey joined in Edmond's laughter.

'We shall say no more,' Aubrey said.

Edmond rose.

'You will stay for luncheon, will you not, Aubrey?'

Aubrey grinned. 'I had hoped you would ask, Edmond. I enjoyed y'r company, and that of y'r family, the last time I was here.'

Edmond pulled the bell cord.

'As they did yours, Sir,' Edmond said. 'Today you may only have me for company, however. Simon is at his studio. Perdita and Sophia are out. No doubt they are making inroads into my finances as they add to Sophia's wardrobe,' Edmond said with a chuckle.

Swithun came into the room, 'My Lord?'

'Please inform Mrs Cribb we have a guest for luncheon, Swithun,' Edmond said.

'Yes, my Lord' he said, bowed and left.

'And how are ya coping with being a true civilian, Edmond?' Aubrey asked.

Edmond replenished their glasses.

'Surprisingly well, Aubrey. I am studying the plans of my estate and making notes. We are going there within a short while. Have you given more thought to your own resignation?'

'Yes, Edmond, I can think of nothing else. I am definitely considering it,' Aubrey said.

'I considered resigning many times for over a year, Aubrey. It was the death of Colonel Erdington and my promise to care for his daughter which finally caused me to make up my mind.'

Aubrey looked thoughtful.

'Ah, Edmond. I shall not be considering it for long, I

assure ya. I feel like a village pond. Stagnant.'

Edmond laughed.

'I was certainly not stagnant. I was thoroughly occupied. It was the stagnating influence of officialdom that drove me out of my mind.'

Furlong entered. 'Luncheon is served, my Lord,' he intoned and retired.

As he and Edmond made their way to the dining room, Aubrey made a suggestion.

'I have brought ya a bottle of Beaumont's port, Edmond. Perhaps ya would be so good as to swap it with me for a bottle of Wilson's brandy.'

Edmond gave a quiet laugh.

'With pleasure, my friend.' He said as he accompanied Aubrey Courtney to the dining room.

The following day, Swithun came to Edmond's study.

'My Lord, a young soldier by the name of Benson is at the kitchen door asking to see you,' he said, his expression disdainful.

Edmond closed the books he was perusing and smiled.

'That is good news, Swithun. Please show him in,' Edmond said.

'Yes, my Lord,' Swithun said, barely hiding his surprise.

When Benson entered his study, Edmond rose and coming around his desk held out his hand.

'Benson, how pleased I am to see you, a free man,' he said.

Benson shook Edmond's hand.

'Thank you, Major,' he said, as surprised as Swithun had been at Edmond's informality.

'I am no longer a major, Benson, I have resigned. Take a seat,' Edmond said, drawing one forward from against the wall.

'What can I do for you, Benson?' he said as he went to stand behind his desk.

'Well first, Sir, I want to thank you for your help.

Without you and Colonel Courtney, Sir, I'd be a dead man,' Benson said with a serious frown.

Edmond nodded.

'I hate injustice, Benson. I also dislike Captain Anderson's behaviour. It was a pleasure to help you,' Edmond said, resuming his seat.

'You said, "The first thing", is there something else?' he asked.

Benson sat on the edge of the chair that Edmond had provided.

'Yes, Sir. I hardly dare ask for your help,' he replied.

Bowing his head, he glanced up once or twice at Edmond.

'I cannot help you unless I know what you want me to do,' Edmond said, giving Benson a wry look.

'No, Sir.'

Benson paused, then burst out, 'Well, the truth of it is, I want to leave the Army.'

Edmond stroked his chin, looking fixedly at Benson.

'No difficulty there, Benson,' Edmond said. 'I have already bought my batman out without much trouble. I can probably do the same for you.'

'You can, Sir?' Benson said, looking up, his eyes bright and a smile on his lips.

'What do you intend to do with yourself?' Edmond asked, 'You will need employment. What are you good at?'

'Horses, Sir. Me father was a blacksmith, and I grew up with 'em.'

'Of course. You are a farrier, are you not?' Edmond said. He pursed his lips and frowned as he thought, tapping his lips with a knuckle. He gave Benson a broad smile.

'I can help you again, Benson. I am about to go to my estate in Oxfordshire to organise its refurbishment. I keep no horses there, as I have not yet employed anyone to care for them. The position is yours if you want it.'

Benson's eyes widened. He couldn't speak. He rose from his seat, looking at Edmond, open-mouthed.

Eventually, he found his voice.

'Sir! Do you mean it? I can't believe you'd do such a thing for me. If I want it, you say? Indeed, Sir, I surely do want it. Thank you, Sir.'

He stood and swayed gently from foot to foot, his face a picture of ecstasy.

'Before you become too excited, Benson, I must warn you. If you prove incompetent, you will be out of my employ.'

'No fear o' that, Sir. I'm good at me job. Ask anyone in the company.'

Edmond rose and held out his hand once again to Benson. Benson took it in both of his and pumped it vigorously, laughing.

'Thank you, Major, I mean, my Lord. Thank you.'

CHAPTER TWENTY NINE

Standing on the terrace, Simon saw Sophia in the distance, by the lake. As he watched, she turned and seeing him, waved her hand. He descended the steps to the lawn and walked towards her.

'Good morning Simon,' she said as he approached.

'Good morning Sophia. I might have known you would be by the lake. Edmond has told me you are to journey to Crawford Lees within a week or two. I believe it has a lake too, so you will feel at home,' Simon said.

'I am looking forward to seeing Crawford Lees, although Edmond tells me it needs much attention. Have you been there?' Sophia asked, linking her arm in Simon's.

'No, Sophia; although my mother described it to me. Mr Reynolds has asked me to complete several pieces this month,' Simon said. 'Otherwise, I would come to Crawford Lees with you for a week or two. I would enjoy a visit to the country.'

'Will Perdita not mind being here in the house by herself while you are at the studio?' Sophia asked.

'Not a bit of it. Did she not say recently that she wants to renew old acquaintances? She plans to send her card to people she used to know. Her hope is they will return their cards to her so that she may call on them. She will undoubtedly pour her heart and soul into renewing old friendships, and making new ones.'

They stopped beneath the stand of cedar trees to look at the bluebell carpet beneath them. Simon disengaged his arm from Sophia's. He took a small sketchpad and a little silver box, containing charcoal, from his pocket. Choosing a thin stick, he replaced the box in his pocket and began sketching an especially charming patch of snowdrops growing under the trees a little way from the bluebells.

He was silent a short while, intent on his sketch. Then he spoke again.

'My mother will not, of course, presume to host a dinner party without Edmond being here.'

He looked up from his sketch, gazing intently at the snowdrops, his head to one side.

'She thinks, by the time you and Edmond return, her contacts will be numerous enough to hold a soiree. I trust such a thing will not cause Edmond discomfort.'

He held the small sketch before him at arm's length. Comparing it with the original, glancing from one to the other.

Sophia looked at it over his arm. She wondered how Simon brought things to life on the page so adeptly. The sketch captured the charm of the little white flowers to perfection.

'I am sure Edmond will not mind,' Sophia said. 'When he was with his regiment, he often attended social gatherings. Perhaps he misses such things. I do. Of course, father did not allow me to go to balls or Soirees. He often had a few officers to dinner in his quarters where I was allowed to attend. When invited to dinner by other officers, I sometimes went, too.'

As she spoke, Simon added a touch here and there to what he had drawn.

Sophia knelt, and lightly touched the delicate snowdrops with a gentle finger. Simon watched her and began another sketch.

Sophia looked up into the trees, and beyond to the house.

A gentle breeze moved the reeds at the edge of the water and caused the trees to whisper. It caught the tips of Sophia's hair, which floated in a gauzy veil around her shoulders.

'I think I know every inch of this garden. I love it and always will,' she said, breathing the sense of the imminent season. 'I have little else to occupy me here. Edmond says there is much to explore at Crawford Lees.'

Simon's charcoal scraped lightly as he worked on his picture.

'What of your education, Sophia? Does Edmond mean to employ a governess for you?'

Simon looked with serious concentration from her to his sketch.

'He says he intends to arrange that when we return from Crawford Lees.'

Sophia sighed.

'I miss my governess, Miss Roseberry, and her lessons. I do not think anyone can replace her.'

She looked up at Simon who was smoothing a harsh shadow with a practised finger.

'As to my education, I have made one proviso: I do not want drawing or sewing to be part of what I must learn. They were things Miss Roseberry and I despaired of my accomplishing. I was never proficient in either.'

Simon held up his sketch before him again. Sophia quickly rose to see what he had done.

'Simon, it is of *me*,' she exclaimed in delight, regarding the sketch with her head tilted to one side.

'You make me look so pretty. I am sure I am not like that.'

'You *are* pretty, Sophia, especially with your hair tumbling as it does,' he stated, looking intently at her, appraising her features.

'You know, one day you will be an exceptionally beautiful woman.'

A mischievous twinkle sparkled in Sophia's eyes.

'And will you then fall in love with me, Simon?'

'Ah! … No, Sophia, you are too much a sister to me. I am fond of you and trust you. But nothing in you attracts me in a romantic way—oh, I beg your pardon, I do not mean to offend.'

Simon blushed.

'Do not apologise, Simon. I am very fond of you, to be sure. But you are more like a brother than a beau. I do believe we shall always be friends.'

Simon closed his sketch pad and put his charcoal in its box, placing both in his pocket.

Sophia smiled up at him taking his hand in hers.

Simon tilted his chin, regarding her.

'Ours is, indeed, a comfortable friendship, Sophia.'

No shyness hampered him as he moved to link her arm in his again.

They walked back to the house in companionable silence both thinking on the easy, gentle relationship that had grown between them over the past months.

Simon spoke into the haven of silence.

'Sophia, would you like me to teach you to draw? I cannot believe you have no capacity at all. What sort of things did your governess teach you?'

'Oh, she tried everything—still life, landscapes, portraits—everything. And I could not make good with any.'

'Did she explain perspective or proportion?'

'I think she did speak of them, but I did not grasp what she meant,' Sophia said, turning despairing eyes on him.

'Well, my dear sister …' he paused to glance at her. 'I am willing to explain if you wish.'

'You may try, Simon. I do believe I would be such a trial to you; we might fall out.'

Simon's rare laugh rang forth.

'You cannot be that bad, Sophia. When you return from Crawford Lees, I shall begin. We shall start with half an hour, two or three times a week. And if you are utterly hopeless, we shall not continue, for I should indeed hate to fall out with you.'

They paused, laughing.

Her hand rested in the crook of his arm as she looked up at him,

He put his hand on hers and gave it a gentle squeeze.

'I must say, Simon, since you became apprenticed to Mr Reynolds, you have lost much of your shyness. You have gained in confidence. Do you feel it in yourself?'

They had reached the house. Simon held the door open for her.

'I do, Sophia. I am at peace and filled with pleasure and

fulfilment. I have never been happier.'

She caught his eye.

He smiled at her.

'I am so glad, Simon,' Sophia said, reaching up to kiss his cheek.

Perdita, descending the stairs, caught the tail of their conversation. She glimpsed the kiss with delight. Of all things, a romantic attachment between her son and Sophia would be most welcome to her. The idea became fixed in her mind.

They are young yet. Time enough to nurture such thoughts when they reach a more appropriate age, she thought.

On the day before Edmond and Sophia's departure, organised confusion enveloped the household.

Furlong ordered the travelling arrangements.

'Mrs Narrowby and Mrs Cribb will travel with Meg, Lizzie and Clara,' Furlong informed them.

'Far be it from me, Mr Furlong, to be on my dignity, but I do think I should be the one to travel with Miss Sophia and not Dora. And I am sure Mrs Cribb will not relish being cooped up with three young maids of lower status than herself,' Mrs Narrowby informed Furlong, her head held so high her nose pointed almost to the ceiling.

'I am sorry Mrs Narrowby, but Miss Sophia made it plain that she would prefer to travel with her maid,' Furlong intoned, with awe-inspiring solemnity.

'And who, I wonder, put such a notion into her head,' Mrs Narrowby said with a derogatory sniff.

Furlong sighed. 'His Lordship will be travelling on horseback with Wilson. It is only right that Miss Sophia travel with her Lady's maid.'

'It's all right for *you*, Mr Furlong. There will only be four in your coach. There will be five in ours.'

'Four *men*, Mrs Narrowby. Four men and two of them on the large side. Whereas the three maids are small and will fit on one seat,' Mr Furlong explained with forced patience and decided firmness.

'Fagh! Mrs Narrowby said and left Mr Furlong's room in disgust.

Apart from seeing to Sophia and Edmond's baggage plus their own, various household implements and cookware were considered essential. Decanters, trays, and a variety of clothes brushes and boot cleaning equipment; bedding and table napery; pots, pans, dishes and Mrs Cribb's favourite rolling pin. All were packed in boxes and trunks to be transported in two closed carts.

Mrs Cribb, Mrs Narrowby and Furlong were aware that once they arrived at Crawford Lees, they were expected to assess conditions there, with the help of some staff from the lodge.

'If the house is in such a bad state, where will we all sleep, Mrs Narrowby, I would like to know,' Mrs Cribb said, folding her hands under her bosom.

'The lodge is large, Mrs Cribb. It is, of course, not as big as the main house, but it will easily accommodate us all,' Mrs Narrowby said, proud that she, apart from Furlong, was the only member of staff to have been there.

'It has its own housekeeper, of course, so I shall not have as many duties as I do here. I do not know whether they have a cook in residence,' she added, looking at Mrs Cribb sidelong.

Mrs Cribb straightened her apron.

'Well, Mrs Narrowby' she said. 'I have a lot more to do and the dinner to cook as well. I must get on.'

The last thing she wanted was to be at odds with the housekeeper who always became somewhat sharp when pressure was upon her.

Edmond put to rest his worries for his horses. In anticipation of Benson being there to see to them, he had recently increased their number. Some could now be stabled permanently at Crawford Lees. Edmond had told Benson that the head groom, Greer, would stay at Vere House. An elderly man who had served Edmond's father and brother, Greer was glad that some of his responsibility was taken from his shoulders.

Excitement filled Benson when he thought of his new duties—his new life. Yet, he worried. He didn't feel completely secure. He hoped he wouldn't commit some terrible mistake and lose his perfect job.

Edmond had picked up on the man's unease.

'I hope you will be comfortable at Crawford Lees, Benson. It sometimes takes time for city dwellers to acclimatise themselves to living in the country,' Edmond said. He had come to the stables to see how things were going.

Benson was busy rubbing down a horse. With a brush in his hand, he turned to Edmond.

'My Lord, I weren't born a city dweller. Me father was blacksmith in Loxford village. He died when I were sixteen, and that's when I joined the Army. I'd be glad to live in Crawford Lees. Mr Greer's been tellin me of it. It sounds grand,' Benson said. Turning back to the horse, he continued brushing its coat.

As he finished, he decided to point out some of his good points in case Edmond hadn't noticed.

'I've finished sorting out the carriages and got em clean as a new pin, Sir. I've inspected all the horse's shoes, and none of em needs renewing. Being a farrier, see, my Lord, you got two for the price of one in me. I'm a groom, but I'm also a farrier and can do a bit o' blacksmithin' as well.'

'I am fortunate to have you, Benson, and am pleased you are working for me. I wanted to be sure all was ready for our journey tomorrow. I see it is. Thank you, Benson. Good morning to you,' Edmond said and walked towards the house.

He was hungry and made his way to the morning room for his breakfast.

He found Perdita there, reading a periodical. It contained reports of exclusive social gatherings, which fuelled her desire to enter circles of society that had once been open to her. Her mind ran through the people she had already added to her list of friends, comparing them with those mentioned in an article, which told of those who had attended a *haut ton* ball.

Edmond was of a mind to share his thoughts.

'I have been thinking on our domestic arrangements at Crawford Lees,' he said as Furlong put a plate of kedgeree before him.

'I am wondering about which servants will come with us when we finally move. I have been giving this much consideration. I think perhaps they should make the choice themselves.'

Perdita listened with feigned interest. Her thoughts were elsewhere.

'People will not be comfortable if forced to move from town to country,' Edmond continued. 'I find when employees are uncomfortable their work suffers. I want those about me to be at peace with their surroundings, which is what I desire for myself.'

Perdita looked up for a moment from her periodical to take a sip of her tea. She had heard Edmond speak of his staff in this way before and found his care of them excessive. On previous occasions, she vehemently voiced her opinions. Today she was far too preoccupied with her own plans to comment. Continuing with her breakfast, she acknowledged his statement with the glimpse of a smile and a sociable nod.

Edmond had brought the subject up with Mrs Cribb and Mrs Narrowby. Although appreciating Edmond's attitude towards his staff, they were of the same opinion as Perdita. They thought Edmond's treatment of the lower servant indulgent and unwarranted. Without consultation, they chose the maids and footmen to accompany them.

Early in the morning of the following day, three carriages and two carts piled with luggage and people set off for Crawford Lees. Edmond, Wilson and Benson rode.

The entire cortege stopped twice overnight on the

journey.

The week before, Edmond had sent Wilson to find suitable inns along the way. He hoped to avoid a repeat of Sophia's discomfort when they first travelled from Weymouth to Kensington.

Their stay at both inns was uneventful. On the last stretch of the journey, everyone looked forward eagerly for their first sight of Crawford Lees.

Situated in a hamlet, they approached the house from a high point in the road.

The house looked beautiful from this angle, its honey-hued sandstone glowing in the bright spring light. Two-storey wings lay at right angles to the main three-storey house. Trees surrounded it, and at some distance behind the house, the sun sparkled on a large lake.

When they saw the house without distance lending it appeal, disappointment filled them. They could see it was uninhabitable. The west wing was in the sorriest state. Where windows were broken, birds flew in and out. The top of a big, heavy chimney pot had broken off. The roof was damaged where pieces of the chimney pot had penetrated it. In other places, part of the brickwork had crumbled. Dead ivy clung to one wall of the south wing.

The wonderful sweep of the gravel drive was infested with weeds. The grass enclosed by the drive's oval was home to a carpet of colourful, wild, meadow flowers rioting through it.

The inhabitants of the coaches were speechless as they gazed on the dilapidation.

'I have not seen it in three years,' Edmond said to Wilson. 'It is far worse than I expected. Much work and dedication will be needed to put all this to rights.'

'It'll definitely keep you occupied, Sir,' Wilson remarked.

'That it will, Wilson,' Edmond said as he turned his horse around to face the coaches.

He raised his voice.

'No doubt you know that we shall be staying at the

lodge. I shall show you the way. Will you all please follow me.'

He rode back the way they had come and turned off to the left, half way down an avenue of lime trees.

At the end of the avenue, they came to a large foursquare red-brick building. The windows shone, the paintwork everywhere was fresh and clean. The gravel drive leading to the front door was well kept, not a weed in sight.

Several footmen descended the lodge steps and began taking the luggage into the house.

Edmond dismounted. 'You will find the stables behind the house, Benson. Please take charge of my horse and Wilson's.'

Everyone erupted from the coaches, the women shaking out their skirts, the men adjusting their coats.

A small fair woman in a plain, light brown gown came to stand at the top of the steps.

Mrs Narrowby recognised the housekeeper, Agnes Eldridge, and went to her.

Sophia went to Edmond who stood to one side watching the people scurrying about before him.

No doubt the housekeeper and Mrs Narrowby will sort them out, he thought, unwilling to impose his authority on them just yet.

'The house is in a dreadful state, is it not, Edmond?' Sophia said.

'Yes, Sophia. But take heart. I mean to put everything to rights. It may take some time, but it will happen,' Edmond said, hoping his words were true.

If Edmond hadn't informed those living at the lodge to expect an influx of people, no one would have had a place to sleep. As it was, Mrs Eldridge, the housekeeper, had everything in hand and sent the lodge's head footman to show the Vere House men their rooms, and she, herself, showed the maids to theirs.

Within the hour, all the serving men and women, including Wilson, sat in the servant's hall eating their luncheon.

Edmond and Sophia ate theirs in the airy dining room on the first floor of the lodge.

After they had all eaten, Edmond sent word to the staff that he wished them to attend him in the hall.

Standing on the polished wooden stairs, a hand on the shining balustrade, he addressed the servants gathered below him.

'You must all appreciate the daunting task we have before us. I know it will be a long time before we can make the main house fit to live in,' Edmond began.

'This is not something we can accomplish overnight. Initially, we must discover what needs to be done. I hope you will all make a thorough assessment.'

His eyes sought Mrs Narrowby.

'Mrs Narrowby?'

She raised her hand.

Ah, yes, there you are. You will assess the state of the drapery, upholstery, table napery, linen and such.'

Mrs Narrowby gave a small curtsy and nodded her assent.

Mrs Cribb was standing not far from him.

'You, Mrs Cribb, evaluate the state of the kitchen if you please.'

'Yes my Lord,' she said with a nod.

'Furlong? Where is Furlong?'

'I am here, my Lord,' Furlong said from the back of the hall. He held himself a little apart from the rest of the staff.

'Furlong, please look at the overall condition of the rooms in the main house and in the east and west wings.'

'I shall, my Lord. I wonder whether …?'

Edmond was used to speaking to groups of trained soldiers under his command; to be interrupted gave him a jolt.

'Speak to me later, Furlong,' Edmond said, trying to hide his irritation.

Furlong did little to hide his.

'Benson?' Edmond called.

'Sir!' Benson replied, standing to attention.

'Benson, please report on the condition of the stables,' Edmond said.

'Yes, Sir,' Benson said, feeling as if he should salute.

Edmond gave him an appreciative look. If only they could all take orders like soldiers.

'Mrs Narrowby, Mrs Cribb, Mr Furlong, Mr Benson, choose people to assist you.

He now addressed the whole group.

'Those of you who can write, please make notes on what you see—everything you see—and when all our evaluations are complete, we may tackle the task methodically.

'Eventually, we will turn this dilapidation around and make Crawford Lees a place that is a pleasure to live in.'

Edmond delivered his speech as if he were addressing troops about to go into battle. He was surprised to find it had the same effect. The expressions on the faces of the people standing before him ranged from eager anticipation to determination. He felt he had encouraged them. Indeed, they *were* all encouraged.

The following day, Edmond called Furlong, Mrs Narrowby, Mrs Cribb and Benson to the study to discuss their findings.

Their faces didn't show quite the same enthusiasm as the day before.

Edmond sat behind his desk. He had asked his agent, Henry Lambert, and Henry's secretary, Joe Martin to be present at the meeting. They sat at either end of the desk. The four servants stood before Edmond.

'No doubt you are wondering who these gentlemen are. May I now introduce them to you. This is Mr Lambert, my agent,' Edmond said, indicating Henry with a hand waved in his direction.

Henry Lambert was tall and fair, with myopic blue eyes, over which he wore wire-rimmed spectacles. Fidgety and anxious, he frequently adjusted these on his nose.

Henry rose, nodded to the group and took his seat

303

again.

'And this is Mr Martin, his secretary.'

Joe Martin was a small, bright man, with intelligent eyes. His brisk manner gave off an air of efficiency.

Joe remained seated.

'Good morning,' he said, smiling.

'Mrs Narrowby, will you speak first?' Edmond said.

Today Mrs Narrowby looked more neat than usual. She had dispensed with her white cap. She wore her Sunday best dress which she had unearthed from her trunk. The dress was black, made of heavy satin with narrow black lace in strips adorning the high neck, the front, and above the hem. Tiny black jet buttons ran up the sides of the narrow sleeves, almost to her elbow. The sleeves puffed out before they met the shoulder. She carried herself with more than usual self-possession.

Mrs Narrowby took a step forward, glancing at the notes in her hand.

'The upholstery is threadbare and sadly sagging. The wood everywhere is scratched and stained beyond repair. All the rooms will need new carpets, and drapery at the windows, and on the beds. And the linen,' her face wore a worried frown as she looked up from her notes. 'Goodness, my Lord, it is so moth-eaten, I despair of any being of use.'

She curtsied taking a step back.

'Thank you, Mrs Narrowby,' Edmond said.

'Mrs Cribb, will you tell us, if you please, what you have found?'

Mrs Cribb was dressed in her usual kitchen garb, a dark pink gown covered by a white apron with her cap covering most of her hair. Her sleeves were unrolled and buttoned at her wrists, her only tribute to the formality of the occasion.

Furlong felt slighted. He should have spoken before the housekeeper. He had let the breach pass. Now the cook was given precedence before him. His lips drew together in a thin line.

Mrs Cribb pulled at her sleeves.

'Well, my lord, first the good part, all the china and crockery needs cleaning, of course, so dusty are they. Other than that, it is all complete and nothing wrong with it—apart from being sadly out of style, my lord. The pots, pans, and other utensils are dusty too, but in good condition. If everything were cleaned, I would be happy to work with it.'

She folded her hands beneath her ample bosom.

'Now to the bad things. The range is…unusable.'

She added in a rush, 'Would it be possible to have one of those new ones they talk of? I hear they are far more efficient. Perhaps Mr Lambert could look into that?' she said, glancing in his direction.

Edmond nodded and turned to Furlong who cleared his throat ready to speak.

'I haven't finished, my Lord,' Mrs Cribb said, glaring at Furlong.

'I beg your pardon, Mrs Cribb,' Edmond said, hiding his amusement.

He was well aware of the rivalry between Furlong and Mrs Cribb.

'Pray continue,' Edmond said.

Mrs Cribb took a breath, pointedly ignoring Furlong.

'I am sorry to say the kitchen floor is badly cracked and chipped. I think a new one needs to be laid. Also, the cupboards in the kitchen have …'

For the next word, she leant forward and lowered her voice to a whisper.

'… Woodworm. I think we must have new ones.'

She straightened and continued.

'The kitchen itself is sizeable—fine and large. Nevertheless, my Lord, none of the rooms leading off it are big enough. The scullery, the larder, the pantry and buttery, all of them, are far smaller than at Vere House. Would it be possible to make them bigger?'

Edmond took a look at Mr Lambert, who nodded to Mr Martin who made a note in his book.

'Then there is the laundry and the dairy. I would not be

surprised if they have not been touched since the first King James was on the throne! Something must be done with those.'

Joe Martin laughed. He coughed and, blushing, bent his head over his book.

Mrs Cribb curtsied, looking at her Master, who rewarded her with an encouraging smile.

'Thank you, Mrs, Cribb. A most comprehensive assessment. Now, Furlong, your report, if you please.'

Furlong cleared his throat again, glancing sidelong at Mrs Cribb.

'I have walked around the whole house, my Lord,' Furlong began, in his usual mournful tone. 'I find the west wing in such a state of dilapidation pulling down and rebuilding is all that could be done. However, as regards the east wing, it would be possible to renovate.

'The Main House itself is sturdy. Refurbishment and redecoration of the rooms would suffice. But it will need to be done on a grand scale.'

Furlong bowed his head elegantly to indicate his report was complete.

'Thank you, Furlong,' Edmond said.

Furlong has told me nothing I have not seen for myself. I shall go with Lambert to look at it again, Edmond thought.

'Benson, what have you found?' Edmond asked.

Benson stood to attention. Edmond felt like telling him to stand easy.

'The stable buildings themselves, my Lord, are strong and in reasonable condition. However, everything within them needs renovating. I have written out a list, Sir, and have presented it to Mr Martin.'

'Thank you, Benson. Most efficient of you,' Edmond said.

Benson took a glance around at the other three, wondering why they hadn't done the same. *Perhaps they can't write*, he thought, proud that he could.

'Thank you all for your work,' Edmond said. 'You may

go, now. Mr Martin will speak to you individually tomorrow.'

Edmond dismissed them with a nod as he turned to Joe Martin.

'Mr Martin, have you noted all that has been said?'

'Yes, my Lord,' Joe said with a bright smile.

Edmond realised the amount of work that needed to be done would cost a great deal. For the first time since he inherited, he appreciated the size of his fortune. The work was necessary if he wanted to make Crawford Lees his permanent home. He also realised it would be some time before it would be possible to take up residence.

He rose to leave the study and go to the dining room. Hunger told him it was time for his luncheon.

'Go, gentlemen. Have something to eat. After our meal, I wish to inspect the nearest area of the estate. Will you accompany me, if you please? I will meet you in front of the lodge under the plane tree.' Edmond said and left them to themselves.

'I am not looking forward to this, Joe,' Henry Lambert confided, as they left the study and crossed to the hall door.

'No Henry. None of it is our fault. Remember that. We must not allow the blame to fall on us. Whether he likes it or not, Lord Edmond must be told the truth,' Joe said, with a decisive nod.

'Where do you think we should go to take our lunch?' Henry asked. 'I don't mind lunching in the servant's hall, but maybe we are expected to go somewhere else.'

While they discussed the matter, Benson approached them from the back of the hall.

'Mr Martin, Mr Lambert,' Ned said nodding to each man in turn.

'I couldn't help overhearing your conversation, gentlemen. I am about to take luncheon. I wonder whether you'd like to eat with me? One of the girls from the lodge brought me meal to me there yesterday. There was far too much for one. Would you care to share it?' Benson asked, glad of the company, but wondering if the two would feel too far above him to accept.

'Thank you, Benson,' Henry said, 'What say you, Joe?'

'A most welcome invitation, Benson, thank you,' Joe replied.

Benson led them to the coach house, and up to the long room above it. One end was filled with lumber, the other end neat and tidy, with a polished table in the middle of the room. A comfortable easy-chair stood by the hearth.

'This used to be the coachman's quarters. I mean to make it mine. It is cluttered now, but I'll soon bring it up to scratch,' Benson explained as he showed Henry and Joe into the room.

A pretty fair-haired girl was laying the table for Benson.

'Mary-Anne, I've guests for luncheon. Is there plates enough to go round?' He asked.

Mary-Anne looked up with a smile.

'Good afternoon, Sirs. Of course, there is, Ned, er … Mr Benson. Just a minute.'

She went to a cupboard hidden behind the door and took out knives and forks, two plates and two mugs. She set them on the table where Benson's place was already laid out. In the middle of the table stood three covered dishes and a large brown jug.

Mary-Anne put her hands to her mouth.

'Napkins. There aren't napkins!' she lamented.

Benson smiled.

'Mary-Anne,' he said, laying a large hand gently on her shoulder. 'I'm not used to napkins, and I'm sure we can all manage with our handkerchiefs if need be. Don't trouble yourself.'

Mary-Anne blushed and smiled up at him.

Henry and Joe exchanged looks. Later they agreed that within a year, Benson would be married to Mary-Anne. All the signs were there.

'I'll leave you then, Sirs,' she said, bobbing a curtsy and adding, 'I hope you enjoy your food. I cooked it myself.' She glanced at Benson, blushed, and hurried away.

The three dined well on the plane fare. Rabbit stew, boiled potatoes and beans, with ale from the jug to wash it down.

After luncheon, outside the lodge, Joe and Henry, mounted on their horses, waited for Edmond.

Benson stood with them holding Edmond's horse.

They saw him leaving the lodge, his riding crop under his arm. He put on his gloves as he walked purposefully towards them, his boots crunching on the gravel drive.

'Good afternoon gentlemen. I propose starting by riding to the home farm. I want to inspect the houses. I shall finish by interviewing the tenants,' Edmond informed them as he took the bridle from Ned.

'Thank you, Benson,' he said.

Benson lowered his head. At night, he stayed in a cottage on the home farm with Silas Jup, a farmer.

Benson hoped Edmond would speak to Silas. Although Silas did his best, the cottage was in a state of disrepair, with, among other things, a leaky roof, a smoking chimney, and broken flagstones on the kitchen floor.

As he rode through the home farm area, Edmond became increasingly infuriated with what he found. Some of the accommodation was in fine shape. Some was adequate. Most was poorly maintained. Many of his tenants lived in a state of virtual squalor.

At the farthest point of the home farm dwellings, in a little copse of birch trees, Edmond reined in his horse and dismounted. Lambert and Martin followed suit.

Edmond turned to Henry. 'Is it all like this, Lambert?' Edmond asked, his eyebrows drawn together.

'Some is better kept up than the rest. On the whole, much needs attention,' Lambert replied, his fussy hands moving nervously on his horse's reins.

'Why the devil has nothing been done about it, man?' Edmond demanded, his voice raised in annoyance.

Edmond's horse vigorously shook its head.

He took hold of the bridle, running his hand automatically along its neck, momentarily distracted.

'My Lord, when you first inherited, Mr Treadwell was the agent, and I his assistant. You made some remarks to him regarding the upkeep of the cottages that they should all be kept in a state of good repair, as I remember. Mr Treadwell thought it best we should carry on as we had under the old Master and took no notice of your instructions,' he said, the corners of his thin lips turned down.

Edmond was speechless. His dark brows came together, his eyes blazed.

The horse moved his head again as Edmond's hand tightened on the bridle.

Lambert's eyes wandered as if looking for a means of escape. He stood his ground as his uneasy eyes and Edmond's angry ones met.

'As I remember, my Lord, he showed you only the parts in best repair, and paid the tenants to say nothing in complaint,' Henry stated, wishing he was one hundred miles away.

'Did he, by God!' Edmond uttered through gritted teeth. 'And my tenants suffer because of him. I swear, were he not dead, I would bring him near it.'

Eyes glinting, nostrils flaring, Edmond turned on the unfortunate Mr Lambert.

'Have you done anything, anything at all, to rectify his mismanagement?'

Henry swallowed. 'I did my best, my Lord. I began a scheme of building new cottages, near the home farm. The work has been slow, as Mr Ogden Carterett, your accountant, was reluctant to spend money on what he termed "unnecessary work", he being of the same mind as Mr Treadwell.'

Edmond's face darkened, his expression thunderous. The situation reminded him of conditions within the Army. Enlisted Men going hungry and ill-clad when government funds were withheld.

He took a deep breath and let it out slowly, trying to control his anger. He turned to Joe.

'Mr Martin, will you please write to Mr Carterett. Require him to come to me here, at the lodge, as soon as he receives my letter.'

'Yes, my Lord,' Joe Martin said, scribbling quickly in his notebook.

Edmond stood, hands on his hips, and took stock of the two young men before him.

'Gentlemen, I believe the entire estate probably needs an overhaul. It may take some years to achieve. The quicker it commences, the quicker we shall succeed. Are you in agreement with me?'

'Certainly, my Lord,' Lambert said, a smile appearing on his fresh, young face. 'I would have done far more to set things right if my hands weren't tied.'

'I am at your service, my Lord,' Martin said, flicking his eyes from Lambert to Edmond.

'Ogden Carterett thwarted Henry in everything he tried to do,' Joe explained.

Glancing around him furtively, he added in an under voice, 'I would be surprised if some corruption was not involved. I shall say no more.'

He shook his head sagely.

Edmond gave him a narrow look.

'Where does Mr Carterett live, Mr Martin?'

'In a large house in Oxford Town, my Lord.'

'Hmm,' Edmond said, rubbing his chin. 'Forget the letter, Mr Martin. I think I shall pay him a visit. Will you accompany me early tomorrow, gentlemen?'

The two looked at each other, grinning. They turned towards Edmond, saying together.

'Yes, my Lord.'

Edmond spoke to Joe Martin.

'Ogden Carterett has no information regarding my coming here—I doubt whether he knows I am in England. He has had no time to cover his tracks. While Mr Lambert and I are speaking with Mr Carterett, will you please go to the chief clerk er …?

'Denton, my Lord,' Martin supplied

'Yes, Denton. Require him to produce the Crawford Lees estate's ledgers. If Denton refuses, you must tell him I am about to bring Mr Carterett before a magistrate, and if he does not comply, he too will be implicated.'

Mr Martin's face slowly broke into a wide grin.

'It will be a pleasure, my Lord.'

'We shall meet tomorrow before the Lodge at Seven,' Edmond said.

'Yes, my Lord,' Martin and Lambert said.

'Until tomorrow, then, Gentlemen,' Edmond said before mounting his horse and taking off towards the lodge.

When Edmond was out of sight, the two shook hands and beat each other on the back, laughing.

Carterett would get his comeuppance at last.

On arriving at the lodge, Edmond returned to his study. He was still furious. He took a glass and a bottle of brandy from his cupboard and downed several glasses before he was calm enough to visit the estate's office which hadn't been touched in years. Everything was covered in dust. Edmond lost himself in the task of trying to sort it out.

The following morning, Edmond, Joe Martin and Henry Lambert met in front of the Lodge, at seven, as arranged.

'A fine morning, my Lord,' Joe Martin remarked.

'Indeed, Joe. A good day to get things done,' Edmond replied.

They spoke as they walked their horses towards the gate.

'You know what you must do, Joe?' Edmond asked.

'Yes, my Lord. I shall demand the ledgers and frighten the hell out of him if he refuses,' Martin said.

Edmond controlled his laughter. 'Ha, in short, Joe, that is right.'

Edmond couldn't help smiling.

'One thing troubles me, however, Joe. How will you

find Mr Denton?'

'Mr Lambert and I have been there several times before, Sir. I know the layout of the place,' Joe said, grinning.

'Good,' Edmond said.

'Must we not keep Carterett occupied, to give Joe a chance to get at the ledgers?' Henry asked.

'Correct, Henry,' Edmond replied

They reached the gate.

'Let us away, then, gentlemen,' Edmond said, mounting his horse and setting off at a cracking rate. Joe and Henry glanced at each other, mounted their horses, and followed.

When they arrived in Oxford town, Mr Martin led them towards Mr Ogden Carterett's house.

The three rode to the stables at the back of the house, where they left their horses. Going around to the front, they knocked at the door.

A lackey opened it.

'Good morning. May I help you?' he said.

Henry stepped forward, handing him Edmond's card.

'We have come to see Mr Carterett,' Henry said.

'Have you an appointment? Mr Carterett does not see anyone without an appointment and never before ten o'clock,' the lackey intoned, in a Furlongish way.

Edmond gently pushed Henry out of the way.

'I am Lord Edmond St Vere, Major in the second of foot, Queen's own infantry. Mr Carterett is my accountant. I do *not* need an appointment.'

Edmond spoke quietly, but with such force that the lackey turned white.

'I shall tell Mr Carterett you are here, Major... er... my Lord. Will you step this way?'

Edmond turned his head a little and winked at Joe who had difficulty keeping a serious face. Henry looked anxious.

They were shown into a well-appointed Salon, decorated in pink and gold. Sheraton furniture stood about the room. On the mantel shelf, Limoges porcelain ornaments.

Noticing the opulence, Edmond scowled, his eyes frosty.

The Lackey returned.

'Follow me please, my Lord,' he said, his tone far different.

Edmond and Lambert walked behind the lackey while Martin hung back.

When no one was in sight, with his saddlebags slung over his shoulder, he made his way to the back of the house where Ogden Carterett's three clerks worked.

Without knocking, Martin went straight into the room and up to Mr Denton's desk.

'May I please have the ledgers for any and all business to do with the Crawford Lees estate,' he asked, his chin up, a determined look in his eye.

Mr Denton was taken aback.

'Who *are* you, Sir?' he asked, blinking behind his spectacles.

Martin took a stance. He leant slightly forward, one hand on his hip, the other fist resting on Denton's desk.

'I am Mr Joseph Martin, secretary to Mr Henry Lambert, Lord St Vere's agent,' Joe informed him.

Mr Denton regarded Joe in astonishment. It took him a moment's thought to decide what to do. He removed his spectacles and rose from his chair.

'I'm not about to allow you to peruse private accounts. Be off with you!' Denton cautioned, towering over little Mr Martin.

The other two clerk's heads rose as they looked at each other.

Undaunted, Joe straightened and launched into the speech he had carefully rehearsed in his head all the way from Crawford Lees.

'We know that Mr Treadwell was involved in corrupt dealings in the affairs of Crawford Lees. We also have reason to believe that Mr Carterett conspired with him in the corruption. If you do not cooperate, we, that is, Mr Lambert, Lord St Vere, and I, shall have no other option than to expose you as complicit in their criminal activities.'

Mr Denton blanched. His eyes narrowed.

'I have nothing to do with whatever Ogden Carterett is about. He keeps those books himself.'

Denton walked to a cupboard at the other side of the room and unlocked it. He took out six large ledgers and gave them to Joe.

'You may take them and welcome, as long as I'm not implicated,' he said, with a furtive look at the other two clerks. They glanced at each other again and lowered their eyes to their work.

Joe put the books in the saddlebags.

'Is there a back way out to the stables, Mr Denton?' Joe asked.

'Through the kitchen garden; I'll get someone to show you the way,' Denton said, tugging the bell rope.

While waiting, Joe turned to one of the clerks.

'Will you lend me a pen and a sheet of paper, if you please, Sir?'

The clerk handed Joe his own pen, and a sheet of paper, which he took from his desk drawer.

Joe took them from the clerk's hand to scribble a note.

A small servant girl with dark hair and big blue eyes appeared.

'Please show Mr Martin to the stables, Sally,' Denton said to her.

'Yes, Mr Denton,' she said before turning to Joe.

'Follow me please, Mr Martin,' she said, looking up into Joe's dark eyes. She smiled, showing her dimples and bobbed a curtsy.

Mr Martin was immune to her allure. He had already given his heart.

Once in the stables, Joe took the note he had scribbled, attaching it to Edmond's saddle. He mounted his own horse and took the road back to Crawford Lees, well before Edmond and Henry had finished with Carterett.

While Joe visited Mr Denton, Edmond and Henry were shown to Ogden Carterett's office.

'Lord St Vere and his agent to see you, Mr Carterett,' the lackey intoned.

Carterett rose.

'Thank you, Culver,' he said and moved forward.

He bowed.

'Good morning, my Lord. I was not aware of your being in England. How long is the duration of your stay?' he enquired, a false, smarmy simper plastering his face.

Edmond took a grip on his anger, schooled his face to affability, and smiled.

'Good morning Mr Carterett. I am not sure how long I will stay, Sir. Probably some while,' Edmond replied, thinking to give the slimy creature as little information as possible.

'What may I do for you, my Lord?' Carterett asked.

He pursed his lips primly, clasping his hands on his chest.

Parted in the middle, Mr Carterett's pale hair hung, in wisps, either side of his head. He had forgotten to replace his wig, which rested on a chair by his desk. His clothes were of the finest quality, but his figure was long and gaunt. From his concave chest to his spindly legs, there was nothing to admire in his appearance.

'I would like to see the ledgers of the Crawford Lees estate, if you please, Mr Carterett,' Edmond announced brightly, the corners of his mouth lifting.

Ogden Carterett's expression lost its shine. His eyes turned cold. He paused a long moment before answering.

'Ahh … I am sorry to say, my Lord, you have had a wasted journey. The ledgers are in London. In fact, all the ledgers pertaining to your estate are in London.'

Edmond's smile vanished. His eyes darkened. His face became more serious.

'What are they doing in London, Mr Carterett?' he

asked.

'Oh, for safe-keeping, yes, safe-keeping. I could not risk them falling into unscrupulous hands. Oh, goodness me, no, indeed.'

'I see,' Edmond said. A sweet smile appeared again on his face. His eyes remained sharp.

'Then, Mr Carterett, will you please send to London, and have them delivered to me at Crawford Lees? I would be much obliged.'

'Of course, my Lord, I am entirely at your service. May I offer you refreshment?'

'Thank you, no, Sir. I shall welcome you at Crawford Lees when the ledgers arrive. Good day to you.'

Edmond bowed. He left the room followed by Lambert.

In the stables, Edmond plucked the note from his saddle, letting out an exclamation.

'Ah, good lad, Joe!' He turned to Lambert. 'He has taken the ledgers to Crawford Lees.'

Lambert laughed.

'How are you with figures, Lambert?' Edmond asked.

Lambert mounted his horse.

'I have a good knowledge of them, my Lord,' he said, with an air of confidence. 'I assume you want me to look at the accounts?'

'Yes, Lambert,' Edmond replied.

Edmond led his horse out of the stables. Henry followed him.

'I think it is time to seek the Magistrate's advice,' he said as he mounted.

'I shall ask him to visit us tomorrow. We shall then see what is to be done. Do you know where he lives?' Edmond enquired.

'I do, my Lord. Do you want to visit him now, Sir?'

'Yes, Lambert, the sooner the better.'

When Edmond and Henry arrived at Crawford Lees, they found Joe Martin in Edmond's study, glancing through the ledgers he had acquired from Denton.

'Did you have much difficulty in persuading Denton to let you have the books, Mr Martin?' Edmond asked.

'Once I told him he would be implicated if he did not cooperate, he handed them over like a lamb, my Lord,' Joe said, his ready smile beaming.

'Have you seen anything suspicious in them?' Edmond asked.

'No, sir. I'm not as good with figures as Henry. He is most proficient. If there is anything there, he will find it, my Lord,' Joe said, gathering up the books and handing them over to Henry.

'I hope you can find something by tomorrow, Mr Lambert,' Edmond said.

'Well, my Lord, I shall do my best. May I use this room, sir?'

'Of course. Everything here is at your disposal,' Edmond replied.

Henry took up residence in Edmond's office and pored over the ledgers well into the night.

In the morning, Edmond invited Henry Lambert to breakfast with him.

'So, Henry, what have you found?' Edmond asked, putting his napkin on his lap. Over their meal, Lambert told Edmond what he had discovered.

'Untold discrepancies, my Lord. Money has been taken from one account and put into another in a … em … creative way. I am sure Ogden Carterett has been lining his pockets for years,' he confided.

'Thank you, Henry. I felt sure that would be the case. It is not so much for myself I am annoyed, but for the tenants who have suffered hardship because of him. How do you feel about becoming my accountant, Sir? Do you think you are up to it?'

'Indeed I am, my Lord. Nothing would give me greater pleasure. But what of the agency? Who would fill the gap?'

'I think young Martin is more than capable, do you

not?'

'Well, my Lord, he has been at my elbow ever since Treadwell's demise and knows as much of the business I conduct as I do myself. I think he would make an excellent agent. Of course, he can always come to me for advice, should he have difficulty,' Lambert said.

During the morning, Sir James Hawtree, the Magistrate, kept the appointment they had arranged the previous day. Sir James, Henry Lambert and Edmond sat together in the drawing-room.

Edmond took his brandy and three glasses from a cabinet.

'May I offer you brandy, Sir James? Edmond asked.

'Most kind,' Sir James said accepting the proffered glass.

Henry was surprised at being given one too.

Edmond and Henry told Sir James of Carterett's duplicity. When they had finished, Sir James shook his head and sighed.

'Let me go over the facts, my Lord. You specifically asked Mr Ogden Carterett for the ledgers. He told you they were in London. Mr Lambert is a witness to that?'

'He is, Sir,' Edmond said.

'We must have an affidavit from you, Mr Lambert, to that effect. And you say Mr Martin was given the said ledgers by Mr Denton?'

'Yes, Sir,' Edmond replied.

'He must provide an affidavit, too.'

Sir James took snuff and continued.

'You have also stated how Mr Lambert has now discovered discrepancies in the ledgers, which suggest Mr Ogden Carterett has been misappropriating monies from your estate?'

'Yes, Sir. So it would seem.'

Edmond nodded, sitting back in his seat.

'I assume you would wish Carterett to be prosecuted for his crimes?'

'Will that not take a long time, Sir James? I am here for a month or two only,' Edmond said.

Sir James brushed a particle of snuff from the lace at his wrist. He looked earnestly into Edmond's face.

'This sort of crime is something I abhor, my Lord. It would give me pleasure to hurry things along, so to speak. He has probably treated others in a similar way. No, I do not think a prosecution will take long. I shall set the wheels in motion.'

He picked up his glass to sip Edmond's excellent brandy.

'First, I shall have him arrested. We shall then go from there.'

The last of the brandy in his glass gone, he looked at the bottle appreciatively.

'I must say, Sir, this is a most superior brandy. Where did you come by it?' Sir James enquired, holding his glass and inspecting the bottle, in hope of more.

'Oh, I leave all that to my man, Sir James. He is an exceptional fellow,' Edmond said.

He poured another measure into the magistrate's glass, trusting there would be no further comments in that direction. Wilson had his own ideas about procuring liquor, as Edmond knew. He didn't think the magistrate would approve of them.

CHAPTER THIRTY

While Edmond consulted with Sir James, Sophia decided to explore the gardens. Leaving the lodge, she walked along the Avenue and found her way to the sweep of the drive before the house. There she pulled up short.

Her first impression was one of chaos.

A leaf-strewn path ran around the house. She followed it and found herself in the remnants of the kitchen garden where straggly vegetables were just discernible among the weeds. A huge rosemary bush dominated the patch where herbs had once been lovingly cultivated. Mint and thyme struggled for dominance. Lemon balm sprung up in the cracks of the paved path, which ran through the middle of the area. The high walls, which protected the spot, couldn't be seen for ivy clinging to the bricks. She kicked a big stone and jumped when a huge beetle scurried off into the grass. She bent down to see where it had gone and found an old bucket buried beneath the overgrown cabbage patch. She looked inside it and found a nest of baby mice. Not wishing to disturb "nature" Sophia carefully put it back the way she found it and moved on.

She heard the chirring squawk of a magpie and looked up to see his black and white flight.

Another landed on a branch above her head.

'One for sorrow, two for joy,' she repeated.

'Hmm,' she said, gratified that there had been two.

She walked farther around the house and arrived at a terrace. The grey stone had patches of emerald moss and yellow lichen here and there. Steps led down into what had once been a knot garden.

Uncut branches sprouted at strange angles from the pleached yew trees surrounding it. Various shrubs that once stood, carefully clipped into neat rows, now embraced each other riotously.

A path led from the knot garden to a meadow. Sophia surmised it had been the lawn. A patch in the middle seemed less overgrown. Sophia discovered that beneath its sparse coat of weeds was a brick path. If the path hadn't been laid to run towards the lake, Sophia wouldn't have been able to fight her way through the high, wild weeds, some as tall as herself.

She walked towards the lake, thinking to walk around it, inspecting it as she had the one at Vere House.

Disappointment filled her when she reached the stretch of water. It was covered with green slime and waterweeds by the bank, but towards the middle, Sophia saw clear water. The slime was scummy. Dead leaves, odd branches, feathers and unidentifiable rubbish floating in it. The decaying muck gave off a faint green smell.

Sophia shook her head. No, she didn't wish to explore here.

Around the edge, the once-beautiful trees ran riot. If pruned, Sophia imagined they would form a lovely aspect when seen from the house.

As she stood contemplating what once was, she heard a movement near her. She stood very still, listening, telling herself it could be nothing to fear.

'Good morning, Miss, what might you be wanting?' a gentle voice inquired.

Glancing about, she saw a wizened old man nearby, leaning on a staff.

He wore a battered, old, shapeless, brown hat, a brown waistcoat and breeches, with a slim black coat down to his knees. Around his neck was knotted a spotlessly white kerchief.

'Good morning, Sir. I came to explore the garden,' she explained, scrutinising him.

He peered at her. A frown drew his eyebrows together causing him to appear somewhat forbidding.

Sophia determined not to be intimidated.

'What a pity it has been let run wild. It must have been magnificent once.'

The old man's expression changed to one of friendliness.

'Aye, that it was, Miss,' the old man said, looking about, nodding. Although his eyes were old, they were incredibly blue. A look of sadness passed across them.

Sophia looked about her at the overgrown muddle and wanted to cheer him, to take away his melancholy.

'It will not be like this for long, you know. Edmond is determined to restore it to what it was.'

'Oh aye?' the man said without enthusiasm. 'And who be this Edmond person when he be at home?'

'He is Lord St Vere. May I ask who you are, Sir?'

His old face crinkled into a smile as he considered her.

'I'm Gabriel Bothing.'

He nodded and pulled the front of his wispy hair.

'You must be Miss Sophia.'

'Yes, I am,' Sophia said, delight in her voice. 'How did you know?'

'My sister, Agnes—she looks after the lodge, Miss— she told me of you. The Master is your guardian, ain't he? And when they've fixed up the house, you'll live here, won't you?'

Sophia glanced at Bothing and sighed.

'I shall, but repairing the house will take a long time. I think the garden will have to wait 'til the house is put in order.'

Gabriel leant on his staff and stroked his chin. He gave Sophia a hard stare. Smiling, he nodded his head slowly.

'I'll tell you what it is, Miss, if I had enough help, say, seven strong men, just at first, like, I know what must be done, and I could tell 'em.'

Gabriel peered around, shaking his head.

'I was one of the gardeners here in the old Master's time, and I don't mean the present Master's father, but his grandfather. The Old Master loved his garden, he did—ah, I were just a boy then, but I remember how it was.'

He gazed at the long grass, at the choked lake, at the trees and back to Sophia.

'Could you, Mr Bothing?' Sophia said, her eyes bright, her hands clasped beneath her chin.

'Could you really oversee putting the place back to rights? Oh, that would be wonderful.'

She clapped her hands, then paused. 'I must tell Edmond—I mean, Lord St Vere—I am sure he would appreciate your help with the restoration,' Sophia said, giving Bothing her most charming smile.

'Where can Lord St Vere find you if he wants to talk to you about it?' she asked.

'Oh, my house in't far, Miss. Do you want me to show you?'

'Yes, please, Mr Bothing.'

'Ere! Don't you go "Mister-ing" me, Miss,' he said gruffly. 'If you want to call me anythin', me name's Gabriel. Only Agnes, me sister, ever calls me that now. But I'd count it an honour if you'd use me name,' he said, his old eyes twinkling as he smiled.

'And I should be honoured if you allowed it … Gabriel.'

Gabriel's smile deepened.

'This way, then, Miss Sophia,' he said, gesturing the direction they must go. 'Follow me.'

Bothing had taken a fancy to Sophia. She reminded him of his granddaughter when she was young. Sophia's exuberance for the garden's restoration won his heart.

'I bin dreamin' about these gardens, and I thought, afore I die, I'd like to see 'em as they used to be. Reckon I doesn't have too many years left in me. Ah, but 'tis a shame it's been allowed to get this way. Fair brings a tear to me eye, and that's the truth,' he said, taking out a tattered handkerchief and wiping his eyes.

Thinking his dream of restoring the gardens might become a reality, his heart was full.

He led her along a path, one footfall wide, through the long grass and weeds, which he had trodden often.

Sophia found herself at the edge of a wooded area, in front of her, a thatched cottage, the outside painted white and the door and window frames light blue.

'Oh, what a pretty-little house, Gabriel. And the garden

is lovely with all the different flowers growing about it—what are those little-pointed things, like small hay stooks?'

'They's me bees, Miss Sophia. If you care to come in, I'll give you a cup o' milk and a slice o' bread, spread with their honey.'

'Wonderful, Gabriel. Yes, please.'

He held the door open for her.

Inside, the furniture was plain and serviceable, with a cushion on each chair. On the table, a blue tablecloth to match the cushion covers. A bowl of flowers stood in the middle of the table, and a fire burned in the black-leaded grate. The place was spotless.

'Oh, how delightful,' Sophia exclaimed, gazing around the cosy room.

'My sister, Agnes, comes and cleans up for me every morning. She gives me a bit o' butter and brings me a pitcher o' milk. But I bake me own bread, *and* I grows me own vegetables,' Gabriel said with pride, his old eyes shining.

'Sit you down there by the fire, Miss Sophia, while I sort things out.'

Gabriel busied himself in his slow, quiet way, taking two white cups, saucers, and matching plates from the dresser, and setting them on the table. He cut two slices of new bread, spread them with butter and his precious honey, and poured fresh milk into the cups, while Sophia watched him. She thought to help him but

. But I missed the garden and went back after a year.'

'Have you lived here all your life, Gabriel?' was sensitive enough to realise the old man was taking pleasure in playing host to her.

'Come you now, Miss, and sit up to the table. You can tell me how you like me bread and honey,' he said, pulling out a chair for her.

He went to a drawer and to her surprise, pulled out two blue napkins, and placed one on her lap.

'I won't have anyone say I don't know how to serve at table. I worked as a footman when I were a lad

'That I have, Miss, man and boy.'

'Did you ever marry?'

'I did. And I have a son, and he has six childer of his own. Works on the home farm he does. Don't make much of a livin', though. Mr Lambert tried to do his best for the farmers, but that old miser, Ogden Carterett, keeps his purse strings pulled tight, blast him.'

'Well, Gabriel, you will be pleased to know, Edmond intends to make many improvements on the estate, and that includes making his tenants more comfortable.'

'That's grand news, to be sure, Miss,' Gabriel said, slowly nodding.

Sophia took a tentative bite of bread. When she tasted it, her eyes opened wide.

'Gabriel, this bread is the finest. And the honey the most delicious I have ever eaten. And I am not saying it to be polite—it is true,' she said, catching an escaping crumb.

She took a sip from her cup and found the milk cool and creamy.

'Mmm, Gabriel,' she said. 'Will you let me come again? This is all so flavoursome.'

She continued eating, then looked at Gabriel as a thought came to her.

'When Simon comes, you must meet him, too.'

'Simon? Who's that, then?' Gabriel asked, his eyes narrowing.

'He is Edmond's nephew, and he is an artist. I thought, would it not be wonderful if he were to paint a picture of you.'

'Paint me?' Gabriel said, and gave out a wheezing laugh. 'Who'd want to paint an ugly ol' varmint like me?'

'You are not ugly. You have an interesting face. Just the kind of face Simon loves to capture.'

Gabriel wheezed again.

'He-he-he, well I'm blowed. Fancy that? Me, with me picture painted. I reckon I'd enjoy that, Miss,' and he wheezed again.

They sat eating their bread and honey, then talked for

another half an hour.

As they talked, Sophia looked about her. At the blue painted dresser beside the window; at the two rocking chairs by the fire; an old wooden clock on the mantelpiece, on either side of it a two-branched candle stick; at the heavy valance along the edge of the mantel.

An old rug, as spotlessly clean as everything else, rested on the floor before the fire. A coal box next to the fire with a poker on top of it.

Suddenly, Sophia jumped up.

'Gabriel, I must go. I have not told anyone where I am. Edmond says I may go wherever I wish, but I must tell them where I am, and I have not. Will you guide me back to the lodge, if you please?'

'Right you are, Miss Sophia. I know the shortest way,' he said, as he gathered up the plates and cups and deposited them in the scullery, while Sophia folded the napkins and put the chairs back at the table.

'I can go in and tell Agnes about the garden and the Master's plans. She'll be pleased, I'll be bound,' he said, as he put on his hat and opened the door.

They walked back the way they had come, and soon the lodge came into view.

'I'll leave you now, Miss,' he said, 'and go in the back way to Agnes. You'll be all right, won't you?'

'Yes, Gabriel, thank you. I must also thank you for the delicious bread and honey, and the milk. I am most happy I met you. Visiting with you has been a great pleasure.' She grabbed his hand in hers, shook it, then walked briskly off up to the house.

Gabriel stood watching her go.

'Well I never!' he said. 'If she in't the sweetest, kindest little maid I ever did see.'

Sophia gently pushed open the front door and tiptoed into the hall. She closed the door noiselessly behind her and headed towards the stairs. With stealthy steps, she crept up them.

Moving softly past the drawing room, she could hear men's voices talking.

Without a sound, she made for her room.

She breathed a sigh of relief as she closed the door and leant against it. Dora moved from the anteroom into the bedroom.

'Where have you been, Miss Sophia?' she asked.

Sophia was alarmed. 'Why, Dora, have I been missed?'

'Oh, no, Miss. I was just wondering,' she said.

Having no one else to tell, Sophia recounted to Dora what she called "an enchanting experience".

When Sophia had finished, Dora said, 'I've heard of Mr Bothing. He's the housekeeper's brother. I also heard bad things in the village about the way the estate is run, Miss Sophia. My Lord will put everything to rights, and so I told Mr Martin.'

'I am sure he will, Dora. I shall tell Edmond of Gabriel and his dreams of restoring the garden; Edmond will find his knowledge helpful. Do you know where he is?'

'Joe… Mr Martin… told me he is with Sir James, the magistrate, in the drawing room, and they are discussing Mr Carterett's underhanded dealings, Miss. Mr Martin has been suspicious of him for a long time and told my Lord of it, and my Lord believed him.'

She bent her head in a sideways nod, her lips folded in a prim line.

'Mr Martin said Mr Lambert is with them … Mr Martin says he thinks my Lord is a very fair man.'

Sophia glanced at Dora and wondered whether this "Mr Martin" had taken her fancy. Four times, she mentioned him as she spoke, and had called him Joe. Sophia wondered if Mr Martin was the affable young man she had seen Dora talking to yesterday afternoon, by the stables. She said nothing but smiled to herself.

Edmond concluded his business with Sir James and, having seen him off in his coach, walked back into the house in time to see Sophia coming down the stairs.

'Was that the magistrate, Edmond?' she asked.

'Yes, Sophia. How do you know of it?'

'Dora told me you were speaking to him of Mr Carterett, who has been involved in "underhanded" dealings. Do tell me all about it, Edmond,' she said, her eyes dancing with curiosity.

Edmond decided she should hear his version instead of a garbled account from the servants. He led her to the drawing room and proceeded to explain.

When he had finished, Sophia's face wore a serious expression.

'Edmond, what will happen to Carterett? He should be made to live in poverty for the rest of his life, so he may experience the hardships he has caused your tenants.'

'A fitting punishment, Sophia. However, I presume he will be imprisoned, at the very least, and he could be hanged. The punishment for such an offence is harsh.'

'Oh, no, Edmond, I would not wish the man to lose his life. Think of his family.'

'His family will suffer whatever his punishment might be. He should have thought of his family before he embezzled monies from my estate, which he has been doing for the past three years, ever since my father died. He would have continued, with Mr Treadwell as his accomplice if Treadwell had not died. After his death, it was but a matter of time before we discovered his crime. Lambert and Martin have done their best to combat his insistence on not supplying money to them for the upkeep of the estate.'

'I wonder how many landowners are swindled in this way,' Sophia said.

'A good many, without a doubt. However, *we* need worry no more, as one could not find two more honest men in England than Mr Lambert and Mr Martin. I intend to put all the financial matters into Mr Lambert's hands and give the duties of agent to Mr Martin. I shall leave them to decide whether they employ staff to assist them.'

'Dora will be pleased,' Sophia said, wiggling her

shoulders.

'Dora? Your maid? Why should she be pleased?' Edmond asked.

'Well, Edmond, I am not sure, but I do believe a *tendre* is developing between Dora and Joe Martin.'

'And why do you think so, Sophia?'

'Because of the way she spoke of him just now,' she said, smiling demurely.

'Sophia, you are developing a fondness for intrigue. Twill not be long before you become a regular gossip,' Edmond said, with a narrow look and a twist to his lips, as he tried to be serious.

'Is that not a common trait in women, Edmond?'

'You may be right, Sophia, but you appear to be starting young.'

'Perhaps it stems from my love of adventure—which reminds me—I had a very pleasant adventure this morning,' she said and paused for effect.

'Did you?' Edmond said, feigning disinterest by taking snuff, just to tease her.

Sophia sat silent. After a few moments, she couldn't contain her desire to share her experience.

'I met an old man called Gabriel Bothing, who used to be a gardener here in your grandfather's time. He took me to his cottage and gave me bread and honey—honey from his own bees—and a cup of milk. He made the bread himself. Everything was most delicious.

'His sister is housekeeper here at the lodge, and he said if you gave him seven strong men to work with him, he could put the gardens back to their former loveliness.

'There, was that not an adventure?'

'Indeed, Sophia,' Edmond said, his interest engaged. 'Where is his cottage?'

'I am not sure. Beside a wooded area, but his sister, Agnes, she could tell you,' Sophia said.

Edmond pulled the bell rope.

Swithun appeared almost instantly.

'Yes, my Lord?' he said.

'Ah, Swithun. Will you ask the housekeeper to come to me here, if you please?'

'Yes, my Lord,' Swithun said, leaving the room and wondering why Edmond wanted to see her.

A few minutes later, a knock sounded. Agnes, the housekeeper, entered. She fiddled with the front of her apron, overawed at the summons of "the Master".

Coming forward she curtsied and looked at Edmond with anxious eyes.

Sophia wondered whether she assumed she was in trouble.

'You sent for me, my Lord?' she said, standing in front of him, her hands folded before her, her brow wrinkled, her lips pressed together.

'You are Agnes Bothing?'

'I am … I mean, I was, my Lord. I am Agnes Eldridge now. Is something wrong?'

'Quite the reverse, Mrs Eldridge, I am very pleased. Miss Sophia has become acquainted with your brother, and I would like you to take me to see him.'

'You would, my Lord? When, my Lord?' she said, the worried look on her face clearing, and replaced with a happy, puzzled smile.

'If it is no trouble, Agnes, I want to see him now, if you please,' Edmond said.

Sophia's face was a picture of delight. She could imagine Gabriel's expression at receiving a visit from "The Master".

'May I come too, Edmond?' she asked.

'Of course, you may. You might make the introductions,' Edmond said.

Agnes led the way down the avenue to her well-trodden path through the jungle of weeds. They emerged into the clearing before Gabriel's house.

'I shall go and tell him you are here, my Lord, so he doesn't get flustered,' she said, going into the house.

In a moment, Agnes came to the door to beckon them in. Edmond stooped as he entered the door. Sophia followed him.

Gabriel stepped forward bowing to "The Master".

'My Lord, I am pleased to welcome you to my house. May I offer you a little ale, or a cup of milk, to refresh you?'

'A cup of milk would be most welcome, Mr Bothing, thank you,' Edmond said.

He disliked drinking milk, yet couldn't bring himself to take the old man's ale.

A smile gradually appeared on Gabriel's face when he caught sight of Sophia.

'And you've brought your little maid with you, my Lord. Such a sweet girl, you must be proud of her,' he said.

'I am, Mr Bothing, and I have come because of what she told me of you,' Edmond said.

'Oh, aye, my Lord? And what was that?' Gabriel said, pausing with the pitcher of milk in one hand and the cup in the other.

Agnes intervened.

'Give them to me, Gabriel dear, and sit down. And you too, my Lord,' she said.

Gabriel went to one of the rocking chairs.

'You may sit here, my Lord. The other chair is a bit rickety.'

'Thank you, Mr Bothing,' Edmond said and made himself comfortable.

They sat in the two rocking chairs on either side of the fire, while Edmond explained to Gabriel why he had come.

'Sophia has told me you were once a gardener here, and you can help me restore the grounds to their former glory,' Edmond said.

'That I could, my Lord, given enough men to help me. And I would enjoy the doing of it.'

'Are there men on the estate who could help?' Edmond asked.

'Aye, my Lord, and glad of the work. Why, my own son and his two sons would come, I know.'

They talked a long time of how the land was in Edmond's grandfather's day, and what needed to be done now.

Sophia sat at the table, listening to them, enthralled.

After serving Edmond with his milk, Agnes bustled about in the other rooms cleaning, tidying, and keeping out of the way.

Having agreed to talk to Joss Bothing, Gabriel's son, who worked on the home farm, Edmond drained the rest of the milk in his cup, rose, and put the cup on the table.

'Good day, Mr Bothing. It has been a true pleasure talking to you. If I may, I shall come again when I have spoken to Joss,' Edmond said, shaking Gabriel's hand.

'Good day, my Lord. It'll be a great joy working with you.'

'And I, with you, Mr Bothing,' Edmond said.

He bowed his head graciously to the old man and left.

Sophia hung back.

'I am so glad you are going to help Edmond, Gabriel. I knew you would get on well together. Good day,' Sophia said, bestowing on him her sweetest smile, and was gone.

'Well, Gabriel Bothing,' Agnes said, as she came from the kitchen, wiping her hands on her apron, 'Did you ever think to see the day when you would welcome my Lord into your house?'

'No, Agnes, I didn't, and I never thought to see a Lord speak to me as if I were over him, instead o' t'other way round. So respectful was he, and listened to everything I had to say, and wants me to oversee it all.

'"No," I says, "I'm not capable of ordering men around." So, I suggested Joss should be overseer, and me tell him what needs doin. Says he's goin' to pay a shilling and thrupence a day to any man who helps, and a bonus at the end of the work, and that's to make up for the hardship Treadwell and Carterett caused us. Me and Joss is to have an extra three shillings each week as overseers. By, but he's a good landlord and no mistake. I won't have any layabouts working with us, mind. They'll all have to be decent, upright, hardworking men, and I won't stand for anything less, and so I'll tell Joss.'

Gabriel sat thinking a moment, then continued.

'Aye, it were a good day when Lord Edmond St Vere came to us. That it was,' Gabriel said.

He sighed deeply, took out his pipe and sat by the fire to enjoy a contented smoke.

CHAPTER THIRTY ONE

Joe Martin entered Edmond's office carrying several dusty books, and a sheaf of papers in his arms. He stood before Edmond's desk, placed the books on it, knocked the papers into a neat pile, and put them on top of the books.

In his shirt sleeves, his waistcoat undone, Edmond didn't look up, but continued with his reading and note taking. Mr Martin stood by his desk. He heard a bird twittering plaintively outside the window. The clock ticked on the mantel. The fire crackled in the grate. He gave a little cough.

Edmond looked up, his concentration disturbed.

'Good morning, Mr Martin. What can I do for you?' Edmond said, as he put down his pen and eased his shoulders.

'I found more farm records, my Lord. I thought you would want to look at them. These documents were with them, so I brought them, too, Sir.'

'Thank you, Joe. I am looking into the farm records now. The books you have found are probably those that are missing. A good find. Thank you,' Edmond said.

Edmond picked up the top sheet in the pile of documents, glancing at it.

'What are these documents?'

'They look like copies of correspondence, Sir. I'm not sure of their relevance.'

'Hmm,' Edmond said, placing the sheet back on the pile.

'I shall look at them more closely when I have finished gleaning information from these books. Thank you, Mr Martin,' Edmond said, returning to what he had been reading.

Joe stayed by the desk.

Edmond looked up again and sat back in his chair.

'Was there something else, Mr Martin?'

'Yes, my Lord. I have been meaning to ask you, Sir.

My brother, Owen, is most efficient. I would like to hire him as my secretary, if I may,' Joe said, looking at Edmond with hopeful anticipation in his eyes.

'If you and Henry need to hire people to help you, and you know they are trustworthy, you may do so,' Edmond said, smiling at the eager young man.

'Thank you, my Lord,' Joe said, surprised at being given so much responsibility.

Edmond's head bent over the books again.

Joe cleared his throat.

'There is one other thing, my Lord.'

Edmond, somewhat impatient to continue with what he was doing, looked up again.

'What is it?'

Joe paused, gathering his courage.

'It is a personal matter, my Lord. I have formed an attachment to Dora Lester, Miss Sophia's lady's maid.'

Edmond's eyebrows rose.

'Have you? Indeed!' he said, remembering his conversation with Sophia.

'I would like to ask her to marry me, my Lord.'

'You are free to do so, Mr Martin. You do not need my permission,' Edmond said, amused, but keeping his face serious.

'No, my Lord. But if I am here and Dora is in Vere House, well, Sir, you must understand the difficulty,' Joe said, lowering his eyes.

'Dora must stay here with you, then, Mr Martin. I suppose I had better find a new lady's maid for Sophia. I suppose I must find accommodation for the pair of you, as well,' Edmond said, rising from his seat. 'Congratulations, Joe. I hope you will be very happy,' he said, holding out his hand.

The sun seemed to shine from Joe's face.

'Thank you, my Lord. Thank you very much indeed,' Joe said, shaking Edmond's proffered hand.

A beaming smile covered Joe's face, as he moved from foot to foot.

'Was there something else, Joe?' Edmond asked.

'No, Sir, no. Thank you again,' Joe said, backing towards the door. He gave a final nod and was gone.

Edmond stood by the window, thinking. Turning, he looked out and saw a robin busily flit from ground to bush to tree and back again.

A slow smile came to his face as he thought of the ideal lady's maid to replace Dora.

He heard the robin's plaintive little song.

A robin is a sign of good luck, so I am told, Edmond thought.

The clock on the mantel shelf chimed.

Edmond turned away from the window.

Tempus fugit, I must get on.

He moved to sit behind his desk again and continued perusing the old farm records.

Edmond, experienced in surveying the terrain when planning battle strategies, had drawn up a plan of the area of the gardens. Gabriel had told him in detail the lay out of the gardens, the way everything had been. Edmond presented these plans to Joss, a broad, stocky man, with muscles of steel, and an intelligent face.

Joss had scratched his head and looked bemused. He had learned to read, but had never seen a map, and had difficulty comprehending it.

'Let me explain it to you, Joss,' Edmond said patiently. 'This line on the outside is the perimeter of the garden. All the little circles are existing trees and shrubs. This large oval shape, coloured blue, is the lake. These wavy lines tell us how the land rises and falls. The closer the lines, the steeper the incline. The paths I have represented in red.'

Joss pored over the drawing, and when he came to understand what it all meant, gave Edmond a long, slow grin.

'Is they little square pictures the summer house and the folly, Sir?' he asked.

'Yes, Joss, they are. I have divided the area into

sections, and we shall work on them in turn,' Edmond replied.

'Eh, my Lord, we'll have it done easy with knowin' exactly what we're doin'.'

Within two weeks of having spoken to Gabriel, men were hired, and work started on the garden.

Joss took delight in having the plan pinned up on the wall in his cottage. He brought men, a few at a time, to see it and have it explained to them, proud that he was the first to understand it.

The rest of the estate, the farm and the dwellings, now took priority with Edmond.

As a leader of men, Edmond knew the value of delegation and was a good judge of character. In every area of enterprise, his strategy was to pick a man to be in charge and require them to report to Joe Martin.

Edmond consulted Joss.

'Well, Joss, now that we have set in motion the renovation of the gardens, we may start on the more important work of renovating the rest of the estate.'

'But that be good news, my Lord,' Joss responded, bestowed his big grin on Edmond, then drew his brows together.

'It'll be a big job, Sir, and it'll take a deal o' time. The farmland itself is in good order. Carterett and Treadwell made sure of that. The land produced income, so wasn't neglected. Just us what worked it was left to rot.'

Joss was tempted to spit in derision, but didn't give in to the inclination before "The Master".

'I still think improvements can be made, Joss. I have written to a farming expert. He will inspect the land, and make suggestions.'

Joss gave Edmond a dubious look.

'Yes, yes, Joss. I anticipate the farmers may resent change. Things have been done the same way for many years, and they may not relish it.'

'You have the right of it, Sir,' Joss said, squaring his shoulders.

'I have been looking into this, Joss. According to the farm records, in my Grandfather's time, they introduced crop rotation, with turnip, clover, and grain in rotation. After about ten years it stopped. I wonder why?'

'My father might know, Sir. Do you want me to ask him?' Joss offered.

'Ah, no, Joss. He has his head full of the garden. We won't confuse him,' Edmond said, rubbing his chin. 'I do not mind why. The important thing is to get it started again. I want you to call all the farm labourers to a meeting in the church to discuss the matter. Before we organise the meeting, I want you to ask around and tell me how they feel about it.'

'Yes, my Lord,' Joss said.

He had a thought.

'If there are those around who remember the—what did you call it, Sir?'

'Crop rotation,' Edmond supplied.

'Yes, that. If the older men remember crop rotation, they mayn't be so against it. I'll speak to a few of the ol' fellas and get em on our side,' Joss said.

He had great respect for Edmond and had, many weeks before, decided to go along with him in all he planned to do.

Edmond noted the "our side" with satisfaction.

'The other thing I want to do, Joss, is to find people within my estate, who have skill enough to help with the renovation of the run-down cottages and farm buildings.'

Impressed, Joss raised his chin in a gesture of approval.

'I'll put the word about, my Lord,' Joss said.

'Perhaps you could tell any of them who have useful skills, to present themselves in the hall here on Monday morning. They can give their names to Joe Martin, with a list of their abilities,' Edmond suggested.

Joss nodded in agreement.

Monday dawned with a light drizzle falling.

'Good morning, Mr Martin,' Edmond said, as he

entered the hall from the morning room having finished his breakfast.

'Good morning, my Lord. I hope the weather won't deter men from coming,' he remarked, with a small frown.

'I doubt it will, Mr Martin. Times are hard, and they need work. Besides, I am sure it will clear up by lunchtime,' Edmond said. Nothing could dampen his enthusiasm today.

Furlong passed through the hall. Edmond stopped him.

'Ah, Furlong. Will you please send me two footmen to move some furniture, if you please. Swithun is a strong young fellow, he will do, and one other,' Edmond said.

'Yes, my Lord,' Furlong said, wondering what furniture Edmond wanted to shift.

Joe wondered, too, and gave Edmond a questioning look.

'I think it best we see the men here in the hall, Joe. I mean to watch from the gallery, and look for men who stand out as competent and reliable, and who might be suitable as overseers,' Edmond explained.

Joe smiled.

'Ah, I understand, my Lord,' he said.

Swithun and Jacobs entered the hall.

'You want us to move furniture, my Lord?' Swithun asked.

'I do, Swithun. There is a small desk in the blue salon. I want you to go there, take everything off it, and put it all neatly on the floor. Then, I want you to carry the desk here, and place it to the right of the stairs.'

'Yes, my Lord,' Swithun said. 'Do you want a chair to go with it?' he inquired.

'If you please, Swithun, yes, and I want you to stay at the door and let the men in one at a time,' Edmond said and turned to Mr Martin.

'Joe, I want you to make a note of each man who comes before you. His name, his age, and his experience, and anything relevant you think might be of help in assessing the man,' Edmond said.

'Yes, my Lord,' Jo said, and placed a ledger on the desk before him. He went to the room from where the desk had been taken and retrieved the inkstand from the floor.

Sitting behind the desk, he awaited the entrance of the first candidate.

Within the following few days, Edmond had chosen a man, Isaiah Sayle, to oversee rebuilding and refurbishment. Edmond chose another man, Dick Ellingham, to take charge of matters to do with farming.

He left these men to make choice from the workers who had presented themselves to Jo Martin.

CHAPTER THIRTY TWO

Edmond's efficiency amazed Sophia. Moreover, the way the men recognised his authority and obeyed him without question put her in new awe of him. Everything he set his hand to was a success and by the end of their two-month stay, the estate was set to be more habitable for the tenants and a more efficient farming enterprise.

'What of the house?' Sophia asked him one evening over dinner.

'That must wait awhile, Sophia,' Edmond said, pausing to pat his mouth with his napkin.

'I shall hire masters to accomplish what I want done with the house. Builders, plasterers, painters and carpenters—I think I shall employ Mr Sayle in that capacity, as he is a master carpenter. Nonetheless, I must put my tenants' welfare before the house.'

He noted her disappointed expression, her eyes sad, and her mouth pulled down.

'In about six months, I think we shall be ready to start on it,' he continued. 'But I do not think it will be habitable for over a year, maybe two.'

'Oh dear, Edmond. I thought we could come to live here much sooner than that,' Sophia said, putting down her fork.

'I have spent much time in Gabriel's company and looked forward to seeing the gardens completed. I have learned so much about plants and garden maintenance from him; I feel I am quite the expert. Must we go home next week? Could we not stay another month or two? I do so love being here,' she pleaded, her shoulders drooping.

'I thought you liked the gardens at Vere House?'

'I do. I love them. But these will be much bigger and have more variety. I wanted to see it taking shape. Vere House is mature; I feel the garden here is an infant about to be born.'

'More like resurrected,' Edmond murmured. He tried to

use a lighter tone.

'But, you must know, "Miss Erdington", as your guardian I am responsible for your education, and I have hired several people to take care of it. In a few weeks, it will all begin for you. I have already hired a governess to supervise you.'

Sophia looked more unhappy. She shook her head.

'Am I never to see Crawford Lees again?'

'Of course, you are, Sophia,' Edmond said, patting her hand. 'I shall be paying regular visits here, and sometimes you may accompany me.'

Sophia sighed and gave Edmond a direct look.

'With all your plans for me, Edmond, you seem to have forgotten something.'

'And what is that, Sophia?' He looked back at her, questioning.

'I am not Miss Erdington,' she stated, her chin tucked in, her lips pressed together.

'I could never forget that, my dear,' Edmond said gently. 'Is it not more reason to do my best for you?' he said, taking her hand in his. 'As I have often said to you, I promised your father I would look after you, and that is what I am doing.'

Swithun came to remove the dishes from their first course, and serve the second.

After he had gone, Edmond continued.

'You will enjoy it, my dear. And do not think you will not have time to yourself. You can still spend time in the garden if you wish.'

'I shall not be free, though, Edmond. I shall be confined to doing things at certain times—I have always hated that.' She placed a morsel of chicken on her fork but held it suspended over the plate.

Edmond swallowed his food before answering.

'All I can say, Sophia, is, if anything becomes too irksome for you, you may come and tell me, and I shall do my best to rectify things—does that not make you feel better?'

Sophia gave him a wan smile.

'A little, Edmond.'

She was silent a moment.

'Oh, but I am behaving badly, am I not?' she said, her conscience pricking her. 'Here you are, arranging everything for my good. You must think me so ungrateful. I shall do as you say, and yes, I shall come to you if there is anything I do not like,' she said, took a sip of her wine and continued eating her dinner.

The following morning, Dora came to Sophia, her eyes shining with pleasure.

'Oh Miss, Oh Miss, the greatest thing has happened to me!' she said, standing before Sophia gripping her hands together in front of her.

'Dora, do tell me what it is. At once!' Sophia said, almost as excited as Dora.

'It's Mr Martin, Miss. He has proposed to me!' Dora said, breathless with excitement.

'There! I knew there was something in the wind. How wonderful, Dora. I presume you said yes?'

'Oh, I did, Miss. I can't say how much I love him. And he says he loves me too. There is a problem, though, Miss. I wouldn't be able to come back to London with you. You will need a new lady's maid.'

'Do not worry about me, Dora. I am sure Edmond will see to that. Does he know?'

'He does, Miss. Joe spoke to him before he asked me. My Lord gave us his blessing. He said we can stay at the lodge when you have left 'til a cottage can be found for us. There are several on the home farm that are empty. Joe can get the new overseer, Mr Sayle, to make it liveable. Ooh, Miss Sophia, I am so excited!'

Sophia hugged Dora and didn't let her see her disappointment. She had become fond of her maid and would miss her.

She went to his study to speak to Edmond.

'I have heard about Dora and Joe, Edmond. I am

delighted, naturally. Yet, who will be my lady's maid now?' she said, chewing her lower lip.

'Do not worry, Sophia. I have someone in mind for you already. If I can persuade her to come to you, I am sure you will be pleased with my choice.'

Edmond gave her a guarded smile.

'Who is it, Edmond?' Sophia asked, all curiosity.

'It is a surprise, Sophia. I shall not tell you in case she will not come,' Edmond answered, one eyebrow askew.

All day, Sophia probed Edmond to tell her who the new maid would be. He took delight in *not* telling her. No matter whether she became wheedling or vexed, excessively sweet or pouting, still he wouldn't tell her. She, therefore, gave up.

While undressing that evening, Edmond spoke to Wilson.

'How difficult would it be to contact Bonnaire?'

'Not difficult at all, my Lord, if we were in London,' Wilson answered. He assumed Edmond required brandy or port.

'I shall tell you the situation, Wilson. Dora, Sophia's maid, is to marry my agent, Joe Martin. She will be living here with him, so I need to find a new lady's maid for Sophia. I notice she has been in correspondence with the housekeeper, Clothilde, from the billet in Membillier.'

Wilson's face turned white.

'I mean to ask Clothilde to come to England to be Sophia's maid,' Edmond said.

Wilson turned towards the armoire to hang up Edmond's coat, and to hide his face as his eyes widened, and his heart beat a tattoo in his chest.

Wilson had also been corresponding with Clothilde, whose letters he kept under his pillow, and which he read every night before he went to sleep.

The last letter she had written to him was a sad one for her. Yet, for him, it held hope.

345

Chér Daniel,

It is with sad heart I tell you my mother died.
She was very ill. Le Bon Dieu has kind been
and taken her to Himself. I am sad. I miss her.
I miss you, Daniel. I wish you here to comfort me.
I pray God someday He bring us together.
Even though we only met for moments,
and we are far apart, I love you very much.

Clothilde.

Edmond broke in on Wilson's thoughts.

'Are you listening, Wilson?' Edmond asked.

Wilson coughed. 'Yes my Lord, I'm all ears,' he answered.

'You have met Clothilde, I think. You would be known to her?'

Wilson swallowed.

'Yes, sir. We have met,' he said.

'Good. Now, what I want you to do is to go to London and find Bonnaire, ask him to transport you to France, and escort you to Membillier. There you will invite Clothilde to come to England to be Sophia's lady's maid. If she will not come, then so be it. If she will come, then you must ask Bonnaire to transport her and yourself back to England. Can you do that, Wilson?'

'Oh. Well. Hmm. Yes, my Lord. I can but try. When would you like me to go?'

'Tomorrow, Wilson, if you please. We shall be here for another two weeks only. I hope Mademoiselle Clothilde will be at Vere House for Sophia when we return.'

I hope so, too, Wilson thought.

'I'll do me best for you, Sir,' Wilson said.

The next day, Edmond called Swithun to him.

'Swithun. Wilson has gone to London on an important errand. I would be grateful if you could perform his duties as my valet while he is away.'

'*Me*, my Lord?' Swithun exclaimed. 'I have no experience, Sir.'

His eyes were big, his hand slightly trembled.

'This, then, is your chance to gain some, Swithun. I am not a difficult man to valet for. All you need do is clean my boots, lay out my clothes, and make sure I have a good supply of hot water in the morning. Oh, and sometimes I need help with putting on and taking off my boots. I can manage everything else myself.

'Yes, my Lord,' Swithun uttered in a small voice, his face resembling a frightened rabbit.

Edmond laughed.

'Oh, come, man. Am I such an ogre? I shall not eat you if you do something wrong.'

'Would not Mr Furlong be a better choice, Sir?' Swithun said, still dubious.

'Probably, Swithun. Yet, how would *you* feel if you had to face his dour countenance first thing in the morning, and last thing at night? Hmmm?'

Swithun, despite his fear, smiled and lowered his head.

'I'll do my best, my Lord,' Swithun said, resigning himself to the task.

Two weeks later, the household returned to Vere House, where there were two surprises awaiting Sophia, and one awaiting Edmond.

Edmond had found Miss Roseberry, Sophia's former governess. He had asked her to come to teach Sophia again, and the lady had accepted.

Charlotte Roseberry was of medium height. A pretty, young woman in her late twenties. Her bright blue eyes twinkled with fun. With a neat figure, blond hair, which she wore in a simple style, her clothes were neither unfashionable nor ostentatious, as befitted a governess. A rosebud mouth that often smiled added to her charm. She was exactly suited to Sophia's temperament.

On arrival at Vere House, after the tedious journey

from Crawford Lees, Sophia immediately went to the drawing room.

To her great surprise, she came face to face with her former governess.

Sophia stood, incredulous at sight of her.

'Miss Roseberry! Oh, Miss Roseberry. Can it really be you?'

Charlotte nodded, offering Sophia a beaming smile with her arms outstretched.

Sophia ran forward to embrace her warmly, happily inhaling her governess's familiar lavender scent. Standing back, Sophia gazed at her in disbelief, tears in her eyes.

'Oh, Miss Roseberry, how on earth did Edmond find you?' she asked.

Miss Roseberry, smiling, patted Sophia's cheek.

'He put many advertisements in periodicals and newspapers. One of my friends saw one and wrote to tell me. I wrote to Lord St Vere. He sent for me. So here I am, my dear Sophia.'

They hugged again.

'And how happy I am that you are,' Sophia said, taking Miss Roseberry's hand, leading Charlotte to sit on a couch.

'I have dreaded starting lessons again as no one could make things as interesting as you.'

Miss Roseberry smiled, shaking her head, embarrassed by such praise.

'I was most relieved when Lord St Vere sent for me. I have been working in Yorkshire, employed by a dragon-of-a-woman with three spoiled little girls, who never would mind me. I could see myself going into a decline if I had to stay there much longer.'

Sophia laughed and so did Charlotte Roseberry.

'Edmond means for me to learn to dance, and to play a musical instrument, and to sing,' Sophia told her, wearing a pouting, sceptical expression. 'I am not sure whether I want to do all that.'

'Oh, nonsense, Sophia, you will enjoy it immensely, I promise you,' Miss Roseberry said, taking Sophia's hand in hers.

'But look at you. How fine you are, and your hair is beautiful. You are quite a young lady.'

Sophia blushed and smiled.

'How long have you been here, Miss Roseberry?'

'Several weeks. Mrs Luxton has been most welcoming. She has told me where I may set up our schoolroom, and helped me buy books and equipment.

'Lord St Vere said to spare no expense and, dear me, Mrs Luxton has certainly taken him at his word,' she said, and caught her lower lip between her teeth, her bright eyes wide.

'I think we have the best-equipped schoolroom in England.'

Charlotte Roseberry laughed and smiled.

Sophia laughed with her.

'I like Perdita; we get on well together. But I am determined not to let her think she has me under her thumb,' she said, with a decisive nod.

'I raised objection to buying a new piano. We need an expert to advise us, and until Lord St Vere employs a music master, I think purchasing a piano can wait.'

She rose from the couch.

'But come, Sophia, you must be tired from your journey. You must go to your room to refresh yourself. After that, I shall show you your schoolroom,' she said and led Sophia across the gallery.

Sophia opened the door to her bedroom.

'I *am* a little weary, Miss Roseberry, perhaps I shall lie down to rest for half an hour,' she said over her shoulder as she entered her room.

She turned her head, walking farther into the room and stopped short.

Standing at the foot of Sophia's bed, a smile on her face, her arms outstretched, stood Sophia's new Lady's maid.

'Clothilde!'

Sophia ran into Clothilde's arms, hugging and kissing

her. She stood back from Clothilde, her hands over her mouth, tears streaming down her face. She turned to Miss Roseberry.

'You knew, and you did not tell me!'

Sophia looked from one woman to the other.

'Oh! Oh! This is the happiest of days. Two of my favourite people in all the world, here with me. I cannot believe it!'

Clothilde moved to put her arm around the girl's shoulders. With a handkerchief, she wiped the tears from Sophia's cheeks.

'Well, Sophia. You will be envied by all the girls in London. It is quite the status symbol for a young lady to have a French maid,' Miss Roseberry said with a laugh.

'I care nothing for that,' Sophia said, taking the handkerchief and further drying her eyes.

'How did you get here, Clothilde? How did you know I needed a new maid?'

'The Major sent Daniell ... Weelson... to fetch me. I wrote to you a month ago to say my mother had died, did I not?'

Sophia nodded. 'You did, yes.'

'*Alors*, when Weelson came to ask me to be your maid, I was free to come,' she said.

'How delighted I am that you did,' Sophia said, wiggling her shoulders.

'But how did you get out of France?' Sophia asked.

'Weelson has friends who are *contrebandiers*, Messieurs Bonnaire and Renaud…'

'Oh, yes. We came to England on Monsieur Renaud's ship…'

'*Vraiment.* So here I am to be with you, Miss Sophie,' Clothilde said.

Miss Roseberry had looked on at the reunion, tears of happiness in her own eyes. She now stepped forward.

'Clothilde, my dear, you must tell Sophia your other news,' she said gently.

'Oh, yes. *Bien sûr*. But you must say not a word to

350

Major Edmond till Weelson has told him.'

'Told him what, Clothilde?' Sophia asked, her eyes wide with curiosity.

'*Pere Alain* married us before we left France.' Clothilde disclosed, her eyes shining, her smile beaming.

'Oh, Clothilde!' Sophia exclaimed. She could say no more.

CHAPTER THIRTY THREE

In Sophia and Edmond's absence, Charlotte Roseberry had become part of the household.

Perdita liked her.

'Edmond, she is the sweetest girl. I have become quite fond of her,' Perdita said to her brother, as they gathered in the drawing room to wait for dinner to be served.

'We have corresponded, Perdy. Her letters were a pleasure to read, but I have not yet met her,' Edmond said, as he poured another glass of canary for his sister.

They heard a knock at the front door, and a male voice talking to Furlong.

'Oh, dear me, Edmond, I forgot! I should have mentioned it. I invited Aubrey to dinner to welcome you home,' Perdita said, casting a speculative glance at him.

'Why, how thoughtful of you, Perdita. I shall enjoy his company,' Edmond said, as Furlong came into the room.

'Sir Aubrey Courtney, my Lord,' he announced.

As Aubrey entered, Edmond moved forward to shake his hand.

'My dear friend, I am glad to see you,' Edmond said.

'I am pleased to see ya too, Edmond,' Aubrey said as he shook Edmond's hand, and patted his shoulder.

'But what is this, Sir? Furlong announced you as "Sir Aubrey" and not "Colonel",' Edmond enquired.

'I have followed in y'r footsteps, Edmond, and resigned ma commission. There was little to do in ma own house, so I have visited your sister quite often. She has brought me to several musical evenings, and soirees. She is determined to get me a wife,' Aubrey said making a face, but then laughing.

'Oh, come now, Sir,' Perdita said, blushing. 'Have you not enjoyed our little outings?'

'Not so much the musical evenings, ma'am, but the soirees were pleasant enough.'

Perdita turned from him to Edmond.

'I have also suggested Miss Roseberry join us for dinner, Edmond. She dines with me most evenings. Do you mind?'

'Of course not, Perdy. I believe her to be a most cultured woman. Her conversation will be welcome,' Edmond replied.

Simon entered the room, and while he went to say good evening to Aubrey, Perdita spoke to Edmond in an under voice.

'It is perfect is it not, Edmond. Three men and three women to dinner, so there is no difficulty in the seating arrangements.'

The niceties of etiquette were of little importance to Edmond. Yet, he knew it was the breath of life to Perdita.

'Perfect, indeed, Perdy,' he said, an amused smile hovering on his lips.

It was at that moment Sophia and Miss Roseberry entered the room.

Perdita hurried forward to introduce Charlotte to Edmond.

'May I make known to you, Edmond, Miss Charlotte Roseberry. Miss Roseberry, Lord Edmond St Vere.'

Charlotte curtsied to just the right depth, and rising, proffered her hand to Edmond.

'Your servant, ma'am,' Edmond said, bowing over her hand.

'I am pleased to meet you, my Lord,' Charlotte said, smiling in genuine pleasure at meeting Sophia's guardian at last.

Perdita watched Aubrey out of the corner of her eye. Over the short period Miss Roseberry had been in the household, Perdita had noticed Aubrey's partiality for her, and had decided to nurture it.

Seeing Edmond look at her in such an appreciative way now, she wondered whether there would be something here to nurture instead.

Simon liked Miss Roseberry, too. He had already sketched her, and prepared a canvas, planning to paint her portrait. Miss Roseberry's personality was informal and jolly, so Simon's initial reserve was soon lost as he conversed with her with ease.

'Well, this is very pleasant, I must say,' Aubrey said, coming over to join the group.

'Good evening to you, ma'am,' he said his eyes glowing as he spoke to Charlotte.

'Good evening to you, Sir,' she said, with her brightest smile.

Is that a hint of pink in her cheeks? Perdita wondered.

'And Miss Sophia. How do you do, ma dear?'

'I am very well, Aubrey, thank you,' she replied.

Furlong entered.

'Dinner is served, my Lord,' he intoned.

Perdita took Edmond's arm as they processed to the dining room. Aubrey offered his arm to Miss Roseberry.

'So, that leaves us,' Sophia said, taking Simon's arm.

'How are you, Sophia?' Simon asked.

'I did not want to leave Crawford Lees, but now I am here, I am glad to be home again,' Sophia said. 'Have you missed me, Simon?'

'I have, Sophia, but I have been very busy, so the time has flown,' Simon said, as he stood back to allow Sophia to enter the dining room.

Edmond sat at the head of the table. The rest of the party were grouped perfectly about him.

A chine of beef, accompanied by winter vegetables, and a large dish of boiled, buttered potatoes, appeared after the soup. Finally, a variety of tarts, fruit, and little cakes, were served for desert.

Edmond sat looking around the table, happy to have extra company. A warm satisfaction filled him. He wondered how Sophia had reacted to seeing Clothilde. He hadn't had the opportunity to speak to Sophia. He turned to Miss Roseberry.

'Sophia looks pleased with herself,' he remarked

'She is, my Lord. She was happy to see me, but she wept when she saw Clothilde. She is fortunate to have such a thoughtful guardian as you, Sir,' Charlotte said.

'Oh, she is such an exuberant child. It is a pleasure to make her happy. Perdita tells me, you and she have furnished and stocked the schoolroom.'

'We have, Sir. All we need now is a new piano, a small one for Sophia to use in our schoolroom. I have put off purchasing it till Sophia's music master arrives.'

'Very wise Miss Roseberry,' Edmond said. Aubrey said something to Charlotte, and Perdita claimed her brother's attention.

'Edmond, I have amassed quite a circle of friends while you have been away. I wondered whether you would allow me to organise a soiree in a few weeks' time.'

Edmond, although reserved in company, enjoyed social gatherings.

'I have no objection. In fact, I think I would enjoy it. I feel I would like Sophia to attend,' he added and waited for Perdita to disagree.

'It will be a small affair, Edmond, so I think there can be no objection. A ball is a different matter. Yes, I think she should be allowed to be there,' Perdita said.

Edmond sat back in his chair, sipping his wine, glancing at Perdita over the rim.

He saw her looking at Aubrey and Charlotte together.

What is she planning? Of making a match? If she interferes too much, she will scotch anything that might have been. They do seem remarkably well suited, though, Edmond thought.

Perdita rose when the covers were cleared, and the ladies left the men to their port.

After a short while, the men joined the ladies.

Aubrey made a beeline for Miss Roseberry.

'Will you sing for us, ma dear?' he asked her.

'I shall, if you turn the pages of my music for me, Sir Aubrey,' she replied.

Aubrey went to the piano, pulled out the stool, and opened the lid of the keyboard.

'Miss Roseberry has agreed to sing for us,' he

announced.

Sophia smiled, and whispered to Edmond, 'Miss Roseberry is a most accomplished pianist, and her voice is sweet. I am sure you will enjoy it.'

Sophia was right. Charlotte's singing and playing were delightful, and everyone clapped when she had finished.

'Come, Sophia. You must sing now. I shall play a tune I am sure you remember, and you must sing,' Charlotte said.

Sophia looked around the group. They all looked surprised.

'My voice is not as pleasant as Miss Roseberry's, but since she has asked, I shall not refuse,' Sophia said, her cheeks bright pink.

Charlotte played an introduction.

'Oh yes, I do remember this,' Sophia said.

It was a French country song. Sophia sang it well.

They all laughed and clapped when Sophia had finished.

Everyone stood around the piano discussing who should sing next. But Edmond saw Sophia stifling a yawn, and had to admit that he, too, was somewhat fatigued after his journey, so decided to retire early.

The party broke up and slowly went to their separate rooms, Aubrey having made claim to the best spare bedroom.

When Edmond opened the door to his room, he was surprised when he found Wilson wasn't there.

Curious, he went in search of him.

Without knocking, Edmond opened Wilson's door.

Wilson didn't hear him.

Edmond stood staring at what he saw.

Wilson, in a close embrace with a woman.

Edmond watched the pair for a moment, a menacing expression on his face, his eyebrows drawn together, and his mouth pursed.

'Good evening, Wilson,' he said, with ominous gravity.

Clothilde gave a small shriek.

Wilson turned.

'Good evening my Lord,' he said with great éclat.

Edmond paused, gathering his anger.

'Wilson, in all the years I have known you, I have never caught you behaving with such disrespect. What do you think you are doing?'

'Now, my Lord, don't get angry. It's not as bad as it looks,' Wilson said.

Clothilde stood behind him, peering at Edmond from around Wilson's arm.

'Good God, Wilson! Is that Clothilde?' Edmond's ire increased.

Clothilde stepped forward.

'You must not be angry at Weelson, Major. Please, let him explain,' she said.

Seething with anger, Edmond spoke with measured calm,

'Very well. *Explain,* Wilson, if you please.'

Wilson gave Clothilde an appreciative look, then turned with his head held high.

'The long and the short of it, my Lord, is me and Clothilde was married before we left France,' Wilson "explained".

There, that'll take the wind out o' yer sails, he thought.

Edmond stood in silence, observing Wilson with eyes narrowed, and chin up.

At last, he said, 'Why did you not tell me?'

'I wanted to, Sir, but I haven't seen you all day. It ain't no secret, my Lord.'

'Where do you intend living?' Edmond asked, his anger subsiding.

'Right here, Sir. We thought I would still be on hand for you, an' Clothilde would be nearby all the time for Miss Sophia,' Wilson said, pausing for Edmond to take it in.

'But if you've got a better notion, Sir, we'll be happy to go along with it, won't we, Tildy?'

'*Certainement*, Major,' Clothilde said, nodding.

Edmond sighed deeply.

'Leave things as they are, for now, Wilson. I shall think on it,' he said and returned to his room.

In a short while, Wilson joined him. Edmond sat on his upright chair, slowly undoing his neck cloth, staring in front of him.

'May I come in, my Lord?' Wilson asked.

Edmond glanced at him.

'Yes, Wilson. Be so good as to help me off with my boots,' he said.

Wilson knelt before him and heaved at Edmond's high boots.

'I didn't set out to deceive you, Sir, honest,' Wilson said in a hushed tone.

'I am sure you did not, Wilson. I am sorry I became angry with you. It was a great shock to see you like that. I suppose you have had women over the years, but I never knew of it, or even thought about it. How did it come about that you married a virtual stranger?' Edmond said, undoing the buttons at the cuff of his breeches, and peeling off his stockings.

'Well, my Lord, I can hardly credit it meself,' he said, taking Edmond's stockings from him.

'You see, me and Clothilde met the day I came to transport Miss Sophia to the Encampment. Somethin' just fell into place between us. I thought she was the most wonderful girl I'd ever seen. And, God help her, she felt the same about me.'

Wilson helped Edmond off with his coat and waistcoat, as he continued to tell his story.

'I wrote to her, and she wrote to me and, well, when you sent me over there to bring her back, I asked her to marry me, she said yes, and the priest married us, Sir.'

Edmond gave a short laugh.

'Quick work, Wilson. God in heaven, though, man, you could have told me!' Edmond said, as he took off his breeches and handed them to Wilson.

'I didn't know meself till I got there, Sir. And then I

358

were out when you arrived today, and when I got back you was at dinner and …'

'All right, Wilson, I understand. But do you think it will work, the two of you living in my anterooms?'

'There's many a house smaller than *one* of your anterooms, Sir. Course it'll work,' Wilson said, smiling broadly at Edmond.

Edmond removed his shirt.

'I shall see to it that when Crawford Lees is refurbished, a better arrangement may be accommodated,' Edmond said, slipping his nightshirt over his head.

'You had better get back to Clothilde, now, or she will think you have abandoned her. Goodnight, Wilson.'

'Goodnight, my Lord,' Wilson said. He snuffed the candle and slipped into the hall, breathing a hefty sigh of relief.

A smile came over his face as he went to the next room where Clothilde waited for him.

Edmond lay in the near darkness of his room, on his back, with his hands behind his head. A chink in the curtains let in a sliver of silver moonlight.

He thought of how his new life was taking shape.

Perdita was planning to give him a social life. Edmond was not sure he wanted one.

Although I enjoyed this evening's small gathering, he thought.

Aubrey looked set fair to marrying Miss Roseberry. Whether this would be soon, or in the not too distant future, he could not tell.

Simon was making good progress with his apprenticeship.

Sophia had Miss Roseberry to educate her.

I must advertise for a dancing master and a music teacher for her.

Wilson. Ah, Wilson! What a surprise, the old dog. Imagine, at his age falling prey to romance.

What of myself? By all the saints! I have not thought of

the Army for weeks, he thought.

Crawford Lees had taken up all his time. It satisfied him. It was not unlike what he did as Major. Instructing men in what must be done; delegating responsibility to the most competent; drawing up plans of strategy.

Ha! And with no interference from on high, he thought.

In three or four years, he would have the marriage annulled. Sophia would marry and produce children of her own.

Perhaps I should find a wife for myself, then, and produce children too, he thought.

For now, despite his earlier misgivings, he was content.

TO BE CONTINUED…….